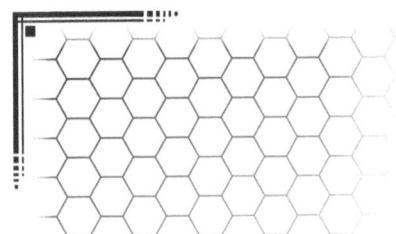

THE
TIME REFUGEE

THE EVARAN CHRONICLES

BOOK 4

ADAIR HART

Editing done by Laura Petrella

Cover done by Tom Edwards

Interior design done by Colleen Sheehan

Proofread by Red Adept Publishing

Published by Quantum Edge Publishing

ISBN: 978-0-9967172-3-6

www.AdairHart.com

To get updates on new books and other notifications, sign up for my mailing list at

www.AdairHart.com/MailingList.aspx

THE
TIME REFUGEE

THE STORY SO FAR

Dr. Albert Snowden and his niece, Emily, were abducted by an alien race known as the Krotovore. They were rescued by a space- and time-traveling being known as Evaran, who dropped them back off on Earth.

When Evaran returned to check on them, they asked to travel with him, and Evaran accepted. Since then, they have helped the people of Fredoria, a planet of human ex-slaves, become a full trade partner with the Kreagan Star Empire, the local galactic superpower in Earth's region of the galaxy. They have also fought the timeline invaders known as the Purifiers, a human-supremacist group.

This book continues with their adventures.

EVARAN'S TECHNOLOGY

Torvatta—his ship that can travel through time and space

Universal interface card (UIC)—a credit-card-sized device carried on his belt that allows access to any technological system

Augmented reality interface (ARI)—an interface that only he can see around him

Utility handle—a hilt-like device carried on his belt that can extend morphable matter in any shape, typically extended into a baton or staff; can also fire repulsion, grappling, heat, and stun beams

Illumination orbs—small orbs on his belt that provide lighting and can hover

Projection orb—an orb that allows projections to be sent to it from remote sources, such as Evaran's ring or the Torvatta

Ring—a ring that can provide holographic projection and also scan

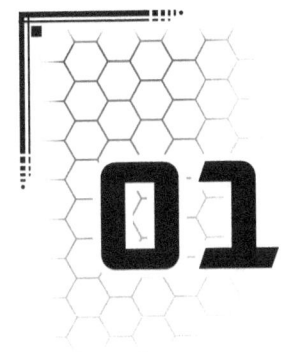

01

Dr. Albert Snowden gazed into the clear sky lit by two suns. Looking around, it could have been any beach on Earth, but this was the resort planet known as Kamala. Coming out in swimming trunks was not his first choice, but after seeing how many bare-skinned aliens were around with their unusual bodies, it was an easier decision. His fair skin was taking a beating while soaking in the rays, but the cool wind helped even it out. The smell of salt water caressed his nostrils.

A loud guttural sound caught his ear. Off in the distance, a small group of reptilian birdlike creatures were hopping around. The birds on Kamala were larger and generally louder than what he knew from Earth. He ran a hand over his gray tufts of hair and bald spot. The other hand scooped up some sand, then let it slip through his fingers as he eyed his early twenties fair-skinned niece, Emily, sitting a few feet away. Her long dirty-blond hair was pulled back in a ponytail and swayed in the wind.

He and Emily were traveling companions with Evaran, a powerful being who traveled through space and time in his ship, the Torvatta. The Torvatta was disc shaped and reminded him of a hockey puck that sat between two thin layers on top of a wide-based cone. Evaran had rescued them from an alien abduction, and they had traveled with him ever since. They had traveled to a distant galaxy and several thousand years into the past to get to Kamala relative to the year 2012. It had become routine to travel like that, and he had learned much in his journeys with Evaran.

Emily's guarded face was no surprise to him as a raptor-like couple walked by. She had been on a rough journey in their last adventure. Being separated for nine months and having to survive on a prison planet in a pocket universe had taken its toll. A lump formed in his throat at the thought that the full-of-life Emily he had grown up with was gone, and in her place was a much more serious version.

Emily turned her head toward Dr. Snowden. "You're giving me that look again."

Dr. Snowden snorted. "Well . . . I don't think that couple is a threat. Relax. It's why we're here."

"You never know," said Emily with narrowed eyes. "It doesn't hurt to be prepared."

Dr. Snowden glanced at the survival suit lying next to her. She had picked it up on the previous adventure, and Evaran had tweaked it so that it was more durable and space worthy. Next to it was her personal support device. Her PSD, which was shaped like a pen, had the ability to open a small interface, shoot repulsion and stun beams, extend morphable metal, and store more than it was capable of, due to dimensional mechanics. It was her constant companion, and even now, her hand rested on it. Although she had on a swimsuit, she looked like she could jump into the suit and whip out the PSD at a moment's notice.

"I think we're safe," said Dr. Snowden, chuckling. "We've been here for five weeks now, and I haven't seen any sign of trouble."

Emily exhaled from her nose as her eyes followed the couple.

Dr. Snowden raised his eyebrows as he wagged a finger at her. "They might think you're a threat if you keep staring at them."

Emily glanced away for a moment, then focused on Dr. Snowden. "Sorry. I'm . . . still getting used to being around others."

Dr. Snowden sighed. He wished he could do more. Being available to her at any time was his top priority. He had tried to participate in her nonstop training in the holographic room, or holo room as he called it, on the Torvatta. Four to five hours a day was too much for him. He did enjoy some of it, whether it was fighting one creature or another or running across terrain and shooting with their PSDs. Although they both had nanobots that gave them heightened abilities and senses, she was in command of hers more so than he was of his.

Dr. Snowden looked around and spotted Evaran talking with animated hand motions to a lizard-like humanoid alien near a metallic high-tech shack. Evaran had mentioned that most residents of Kamala would have never seen a human, so there would be some interest from others wanting to know about them.

During this visit, Dr. Snowden had talked with dozens of different aliens from across the stars. The most common question was how humans could evolve with such soft skin. Sometimes they would ask to touch it or ask him and Emily to undress completely for further inspection. Touching was okay, undressing was not. He had told them that humans had intelligence and were good endurance runners. That often drew laughter, and he could never tell if they were laughing at him or with him. He was just glad that they had a spot to go where nothing was trying to destroy or capture them.

Evaran waved at the alien and turned to walk toward Dr. Snowden and Emily.

Dr. Snowden studied Evaran. Evaran strolled as if he did not have a care in the world, but Dr. Snowden knew that to be far from the truth. Evaran looked human, but was not. Even his dirty-blond hair with a small wave out front was unnatural in that it never seemed to move. He always wore a light-gray suit with rubberlike armor pads. Dr. Snowden thought Evaran might have had some swimming clothes, but Evaran had gone into the water with his suit. The pads with multicolored lines around the edges were visible even when Evaran was under water.

Dr. Snowden liked the metallic neck guard, boots, forearm guards, and utility belt. They always seemed shiny and free of scuffs. The belt had a utility handle similar to his PSD, except Evaran's was much more powerful, and the handle was larger, akin to the hilt of a sword. He had seen the utility handle exhibit abilities not present in his or Emily's PSD, such as an orange heat beam. There were also small orbs and a universal interface card on the belt. The UIC allowed Evaran to access any technological system, which he could then view through his augmented reality interface. The ARI could only be seen by Evaran. It did not surprise Dr. Snowden that even under two suns, Evaran did not tan. His fair skin was a constant.

Evaran arrived and took a seat in the sand. He crooked a thumb back at the alien he had been talking to. "They are an interesting species."

Dr. Snowden looked at the alien, who had gone back to doing whatever it did in the shack. He had learned that the native denizens of this planet called themselves Rokki. Given how warm the planet seemed year round and in their history, it was not too much of a surprise they would have evolved here. The fact that they were humanoid was a data point that he would have found puzzling, but after traveling with Evaran, he knew that there were other forces at work promoting the humanoid form.

The Rokki did not deal only in rest and relaxation; they had a burgeoning scientific community, with many alien races participating. The warm weather and accommodations alone would have been a great lure. Dr. Snowden did not mind it at all and liked touring some of the scientific events they had.

"Are you enjoying the beach?" asked Evaran.

"Heck yeah. There's science and good weather—doesn't get much better than that," said Dr. Snowden. He pointed at Emily. "I even think I saw her crack a smile once."

Emily raised an eyebrow.

"It's much better than, say . . . a space station with a timeline change," said Dr. Snowden.

"Understandable," said Evaran.

The memory of their last adventure shot through Dr. Snowden's mind. Although everything worked out, there were many complications. He had learned a lot more about Evaran, but it led to more questions. The one thing that stood out to him was that they had discovered there was a different, female version of Evaran who was not a past or future version. It was something that Dr. Snowden had chewed on for over a month.

Evaran pursed his lips. "Kamala is very relaxing, yet you seem deep in thought."

"Well, I was thinking that this is what I thought most of our travels would be like," said Dr. Snowden. "Maybe a few more cultural events or scrounging around ruins."

"I am usually not this active in my travels," said Evaran. "The fact that I am would seem to suggest I am in the right place."

Dr. Snowden glanced over at Emily, who was looking at her feet. She did not want to travel with Evaran at first, but now she did not want to leave. Traveling with Evaran was her safe haven, her new home. He had hoped some time away from everything would change her outlook, but it was not appearing that way.

Evaran drew his lips taut. "After the last few adventures you two have been through, I hope this can make up for some of it."

"If you're taking requests on the next place to go, it would be interesting to go through the various layers of reality you've mentioned in the past," said Dr. Snowden.

Evaran observed Dr. Snowden for a moment. "You wish to investigate my origin."

Dr. Snowden chuckled. "We could do that, and maybe . . . find out more about this other Evaran and the Torvatta."

"Perhaps," said Evaran. "It has been on my mind as well. It could be dangerous, though."

"I'm up for it," said Emily.

"I figured you would be," said Evaran. "Are you not relaxing here?"

Emily shrugged. "There's not much to do other than sit and look at half-naked aliens."

Dr. Snowden wrinkled his eyebrows. "You could interact with others . . ."

Emily shot Dr. Snowden a look.

"Okay, okay, maybe not," said Dr. Snowden. He missed the Emily who would have dove into the history of Kamala and the Rokki. Now it seemed all she was interested in was knowing who was a threat. He shook his head and then looked around for V. Evaran had created V as a flying orb that could scan, stealth, and project holograms and had an extensible segmented arm that could pick up and carry small things. V had taken on a male persona and was made to be Evaran's mobile assistant, but Dr. Snowden considered him a friend. "Where's V?"

V shimmered into view. "I am here, Dr. Snowden. I was observing the organic life-forms from above."

"Did you find anything interesting?"

"Analysis. There are twenty-six different species on this beach. Some were engaging in reproductive activity."

"Oh . . . uhh . . . wow . . . ," said Dr. Snowden as his eyes popped open. He ran a hand down his throat.

"Are you thirsty?"

"Actually . . . yeah. I could use some iced tea."

V scanned Emily. "You both could use some hydration. I will bring some iced tea." He flew off.

Dr. Snowden had raised a hand to stop V. "I was going to suggest we all head back for lunch, but this works too."

Evaran glanced at Dr. Snowden. "V wanted to help you relax."

Dr. Snowden harrumphed as he shook his head. "That's V."

After a few minutes, Dr. Snowden's gaze followed V as he came back in full body mode. It intrigued him that despite the fact V could be in a humanoid robot form, he chose to be in orb mode the majority of the time. Since he had to carry something, robot mode had to be used.

V handed Dr. Snowden a metallic container. "It is chilled, and replicated using your previous pattern."

"Thank you," said Dr. Snowden.

V gave Emily the other one. "This is for you."

"Thanks," said Emily.

V faced Evaran. "A summons has been initiated."

Evaran snapped his head toward V. "When did it activate?"

"It activated one hour ago."

Evaran sighed as he looked up. "Okay. I will check it out once on board." He glanced at Dr. Snowden. "Since I know you will ask, summonses are something that came with the Torvatta. It was part of the package. A summons sends me to a point in space and time where I must intervene in some unknown situation and use my judgment to render a decision. The timeline will adjust to it."

"Whoa," said Dr. Snowden. "You make it sound like the Torvatta's alive."

"I get that feeling sometimes. The Torvatta actually has a list of places for me to investigate. If one activates, I must go, but I have ignored them for a while now," said Evaran.

Dr. Snowden raised his head a bit. "Because of us . . . right?"

"Yes. It would appear the Torvatta does not have patience."

"How does it have a list of places across space and time?"

"I am not sure," said Evaran. "That was never explained when the Torvatta was given to me, and I have not found anything in the Torvatta's database on it. However, it was responsible for me going to the Andromeda galaxy long ago."

Dr. Snowden's eyes narrowed. "Maybe the person who gave you the Torvatta is sending these summons . . ."

"It is possible," said Evaran. "I understand your concern, but the summons I have responded to needed my presence.

The friend who gave me the Torvatta is someone who I would trust my life with."

Dr. Snowden adjusted his glasses. "What happens if you ignore an active summons?"

"The Torvatta will transport itself to that location the next time I step on board. I do have some time before that occurs, though."

Dr. Snowden's eyes widened. "Yeah . . . that should probably be checked out then."

"Will this delay my orb upgrade?" asked V.

"I am afraid so. I still have some work to do on it," said Evaran. "Once this summons is resolved, it will be my top priority. You have my word."

"Acknowledged."

Emily picked up her survival suit and put it in her lap. She glanced at Evaran. "I'm ready to go when you are."

Evaran rubbed his chin. "A summons is potentially dangerous. Maybe you two should stay here. I can handle it and be back in less than ten minutes from your perspective. Then we could take Dr. Snowden's suggestion for our next place to go."

Dr. Snowden grinned at Emily, then shook a fist at Evaran. "No way. We go as a team. Evaran and the gang."

Emily snorted as a smile fought for control of her lips.

Evaran shook his head. "Humanity. Always up for a challenge, even at this young age. Very well. Let us head to the Torvatta."

Dr. Snowden ran his hands over his head as the shower water fell over him. Although Kamala was a planet he could see himself retiring on someday, the lure of an adventure sparked his curiosity. He had learned that the Torvatta was given to Evaran by a friend and was continually being upgraded. Of course, Evaran had never mentioned who the friend was, and there were systems that not even Evaran fully understood. This summoning mechanism seemed to be one of them.

After showering and getting dressed, he stood in front of a mirror. His brown twill slacks and white striped shirt with a brown bow tie and cotton vest slipped over it was his uniform on these adventures. Running a hand over his trimmed beard made him think of the nanobots. With them inside him, he aged five weeks for every year. They also provided regeneration, heightened senses, superior strength and speed, and, as of the last adventure, the ability to raise their activity level to give him a boost. Although they were injected into him without his consent during an alien abduction, the nanobots had become a part of his life. He did one final review of his reflection, then headed to the conference room.

When Dr. Snowden arrived at the conference room, he noted Emily had on her survival suit and was already seated. The suit had a solid light-gray material as the base layer, with dark-gray fiberglass-like padding covering the major sections of the body. There was a belt that had several pouches on it and a slot to hold her PSD. It reminded him a bit of Evaran's outfit, but much darker.

Evaran sat at the end of the rectangular conference table, with Emily to his left. V in body mode was seated on the right.

Dr. Snowden had come to enjoy this room. It existed outside normal space and time in its own dimension. Dimensional mechanics as Evaran had called it. The room had matter replicators that could make any type of food it had a pattern for. Dr. Snowden had spent many a morning enjoying his coffee here, and also good conversations over dinner. He took a seat next to Emily.

"Now that we are all here, let me show you where I am being summoned to," said Evaran. He tapped at the embedded console in front of him. A projection shot up from the middle of the table, showing a map of the Milky Way galaxy. He pointed at a red dot on it. "We are going there, in the year 3104. I am not sure what awaits us, but it is approximately seven hundred forty light-years away from Earth."

Emily wrinkled her eyebrows. "Can't you look it up? I thought you had all the milestones of humanity."

"I do. However, they are, for the most part, extremely high level. Most of the events are pulled from sources in the future, and I make sure to only grab the event title, not the details. For instance, with the Fredorian Arkaron event, the title was, 'Fredoria finds the lost Arkaron and grows in power due to trade deal with the Kreagan Star Empire.' That was it. When I first came to Earth, I spent some time traveling humanity's timescape. It is larger than you might realize. What I do know is that Earth was one of the founders of an empire named the United Planets from around this time period. I suspect whatever is waiting for us there will involve that to some degree. I do not know if they have reached this far out into space, but we will find out."

"Oh," said Emily.

Dr. Snowden scooted to the edge of his seat. "It's quite a bit away from Earth. If we did expand out this far, I would think travel time and communications would be rough."

"Indeed. However, humanity has learned the basics of condensed space travel and long-distance communications in this time period," said Evaran. "We will need to be careful."

Dr. Snowden raised his eyebrows. "Even when we *are* careful, danger seems to follow." He glanced at Emily.

Emily shrugged.

"There is always that possibility. Are we ready to go?" asked Evaran.

Dr. Snowden and Emily both nodded and then assembled in the command center.

Dr. Snowden sat in one of the U-shaped seating areas to the sides of Evaran's command chair. He liked the layout of the ship in general. It had an entrance in the back, with three doors on each side that led off to dimensional rooms that existed outside normal space. He remembered seeing the rooms for the first time and trying to figure out if it was a display trick, but they were real. A lift to the roof was in front of the entrance. Ramps hugged the sides of the ship and led to a central walkway that separated the entrance area from the command center.

He had spent a lot of time in the command center. It was roughly one-third of the main area of the ship. Evaran's command chair sat in the top center of it, with ramps leading to a depressed area.

His eyes focused on the immediate front of the ship. V stood before a U-shaped console that had three angled holographic layers above it. Dr. Snowden had learned how to operate it, and it was more intuitive than he had originally thought. The front wall was one screen, but usually split into a left and right screen. He recalled that the left screen showed a real-time view outside the ship and the right was more for tactical views or information.

"V, take us out," said Evaran.

"Acknowledged," said V as his hands flew over the console.

The Torvatta ascended through cloud cover and reached space. It flew a bit away from Kamala before holding position.

It then shot out a gold beam that formed a silver-ringed portal with a light-blue rippled surface.

Dr. Snowden enjoyed seeing the portal formation. He had come to understand that the colors of the beam, the portal ring, and the surface corresponded to where they were going. He had seen it change color when they went to another timeline, and once again when they went to a pocket universe.

The Torvatta flew through the portal into a tunnel with pinpoints of light appearing then disappearing as fast as he could register them. They exited the tunnel into deep space.

Dr. Snowden scanned the front left screen, then the right one. "I don't see anything . . ."

"We are in the interstellar medium outside the solar system of our destination, roughly two light-years away. We need to go forward in time still, then head in," said Evaran.

"Why didn't we head in and time warp there?"

"I do not know what is there. We could be entering into a hostile situation."

"We could stealth," said Dr. Snowden.

Evaran shook his head. "It should appear that we are coming into the solar system like a normal ship. Whatever authority claims the space will then contact us without dealing with something appearing out of nowhere."

Dr. Snowden bobbed his head. "Fair enough."

The left screen showed the stars fade out, then shimmer back into view.

"We have arrived on June 13, 3104 at six a.m., Earth time," said V.

"Excellent," said Evaran.

Dr. Snowden remembered the uneasy feeling that had swept over him the first time he had seen the Torvatta go through time. How it worked was beyond him, and Evaran never fully explained it. Maybe it was a feature of the Torvatta that even he did not understand. Evaran said that he would explain it sometime, which always seemed to be pushed back.

"Now we go in," said Evaran. "V."

"Acknowledged."

The Torvatta angled itself toward the solar system and flew in. After three hours, they passed the first planet, and several red dots appeared on the solar-system map.

"Analysis. Seven ships of unknown configuration headed at an intercept angle."

"Hold position."

"Acknowledged."

Dr. Snowden watched the ship wireframe on the right screen that showed thruster activity. It showed the middle of the Torvatta pivot 180 degrees, then fire the main thrusters. He observed the speedometer decreasing. It made sense that to slow their inertia, they would have to fire in the direction they had momentum in. Being able to rotate the ship quickly to fire in any direction was something the Torvatta had as an advantage. He remembered seeing it in action before but also knew there were thrusters in the front and sides and that they could be angled. Those were probably more for steering.

After twenty minutes, an image of the ships appeared on the left screen. One was much larger than the others.

Dr. Snowden figured they were fighter craft of some sort. The profile of the larger ship was unusual to him. It reminded him a bit of the Torvatta, except the ship's profile was much larger and more flattened. On the backside were two large finlike pieces that looked like they were clamped on. The gap between the top part and the bottom part was a mix between glowing blue panels and what appeared to be metallic ones. He did not see anything that resembled a bridge. If anything, the top surface and underside were smooth, to the point that the only discernible features on them were raised bumps, some segmented lines, and a symbol of three circles with a triangle in the middle.

Dr. Snowden pointed at the symbol. "Umm . . . I hope that's not a derivative of what I think it is."

Evaran shook his head with a smile. "No, it is a United Planets symbol, according to the Torvatta symbol registry."

Dr. Snowden exhaled from his nose. The last time he saw a symbol with circles and triangles, it was the timeline-invading Purifiers. The six smaller ships flying off to the side looked like cylindrical cannons with triangular-shaped wings on the top and bottom and to the sides. Between the wings were slits that were lit blue. He was beginning to sense a pattern in the design. They looked too small to house a human. Probably support drones of some type. He also noticed that the ship was not in front of them, but above them and to the side, relative to their position. Ships meeting face-to-face was something he saw in science fiction, but he knew that in space, it could be in any direction.

Evaran raised a hand. "Set Torvatta scan profile two."

"Acknowledged," said V. His hands went to work on the front console, and after a moment, he said, "Torvatta scan profile two activated. Shields weakening now."

When the lead ship was in range, it shot a beam that washed over the Torvatta.

"They are attempting to contact us. Analyzing communication protocol," said V.

"Once established, transfer it to full screen," said Evaran.

"Acknowledged," said V. After a moment, he said, "Communication protocol established. Transferring visual."

The front screen changed to a live feed of a metallic humanoid sitting in a command chair. In front of him was a row of workstations manned by humanoid robots and other humanoids like the one in the command chair. The robots had polygonal robotic faces with a single red eye encased in a steel cylinder as the main facial feature. Their bodies looked like they had the bare essentials of legs, arms, and a segmented coil that served as a backbone to a semitransparent chest plate.

In contrast, the other robotic humanoids had a white faceplate that mimicked a human face, with a body that had dark-gray metallic skin with lines that segmented it into sections. The humanoid in the command chair had a United Planets symbol emblazoned on the right side of its chest.

It was the furry four-foot humanoids in the back, and some on the side, that caught Dr. Snowden's attention. They reminded him of what a meerkat would look like it if were humanoid. They had on a different type of suit than the humans and robots. His attention focused on the humanoid as he spoke in a soft yet commanding voice.

"I am Z7, a United Planets Bureau of Law Enforcement agent. You have entered Kalesh space. Please identify yourself."

Evaran stood and bowed with his left hand across his stomach. "I am Evaran, and this is my ship, the Torvatta. I have with me Dr. Albert Snowden, Emily Snowden, and V. We are explorers and new to this region of space. We only seek a place to stock up and take a break from our travels." He reached into a small compartment on the side of his chair and pulled out a small device. "If it helps, we do have some identification you may be familiar with."

Dr. Snowden noted it was the device that had been given to them by the Helians, a nonhuman power group that essentially ran Earth in the past. It was meant to identify Evaran to humanity via the Evaran Protocol, something established in their last adventure.

A beam washed over the Torvatta again.

Z7 tilted his head for a moment, then straightened it. "An ancient identification, but it is valid. You have been cleared to enter Kalesh space. I am relaying to you the coordinates of the Corunus station above Roeth, fourth planet from the sun and home world of the Kalesh. Proceed there to receive final clearance. So you are aware, your ship will be monitored at all times. United Planets and Kalesh regulations have been sent. Please confirm you have received them."

Evaran looked at V.

"Regulations received."

"Please read through them prior to your arrival at Corunus," said Z7.

"We will. Thank you," said Evaran.

The screen flashed off.

"Once we are out of range, revert back to Torvatta scan profile one," said Evaran.

"Acknowledged."

"Well, that wasn't too bad," said Dr. Snowden. "I don't think I've ever seen the Torvatta scanned before. What was all that scan profile stuff?"

Evaran raised a finger. "Profile one is the default, and when active, the shields are fully powered and the Torvatta appears to not exist. Profile two weakens the shields and returns to the scanner a small ship with low power, no dimensional rooms or weapons, and cramped quarters."

"Ha!" said Dr. Snowden. "You deceived them."

"If I did not deceive them, they would visually see a ship that should not exist. That may be cause for investigation on their part."

Dr. Snowden looked at Evaran. "Like you did on Kreagus. And I'm going to guess Z7 was an android or something?"

"You are correct. Z7 was an android. The robots around him did not have the same level of sophistication. I suspect the robotic aspect of their form was intentional."

"Who were the furry ones?" asked Emily.

"They were most likely Kalesh. We will learn more on Corunus."

Dr. Snowden smirked. "Well, let's hope this goes a lot smoother than the last time." He remembered the previous time they were given clearance. They were jailed shortly after landing.

"I concur," said Evaran. "V, take us in."

"Acknowledged."

02

After an hour and a half of flying through mostly empty space, the Torvatta reached the Corunus space station that Z7 had directed them to. The left screen showed it in mid orbit over Roeth.

Dr. Snowden was impressed at how fast the Torvatta could move in normal space. Even without portals, it did one light-year in about two hours. He suspected they could have done that entering the system instead of going for three hours until they met something, but if they wanted to appear normal, it made sense to travel at a lower speed until met by whatever authority claimed the space.

Corunus had a spherical center, surrounded by a ring attached by large cylindrical connectors. Extending out from the ring were smaller arms. Larger ships were docked at the end of it, while smaller ships were coming and going from hangar bays on the sides.

While the station was impressive to Dr. Snowden, it was the right screen with the solar-system map that showed blue dots surrounding the sun that caught his attention. He pointed at it and looked at Evaran. "What are those?"

Evaran perused his ARI for a moment, then faced Dr. Snowden. "It appears to be what you would refer to as a Dyson bubble, or at least the beginnings of one."

Dr. Snowden's eyes popped open. "Seriously?"

"Yes. According to the long-range scans, there are one hundred twenty-two structures. I am not sure if they are collectors or habitats or a mix."

Emily wrinkled her eyebrows. "I remember reading something about these long ago. I always thought that they had a shell or something."

Dr. Snowden wagged a finger at her. "In a Dyson sphere, yes. A Dyson bubble is a variant of a Dyson swarm. They are a bunch of geosynchronous structures that are independent of each other. It's a lot more feasible from an engineering perspective, at least from what I know of it."

"We can check them out after this summons is dealt with," said Evaran.

Dr. Snowden's eyes lit up.

"Docking authorization received," said V.

"Take us in," said Evaran.

"Acknowledged."

The Torvatta approached Corunus.

Dr. Snowden watched the left screen highlight the hangar bay they were to go to.

The door slid open, revealing a smoke-colored semitransparent shield. Several small drone ships escorted the Torvatta up to the hangar bay door. The Torvatta passed through the shield and landed.

Dr. Snowden noted that the door was sliding back when they went through the shield, effectively sealing them in. Security and docking protocols seemed much more formalized out here. They did not mess around. At least it would not be another human-supremacist situation.

Evaran stood and waved toward the Torvatta exit. "I do not think you will need your suits. Come."

Dr. Snowden watched Emily follow Evaran. He turned toward V. "Are you coming this time?"

"Yes, but in body mode."

Dr. Snowden grinned. "Great. I'm glad you're coming with us."

V's chest lights glowed a bit brighter. "Acknowledged."

Dr. Snowden knew V would have preferred orb mode, but given they had seen androids and humanoid robots earlier, V's body mode would blend in better. He exited the Torvatta with V and rendezvoused with Evaran and Emily in the now-sealed docking bay.

They headed toward a doorway opposite the hangar bay door. It hissed, then slid to the side, revealing a small tunnel. After everyone stepped in, the door closed.

Dr. Snowden noticed the other side of the tunnel was sealed. He jumped when a flat layer of light rose from the floor to the ceiling and a mist shot out of several points in the ceiling. The smell reminded him of bleach. Looking around, he said, "What is all this?"

"Decontamination," said Evaran. "They are also scanning our internals, or trying to anyways. It is similar to what the Helian structure did on Atlantis."

"Oh . . . ," said Dr. Snowden. "That was after we were outside the ship, though."

Evaran raised a finger. "Not quite. The landing pad scanned us as soon as we stepped out. It would have formed a bubble shield if it detected anything."

"I didn't even notice. Huh. At least this one is more visible."

The door opposite the one they came through slid back. They entered into a large hallway and began to walk down it, following large green arrows on the ground pointed toward the interior ring.

Dr. Snowden wrinkled his nose as they exited the tunnel. The smell of steak seemed soaked into the environment. As they passed by other hangars, he could see other ships, although he did not recognize any of their designs.

After walking the length of the hallway, they entered a room that was dome shaped, with a section off to the right that had a freestanding table surrounded by chairs. To the left were four humanoid robot guards.

Dr. Snowden had expected to see them carrying weapons, but instead they had large forearms that looked like a weapon was fused onto them. One of the meerkat-like humanoids he had seen earlier greeted them. He was not sure if the others noticed it, but the humanoid had a strong musky smell.

The humanoid bowed. "Welcome to Corunus. I'm Jax and will be your registrar."

Evaran bowed with his left hand across his stomach. "I am Evaran, and with me are Dr. Albert Snowden, Emily Snowden, and V."

"Noted! Please follow me," said Jax as he bounded over to the table on the right side.

After they took their seats, Dr. Snowden asked, "Are you . . . a Kalesh?"

Jax looked up from the embedded console in the table that he had been looking at. "You're quite right. From what I've heard, humans say we look like weasels."

Dr. Snowden bobbed his head. "I would say meerkat."

"That's an Earth creature. I have studied Earth's animals to some degree, and I would agree with you. Impressive. I'm even more impressed that you're fluent in Kreagan. Do you use an augment for that?"

Dr. Snowden glanced at Evaran, then back at Jax. "No . . . it's something I picked up."

"Uh-huh," said Jax. He focused back on the console. "This is interesting," he said, stroking his small snout. "There are no Kalesh records on you, but the United Planets has cleared you, but no reason has been given. Give me a moment." He tapped at the console and, after a minute, looked up. "No . . . no . . . it's right. Somehow you've been cleared, and quickly too. I've never seen that before."

Evaran rested his chin on his right hand. "Interesting."

"Very," said Jax. He got up and walked over to a cabinet-like device. He opened the doors and pulled out four wristbands. After returning and handing them out, he said, "These are your physical registrations. They have a language translator for our native tongue as well. To access the interface, just squeeze them."

Emily snapped hers on and twisted her wrist around. "Do they also tell you where we're at all the time?"

"Of course. However . . . only someone of the appropriate authority can actually look at that information. For instance, I couldn't, but law enforcement could."

"I see," said Evaran. "What restrictions do we have in regards to going to the planet?"

"You're cleared, but you're also a new arrival. All new arrivals usually go to Follisat, where I've registered two rooms for all of you and access to a replicator cafeteria. The coordinates are in the bands."

Emily narrowed her eyes. "What if we don't want to go there?"

Jax shrugged. "Your choice . . . but if you're new to Kalesh culture, it would be advisable to go there first."

Dr. Snowden glanced at Evaran. "That sounds good to me." He looked at Jax. "Can we check out the station?"

Jax peeled back his lips and made snickering sounds through his nose.

Dr. Snowden's eyes widened.

Jax showed them his palms. "Don't worry. This is how Kalesh laugh. Most humans are startled by it. You'll get used to it. I enjoy human curiosity. It's one thing we have in common."

"Oh . . . ," said Dr. Snowden. He noticed Emily had instinctively reached for her PSD.

"Nonetheless, given your clearance level, this station is yours to explore."

"I'm looking forward to checking it out," said Dr. Snowden.

"Before you go, I do have one question. According to the scans, you," said Jax, pointing at Evaran, "have mass, but your internals weren't visible." He looked at Dr. Snowden, then Emily. "And you two have nanobots, but not any that I've seen before. Where did you all come from? I'm guessing Earth but . . ."

Evaran raised his head up a bit. "We came from far away."

Jax snickered. "I see . . . well . . . once again, based on your clearance level, you don't have to tell me. I was only curious. You're registered and free to go. I hope you enjoy the station."

Dr. Snowden stood and extended a hand. "Thanks. Any place you recommend to eat at?" He noticed Emily shaking her head.

Jax returned the handshake. "I would suggest checking out Krells. He runs a somewhat exotic eatery. Your wristbands have a map of the station."

Dr. Snowden squeezed his wristband, and a projection shot up with spheres with words in them. He selected the navigation sphere, which expanded to show another series of spheres. After selecting the station one, the projection changed to a layout of the station. He used his other finger to navigate through it. "Where's Krells?" The map zoomed into a location briefly, then zoomed back out with a line from where they were to Krells. "Okay . . . voice activated. That was pretty nifty."

Jax snickered. "It has some other commands, accessible by voice, or augments, if you got them."

"You mentioned that before. What are augments exactly?" asked Emily.

"You know, cybernetic implants. They're quite popular in the United Planets. They've been helping integrate them into Kalesh culture. Since I work here, I've been able to get quite a few useful ones. To be honest, I'm surprised you have nanobots."

"Elaborate," said Evaran.

"No one has been able to get nanobots to stick around in the body for long periods. Augments, yes, nanobots, no." He waved his clawed hand between Dr. Snowden and Emily. "The fact you two have them is very interesting to me."

"I see," said Evaran. "Due to our clearance, I am afraid we cannot go into that."

"Of course, of course. Anyways . . . if you have questions, you can ask one of the metalheads."

V's chest lights lit up as he tilted his head.

Jax raised his hand. "Sorry, sorry, it's nothing personal. Kalesh are not quite as . . . comfortable . . . around robots and androids as humans are."

"Acknowledged."

Evaran stood and gestured toward the room exit. "Come, let us explore the station."

As they exited the room, Dr. Snowden looked back at Jax. Jax was bobbing his head around as if trying to figure out who they were. Dr. Snowden liked Jax. If the Kalesh were like that in general, he figured he would get along great with them.

He wanted to spend more time learning about Kalesh culture, but the summons hung around in the back of his mind. A smile crept onto his face as he looked around. The hustle and bustle of the large open area they were in was a nice change from the last time they were on a space station. He noticed Emily scanning around. She seemed less tense. He wondered if her sense of exploration was fighting her now-guarded nature.

Emily swiveled her head toward Dr. Snowden.

Dr. Snowden half smiled.

Emily raised an eyebrow.

Dr. Snowden smiled as they continued on.

Over the next hour, Dr. Snowden soaked in the environment as they traversed it. The station had spotless floors, but it was the walls that caught his attention. They were metallic and segmented into several sections by thick black strips that showed both holographic and static displays of information.

The design intrigued him, as every twenty feet, a portion of the wall jutted out with a sloped segment. Lights were interspersed throughout. The floor also had lights embedded in it, and the floor area near the base of the walls had a strip that glowed blue. It gave off a very high-tech feel to him. The smell of fresh air wafting by seemed unusual on a space station.

There was no shortage of activity around him. He saw Kalesh, humans, and a variety of aliens he had never seen before. A grin crept onto his face when a Kreagan in a somewhat elaborate robe passed by. Maybe an ambassador.

The humans encased in an advanced heavy armor suit did not escape his attention. They looked like they were ready to fight at a moment's notice. Their forearms were huge, and he could not identify half the items hanging off the armor. One of the items reminded him of Evaran's baton. He suspected that it probably served a more lethal purpose. Unlike the humanoid robots he had seen before, these humans had weapons on their backs. There were also three small drones flying around them at all times.

The amount of humanoid robots and androids intrigued him. The androids were usually flanked by at least two robot guards or flying drones. He remembered that Z7 was essentially border patrol, but wondered what they did other than security. He figured the humans handled the higher-risk areas. The idea of artificial intelligences being common gave him hope that there was not an AI singularity that had destroyed Earth. "Interesting that they have robots for guards given the humans in suits I saw. I wonder if the androids have their own AI."

"They do. Their design is inferior to mine," said V.

Dr. Snowden snorted. "Really? How'd you come to that conclusion?"

"Analysis. They tried to contact me remotely. After an exchange of data, we concluded that I was of superior design."

"You're not modest at all, are you?" asked Dr. Snowden.

V tilted his head.

Dr. Snowden chuckled.

Evaran laid a hand on V's shoulder. "To a human, that would appear arrogant, even if it is true."

V dipped his head. "I did not mean to appear arrogant. I apologize."

"It is okay. Consider it a learning moment."

"Acknowledged."

Dr. Snowden was used to treating V like a human. Although V's logic was objective, Dr. Snowden had made it subjective. He realized that he would need to be more aware of that.

When they were halfway to Krells, Evaran pointed at a hallway with no one in it. When they entered it, he placed his UIC on the embedded console on the wall. After a moment, he pulled it off and perused his ARI. "Intriguing. The station systems are host to many AIs."

"Is that a good or bad thing?" asked Dr. Snowden.

"The UIC has a protocol to avoid AIs and route around them. However, due to the amount of AIs, the UIC was not able to retrieve much."

"Oh . . . I take it you weren't expecting that?" asked Dr. Snowden.

"I was not. I do not recall humanity having this type of AI setup in this time period."

Dr. Snowden gulped. "Okay . . . that doesn't sound good. So humanity is a bit more advanced than it should be. We've seen that before . . ." He shook his head.

"It is possible that maybe it did exist and I was unaware of it," said Evaran.

Dr. Snowden mused over the situation as they continued on. He recalled on their last adventure seeing humanity jump almost three thousand years technology-wise due to a timeline change. Hopefully this was a case of Evaran not knowing about this far-off setup. If not, then maybe it was the first clue on what the summons was for.

Emily tapped Dr. Snowden's arm.

Dr. Snowden looked forward and then swerved to avoid hitting a pillar. "Thanks . . . I was just thinking."

"I know," said Emily. "I got your back."

"What about my front?"

Emily shook her head.

Although Dr. Snowden would have preferred a laugh from her like he was used to, this would have to do. He was happy to have any interaction with her that caused her to do something other than draw her lips flat.

After another hour of journeying across the station, they reached an entryway with a holographic sign above it that displayed Krells.

Dr. Snowden sniffed. "It smells good over here. I wonder how much it costs." He rubbed his chin and looked at Evaran. "Speaking of which, how *are* we going to pay?"

"It is free of charge," said Evaran.

Dr. Snowden chuckled. "Yeah, well, I guess not everyone has a UIC. Did you wire some money or something?"

"I meant that the food here is free of charge. At least the food created by replication rations."

Dr. Snowden glanced at Emily, who shrugged.

"Humanity can replicate matter in this time period," said Evaran. "The resources needed to do it are simply the base elements. The more rations you have, the more you can replicate for yourself." He raised a finger. "However, based on what I saw from what the UIC gathered, it would appear that Krells is paid in replication rations by the United Planets to be here."

"That's an interesting economic model," said Dr. Snowden. "I'd guess then that replication resource gathering is a big industry."

"Yes. It appears the process for converting matter and storing it in this time period and region is a complex process. Perhaps the United Planets has a facility here for that and provides this service to the station as a symbol of good faith," said Evaran. "Shall we enter?"

Dr. Snowden shrugged and gestured forward. His eyes popped open as he surveyed the interior once they were inside. It was spacious and much larger than he expected. It could have easily supported several hundred people. There were segmented dining and lounge areas off the side, with a central eating area. The noise from patrons reverberated throughout.

They sat at a small rectangular table near the entrance. When they sat, holographic menus appeared before them. Touching the food items would switch to them and blow it up full-size.

"Now that is cool," said Emily.

"Yeah," said Dr. Snowden as his hands navigated the menu. "There's a lot of interesting choices." He selected the closest thing to a burger. The menu disappeared, and a timer appeared on the table in front of him. He admired the efficiency of it.

When the timer hit zero after five minutes, the text "Served by Ellix" appeared.

Dr. Snowden shot Evaran a quizzical look. "What's an Ellix?"

Evaran pointed at an alien coming their way. "I would assume him."

Dr. Snowden noted that the plump alien was short with gray skin and big ears. He glanced at Emily, who he thought would be repulsed by Ellix's bug-like face, but Emily showed no emotion. When they were on Kreagus in the past, the food was served up by the table. He wondered why a server was needed.

Ellix arrived pushing a hover slab with the ordered dishes. He unloaded them onto the table. "I hope you enjoy your meal."

Evaran gestured at Ellix. "You are a Crustican."

"I sure am," said Ellix. He paused as he scrutinized Evaran. "Not many people would've known that."

"I have been to Octoris and know several Crusticans. I can speak fluent Oakarish as well."

Ellix laughed. "It's a small galaxy, huh?"

"It is. What brought you out here?"

Ellix turned and waved a hand around in an arc. "This place. The United Planets pays my family quite well to be here. It seems they want the best restaurants from around the empire. I don't have the automated food tables, but I don't mind. I get to interact with others." He tapped his chest. "In short, they chose well."

"They must pay pretty good then," said Dr. Snowden.

"Of course. I'll have enough to replicate my dream cluster back on Octoris in a few years. Where are you all from?"

"Earth," said Evaran.

"Ahh, quite a journey to get here then," said Ellix.

"Indeed. Do you have any recommendations on places to visit while we are here?"

Ellix bobbed his head. "Well, you've probably already been told to go to Follisat. That's a good start. It's the only place I've visited myself." He leaned in. "The Kalesh sorta creep me out. They remind me of a predator from our history"

"A gorbcrad," said Evaran.

Ellix nodded as he leaned back out. "Anyways, there are also space habitats, but those are off-limits."

"Elaborate."

"I'm surprised you haven't heard," said Ellix. "They're all quarantined. Every single station. Advanced Dynamics has pretty much shut down any travel to and from them."

"I would've thought the United Planets owned the habitats," said Dr. Snowden.

"No . . . and one thing you'll find is reverence for Advanced Dynamics on Roeth," said Ellix. "Their technology was the tipping point in the Voss Imperium wars. The Kalesh regard them quite highly. Not to belittle the United Planets. After all, they helped out quite a bit in the war. The United Planets still has some influence. This station is one of their first joint ventures."

Dr. Snowden glanced at Evaran, then Ellix. "So . . . what presence does the United Planets have then?"

"A few United Planets Bureau of Law Enforcement offices on the outskirts of some of the major Kalesh cities. They provide assistance as needed and also serve as a liaison for all alien races on the planet," said Ellix with a chuckle. "I'm glad they're there. The Kalesh . . . are a bit skittish about aliens in general after the war. Their justice system was a bit biased. They wanted to join the United Planets, though, for security reasons."

Emily narrowed her eyes. "Is Follisat a safe place?"

Ellix laughed. "*Safe* is not the word I'd use to describe it. It's a diverse city, and some Kalesh point to it as why aliens visiting is a bad thing."

"Oh . . . ," said Emily with raised eyebrows. "It's nothing we can't handle."

Ellix looked Emily up and down, then surveyed the others. "I can tell you all probably won't have any issues," he said, waving a finger at V. "Especially with a robot bodyguard."

V tilted his head.

A device beeped and lit up on Ellix's wrist. "Looks like I need to get back to work. Enjoy your meal and appreciate the conversation. They're so rare nowadays." He took off toward the back.

Dr. Snowden pondered their discussion. It seemed that there were multiple power factions. The Kalesh, who inhabited Roeth; Advanced Dynamics, who built space habitats and supported the Kalesh in some war; and the United Planets, a latecomer that was slowly integrating. He could not shake the feeling that the summons was going to be messy. "He seems like a nice guy."

"Crusticans generally are. They were one of the first species I met when I arrived in this galaxy," said Evaran.

Dr. Snowden dove into his burger-like food item with green-tinted meat. "I thought you met humans first."

"I met them as well," said Evaran, looking far off.

Dr. Snowden examined Evaran. It occurred to him that he had never asked much about Evaran's previous travels. "I'd be curious to hear about your previous adventures on Earth and around this galaxy."

"That would take a lot of time. However, since you asked about my arrival, now is as good a time as any to tell you."

Dr. Snowden perked up as he glanced at Emily. He noticed she had also sat up and was studying Evaran. It appeared that despite her tough outside, she still had that curiosity streak that Snowdens were known for. Maybe that would be his ticket to reaching her, assuming she let him in. He gulped as Evaran began to talk about his arrival on Earth.

03

Earlier that day at 9:30 a.m. in the city of Da Nesh on the planet Roeth, United Planets Bureau of Law Enforcement Agent Jane Trellis sighed as she swung her legs over the side of her bed. She stretched and yawned as she took stock of her bleak apartment. The familiar smell of Kalesh fruits greeted her.

With a grin, she looked down at her fair-skinned left palm. Using her thumb, she pressed at a barely lit circle under the skin between her middle two fingers. A menu appeared in the air in front of her with several options. She was in the mood for something cheerful. Pressing the apartment button caused various panels to showcase themes. She chose a theme that reminded her of Fredoria, her home world. When she looked around, the furniture was more pleasant.

She loved her augments, especially the ocular ones that gave her augmented reality. With a press of a button, she could change the theme of anything she looked at via an augmented reality interface. However, it was time to clean up and then get to work.

Being a field agent assigned to Da Nesh was not as easy as she had thought it was going to be. Her boss and family friend, Andrew Dotrick, was lenient with her and allowed her a wide berth in terms of how she operated. Cases would be sent to her, and she would work on them out in the city and occasionally check in at the office. Today was one of those check-ins.

Andrew was a father figure to her, and after her parents died, he had watched over her until she was an adult. Growing up was not easy, but Andrew's steady hand guided her through troubled times. When Andrew came out to Roeth, she was initially dismayed that he was going so far away. However, working with him now was natural to her. She would prove that his decision to let her work for him was not a mistake.

She headed to the bathroom and stripped off her undergarments before stepping into a clear cylinder. After locking it, she interacted with her ARI and started the cleaning cycle. Dark-blue water shot down and filled the cylinder up to her chest. It then swirled around her while occasionally rising up to the top of her head to soak her long brown hair. After a few minutes of that, the water dispensed out the bottom. Warm air surrounded her as the drying cycle commenced. After a few moments, she stepped out of the cylinder feeling refreshed.

Next up was to get her power suit on. She walked over to a wall near her bed and tapped at it. A portion of it slid back, and a structure pushed out. It had her suit, boots, and other pieces of standard equipment constrained. This was one of the highlights of her day. The white suit with silver and dark-gray segmented lines was damage resistant, yet flexible.

In addition to the augments she had in her body, the suit made her more effective in the field. The black boots could magnetize to any metal surface, and her skintight black gloves allowed her to grip slippery surfaces.

After putting on her suit and boots, she grabbed her standard-issue firearm. Her fingers ran over the cool metal of it when it was holstered. It had saved her several times. Although stun was the official setting, it could scale up as needed, depending on the fight. She never went anywhere without it.

With a final check over, she went to the balcony. Looking down at the busy street made her smile. What caused the Kalesh to stand out from nonaugmented humans was their rapid movements. They seemed to move faster in general, in all aspects, and were formidable close-quarter combatants.

The Kalesh had come a long way since integration. Their past was not as peaceful. They had advanced far enough to build a condensed space drive and attracted the attention of the nearby Voss Imperium, a vicious jackal-like humanoid race that saw Roeth as a resource to be taken. They would have taken it completely over due to their technological advantage, but Advanced Dynamics stepped in and evened the technological playing field. The war ended when the Kalesh petitioned to join the United Planets, led by Earth and Fredoria.

After the United Planets had stepped in, they handed the Voss Imperium a commanding defeat. Ever since then, the Kalesh had embraced the United Planets and requested integration shortly afterward. It was a long process, and the establishment of the Corunus space station and incorporation of offices was the first step. The Da Nesh office she was at had become her new home, and she enjoyed working with the Kalesh employed there.

She had made many friends among the Kalesh, and they were excited to help her get acquainted with Da Nesh. The Kalesh were perennially optimistic, and her guest presentations on the United Planets at the local schools were a hit among the children. She also played with them on the playground, even if she could barely keep up with them.

Her smile wound down as she ran her hand over her necklace. It had been given to her by her husband, Chris, after their first year of marriage. He had been killed almost six years earlier due to an accident when working on one of the space habitats around the sun. She remembered how excited he had been to be hired to work on it. They had only spent one year together on Fredoria before he left. Looking back, she wished she had come to Roeth then. All she wanted was a family, a good career, and to be happy.

Her eyes narrowed as she thought of his employer. Advanced Dynamics. Many Kalesh considered them to be the more important factor in the Voss Imperium war than the United Planets. A corporation operating in and around United Planets space that always seemed to be one step ahead of the United Planets in terms of first contact. Advanced Dynamics was run by Billozein, who had specifically picked Chris due to his exceptional engineering skill set. Chris would have come out anyways and applied to work with whoever was building the Dyson bubble. She gritted her teeth as she recalled trying to find out details on Chris's death. Advanced Dynamics, and Billozein in particular, had been less than forthcoming and deflected any attempt to learn more about it.

Determination flared in her brown eyes. Roeth was the perfect spot for her to find out what really happened to Chris. She had requested a transfer to Roeth and used up most of her political capital to get out of the office she was at. Andrew had been her biggest supporter and welcomed the opportunity to spend time with her. Her stint here would not be wasted.

She shook her head as she swiped through updates on her ARI from across the local and global network. As she swept her eyes over them, a blinking note caught her attention. Her eyebrows wrinkled as she tapped at the update. It expanded to full-size in front of her. The update had one message:

Evaran Protocol Initiated.

She rubbed her chin as she contemplated it. With a gesture, the update changed to a security-clearance-required message. Her head jerked back. This was unusual. Why would it notify her, then reject her when she accessed it? It was probably intended for Andrew, who had a higher security clearance. If that was the case, it should not have shown up on her holo screen. She tapped at her ARI and contacted Andrew.

Andrew's face appeared in front of her. "You're up! When are you headed over?"

"In a bit. I need to check in with our informant, but . . . I have a question."

"Shoot."

Jane flicked a finger at the note.

Andrew looked around for a moment, then reared his head a bit. "Oh . . . I didn't see that one. How'd you get it?"

Jane shrugged. "I don't know. It was there, and it required a higher security clearance than mine. That's kinda unusual."

Andrew raised a finger as he turned to the side for a moment. His hands flew over his ARI. He turned back to face her. "Okay . . . that was supposed to go to me. There was a system update last night, and it looks like they messed up the routing information." He narrowed his eyes. "Was there anything else . . ."

"I didn't look much beyond that one," said Jane with a small grin. "I can look around more if you want . . ."

Andrew swiped at his ARI.

The updates disappeared from Jane's view.

"I'll have a chat with the Kalesh engineers," said Andrew. "This is not the first time they've messed up United Planets message routing."

"I do have more questions about that Evaran Protocol, but will ask in person when I stop by," said Jane.

Andrew smiled. "That would be better. I'll see you then." His image dissipated.

Jane scrunched her eyebrows. Something bothered Andrew. She could see it in his face. Imperceptible to others, but she had known him all her life. Whatever this Evaran Protocol was, it worried him.

She exited her building and closed her eyes as fresh air washed over her. One thing she liked about Roeth was that despite its evolving technological state, the Kalesh always tried to integrate the natural surroundings into their technology. Even in the enclosed United Planets office building, there were trees interspersed everywhere. The smell of the forest mixed with Kalesh spices wafted through the air.

She smiled and headed to a nearby transportation hub. It was underground since most of the above-ground city design was meant to be walked. Easy for the Kalesh since they could move quickly, not so much for a human needing to go a few miles. The transportation hub for the base tied into the cities and was used mostly by the Kalesh employees on the base.

The United Planets office was on the outskirts of Da Nesh, but she was headed to Hillti, a rough area not too far away.

After reaching the hub, she approached one of the transportation units. Raising her left forearm caused a beam from the unit to scan it. The unit's door opened, and she stepped into the small space and took a seat. An interface appeared before her. She selected a spot in Hillti that was less monitored.

Hillti was not a safe district, but it was where her informant was. The interface changed to a smattering of entertainment options as the pod shuddered, then took off down a vacuum-sealed tunnel. She enjoyed the rides and appreciated the ease at which she could get around the city without needing a personal flying craft. If she needed one, she had one, but often it was easier to use the underground transportation system.

When she reached her destination, she disembarked and headed above ground. After fifteen minutes of navigating the back alleys, she reached one behind the packed metal buildings that circled Hillti. A large patch of forest was less than ten feet away. The odor of Hillti versus Da Nesh proper was stark. Hillti reminded her of a garbage dump with buildings. The fecal matter in the alleys did not help things.

Her attention focused on a frail Kalesh male who hobbled by and focused his gaze on her, then continued walking. She headed out of the alley and into the forest a bit. After several minutes, the Kalesh she had seen earlier rushed in. She always got a kick out of seeing Karus and his disguises. She was glad he chose the nickname Karus, since the original long names felt more like a ritual to say rather than an acknowledgment. Karus was much better to say than Karuustogedarne with associated facial and hand movements.

"You're early," said Karus.

"I'm on an accelerated schedule. What do you got?" asked Jane.

Karus shook his furry head. "I don't have much this time. However . . . there has been a lot of underground chatter."

Jane narrowed her eyes. "About what?"

Karus shrugged. "I have no idea, but when communication jumps like that, something big is happening or has happened. You see or hear anything unusual this morning?"

"None, just the usual. I do have to check in with Andrew today, though. I'll tell him you said hi."

Karus smirked as he grabbed his crotch. "You can tell him to eat my—"

Jane extended a hand. "Okay, okay, I get the drift." She knew Karus and Andrew had a long history. Andrew busted Karus so often that Andrew let Karus walk provided he offer local information as needed. Karus preferred that to incarceration. Kalesh in general despised confinement. "All right, anything else before I head out?"

Karus licked his lips. "Be careful."

"Of course," said Jane. "You don't need to worry about me."

Karus sighed. "You're one of the few aliens I can stomach. I'd hate to lose you."

Jane chuckled. "That's a little out of character for you."

"Yeah . . . well . . . there's a lot of nervousness about. Something doesn't feel right." Karus jabbed the air in front of him. "Can't put a claw on it."

Jane tapped her lips with a finger for a moment. "All right. I'd hate to lose my excuse to come out here."

Karus laughed.

Jane always liked the way the Kalesh laughed. They bared their teeth with raised lips and breathed through their nose. It sounded more like snickering than laughing.

Karus dipped his head, then took off.

Jane watched him move effortlessly through the forest. It was no surprise to her that the Kalesh were the masters of their environment. Her attention focused on what Karus had said. She knew that communication spikes were usually precursors to some type of activity. Maybe it was related to the Evaran Protocol. She shook her head as she headed back to the transportation hub. Time to find out.

It did not take Jane long to get to the United Planets Da Nesh building and then to Andrew's office. She always marveled at the distinction between United Planets architecture and the Kalesh take on it. The United Planets building had a wide circular base that narrowed as it went up. The sides were covered in a material that could soak up sunlight and purify the air and was hydrophobic. Its shininess stood out next to the more grungy Kalesh buildings built around it to support the base.

She approached the building entrance, which had two humanoid robot guards standing outside. Several hovering machines whirred around above them. When she was within a few feet of them, she extended her left forearm in front of her. A beam shot at it from above the door.

"Good afternoon, Agent Jane Trellis," said one of the robots with a digital rasp.

Jane nodded and passed between them into the building. She was comfortable with robots in her life. They were not sentient, but mimicked it very well.

As she walked through the large circular hub just inside the building and toward the transport pods, she noticed several humans at the replicator area off to the side. They stood out to her because her ARI showed that they had no augments. All United Planets employees had augments, so these were probably visitors. It was not uncommon to see humans swing by the United Planets office if they had an issue to deal with. She smirked. The fear of augments was something she never understood. She knew that some humans traveled to new planets to get away from the burgeoning trade of augments and their acceptance.

Her ARI revealed them to be members of an obscure group known as the Purists. They believed any alteration of the human body was an abomination and that an overlord would purify the human race. She shook her head. Thankfully they held no power and mainly consisted of small roving bands of members. Why they traveled to alien planets was odd given their human-supremacist views, but she had heard rumors that they were looking for some type of gate.

She arrived at the transportation pod hub, selected one, and then entered it. After interacting with its console, she was on her way to Andrew's office. The pod system was specific to internal buildings, but operated similarly to the outside transportation system. It was a key feature of Kalesh design and one of the few things that the United Planets architecture absorbed.

After a few minutes, the pod stopped. She exited it and headed to Andrew's office. When she arrived, she walked up to the solid door that looked like it was part of the wall. She interacted with her ARI and selected Andrew's office. The doorway formed a glowing hexagonal cell pattern over it, then faded away. She peeked her head in.

Andrew sat in a hover chair in the middle of a blank dome-shaped room. He was moving his hands around in the air and, after a moment, extended an arm and waved her in. "It's Lil Jane! Come on in!"

Jane smirked. He called her that due to her five-foot-eight stature, and she believed also due him thinking of her as a little sister. "I didn't surprise you, did I?"

"Not at all," said Andrew, pivoting his hovering chair toward her.

Jane entered the room, and the door behind her became a solid wall again. The blankness of the room changed to the default theme that Andrew had selected. The room was now a high-tech paradise filled with floating screens, holographic models, and swirling local, global, and space maps.

She tapped at her ARI and selected Andrew's room on the contextually aware menu. After several options appeared, she selected a hover chair similar to Andrew's. A part of the side wall slid up, and a hover chair floated over to her. She sat in it when it got to her, then moved over opposite Andrew. Andrew was tan skinned and seven feet tall, and his chair was larger to compensate. She liked his scruffy appearance, even in a United Planets uniform.

"How is everything?" asked Andrew.

"Good," said Jane, nodding. "This morning was a bit unusual, though."

Andrew focused on Jane. "Unusual . . . huh?"

"Yeah. I met with Karus, who, by the way, said for you to eat something, and he said there's been a communication spike in the underground."

Andrew smirked. "Ole Karus. Still bitter, I see." He clasped his hands in front of him. "So a communication spike. That means something big is happening or about to happen usually."

"That's what I thought. It might tie into the second unusual thing that happened this morning, but you already know what that is."

Andrew ran his hand back and forth over his mouth and cheek several times while gazing at Jane. "About that . . . You shouldn't have seen it."

Jane observed Andrew. His initial reaction earlier was unusual for someone like him. It was not often he was surprised. She stiffened when the room changed back to its blank slate. The only thing in the room besides them and their chairs was a light that hovered above them. She knew this meant the room was secured. Whatever was going to be said would not be recorded. "So . . . this Evaran Protocol . . . What is it?"

Andrew faced Jane. "I'm not supposed to say anything, but as you guessed by the change in theme, I'm going to. That's actually part of the protocol. However, I trust you, so I'm going to fill you in. How much do you know about temporal mechanics?"

"Only what I studied," said Jane with a shrug. "Outside of the actual science parts, it's mostly conjecture."

Andrew licked his lips as he paused for a moment. "What if I told you . . . it wasn't?"

Jane narrowed her eyes. "Okay . . . what parts?"

"Rift doors, space-time rifts, and . . . time travelers."

Jane chuckled. "There's no evidence of any of that. I know the Kreagans purport to have some evidence of rifts, but they also say they can talk to great selectors." Her smile wound down after a moment of silence. "You're serious."

"I'm afraid it's all true. In this case, the Evaran Protocol refers to a time traveler. The fact that the protocol was initiated means he's arrived somewhere nearby."

Jane wrinkled her eyebrows. "Hypothetically, let's assume he's a time traveler. Why would he be here?"

"I don't know," said Andrew, shrugging. "But he is. That means he's here to fix something, most likely."

"So he travels through space and time and fixes things?"

"I know, it sounds crazy," said Andrew. He cocked his head at Jane. "How well do you know your Fredorian history?"

"Fairly well. It's not too complex," said Jane. "It was a refugee planet for human slaves that had been freed. They became full trade partners with the Kreagans, and when Earth finally entered as a member state, they joined with them later to form the United Planets."

"And . . . how do you think they became a full trade partner?"

Jane placed her hand on her chin with a finger over her lips. Her eyes looked upward and moved back and forth as she thought about it. She wagged a finger at Andrew. "It happened because of Andia Kiggs. She was uhh . . . an ambassador. A prime ambassador! And she found the Arkaron. It's coming back to me now."

"You know your history," said Andrew. "So a prime ambassador found the Arkaron. Doesn't that sound a bit unusual to you? The Kreagans had been looking for it for thousands of years, with the vast resources of a galactic empire, and yet, Andia Kiggs found it? Somehow?"

Jane exhaled from her nose. "So . . . you're implying this Evaran person stepped in and helped her."

Andrew raised a finger. "That was one event. He's been involved in several others. The United Planets only started tracking events after it was formed, but some events prior to that were added. Those prior ones don't have a lot of evidence, like the Fredorian one, but more than likely happened."

"Huh," said Jane. "So . . . what does the protocol actually say then?"

Andrew smirked. "For starters, we aren't even supposed to have any recorded events, but that's been violated. Other things include not mentioning anything about events to him unless he asks, keep his existence known as minimally as possible, and if he decides to interfere, help him if he asks."

Jane noticed Andrew fidgeting in his seat. "This excites you, doesn't it?"

"You know me . . . I love all this mysterious stuff. I know the Evaran Protocol and several other protocols by heart."

Jane placed the palms of her hands in front of her and touched her lips with them. She pondered why Evaran was here. With pursed lips, she looked at Andrew. "You don't think he's here about the space habitat quarantine and illegal augment trade, do you?"

Andrew shook his head. "I don't know, it's possible." He eyed Jane. "You're thinking of contacting him, aren't you?"

Jane smiled. "Am I that easy to read?"

"Maybe not to others," said Andrew with a smile. "I can't tell you what to do in your off hours, and I should tell you to stay away. However . . . maybe you can see what he's up to."

"You just want to meet him."

Andrew chuckled. "Okay, maybe I do. Still, if he's in the area, we do represent the United Planets, so if he does need help, we should offer it. There's another aspect of his arrival that's dangerous. He tends to attract the attention of powerful groups. If I got the message, or you in this case, you can be sure that they did too."

Jane inspected Andrew for a moment. "I bet that was the communication spike in the underground. They're probably wondering why he's here too. They may even try to attack him."

Andrew laughed. "From the outcomes of the events he's been in and who he's fought, they would be in a world of trouble if they did."

"Where's he headed? He's not coming to Da Nesh, is he?"

"No, although that would be better than where he is going. Follisat."

Jane drew her head back. "That's a pretty dangerous place. I mean . . . I know new arrivals to the planet go there, but I would've thought they would have routed him somewhere better." She knew that Follisat had a small United Planets presence. New arrivals tended to be sent there, since it was one of the major trade hubs with a viable spaceport, but it was also a place of corruption. It seemed to her that every Kalesh criminal organization, and even some alien ones, had a presence there. The difference between Follisat and Da Nesh was like night and day. "How'd they verify it was him?"

"Looking at the registration, it appears to be from a device given to him around 2635 BC. That was back when the Helians ran things."

Jane's eyes widened. "That's . . . pretty incredible. The Helians have been gone for a long time."

"Yeah . . . anyways, outside of what's been discussed, are there any other updates?"

"Of course," said Jane. She spent the next hour filling Andrew in on her current case workload. Although she was trying to focus on her presentation, her mind kept drifting to thoughts of Evaran. What if he was there to figure out what was going on with the quarantine? It was a high-profile event and one that spanned the solar system, from a corrupt corporation to powerful factions possibly being involved.

There was also her investigation into the illegal augment trade, which all pointed to the habitats. Maybe if she could convince Evaran to help her for professional reasons, she could also get help for a more personal matter: seeing where Chris died on the habitat and getting some closure. After she was done, she gave Andrew a hug as she always had since she was a kid, then exited the building. She headed toward the transportation hub with the intent of stopping by her apartment. If she was going to Follisat, she would need to see where Evaran was staying and prepare.

04

After Evaran and the others finished their meal at Krells, a decision was reached to head to the planet. They returned to the Torvatta and proceeded toward Roeth.

Dr. Snowden repeatedly glanced between both front screens in the Torvatta as it broke cloud cover and approached Follisat. He noted that there were a lot of forests, but the intriguing aspect to him was that the cities he saw appeared to be integrated into the environment. This was a departure from the advanced cities he had seen before. He glanced at Evaran. "Interesting city designs."

"It may be wise to wear your survival suit," said Evaran.

Dr. Snowden snorted. "No argument from me. I know we've been cleared for contamination, but no idea what we might pick up."

"There is that," said Evaran. "However, I was referring to the reputation of the city. I am hoping there will be no issues, but it does not hurt to be prepared."

"You make it sound like it's going to be the Wild West or something."

V looked at Dr. Snowden.

"Umm . . . you know . . . frontier, lawlessness, and all that."

"Analysis. A period of time that refers to the American West in the nineteenth century."

"You got it. Let's hope it isn't that wild."

"Acknowledged. I hope it is not too wild either."

Dr. Snowden chuckled while he saw a grin fight to get out on Emily's face.

Evaran shook his head. "To be out here and build these cities, there would need to be some order present. Since the United Planets is present here, I would expect there to be tighter security in general."

"I guess so," said Dr. Snowden.

"Approaching landing coordinates," said V.

Dr. Snowden surveyed the city they were approaching. Outside the city was a spaceport with a variety of ships parked in a large grid. It reminded him of a parking lot, except the cells on the grid seemed to vary in size and were mostly square, except for a section that had rectangular ones. A vacant cell was highlighted in green. It was about half a mile from the city, according to the distance metric the screen projected. As with the city, large trees were at every corner. The Kalesh loved their trees.

After the Torvatta landed, Evaran said, "Get your suits on and meet me outside."

Dr. Snowden and Emily took off toward the research lab.

Dr. Snowden liked the survival suits. Although Emily had a custom one, he had become familiar with the one he had learned on. They were formfitting and space worthy and could tie into his PSD. There was also an energy shield with a repulsion beam weapon as needed.

His favorite aspect was the helm. It was stored in the neck collar and shot up on demand. Once on, it displayed information on the interior of the helm as a heads-up display. The HUD itself was amazing, but the fact that it could also tie into V and Evaran's ring meant he got to see what they were analyzing or scanning as it happened. It gave him some insight into their decision making.

With his suit on and helmet raised, Dr. Snowden joined Evaran, Emily, and V in body mode outside the Torvatta. He examined the visuals on his HUD. The atmosphere was breathable, and the temperature was around eighty degrees Fahrenheit. Other humans and aliens without helmets were outlined as they scurried between their ships and the city. The trees surprised him. He had expected it to show organic information, but it also showed that there was technology built into them. Upon closer investigation, he could see small panels throughout, with barely lit lines running the height of the tree.

"The air looks breathable, and the temperature isn't too bad," said Emily.

"It is an ideal environment for humans," said Evaran.

Emily nodded.

As they walked down the green walkway, Dr. Snowden scanned the ships and people around them. Most were alien, with a sprinkling of humans. The most common presence was Kalesh scurrying about. The ship designs varied but all looked like they had atmospheric travel as a consideration. His thoughts were interrupted by a group of scruffy-looking Kalesh wearing patchwork light armor. Some of them had their weapons holstered, and others had them in their hands. Their fur looked greasy, giving Dr. Snowden the impression these Kalesh were not friendly.

One of the Kalesh, with black fur, yellow spots, and a chipped tooth, stepped forward. "New here, huh?"

"We are," said Evaran as his eyes darted around the Kalesh.

The Kalesh smirked. "See . . . we don't want aliens here." He pointed at Evaran's utility handle. "So you can fly away . . . in your little ship . . . after you give me whatever that is."

Evaran scanned the Kalesh with his ring, causing the Kalesh to step back. "I do not believe you have any authority here. We do not want any trouble."

"It wasn't a suggestion," said the Kalesh with a snarl. The other Kalesh spread out behind him.

Evaran pulled his utility handle out and rested it on his extended hand, palm up. "Are you sure you wish to go down this route?"

The Kalesh laughed.

"Very well," said Evaran. He gripped his utility handle and pressed a button. A rod extended with a white end. *Boom!* The Kalesh went tumbling as a repulsion blast swept over them.

Dr. Snowden jumped as Emily pushed past him and fired a stun beam at all but one of the Kalesh.

The last Kalesh had closed his yellow eyes, but opened them when it got silent. He trembled as he looked around at his fallen group, then looked at Evaran. "Look . . . Jimus was messing around. Please don't kill me."

"They are only stunned," said Evaran. "In the future, you should refrain from this type of activity. Others may not be as lenient."

The Kalesh vigorously nodded.

"Why did you select us?"

The Kalesh shrugged. "You aren't Kalesh."

"We have heard that there is some resentment toward aliens here. Are you a part of that group?"

"Look . . . I get paid to harass aliens. I don't really have anything against them."

"Who pays you?" asked Evaran.

"Warlord Okon."

"Noted," said Evaran. "You can tell the others to avoid us. If I catch you out here again, I may not be as forgiving."

The Kalesh gulped, spun around, then took off running.

"That was easy pickings," said Emily, cocking her head.

Dr. Snowden sighed. He could tell this was going to be another rough visit. That seemed to be the nature of Evaran's travels in general. Emily's quick response had startled him. By the time he had given thought to getting his PSD out, she had reacted. Maybe he would need to train more with her.

"The city is ahead. We should have no more issues getting there," said Evaran.

Dr. Snowden noticed other groups stepping back a bit. "Well, at least we've made an impression, it seems."

"It would appear so. This Warlord Okon will know of this event, so this may not be over."

Dr. Snowden looked around. He wondered what new players they would meet. Although he was excited to see a new culture and an advanced humanity, he was apprehensive. Evaran tended to attract powerful factions and people. Hopefully it would be over quickly, and maybe they could spend some time here without being bothered. He sighed as he trudged alongside Evaran and Emily.

They spent the next three hours navigating the city.

Dr. Snowden enjoyed the various smells of the trees. He had expected them to have a leafy odor, but instead it was slightly sweet. There was a hint of something spicy mixed in, but he could not identify it. Small patches of trees blanketed the city between high-tech buildings. The greenness of the areas made it feel like it was full of life, something he appreciated.

The lack of insects everywhere was a surprise to him. Maybe the tree smells were a repellent of some sort. As they passed by various Kalesh, the Kalesh would raise their lips, exposing their teeth, and nod their heads. He almost burst out laughing the first time he saw it. Emily going into a defensive stance did not help that.

When they arrived at the three-story building that had their living arrangements, they paused to survey the environment.

"Are you sure this is it?" asked Dr. Snowden.

Evaran perused his ARI. "I am sure. We are on the top floor and have two rooms."

Dr. Snowden pointed to the thin cylindrical pillars that towered over the building. It had rings that jutted out every ten feet or so. "What the heck are those?"

Evaran scanned it with his ring, then monitored his ARI. After a moment, he said, "It is a moisture harvester. It uses nanorods to collect water."

"Oh," said Dr. Snowden. "I remember reading about research into that on Earth. The Kalesh are more advanced than I thought."

"It is a United Planets structure and packed with monitoring equipment. Quite a bit of it, actually."

"Maybe it's for security," said Dr. Snowden.

Emily narrowed her eyes. "Or maybe it's for mass surveillance."

Evaran rubbed his chin. "It probably serves both purposes. I do not know if the Kalesh are aware of this. We can check both of our rooms for any surveillance once we get there."

Emily glanced at Evaran. "V and I will take a room. You two can have the other."

V tilted his head at Emily.

Dr. Snowden gulped. He understood Emily would want her space, but it still stung that she decided to room with V. Maybe she felt that if something were to occur, V would be more effective at helping her. He looked at Evaran. "It looks like it's you and me tonight then."

"You can sleep while I research then."

Dr. Snowden nodded.

They reached the top floor and walked down the hallway toward their rooms.

Dr. Snowden watched several Kalesh scamper away at their approach. Although he figured that maybe they were skittish, it seemed unusual given the reaction he had seen with the other Kalesh they had passed on their way in. Maybe they were in a hurry, or as he probably thought, not all Kalesh were the same. One of the observations he had made since traveling with Evaran was that most races that he had encountered possessed a similar diversity in personality to humanity. Having grown up seeing all aliens defined by one trait, ideology, or style of dress seemed unusual to him now.

They reached their respective rooms and settled in.

Dr. Snowden slipped off his survival suit and kicked off his shoes. After tapping one of the two beds, he lay down and placed his hands behind his head. His PSD showed it to be around 9:00 p.m. on Earth. The sterile smell and soothing silence of the room comforted him. Maybe they had soundproof walls. He watched as Evaran pulled up a chair on the opposite side of the room and begin to interact with his ARI. Dr. Snowden snorted. "You really are going to work all night, aren't you?"

"As you know, I do not require sleep. There is a lot of information to go through, even if it is public information. This is a good opportunity to go through it. Please, feel free to relax."

Dr. Snowden sighed as he stared at the ceiling. After a few minutes, he got the feeling Evaran was staring at him. He glanced over and saw Evaran was studying him.

"Is everything okay?" asked Evaran.

"Yeah . . . why do you ask?"

"You seem troubled."

Dr. Snowden sat up on the bed and scooted back so that he was resting against the wall. A memory of Evaran saying that when he came back after their abduction floated through his mind. He raised a hand off to the side. "It's . . . I dunno. Emily chose V to stay with her. I know . . . I know . . . it's trivial, but it stung a little. You know?"

"Emily and V have a strong bond. He joins her daily in her training, and he bonded with her nanobot version when she was around. I suspect Emily enjoys his objective perspective."

Dr. Snowden rubbed his hands. "I guess. I wish she was the way she was before she got sent to that damn prison planet."

"I believe that another reason she likes being around V is that he accepts her in her current state. To him, she is still Emily, but with an altered personality that he has adjusted to."

Dr. Snowden wrinkled his eyebrows. "Interesting thought. Maybe I'm the one who needs changing."

"You must still be her anchor. I think what you are feeling is natural. Emily has changed since we rescued her, and she is beginning to relax a bit more. Keep doing what you are doing and stay true to who you are."

Dr. Snowden chuckled while shaking his head. "This must seem so illogical to you."

Evaran raised his head a bit. "Not at all. I have come to understand humanity better, and I think what you are showing is a sign of resilience in your species. You do not stop caring or trying. It is an admirable trait. Other species would consider Emily a defect or damaged and treat her as such. I have seen that firsthand."

"Well then. I'll keep on trucking. I guess I could always fire up my nanobots when I'm down, but that state I go into, while powerful, seems to remove any emotional context. That worries me a bit, to be honest."

"It is a side effect of processing everything in a logical and efficient manner, like a computer," said Evaran as he rubbed his chin. "Thankfully, you can use it as a sort of brake when you believe emotions are clouding or affecting your judgment. In the future, humanity changes when they fully embrace nanobots and cybernetic enhancement. *Colder* would be a good word to describe it."

"I love my nanobots," said Dr. Snowden. "Even with the ramping-up issue, they make me feel stronger and more focused. I feel like I can do anything, but hope I never get colder. Speaking of which . . . and you don't need to answer if you don't want to but . . . after our last adventure, you had a part of you taken. How are you holding up?"

Evaran looked down for a moment, then back up at Dr. Snowden. "I still think about it. It was a sort of pain that is hard to describe. I am bothered by it, but now I know that rift technology can have an adverse effect on me when it is utilized in a certain manner. I will need to be more cautious around it."

"You said it sapped your strength. Is it noticeable?"

Evaran drew his lips flat. "Yes. I am seventeen point seven four percent weaker."

"That's kinda precise . . ."

"I have a set of experiments that help me to measure my abilities," said Evaran. "When I ran through them after the fight, that was how much weaker I was. I can feel a difference in my physical aspect."

Dr. Snowden sighed. "I wish that didn't have to go down like that. I bet you're regretting coming to Earth and running into all these crazies."

"Not at all," said Evaran. "If anything, it is good to be where I can affect change more often, as opposed to merely observing."

Dr. Snowden snorted. "I just realized that jumping around space and time must be like visiting snapshots in a history book to you."

Evaran bobbed his head. "In a way."

"Well . . . I'm glad you decided to visit the one where me and Emily got abducted. Anyways, sleep time for me."

"Have a good night," said Evaran. He turned back to perusing his ARI.

Dr. Snowden half grinned as he lay back down and closed his eyes. Thoughts of Emily, his discussion with Evaran, and his nanobots swirled in his mind. He had considered leaving after Emily's incident, and was surprised she wanted to stay. However, it hit him that this is exactly where he needed to be. Trying to figure out the nanobots, nonhumans, and the new reality without Evaran would have been not only disorienting, but also dangerous. His breathing slowed as he drifted off.

Emily tapped at the grayed-out window in the room. An interface appeared on it with several options for opacity, border, and even some backgrounds. She selected a twilight background and stood back with an approving eye. Although the room seemed small to her, the window added a bit of life to it. The sterile odor of the room reminded her of a hospital. It was the unusual silence that made her uneasy. She glanced at V, who stood next to her, observing quietly. "What do you think?"

V scrutinized the window. "It is appropriate."

"That's it? I think it makes the room more alive."

V scanned the room.

"I meant, as a feeling. Not that the room is actually alive."

"Acknowledged," said V.

Emily shook her head and sat in a chair next to one of the two beds. The chair expanded to her size, and she noted that it had a console embedded in the arm. Her PSD showed it to be about 9:00 p.m. on Earth. She wondered what Dr. Snowden and Evaran were discussing, if anything. Dr. Snowden would be hurt by her decision to choose V, but she felt she could relax with V, whereas with Dr. Snowden, she seemed pressured. She looked around and sighed. "I hope you don't mind I picked you as my roommate for the night."

V swiveled his head toward Emily. "I do not mind at all. I enjoy being in your presence."

"And I . . . yours," said Emily with a smile. "Your emotional range has grown a lot since I first met you. How are you adjusting to it? And you can sit if you want."

V scrutinized a chair perpendicular to Emily, and then sat in it. With a pivot of his head, he focused on her. "It has been interesting."

"How so?"

"Emotions are adding components to my processing and sometimes override my logical conclusions."

"That's not too unusual. My dad called it thinking from the heart," said Emily as she raised a hand, palm forward at V. "Not in the literal sense. What have been your strongest emotions so far?"

V looked down for a moment, then back up. "Anger registered as the strongest, followed by sadness."

Emily understood that although V was a strong AI, he was alive with a life layer link, or three-L, as Evaran had called it. Evaran had explained the concept of three-Ls as a link from a life layer that existed on the outside of a universe, and that most machines and AIs usually did not have one. V did, though, making him one of the rare ones. She clasped her hands in front of her. "What situations caused those? You don't have to answer if it's too personal."

"Analysis. You are my friend, and I do not mind," said V. He paused for a moment, then spoke. "The strongest anger emotion occurred when Dr. Snowden and Rakar were about to die on the Fredorian colony ship. I was angry at the creatures trying to kill them and wanted to hurt them."

Emily jerked her head back. "They were going to die?"

"I calculated a ninety-six point four percent chance of that occurring if I did not intervene."

Emily's mouth went agape. "I knew you helped them, but didn't know it was that close. Uncle Albert never told me. I guess me running away in fear didn't help things." She smirked. "I bet he asked you not to tell me, right?"

V tilted his head. "I cannot say."

Emily rubbed her chin for a moment as she pondered V's words. "You don't need to. I'm sure that's what happened. Anyways . . . you were protecting those you care for. That's not unusual either."

"Acknowledged," said V. He stared at Emily.

Emily chuckled. "When you look at me like that, you remind me of Kal."

"The virtual intelligence from the prison planet."

"Yeah. He was hard to talk with," said Emily. "He would say something, then stop and stare at me, kinda like you did a moment ago."

V moved his head a bit. "I did not mean to stare at you. I was contemplating the second instance of my anger."

Emily sat forward a bit.

"The second instance was when you were teleported away."

Emily exhaled from her nose. She had tried to put out of her mind the nine months spent on a prison planet in a pocket universe. Surviving there taught her a lot of lessons. What bothered her the most was how she got there.

A moment of exposure to an enemy and she was on her way. That would never happen again, and if it did, she was prepared. A lump formed in her throat. "I was a bit angry about that too." She cleared her throat. "Not at you, but the situation."

"Your heartbeat has increased. Have I caused you pain?"

Emily shook her head. "You're fine. It's . . . a bad memory." She took a deep breath. "So what about the sad situations?"

V looked at the opposite side of the room for a moment, then faced Emily. "The first instance was watching Sanjay's last moment in the holo room."

Emily replayed the scenes in her head where Sanjay, one of the other humans Evaran was trying to rescue from her and Dr. Snowden's alien abduction, had been killed. His nanobots had temporarily resided in her, Dr. Snowden, and Jay, another human who had been abducted. Sanjay's nanobots had the side effect of boosting fear and providing insights that she would not normally have had. After helping the Fredorians achieve their destiny, Evaran removed Sanjay's presence from her, Dr. Snowden, and Jay and let the final moments of Sanjay's nanobots play out in the holo room. It had been devastating for her to watch, not only because it was Sanjay's death, but that it could have easily been her or one of the others.

"The second one was watching Nanobot Emily leave," said V.

Emily gulped. Nanobots that had been taken from her prior to being sent to the prison planet had been weaponized. They killed those who sent her to the planet, then formed a duplicate of her. Nanobot Emily, as Evaran called her. Emily missed her and had grown close to her in the short time that she had been alive. Her throat constricted.

After a moment, V asked, "Is everything okay?"

Emily nodded. "Those were pretty sad moments. When I synced with Nanobot Emily, I saw that you were able to talk wirelessly to her during her time on the ship."

"Correct. She allowed me to experience emotion from her perspective. It was fascinating. She was my friend."

Emily swallowed hard. "Mine too. You treated her like she was me right off the bat, even if the others didn't." She smiled as her eyes watered. "Thank you for being a true friend."

"Acknowledged."

Emily got up and gave V a hug.

V put a hand on her back and then tapped it. "There. There."

Emily laughed as she pulled back and wiped her eyes. "Yeah . . . We need to work on that."

"Acknowledged."

Emily enjoyed being around V. He did not judge her or try to change her. His acceptance had helped her get through the confusing first month back on the Torvatta. She was at ease around him, and he made her laugh. Not that Dr. Snowden was not helping, but he clung to something that was not there. She did not see things the same way anymore. It felt like she had spent a lifetime on the prison planet, and although it did change her, she felt it was for the better.

She knew most people would have broken where she not only survived, but thrived. It was a feeling that she enjoyed. Being able to take command of a situation and not back down was something her deceased father, Dan, was all about. She had confidence in her step, and she was only getting stronger through her daily training.

"Are you going to sleep?" asked V.

"Yeah . . . but being in this new environment, I'm not going to take the suit off. You never know what might happen."

"Analysis. A wise tactical decision."

Emily lay down on the bed and rested her head on the pillow. She had gotten used to sleeping with the suit on, and with her PSD at her side, she could reach for it if needed. After a few minutes, she felt V staring at her. She rolled over and saw that V was standing and looking at the door over the bed. "You can sit if you want."

The lights on V's face lit up. "I apologize. I was processing today's data. I will face in another direction." He turned to the side.

Emily shook her head. She got up and dragged a chair over to the side of her bed that faced the door. "There. You can sit and watch the door while you process data."

"Analysis. Another sound tactical decision," said V as he took a seat. "I am set to continuous scanning."

"I know," said Emily as she laid a hand on his shoulder. "I feel safe with you." She got back into the bed and assumed a sleeping position. After a few moments, her eyes closed.

After four hours, Emily awoke to the sound of the door being kicked in. Her heartbeat shot through the roof as she rolled off the bed to the side away from the door. Her nanobots kicked in, and the surge caused an adrenaline rush to flow through her.

V stood, and a glowing shield emanated from him. "Defensive mode engaged."

Emily peeked out and saw a black-coated Kalesh at the door. He was much larger than the other ones she had seen. He had on advanced-looking heavy armor under his coat and held a weapon in his hand. She recognized the other Kalesh behind the one in the door. It was Jimus.

"Get off our planet, alien trash!" said the Kalesh.

"Analysis. Your request has been denied," said V as he strode forward. When he was within arm's length, he grabbed the Kalesh's hand that held the weapon. With a squeeze, the startled Kalesh growled in pain as the weapon fell to the ground. In one quick motion, V grabbed the Kalesh by the neck and raised him off the floor. He tossed the Kalesh through the door into Jimus and then exited the room.

Emily pulled out her PSD after gaining her bearings. She squatted for a moment as she looked out the kicked-in door.

V tossed the Kalesh off to the left as weapon fire lit up his shielding. Jimus had scrambled off in the direction that the other Kalesh had been tossed.

Emily approached the door. She did not even know V had shielding in body mode, but it appeared to be very effective. Once she reached the door, she heard the familiar sound of Evaran. She peeked out and saw that V had moved to her left with a small group of Kalesh surrounding their crumpled companion. To her right were Evaran and Dr. Snowden. Past them farther down the hallway was another small group of Kalesh. She activated her forearm shield and exited the room. Standing behind V, she glanced over at Evaran and Dr. Snowden as they converged.

Dr. Snowden grabbed Emily's arm. "Are you okay?"

"I'm fine. What's going on? I recognize Jimus."

"We're about to find out."

Evaran exhaled from his nose. "It would appear Warlord Okon was not happy with the previous engagement."

The sound of footsteps could be heard running from around the corner.

05

Jane looked out the window of the aircraft she was in. Follisat was about a seven-hour flight from Da Nesh. She shook her head. The Kalesh, as eager as they were to integrate, had still not upgraded their aircraft, which reminded her of ships Earth used back in the early twenty-first century. They even used chemical fuel still. She suspected that when they upgraded to United Planets technology in the aircraft sector, it would be game changing.

She was unsure of how she would approach Evaran. What would she say and how would she say it? Andrew had painted a picture of an ageless being who ran around space and time helping people. Who was she compared to that? She rubbed her sweaty palms. Maybe it would not be as stressful as she was imagining it. She was sure that Evaran would be interested in a space habitat quarantine, and maybe she would finally get some closure on Chris's death. Maybe he could take her back to see him before he died. Or not. She did not want to push her luck, but the thought swirled in her mind.

When she arrived at Follisat, she checked the time on her palm and noted it was 10:00 p.m. She grabbed some food from a small eatery and went over her game plan. As she chewed on some bread brushed with the spicy oil Kalesh culture was known for, she inspected a map projection in her ARI. It showed that Evaran was in a new-arrival living area not too far away. She smirked. Not the best impression for a new arrival.

If it were up to her, it would be a United Planets new-arrival area. At least then it would appear to be more neutral, as opposed to integrating alien species directly into a population that for thousands of years, believed they were the only sentient race in the universe and that they were chosen. The arrival of the Voss Imperium shattered that quickly.

She pulled up the image taken from the pilot who had scanned Evaran's ship, called the Torvatta. The clothing surprised her. Evaran looked like he was ready for any situation, but it was the humans that caught her eye. From what Andrew had told her, Evaran sometimes traveled with human companions from across time.

The details of the image identified the older man as Dr. Albert Snowden. He wore some ancient clothing, maybe twenty or twenty-first century. She smiled when she saw him. His posture and the look on his face conveyed confidence, something she found attractive. Although he looked mature, she suspected he was probably about ten years older than Chris would have been.

The younger female wore an advanced suit and was identified as Emily Snowden. Maybe she was related to Dr. Snowden, or unrelated and from the future. The defensive way she sat indicated that she was on guard, a position that Jane knew all too well. Maybe she was a bodyguard.

After finishing her bread and the cold coffee-like substance that passed for a stimulant, she surveyed the restaurant she was in. It was late, and she was tired, yet the restaurant was busy. It did not surprise her. New arrivals came in at all times of the day and night. The smells that made Kalesh food unique massaged her nose. It was spicy with a tinge of sweetness.

She checked her reservation at the living area. It was the closest room she could find to Evaran's, but it was one floor under him. Her nerves would not let her sleep anyways. Checking the time showed it to be about midnight.

Her hands ran over the smooth metallic disc in her pocket that functioned as a movement monitor. She had brought it to put on the wall opposite Evaran's door. When he opened the door, an alert would notify her. Satisfied with her plan, she cleaned up the small table where she had been sitting and exited the restaurant.

As she walked through the crisp air toward the living area, she figured it would take her about thirty minutes. The bustling activity on the streets was a change from Da Nesh. She liked the slower pace of Da Nesh. Most Kalesh cities were very casual in their attitude.

Follisat was an example to her of what happens when the United Planets integrates a new planet or species. She had studied the history of first contact and the subsequent integration on other worlds, and it always seemed to follow the same pattern. As the native culture progressed and integration moved forward, the native culture got swallowed by the United Planets culture.

When she reached the building where Evaran was, she hustled up the stairs and set up her monitoring device. After securing it, she headed to her room. As she lay on the bed, she observed it was 12:30 a.m. She did not know how long it would be before they woke up, so she figured she would get a nap in.

An hour later, her eyes popped open. The monitoring alarm had gone off. She yawned as she sat on the edge of the bed. After wiping her eyes and checking her gear, she exited the room. As she walked up the stairs, several crashing noises reverberated throughout the stairwell. She pulled out her weapon and activated her motion sensor. As she reached the top of the stairs, her sensor showed several Kalesh and humans in the hallway around the bend.

She pulled off a flat circular device and tossed it against the wall facing into the hallways. The device gave her a visual of what was going on. Two Kalesh had weapons drawn and were standing over another Kalesh crumpled on the ground. Ahead of them stood Evaran, Dr. Snowden, Emily, and a robotic humanoid who she guessed was V. Behind them was another group of Kalesh. It appeared to be a standoff. Time for her to make her entrance.

She burst around the corner and aimed her weapon at the two nearest Kalesh. "United Planets Security. Drop your weapons."

One of the startled Kalesh spun around and aimed at Jane. She fired, causing the Kalesh to fall. The second one pivoted and raised his hands. The Kalesh on the other side of the hallway took off.

"Against the wall," said Jane as she crept forward while keeping a bead on the Kalesh.

The Kalesh complied.

Jane pulled off two wristbands that glowed. "Turn around! Put your hands behind your back. Now!"

The Kalesh obeyed.

Jane placed a band on each wrist. She then activated the bands from her ARI, causing them to magnetize and snap together. She spun the Kalesh around and pointed down. "Sit."

The Kalesh slid to the ground and sighed.

Jane turned to see that Evaran and the others had walked over to her.

"I am Evaran." He bowed slightly with his left arm across his stomach, then pointed to the others. "With me is Dr. Albert Snowden, his niece, Emily Snowden, and V."

"I'm United Planets Bureau of Law Enforcement Agent Jane Trellis. It's good to meet you. I'm aware of who you are . . . among other things. Is everyone okay?"

"I believe so," said Evaran, looking around.

"Good . . . Do you have some time to talk?"

"We can," said Evaran. "However, we are going to get our things and stay the rest of the night on my ship."

"The Torvatta, right?"

Evaran pulled his head back a bit. "Yes, that is correct. If you wish to talk, that would be an ideal place to do so. There is a lot of surveillance around us."

Jane narrowed her eyes. "There shouldn't be. That's against Kalesh law."

"I would suggest you check your moisture harvesters. The rooms also have them implanted in the walls. Whoever operates them will find them mysteriously offline during our stay. Perhaps we can meet in the morning?"

The Kalesh smirked. "I'm so glad the United Planets respects our rights."

"Silence!" said Jane, snapping her head at the Kalesh. She faced Evaran. "Sure, that'll work. I need to handle this situation anyways. What time?"

Dr. Snowden chuckled. "How about ten in the morning? I should be up by then."

"You're a late sleeper. Okay, I'll be there. I already have the coordinates of your ship."

Evaran eyed Jane for a moment, then exited the hallway with Dr. Snowden and Emily in tow.

Jane looked down at the Kalesh. "Do you know who you were attacking?"

"Who cares who they are. They're human scum. Like you."

"I can tell by the marks on your arms that you work for Warlord Okon. You're actually lucky I arrived."

The Kalesh snorted. "Whatever."

Jane tapped at her ARI and selected the local United Planets law enforcement option.

A woman's head appeared in her ARI. "Logging call from Jane Trellis, Da Nesh Division. How may we be of assistance?"

"I was attacked by Warlord Okon's men outside my current location. There may be more around."

"I have notified a security unit in your area. They should be there shortly. Anything else we can help with?" asked the woman.

Jane shook her head. "I'm good for now."

The woman swiveled her head for a moment, then faced Jane. "I have updated the security unit."

"Thank you."

The projection shut off.

Jane shook her head as she leaned against the wall opposite the Kalesh. Evaran seemed smaller to her in person. Her scans could not read the handle-like device in his hand, nor the pen-like ones in Dr. Snowden's and Emily's hands. She looked at the crumpled Kalesh on the ground. It was still alive, just unconscious. Evaran must have decided to not kill, or maybe that was his modus operandi. She placed wrist restraints on the crumpled Kalesh. Time to wait for her backup, file reports, and get some sleep. Hopefully in the morning, she could convince Evaran to help her, even though she was supposed to offer the help of the United Planets.

Jane exhaled slowly as her eyes began to open to the sun filtering into her room. The unfamiliar smell of the room alerted her awake. After a brief moment of confusion, she remembered that she was not in Da Nesh, but Follisat. She yawned as she sat up and swung her legs off the side of the bed. Her mind raced as she thought about finally getting to sit down and talk with Evaran.

Her morning routine was a speed bump as she cleaned up and got into her suit. After a final look around the room, she exited it. Once outside the building, she used her ARI to show green arrows on the ground to the Torvatta's location. A distance label decreased as she walked. She would reach the Torvatta a bit early, but she did not think that would be an issue. One of the odd things she noticed the previous night was that while Dr. Snowden and Emily looked like they had been awakened, Evaran was alert. She had thought he would be sleeping, but maybe he could not sleep. Follisat can have that impact on someone.

She yawned as she rubbed her left eye. Having to file all the information and store it on the holonet the previous night took time, and she had been lagging to begin with from the flight to Follisat. At least she had gotten six hours of sleep.

Her mind wandered to what she should expect. Andrew had given her a crash course on Evaran, his ship, and some of his adventures. She had a hard time believing any of it was real, but Andrew was serious about it, and he was someone she trusted without hesitation. The one thing that puzzled her was that he mentioned that Evaran may not have done half the adventures listed yet. With a shake of her head, she focused on the green arrows.

After forty-five minutes, she arrived in front of the Torvatta. She examined its unusual disc-shaped design. It was a lot smaller than she thought it would be. Walking around it revealed that it actually sat on a wide angled cone of some type. It should have been leaning, yet it stood perfectly upright.

She squinted at the sunlight reflecting off the mesh sides punctuated by black reflective panes. Looking at the back was more familiar to her. Two large dark-blue horizontal panes stretched for a good fourth of the ship before running into two vertical ones. She ran a hand along the pane, but jumped back when her hand went through it. It was the cold shock more than her hand going through it that had startled her.

"Are you enjoying the view?" asked Evaran from the roof.

"Oh!" said Jane, taking a step back. She raised her hand over her eyes to look up at Evaran. "I didn't see you up there." She made a mental note to have her sensors run a diagnostic analysis. They had not detected Evaran, even though he was nearby.

"I am glad you came," said Evaran. He gestured to the right side of the ship. "Please, come to this side. I will meet you there."

Jane watched as Evaran walked into a shaft that popped up in the center of the roof. The Torvatta seemed to be more than it appeared. She walked over to the side that had a doorway with a light-blue semitransparent shield with a hexagonal pattern overlay.

Evaran appeared on the other side, waving her in. "Please, follow me."

Jane stepped through the doorway. Her eyebrows wrinkled as she perused the room. It was too small to be a long-distance space-faring ship, and she could see no engine room.

Evaran walked to the left and went to the third door. He stopped and extended his arm toward the door.

Jane began to walk toward Evaran. A cool swath of air brushed up against her nostrils. The Torvatta had a comfortable, sterile smell to it. She paused at the first room after sneaking a peek. Her mouth went agape as she tried to make sense of what she was seeing. The door led to a large, open area, that did not exist on the outside of the ship. She waved her arm into it and then stepped back. "How . . ."

"Dimensional mechanics," said Evaran.

"I thought . . . that was theoretical."

"It is to humanity at this age, perhaps."

Jane swallowed hard. She had come to view humanity as being at its peak. Matter replicators, condensed space drives, and the United Planets way of life were a few things that humanity had never had before. A golden period. She was trying to balance what she already knew from Andrew about Evaran and the Torvatta and what she was experiencing. She took a breath and entered the conference room.

"Hello again," said Dr. Snowden as he and Emily rose from the right side of the table.

Jane smiled as V escorted her to a seat across from Dr. Snowden and Emily.

Evaran walked to the head of the table and sat down. After everyone sat, he faced Jane. "Are you hungry?"

"I'm good," said Jane. She pulled a thin orange stick from her belt that was the length of her hand. "I have a vitastick."

Dr. Snowden pointed at the vitastick. "Okay, you got my attention. What's that?"

"It's a vitamin stick. It has everything you need for about eight hours or so. Standard throughout the United Planets." She cocked her head. "What do you eat in the morning?"

"I usually eat eggs and bacon. Or I have a good ham omelet. I always have a cup of coffee."

"It's replicated, though, right?"

Dr. Snowden nodded.

"For a minute there, I thought you actually ate the flesh of animals."

Emily cast a sidelong glance at Dr. Snowden. "Oh, he does, but here on the Torvatta, there is no need to."

Jane jerked her head back as her eyes widened. "Huh. The Kalesh still do that too." She looked at Evaran. "I've read you're a time traveler, and by extension," she said, looking at Dr. Snowden and Emily, "I'm guessing you two are as well. What time period are you from?"

"We began traveling with Evaran in 2012," said Dr. Snowden.

"Just over a thousand years ago . . . ," said Jane. She cocked her head. "That would explain some things, like your clothing and meat desires. The future must be very interesting to you."

Dr. Snowden bobbed his head. "Well, meat desires aside . . ."

"Analysis. I was not aware you had meat desires," said V.

Emily fought a grin from forming.

Dr. Snowden shook his head. "What I was trying to say was that once you've seen one advanced civilization, you begin to get used to it."

The interaction between Dr. Snowden, V, and Emily intrigued Jane. V seemed like he was a young AI. She looked at Evaran. "Not to get off track, but I'm sorry about what happened to you all last night. Please don't let it paint your view on the Kalesh. They are a proud race, but with all races, there are those who . . . like to cause trouble."

Evaran touched his fingertips in front of him. "We ran into some of the attackers earlier that day. We subdued them, but one of the ones we did not stun said they worked for a Warlord Okon. Do you know of him?"

"Yeah," said Jane. "He runs a group that resents the rapid integration of alien culture into theirs. With all the harassment, bombings, and other activity they do, their hope is that it will scare off business and others. I don't think they will bother you anymore."

"I see. It is good that you came when you did. Although we could have handled it, we always prefer the locals to. Are you from the United Planets office nearby?"

"I'm from Da Nesh."

Evaran perused his ARI. "Ahh . . . that is quite a bit away. What brought you to Follisat?"

Jane swallowed hard as her eyes darted between Evaran, Emily, and Dr. Snowden. "This . . . might sound odd . . . but I got a notice yesterday morning about the Evaran Protocol being initiated. It wasn't supposed to go to me." She glanced at Evaran. "It was meant for my boss, Andrew, who had access to what the Evaran Protocol was. He explained the protocol to me and said that if you're here, then you're here to fix something." She noticed Dr. Snowden shoot a look at Emily, then Evaran.

Evaran rubbed his chin. "Intriguing. What do you know of the protocol?"

"For starters, I can't talk about any event unless you bring it up. It would cause problems," said Jane. "It also lists out all the places and times you have been sighted since the United

Planets formed and any events you participated in. Some of those events have who was involved. There are other events listed prior to the United Planets formation, but most are not verified."

Evaran shook his head. "Then the protocol missed the part about not recording any of that. It was meant as an identification tool."

"Andrew mentioned that," said Jane. "I was surprised to learn that help is to be provided upon request, should you ask, and that your clearance level is pretty high. I'm here to offer that assistance if you want it. However . . . and this may be out of line . . . but I came to see if maybe you could help me with something."

"You have my attention," said Evaran with a hand on his chin.

"My husband, Chris, died six years ago, on a space habitat near the sun."

"You mean the Dyson bubble?" asked Dr. Snowden.

"Yeah," said Jane. "I'm surprised you're aware of what that is."

Dr. Snowden chuckled. "We weren't savages back in our time period. We had computers and were making some great strides in science. We saw the structures on the way in. It looked impressive from what little I saw of it."

"It's an engineering marvel, and that's why Chris went there," said Jane, putting a hand on the back of her neck. "He was highly sought after for his technical skills. After he died, I tried to find out details about his death, but the corporation that built the habitats, Advanced Dynamics, obstructed my inquiries. I even tried the official channels to no avail. Advanced Dynamics is entrenched here."

"So you wish to go to the habitat and see what you can find out," said Evaran.

Jane fidgeted in her seat. "I do . . . and I know it's probably improper for me to ask for help, but I'm out of options. I can't fly there, and even if I could, I would be denied access to land. There's another reason I want to check it out as well that is more of a professional one. I suspect that Billozein, the CEO of Advanced Dynamics, is using the quarantine as a cover to sell illegal augments."

Emily sat up in her chair. "What do these augments do?"

Jane bobbed her head. "They enhance the human body. The United Planets has a list of approved augments, and most humans have them. For instance, I have an ocular augment that gives me an augmented reality interface on demand."

Dr. Snowden chuckled. "Seems that everyone has augmented reality interfaces nowadays."

"That's right. I also have two in my legs that give me superior leg strength, and others throughout my body," said Jane, tapping her thigh. "I can turn my ARI on and off from an augment in my hand. Each human can select their own augments, of course, and most go for those that enhance or add senses. For instance, you could hear color if you wanted." She grinned at Dr. Snowden. "Or you could notice when someone's cheeks are flushed."

"What?" said Dr. Snowden as he ran a hand over his cheek.

Jane smiled. "The general idea is to make the body better. The illegal ones go beyond that. They have not undergone rigorous testing, can fail with serious side effects, and generally have a degenerative effect on the body over a period of time. Some reports have said they can also cause mutations."

Evaran placed his elbows on the table and rested his chin on his laced fingers. "Would Warlord Okon know anything about these illegal augments?"

"As part of the criminal underground, I'm sure he has some knowledge of it."

"Then our next step should be to talk to this Warlord Okon and gather what information we can."

Jane's eyes widened. "So . . . you'll help me?"

"Perhaps this is why we are here," said Evaran, sneaking a look at Dr. Snowden and Emily. "If not, at least we can help you find closure, and maybe stop this illegal augment trade." He faced Dr. Snowden and Emily. "Do either of you have any concerns?"

"It sounds like a challenge to me. I'm in," said Emily with a raised chin.

Dr. Snowden smiled. "Well, we found danger, so sounds like we're in the right place."

V swatted Dr. Snowden's arm. "Let us do it!"

Dr. Snowden rubbed his arm. "I think I like it better when Emily does that."

Emily shook her head as Jane chuckled.

"Warlord Okon may not want to talk to us, but I think I can arrange it," said Jane. She bobbed her head. "Maybe. I'd need to go to Da Nesh."

"Excellent," said Evaran. "Give V the coordinates, and we can be off."

Jane looked around. "I'm not sure how to show you."

Evaran stood. "Come to the command center."

After everyone assembled in the command area, Evaran tapped at his chair console, causing the right screen to show an overhead map of Da Nesh. "The Torvatta took these on its way in." He circled a finger clockwise. "Do that to zoom in." He circled his finger counterclockwise. "Circle the other way to zoom out. To move the map, flatten your hand and move it in the direction you want."

"That sounds easy enough," said Jane as she walked up to the screen. After a few moments of dragging and zooming, she located the alleyway in Hillti and pointed at it. "It's there."

"V, take us there," said Evaran.

"Acknowledged."

Jane let out a sigh of relief as she sat next to Dr. Snowden. Evaran was going to help, both personally and professionally. Maybe all the things she had read about him were true. The thought that she would be traveling with someone so legendary, where traveling through space and time was just another adventure, was an exciting proposition. If they were going to help, a lot would need to be done. The thought that she would have to contact Andrew crossed her mind. She would deal with that later. For now, the focus was on setting up a meeting with Warlord Okon, and she knew the person to do it.

06

r. Snowden focused on the front left screen. It showed a view from V in stealthed orb mode as he followed Jane to a remote alley. Dr. Snowden wondered if Karus, the informant Jane was meeting, would be able to get them a meeting with Warlord Okon. He was not sure if it was a great idea to meet a warlord, but Evaran seemed to think it was. If anything, at least he would get to see another slice of Kalesh culture.

His thoughts turned to Jane. He enjoyed seeing Jane's reaction when the Torvatta did the Follisat-to-Da Nesh journey, then to Hillti, a suburb on the outskirts of town. She had said that it was a seven-hour flight usually, maybe two with a United Planets craft. The Torvatta did it in thirty minutes with a few twists and turns. It intrigued him to see her reaction to Evaran's technology. His thoughts frazzled for a moment as he watched Jane walk.

"Do you see something interesting?" said Emily, glancing at Dr. Snowden.

"Yeah . . . me too," said Dr. Snowden with a sigh. His eyes widened as he looked at Emily. "I mean . . . yeah . . . no . . ."

Emily raised an eyebrow.

Dr. Snowden shook his head.

Jane walked into an alley between two metal buildings. After a few minutes, Karus shuffled by in a disguise. Jane ventured a bit out into the forest where Karus joined her shortly thereafter.

Dr. Snowden examined Karus. He was smaller than the average Kalesh that he had seen before. Something about the way Karus looked around made Dr. Snowden uneasy, like Karus was expecting trouble. He focused on the screen.

"Back so soon?" asked Karus.

Jane nodded. "I have a new request. I need you to set up a meeting with Warlord Okon for me."

Karus stepped back and hunched over. "Are you insane? He'd more likely kill you before talking to you."

"I'm aware of that," said Jane. "However . . . I'm setting up this meeting for a friend."

"Then your friends are insane too!"

"These friends are what caused the communication spike. I suspect that Warlord Okon would like to know more about that, don't you?"

Karus sighed. "Maybe. So you want me to risk my life to set this up. What do I get out of it?"

"What do you want?"

Karus paused for a moment as he looked at the ground, then back up. "I want an unregulated Kalesh IL-06 augment."

"And you haven't been waiting for a moment to say that. You know those are hard to come by, and unregulated . . . that's illegal."

"So is meeting with a warlord outside proper United Planets channels."

Jane sighed. "Fair enough. It might take a while to get something like that."

"Take your time, you know how to reach me. You get me that augment, you got your meeting," said Karus. "So you know, I will only put you in contact with the person who can set it up. I'm not traveling out there because . . . I value my life."

Jane narrowed her eyes. "Fine . . . but I don't think Warlord Okon would attack another Kalesh. He's just anti-alien."

Karus chuckled. "Despite his reputation, he's against any who profit off the backs of the disenfranchised. He is also against those who . . . are involved in crimes against the Kalesh in general."

"Okay . . . so why would you be a problem? You're not a dangerous criminal and not profiting off the disenfranchised," said Jane.

Karus licked his lips and looked down.

"I see . . . well . . . won't he know you're involved once you set this up?"

Karus peeled his lips back and snorted. "Do you take me for a fool? I'll do this through proxies."

"All right, all right. I'll get you the augment, and you get the meeting with that person. Deal?"

"Done," said Karus. "I'll check this spot at our usual time daily." He looked around, dipped his head, then scampered out of the forest.

Jane wiggled her jaw for a moment, then headed back to the Torvatta.

Dr. Snowden glanced at Evaran when the screen went blank. "So I guess we're getting an augment then."

"It would appear so," said Evaran. "I will look to Jane on how to procure it."

"Let's hope it doesn't involve finding lost pieces of it," said Dr. Snowden.

After ten minutes, Jane rejoined them in the assembly area. V had changed back into body mode and took his spot at the front console.

Jane took her seat and glanced at Evaran. "Did you catch all that?"

"We did. What is the augment that Karus requested?"

"It's a rapid-learning augment," said Jane. "It goes near the brain stem and enhances memory and recall while boosting focus. It also enhances problem solving and cognitive ability in general."

Dr. Snowden smirked. "It makes you smarter."

"Right. Almost all humans have that augment by the age of ten. The United Planets have a modified version for the Kalesh, but as part of the integration program, they have to go through a process to get one."

"Let me guess . . . Karus would never qualify," said Dr. Snowden.

Jane nodded. "He would not fit the psychological profile, and with his background, there is the possibility he might use it for nefarious purposes."

Dr. Snowden looked at Evaran. "So we need to replicate it and we're good to go, right?"

"Not quite. This augment involves the brain. I suspect the augment is customized, and without the knowledge of the safety and testing process, it could be dangerous."

Jane nodded. "The illegal augment trade has one that is almost a duplicate of what the United Planets has, but it has issues. I have read reports of Kalesh going crazy, some mutating, and some even dying. When the United Planets installs one, there are regular checkups and tweaking that is done post install to ensure it is working as intended. We have a brain scan of Karus from his brief incarceration that's needed to customize it, and he knows that."

"I see," said Evaran. "Are you able to obtain one then?"

"Maybe. I could ask Andrew. They have a secured augment lab in his building. We would need to apply Karus's brain scan onto it. I doubt Andrew would give me one unless . . ."

"Unless I come with you," said Evaran. He interacted with his chair console, causing the right screen to show a map of Da Nesh. "Very well. What are the coordinates?"

Jane walked up to the map and found Andrew's building. She pointed at it. "There."

Evaran examined the map. "There does not appear to be a place to land."

"It's meant to be traveled to using the city transportation system."

Evaran narrowed his eyes. "The roof appears to have an access point. V, take us to the roof, then keep the Torvatta nearby."

"Acknowledged."

"If they see your ship hovering around the building, there could be some problems," said Jane.

"V, engage stealth mode," said Evaran.

"Acknowledged."

The Torvatta took off and headed toward Andrew's building.

"Torvatta stealth mode engaged," said V.

Jane raised her eyebrows. "That'll work. Your ship is quite impressive."

"It makes for a nice place to live too," said Emily. "It also has a great training room."

Jane eyed Emily. "What type of training room?"

"It is a holo room that can convert energy into matter. It can make any training scenario you can imagine."

"I think I'd like to see that before I leave, if that's okay."

Emily glanced at Evaran, who nodded. "Sure. I'm there most mornings, so stop on in whenever."

Dr. Snowden observed Jane and Emily's interaction. He was glad that Emily was opening up more. Maybe Jane would rub off on her some.

After several minutes, the Torvatta hovered just over the roof.

"We have arrived," said V.

"Excellent," said Evaran. He stood and waved toward the entrance. "Let us go."

Everyone except V exited the Torvatta.

Dr. Snowden scanned the surroundings. The contrast between United Planets and Kalesh architecture was more apparent at this height. He could see several other metallic United Planets structures far off in the distance. They were taller than most of the Kalesh ones. He imagined it as a modern-day suburb with mini skyscrapers in their midst.

Emily squeezed his shoulder.

Dr. Snowden jumped. Looking around, he saw that Evaran and Jane were waiting for him at the roof door. He hustled up to them. "Sorry, I was . . . sightseeing."

"It's a great view up here. I come up here sometimes to clear my head," said Jane.

Dr. Snowden watched the light fluctuations from the Torvatta taking off. "I can see why." With a final look around, he entered the building after the others.

After ten minutes of navigating through the building, they reached Andrew's office. Dr. Snowden had scrutinized the building interior on their way in. The transportation pod system intrigued him. It could go horizontal as well as vertical. He wondered how much additional space that must have added. It was convenient, though.

The solid wall they stood in front of seemed impenetrable to Dr. Snowden. He watched as Jane interacted with her ARI, just like Evaran did, and a section of the wall in the shape of a door faded away. Although he had seen shielded doors before, seeing them with solid matter surprised him. Maybe it was a dark-colored shield with a hologram. He ran his hand along the door's edge as he entered the room. It reminded him of rubber.

Everyone else entered Andrew's office.

The first thing Dr. Snowden noticed was that it was an empty dome-shaped room. In the middle sat a man facing away from the door.

"Andrew . . . I hope I'm not bothering," said Jane as she walked up to Andrew.

"Not at all," said Andrew as he spun around. His lips parted and his eyes widened when he saw Evaran, Dr. Snowden, and Emily. "Evaran?"

Evaran bowed. "You are correct."

Andrew stood and walked over to Evaran and looked him over. "It really is you." He tapped at his ARI, causing the room to dim a bit, and then he shook Evaran's hand. "I have so many questions to ask you . . ."

Evaran waved a finger between Dr. Snowden and Emily. "Before we get to that, let me introduce Dr. Albert Snowden and his niece, Emily. We have come to ask for your help."

Andrew shook their hands and then sat back on his chair. "Of course. Sorry . . . not everyday someone you read about appears in your office. How can I help?"

Evaran gestured at Jane.

Jane cleared her throat. "I know you aren't going to like this, but . . . we need an unregulated IL-06 for Karus."

Andrew snorted. "What?"

"It's for a trade. I know . . . I know . . . it isn't legal, but we need it in order to talk with Warlord Okon."

"Why do you want to talk to him?"

Evaran stepped forward. "We are going to the space habitats to investigate the illegal augment trade, but wanted to check first with Warlord Okon. He may be able to provide useful information that might help us."

"Oh . . . ," said Andrew with a grin. "So that's why you're here. Jane can be quite persuasive, can't she?"

Jane cleared her throat while shooting a look at Andrew. "You remember that communication spike when Evaran arrived? I'm betting that Warlord Okon has a pulse on what that's about. If we're going to the space habitat, it would be helpful to know what we're walking into."

"Warlord Okon might know about the communication spike, but do you think he would know anything about the habitats?"

Jane shrugged. "He would know who is supplying the illegal augments."

"You still think they're coming from the habitats . . ."

"All my research points to it," said Jane. "Warlord Okon would know for sure."

"And if the habitat isn't where they're coming from?"

Jane lowered her head.

"You want to see where Chris died," said Andrew. He contemplated Jane for a moment, then stood up. "I'll get one configured for Karus, but don't tell him I helped." He exited the room.

Jane's eyes lit up. "He's going to help us!"

"Excellent," said Evaran.

After several minutes of light talk, Andrew returned with a box. He handed it to Jane. "Here you go. Don't lose it."

Jane smiled. "Thank you. I know you could get in trouble for this, and . . . I really appreciate it."

"I hope it's worth whatever mess I'll have to deal with," said Andrew. "However, if it gives you closure, and there is progress on the illegal augment trade, then it's worth it. Besides, I can say Evaran requested it." He shot a smile at Evaran.

Evaran dipped his head. "Hopefully that will help."

"Oh . . . it would. There would be no questions," said Andrew. "Obviously, I would love to travel with you, but this is Jane's case. I do have a request, though. Once this is all over, I'd like to see your ship and spend a day touring it if possible. There is so much I want to discuss."

"We will make time for it when this is over. You have my word."

"I can't wait."

Jane hugged Andrew. "Thank you so much."

"Watch her," said Andrew, pointing at Evaran.

Evaran bowed. "Of course."

After everyone shook hands with Andrew, they exited the building and assembled in the Torvatta.

The interaction between Evaran and Andrew intrigued Dr. Snowden. He could only imagine reading about someone as epic as Evaran, then having them appear on your doorstep. Still, Andrew was able to wrestle out a visit to the Torvatta. Probably something he would treasure for the rest of his life. It surprised Dr. Snowden that Evaran did not invite Andrew to come along. Maybe after the last several adventures, one extra person was enough. Dr. Snowden shook his head. It was a reminder for him to not take for granted where he was.

After flying to Hillti, Jane went back to the remote alley. V, in stealthed orb mode, hovered over her and relayed an overview to the Torvatta's main screen. A few minutes after her arrival, Karus appeared at the meeting spot right inside the forest.

"I didn't think you would actually do it . . . ," said Karus.

Jane bobbed her head. "Well, now you know how important this is." She handed the small box over to Karus.

Karus studied the box and then opened it. His eyes widened slightly. "Where'd you get it?"

"I can't tell you that."

Karus peeled his lips back and snorted. "Fine . . . fine." He ran a hand over his mouth. "Be back here in four days, same time. Make sure to bring whoever your friends are for that one. The person meeting them will want to know who is coming and what to expect. I won't be around for that, obviously."

"Thanks for setting it up."

Karus nodded and tucked the box into a bag he carried off to his side. He spun around and headed toward the alley exit. As he approached it, he pivoted. "Be careful." He wheeled back around and left the alleyway.

Jane returned to the Torvatta and took her seat in the command area. "Looks like we come back in four days around the same time. Not sure what we can do until then."

Dr. Snowden chuckled.

Jane wrinkled her eyebrows as she glanced at Dr. Snowden. "What?"

"You're on a ship that can travel through time."

Jane pursed her lips as her eyes darted back and forth. "So . . . you're saying we could go four days into the future?"

"Yep. Unless, of course, Evaran sees an issue. It takes a while to adjust to having time travel as an option."

Jane harrumphed as she shot a look at Evaran. "Any concerns?"

"None that I can foresee. V, take us four days into the future. Bring us a bit before we are to meet, and keep us in stealth mode."

"Acknowledged."

Dr. Snowden smiled as he glanced at Evaran. "Can we go to the roof for this?"

"Of course," said Evaran. He headed to the roof, with V following behind him.

"What's on the roof?" asked Jane.

Dr. Snowden stood. "You have to see it to believe it."

Jane gulped. "Okay . . ."

Dr. Snowden bent over a bit and extended his arm toward the elevator. "After you."

"Thanks," said Jane, shooting Dr. Snowden a smile.

Dr. Snowden watched Jane reach the elevator. He was startled when Emily walked by and tapped his arm.

"Focus," said Emily.

"What?"

Emily raised an eyebrow at Dr. Snowden.

Dr. Snowden's face turned a slight shade of red. He followed Emily to the roof. Once he got there, he saw V behind the pop-up console he had grown accustomed to seeing when they traveled on the roof. He still did not understand how it rose out of what he thought was a glass-like floor.

The Torvatta lifted off and streaked toward space.

Evaran stood at the front light-blue shielding that acted as a guardrail. To his right was Jane, while Emily was on the other side.

Dr. Snowden joined Jane on her right. "I think you'll like this."

"I'll admit, it's a little strange to be on the roof as we approach low orbit," said Jane.

Evaran pointed around. "There is a shield around the Torvatta."

"I figured that but . . . did not expect it would hold breathable air," said Jane.

After a few more minutes, they were in space.

Jane gasped as everything faded out, then eased back in. "Was . . . that time travel?"

Dr. Snowden smiled. "Yep. It was pretty neat, huh?"

"I'd say so," said Jane with widened eyes.

Dr. Snowden remembered the first time he saw time travel from the roof. It made the hairs on his neck raise to think that everything went away then came back. Evaran had mentioned that it was merely the perspective from the Torvatta. Anyone outside would see the Torvatta fade away with a noise. He figured Jane maybe would not believe it completely until they went back down.

"You are officially a time traveler now," said Evaran.

Jane chuckled. "I guess I am."

The Torvatta returned to the remote alleyway in Hillti.

Jane stepped back from the guardrail. "Karus said that everyone that is going to see Warlord Okon will need to come with me."

"That is fine," said Evaran. "V, I will need you to stay behind in case we need a fast escape."

"Acknowledged."

"Dr. Snowden, I would suggest you put on your survival suit."

Dr. Snowden nodded as he hustled past Evaran to the research lab. He decided to keep his helmet down for this. After getting the suit on, he did a final check to make sure everything was working, then headed back to the Torvatta main area.

Everyone except V exited the Torvatta and assembled in the alleyway.

Dr. Snowden looked back at the Torvatta and could barely see the light fluctuations that indicated it was in stealthed mode. He wondered if there were those with augments who could detect it like he could.

A large Kalesh with body armor and a weapon slung over his shoulder approached them.

Dr. Snowden noted there were no disguises and double backs like Karus did. This was walk in and all business.

Jane whispered to Dr. Snowden. "We really did travel in time."

"Yep," said Dr. Snowden. He wondered what must be going through her mind.

The Kalesh paused as he looked them over. "I'm Jaklur. Who am I talking to?"

Evaran stepped forward. "I am Evaran, and with me is Dr. Albert Snowden, Emily Snowden, and Jane Trellis. We are here to meet Warlord Okon."

"Warlord Okon would normally charge you for a meeting, but you have piqued his interest," said Jaklur. "Are you ready to go?"

"I thought we were going to get coordinates?" asked Jane.

Jaklur smirked. "So United Planets or whoever else can find and attack us? I don't think so. You'll be transported in one of our ships, which should be . . . arriving . . . about now."

Dr. Snowden put a hand on his forehead as dust swirled around from a ship landing near the forest. The foul smell it kicked up assaulted his nose. He thought the ship looked like a van with boosters on the bottom and back. The only windows he could see were in the front. He jumped a bit as one of the side doors slid back, revealing a dimly lit compartment.

Jaklur walked up to the side and gestured inward. "Let's go."

Once everyone had entered the compartment, Jaklur poked his head in. "It's a four-hour flight." He closed the side door.

Dr. Snowden looked around the compartment. It had benches on all sides except the doorway. "It's a bit cramped in here, and smells kinda bad too. I think it's time to raise the helmet."

Evaran scanned the interior with his ring. "This compartment has surveillance."

Dr. Snowden sighed as he leaned back against the stiff wall. This was going to be a long flight.

07

Four hours later, the craft landed. Dr. Snowden leaned forward and cracked his back. He chuckled at the thought that cushions must be in short supply on Roeth. The craft's movement made it hard to relax. He surveyed the others. Jane and Emily were stretching while Evaran sat motionless like he had all flight. Dr. Snowden wondered what Evaran thought about. His attention focused on the side door as it slid open. He shielded his eyes as the waning sun filtered into the compartment.

"Okay. Out," said Jaklur.

Dr. Snowden gestured forward.

Emily and Jane exited the compartment first, followed by Dr. Snowden and Evaran.

Dr. Snowden lowered his helmet and took in the fresh air. Studying the surroundings showed they were deep in a forest. Around the base of the trees were scattered makeshift buildings made of thin metal with rigid poles. They looked like they could be dismantled and moved in a hurry if need be.

Immediately around him was a large clearing, big enough to fit several Torvattas. It was the mass of heavily armed Kalesh scattered around that drew his attention. They had weapons that looked like assault rifles and wore varying types of light and heavy armor. Some had on helmets, others had goggles. Uniformity was not a key design ingredient here.

Jaklur signaled to some of the other Kalesh.

The Kalesh advanced forward with a small cylinder. One of the Kalesh bent down and began to fidget with a control panel built into the side.

"You'll be talking via holo presence," said Jaklur.

Jane jerked her head back. "We could've done that in Hillti. Why'd we have to fly four hours for that?"

"You'll have to ask Warlord Okon that."

Jane glanced at Evaran. "I'm not liking this . . ."

Evaran extended a hand. "Let us hear what Warlord Okon has to say."

Dr. Snowden grimaced. They were out in the middle of nowhere in the center of a pack of heavily armed Kalesh who hated aliens. And now the person they were supposed to meet was not even there. The feeling that this was a setup pervaded Dr. Snowden. It was not the first time they had walked into a trap. The only reassuring thought was that if he was thinking of this now, then Evaran had probably planned for this already.

The Kalesh who worked on the cylinder nodded at Jaklur.

With a flip of a switch, the cylinder shot up a projection of a heavyset male Kalesh. His fur was brown with streaks of gray, and his armor seemed more decorated than those in the camp. Around him were several female Kalesh in advanced heavy armor. The Kalesh spoke. "I'm Warlord Okon, and welcome to my territory."

Evaran narrowed his eyes. "Why are we not talking in person?"

Warlord Okon focused on Evaran. "Ahh . . . so you're what everyone is talking about." He moved his head from side to side as he inspected Evaran. "You're not much to look at. It seems you've attracted a lot of attention. More attention than Roeth needs."

"Elaborate."

Warlord Okon laughed. "It was hard to find any information on you. Where'd you come from?"

"Far away from here."

Warlord Okon smirked. "You should've stayed there. Roeth was rebuilding fine until you aliens showed up and brought all your damn galactic drama with you. Is it any wonder Follisat, once the jewel of Roeth, is now a cesspool of crime?"

"From what we saw, the only crimes committed were attacks on me and my friends by your group."

Warlord Okon uttered a low growl. After a moment, he spoke. "I heard about Jimus. I'll deal with him later for not finishing the job. I have to give you credit for coming out here. Not many would willingly seek out the leader of the group that attacked them."

"I have some questions that," said Evaran, gesturing at Jane, "she believed you could answer."

"Really . . . ," said Warlord Okon, eying Jane. "A United Planets agent with questions. Imagine that. And what questions would that be then?"

"Less of a question and more of a confirmation about the illegal augment trade," said Jane. "I think they're coming from the space habitats that Advanced Dynamics built. Once they get planetside, they get sold on the black market, and . . . crimes happen."

Warlord Okon rubbed his hands for a moment. "I'm aware of that *filth* being brought in from the space habitats. I even brought it to the authorities' attention. Their response? They tried to assassinate me."

"I have a hard time believing that the Kalesh government would try to silence you," said Jane.

"The Kalesh government?"

The Kalesh watching the exchange laughed.

Warlord Okon shook his head. "You've never dealt with an executioner, have you?"

Jane pursed her lips. "No . . . I've never heard of them."

"Figures. They're a stealthy, tough, and secretive assassin robot. They took out five of my men before we took it down. Then the second one came, and so on and so on. Now here we are."

Jane wrinkled her eyebrows. "Why didn't you contact us?"

"The United Planets? The Kalesh didn't have the technology for executioners . . . but the United Planets does. The United Planets emblem was also on the executioner's arm."

Jane rubbed her chin. "It could've been Advanced Dynamics and they framed the United Planets. I will look into it."

"Right . . . Anyways, no need to look into it. I've made my decision already. None of you are leaving alive."

Evaran narrowed his eyes. "I do not understand. We came to ask for information to help in shutting down the illegal augment trade. This would help your cause."

"It might. However . . . there are over thirty-three verified groups coming to Roeth. Groups like the Tarmidugeon Syndicate, the Jultolik Cartel, and quite a few I haven't even heard of. All of them want you for one reason or another. Roeth doesn't need a second influx of power players, especially those that play in my arena, but that's what's happening."

"Perhaps I can redirect them."

"Even if you left now, they would still come now that a spotlight's on us," said Warlord Okon. "No . . . what's needed is a deterrent. Something big." He jabbed a finger in the air at Evaran. "Show them that if they come, they *will* be in for a fight. Your deaths will be a warning sign to any group that comes here that even the mighty fall."

Evaran interacted with his ARI. "I cannot allow you to kill us."

A wave of snickering fanned out among the Kalesh.

"You can't allow it," said Warlord Okon, shaking while laughing. "Maybe I should keep you around for a good laugh." He exhaled from his mouth. "Nonetheless, you have your answer. Yes, the space habitats are the source of illegal augments. Too bad it won't do you any good."

"I appreciate your answer," said Evaran. "May we have a private moment among ourselves before our deaths?"

Warlord Okon narrowed his eyes. "I'm not a savage. I will allow it."

"It is appreciated," said Evaran. He motioned for Dr. Snowden, Emily, and Jane to huddle. Once everyone was together, he said, "The Torvatta is hovering just above us. It will land in the open area to our left. Once the distraction occurs, run to it."

Dr. Snowden furrowed his eyebrows. "What's the distraction?"

"I left it up to V to decide. You will know it when you see it," said Evaran.

Dr. Snowden glanced at Jane and Emily, who both shrugged. "That beats dying."

After a moment, two United Planets ships appeared above them and began firing at the Kalesh. The Kalesh scattered into the trees. Jaklur fell backward to the ground as he shot upward. The cylinder that projected Warlord Okon tipped over.

"What's going on!" said Warlord Okon. "Put me back up!

"Go!" said Evaran, pointing to the left.

Dr. Snowden could feel his nanobots kick in. Everything around him began to slow down. He took off toward the Torvatta, which he could now see due to the light fluctuations caused by its stealth mode. He noticed that Jane was not able to keep up with him and Emily. Slowing down, he waited for Jane to catch up. His attention was drawn toward Jaklur, who had rolled to his side and fired at Jane. Dr. Snowden ran toward Jane and yanked her forward, out of the way. He blocked Jaklur's shot with his left forearm shield, then wheeled around and ran as Evaran passed by him. Once they were inside the Torvatta's shielding and standing on the extended ramp, the ships disappeared.

A silence spread out over the camp.

Jaklur stood up and then shot at the Torvatta.

The Torvatta's shielding lit up as fire from the other Kalesh poured in.

After a moment, a visibly shaken Jaklur raised his hand, and the firing ceased. He faced Evaran. "Nice illusion." He righted the cylinder, showing an enraged Warlord Okon.

"We must be going," said Evaran.

"This isn't over," said Warlord Okon, growling.

"Perhaps not. Nonetheless, I will see what I can do about your situation given what I know now."

"You've already done enough. Your mere presence causes problems," said Warlord Okon.

Evaran clenched and unclenched his jaw as he eyed Warlord Okon for a moment, then spun around and gestured for the others to enter the Torvatta.

When Dr. Snowden walked in, Jane hugged him.

"Thank you," said Jane with misted eyes.

Dr. Snowden's face turned a slight shade of red. "I'm glad you're safe."

"I didn't even see him firing at me in all the confusion."

Dr. Snowden nodded.

Everyone assembled in the command area as the Torvatta lifted into the air.

"V, take us to Da Nesh and hover over the city," said Evaran.

"Acknowledged."

"V, your timing was impeccable," said Dr. Snowden.

"Analysis. Evaran had me follow behind in stealth mode."

"I figured he had something up his sleeve."

V looked at Evaran's sleeves.

Dr. Snowden chuckled. "Not literally."

"Acknowledged."

Jane glanced at Evaran. "I didn't expect the meeting to go quite in that direction."

"I suspected that our travel in their ship was a ruse. I informed V to follow us."

Jane ran her hand over her right eye. "I'm glad you did. What's the next step?"

"We can break for the night and pick up in the morning," said Evaran. "I will continue to go over some of the data I acquired from Corunus."

Emily exhaled from her nose. "I'm gonna get a workout in, then make it an early night. I'm not really hungry."

Dr. Snowden glanced at Jane. "I could eat alone . . . unless you want to get something to eat."

"Sure," said Jane. "Can we eat it on the roof? The sun should be setting."

Dr. Snowden squared his shoulders. His eyes sagged a bit, but he was not going to pass up an opportunity to eat with Jane. He glanced at Emily, who had a small grin on her face as she passed him.

Jane wrinkled her eyebrows. "So . . ."

"Sure. Let's gets dinner and a sunset."

Dr. Snowden eased back into his chair on the Torvatta's roof. He had V show him how to pull up the console. It could create items like the holo room could. It made him wonder if the roof was another dimensional area, with holo-room capability. A small table was to his right and Jane on the other side in her chair. The sun setting brought a smile to his face. It was no surprise Jane liked Da Nesh.

"I've never really seen the sun setting from this height," said Jane as she dipped into her bowl.

Dr. Snowden peeked at her food. "It's pretty relaxing. I have to ask . . . is that chocolate ice cream or something else?"

"You got it."

"Ahh, no vitastick?"

"I usually eat a vegetable stew with a breadstick when I want something different."

"Huh. Is meat completely phased out in the United Planets?" asked Dr. Snowden as he placed his plate with two slices of pizza and a container with soda on the small table.

"No . . . there is still live meat consumption, but it's rare, and in most places, animals are protected. With replicators, there's no need for animals. Also, it's more efficient to store replicator elements that aren't perishable. Sure, it requires more to store it, but it's much more flexible in what it can do."

"Makes sense," said Dr. Snowden as he took a bite out of his pizza slice.

Jane placed her bowl on the table. "So I've been meaning to ask . . . How exactly did you come to travel with Evaran? Was there a selection process, or was it random?"

Dr. Snowden chuckled. "Long story short, Emily and I were abducted by an alien race. Evaran stepped in, like he always seems to do when something temporal is involved, and rescued us. He dropped us off back on Earth and said he would be back in three months. When he came, we asked to travel with him, and he said yes."

"Your abduction must have been traumatic."

"It was and it took me several hours to even believe we'd been abducted. The aliens had put us in a virtual simulation, and Evaran appeared in it to guide us when it shut down. He called it our awakening."

"What aliens did all this to you?" asked Jane.

"It's a race called the Krotovore. They were from the future and the Sombrero galaxy. Insect-like race. They're who gave us the nanobots."

Jane shuddered.

"However, I think traveling with Evaran has helped put it in perspective."

"Has it been easy?"

Dr. Snowden gulped. "I wish I could say it has. Our first adventure was with the Fredorians when—"

"When you helped Andia Kiggs find and assemble the Arkaron," said Jane.

"That's right. Andia was a great person. She and Emily were . . . very friendly. I came to know the Kreagans well, and the loss of one who traveled with us hit me pretty hard."

"I'm sorry to hear that. I only saw that you helped from the Evaran Protocol details." Jane tilted her head at Dr. Snowden. "So Emily and Andia . . ."

Dr. Snowden nodded. "I was surprised at first, but after I thought about it, it made sense. While Andia seemed authoritarian, she was actually adventurous, beautiful, smart, open to new ideas—"

"You sure it was Emily that liked her?" asked Jane with a chuckle.

Dr. Snowden's face warmed up. "What I mean is . . . Emily bonds with people that have certain characteristics, and Andia had them. The fact that Andia was a woman and older didn't bother Emily. She tends to go for older anyways. With Fredorian culture being what it was with the groups and all . . ."

Jane chuckled. "I'm Fredorian, and that concept hasn't been adopted widely in the United Planets. I was exclusive with Chris." She cast a sidelong glance at Dr. Snowden. "I better watch out then, huh?"

"I don't think you need to worry about that."

"Hey!"

Dr. Snowden jerked his head back and put his hands out front. "I didn't mean it like that. Emily used to be . . . much more open and free-spirited. She spent nine months alone on a prison planet in a pocket universe on our last adventure. As you can probably tell, she is much more guarded now. I don't think any relationship is in her immediate future."

"I noticed that. I actually thought she was your bodyguard."

Dr. Snowden sighed. "That's not too far from the truth anymore. She wants to be alone lately." He looked down.

Jane laid a hand on Dr. Snowden's shoulder. "It must have been a difficult time for the both of you."

"I'm glad she's safe now," said Dr. Snowden. "We even had a duplicate of her made of nanobots for a short while. One thing I have learned traveling with Evaran is that reality is very strange."

"Sounds like it. Evaran seems like a good person, and I'm happy he's helping me," said Jane.

"That's Evaran. He has so much power, but he is the one being I know where power hasn't corrupted him. Speaking of which . . . you think Advanced Dynamics and the illegal augment trade have something to do with your husband's death?"

Jane sighed. "I don't know. I do know they won't give me a straight answer. I'm hoping to find out more when we head up there."

Dr. Snowden took another bite of his pizza slice.

"You know . . . you sorta look like Chris, maybe ten years older."

Dr. Snowden swallowed, then said, "It appears we share similar tastes."

Jane raised her eyebrows.

Dr. Snowden's eyes widened. "I meant . . . umm . . . that he chose to work on a space habitat. I'm an astronomer, but I would have loved to do work on one in any capacity."

Jane smiled.

"On another note, have you been to Earth before?"

"Oh yeah. Fredoria and Earth are two of the four founding members of the United Planets. I was stationed at Austin, in the Texas district, for a year."

"The Texas district?"

"I'm not sure what you would call it in your time period."

"It was a state in the United States of America," said Dr. Snowden. "Emily and I were abducted north of there, near Columbus, Ohio."

"Ahh, the Ohio district."

Dr. Snowden rubbed his chin. "Things sound quite a bit different on Earth in this time period."

"One government with the world divided into districts."

"That makes sense. In my time period, there are over two hundred independent nations, each with their own leader."

Jane cocked her head. "It makes you wonder how any global initiatives got done. I know some about Earth prior to the Third World War, but not too much."

Dr. Snowden chewed on Jane's words. "I don't know anything about that. I look forward to reading up on it, though. It sounds like this United Planets thing is good for Earth. How are relations with the Kreagans?"

"They're good now. Obviously much better than when we broke off from them in 2734. We've come a long way in the last several centuries."

"There's so much for me to learn still. Anyways, I wasn't trying to use all your time up here for a history lesson. I'm hoping you find some answers when we go up to the space habitat."

"Me too," said Jane. She cast a sidelong glance at Dr. Snowden. "I suspect you're still looking for answers too."

"What do you mean?"

"Emily. I can see the pain in your face when you interact with her," said Jane. She tapped the side of her head. "Augments."

Dr. Snowden sighed. He looked out at the setting sun. "I guess I am. She's changed dramatically, and I'm struggling to deal with it. Evaran says I'm supposed to be there for her, but

I get the feeling she's tense around me. I feel like I'm actually hindering her recovery."

"I wouldn't think of it as a recovery. If this is who she is now, you should accept it, and form a new relationship."

"That's what Evaran said too. He said to be myself, and adapt. I'm trying."

"That's all you can do," said Jane.

Dr. Snowden swallowed hard.

"The night's still young. I sure wouldn't mind a tour of the ship."

Dr. Snowden smiled. "It would be my honor." He stood and went to pick up his plate.

"I know I thanked you already, but I really do appreciate what you did back at Warlord Okon's camp."

Dr. Snowden's heartbeat accelerated. "Oh . . . well . . . As Emily would say, I got your back."

"What about my front?" asked Jane with a small smile.

Dr. Snowden stared at Jane for a moment. "Always." He extended his free arm in a flourish. "Shall we?"

"Lead on."

Jane yawned as she sat on the edge of her bed. She could not recall the last time she had slept as peacefully as she had. A grin crept onto her face as she thought about her tour with Dr. Snowden. The Torvatta was impressive. Its dimensional rooms and technology were unlike anything she had ever seen. No wonder Dr. Snowden and Emily enjoyed traveling with Evaran; the Torvatta was a great base to operate from.

After cleaning up and slipping into her light power armor, she took a final look around the room. It was advanced and luxurious, something she could see herself getting used to. The thought of traveling with Evaran had crossed her mind a few times. In the short time she had been with him, she had already met Warlord Okon, someone who was deemed impossible to find, and now she would be going to the space habitat. She cleared her mind as she exited the room.

When she entered the main area of the Torvatta, she saw V headed toward the holo room. Dr. Snowden had showed it to her the previous night, and she had a hard time believing it was real. While replication shared similar capabilities, to have a room that could do the conversion effortlessly surprised her. Dr. Snowden had summoned up a large rock that they sat on as it orbited a gas giant planet. Talking to Dr. Snowden was easy, and several times she had to catch herself from leaning into him. It had been a long while since someone showed an interest in her. She smirked as she caught up with V outside the holo room.

V swiveled his head toward Jane. "Jane Trellis. How are you this morning?"

"You can call me Jane, and I'm doing fine. What are you up to?"

"My morning training session with Emily."

"Do you mind if I watch?"

"Analysis. I do not think Emily would mind."

"After you," said Jane, stepping back. She followed V into the room. Her eyes widened as she sized up the environment Emily had running. It was a large, open area in what appeared to be a space ship. She could see windows with space on the outside. Emily was jumping around and fighting humanoid creatures with leathery skin. Some had unusual appendages sticking out of their bodies. It was not the appearance that startled her, but the quantity of them. There were probably fifty or sixty surrounding her. Emily was a whirlwind of activity with her staff.

The room paused as V and Jane approached Emily.

Emily wiped the sweat off her forehead and took a moment to catch her breath. "You're late."

"I apologize. Evaran had me run some analytics," said V.

Emily raised her head a bit as she looked at Jane. "Want to join us?"

"Sure . . . but what are we fighting and where are we?"

"This is the first Kreagan colony ship we found hurtling in space when we were looking for the Arkaron crystals," said Emily, waving her hand around. "Evaran called these creatures transformed. They were created by an Outsider race called the Malazim. They couldn't enter our reality, so they used an obelisk-like stone to reach out and transform living matter."

Jane's eyes widened. "Okay . . . that sounds unusual. I know of Outsiders, but don't think I've ever heard of them coming through stones before."

"Analysis. The Malazim are what attacked the first Kreagus home world, causing a mass exodus," said V.

Jane scrunched her face. "Huh . . . I didn't know that. I heard there was a major event, but details were sketchy. Nonetheless, I'm ready."

Emily looked Jane over. "Are you sure? What melee weapon are you going to use?"

"I'll use my sidearm," said Jane. "It's all I need."

"Okay . . . ," said Emily. She gestured for V and Jane to stand next to her. After they arrived, she tapped at a console that appeared in the air. "I've tripled the amount of transformed. This should be a good fight."

Jane looked around as the large area populated with more transformed. She was used to fighting two, maybe three opponents at a time, never a swarm. Crowd control was usually meant to subdue, not kill. After setting her weapon to wide beam and lethal, she glanced at Emily and said, "I'm ready."

Emily pressed a button on the midair console, which caused it to disappear.

Jane raised her eyebrows at the growling sounds coming from the creatures. She could smell them. It reminded her of rotting flesh. Her attention focused on the group of transformed rushing her. She aimed ahead and fired.

The transformed in front of her were sliced in half.

She glanced over at Emily, who was spinning around gracefully like a dancer with her staff and tossing transformed around.

V was punching holes in the transformed and kicking them back.

Jane stumbled back as one of the transformed grabbed her arm. With a quick kick that sent it flying, she stepped back and fired, shredding it.

Six more transformed converged on her.

She fired in an arc, but one of the transformed dodged it and was within arm's reach. She hit her belt, causing a rectangular human-height shield to appear in front of her.

The transformed jumped forward, knocking her down. It then jumped on top of her shield.

Her pulse quickened.

Another transformed grabbed her feet and pulled her into a mob. They attacked her shield, and the ones near her feet began to slash at her lower legs under the shield. She struggled to slide back, but more transformed appeared near her head. There were too many. She had underestimated their speed and ferocity. With a panicked look over at Emily and V, she said, "Help!"

Emily and V rushed over.

V grabbed the one trying to get Jane's head and tossed it away. He kicked two more that had tried to fill the gap.

Emily jumped on Jane's shield and, in a swirling motion, knocked the transformed back. Once there was some breathing room, she cleared a spot where they could defend.

V helped Jane up.

"New strategy," said Emily. "Me and V will take the sides. You fire from the center between us."

"Okay," said Jane as she tried to steady her trembling hand. This was more real than she had expected.

Emily had shortened her staff into a baton and was mixing repulsion blasts in with strikes. V had begun to spin at a high velocity and move around. Whatever he hit went flying back or was decapitated.

Jane took advantage of the space they had secured and fired out.

After forty-five minutes, the swarm had been cleared.

Jane sat down. "Whew. That . . . that was intense."

Emily sat next to her and tapped Jane's arm. "That was level eight."

"What?"

"Analysis. There are one hundred levels. Emily has only reached level forty-two."

"That's incredible," said Jane as she looked at Emily. "You move much faster than I would have expected. You're a lot stronger too. I would've expected that from V, but not you."

"I train for four to five hours every day. And of course, the nanobots help."

"Do you train so hard because of . . . what happened?"

Emily snapped her head toward Jane.

"I'm not trying to pry. It was . . . something your uncle mentioned last night."

Emily sighed. "That's part of it. However, I think it boils down to being prepared for whatever life throws at you. I don't just train physically, I train mentally now as well through studying."

"That's a good approach to life. I follow a similar regime, though not quite as hard as you, apparently."

Emily exhaled from her nose. "You performed well for your first time. The first time I did this on the colony ship, I ran away in fear and left Uncle Albert and a friend alone. If V hadn't reached them, they wouldn't have made it. My weakness could've been their death." She clenched her jaw.

"Oh . . . ," said Jane. "If you and V hadn't stepped in, they woulda crawled under my shield and I wouldn't have made it."

"The holo room would have paused before any serious injury. It tracks our health," said Emily.

V swiveled his head toward Emily, then Jane. "The Torvatta has your back."

Emily and Jane chuckled.

"So you do this every morning then for a few hours?" asked Jane.

"I do an hour in the mornings usually if Evaran has a meeting. On other mornings it can be two hours, but overall, still four to five hours a day. You're always welcome to join. I've tried to get Uncle Albert in here, but that'd interfere with his late sleeping."

Jane pursed her lips. "You know . . . he's trying to adjust to the new you."

"I know. He'll have to come to terms with who I am now."

"He will," said Jane with a smile. "Just takes time." She swallowed hard. "At least he has time."

Emily paused as she examined Jane. "How did you adjust after losing your husband?"

"I haven't, really. They say time heals all wounds. I think it's more accurate to say time covers all wounds. It still hurts, but I won't let that event define me. I . . . need to focus on the future."

"Yeah."

"Anyways, I'm going to get cleaned up."

V tilted his head. "Evaran has requested we meet in the conference room at eleven a.m."

"Good. I can get something to eat then too."

"Acknowledged."

Jane exited the holo room and headed to her living quarters. It was obvious to her now that Dr. Snowden and Emily were far more advanced than an augmented human. She did not think they knew their full potential. The United Planets called augmented humans advanced, and nonaugmented humans normal. Dr. Snowden and Emily were something else. Human, yes, but with capabilities far in excess of an augmented human.

Jane enjoyed talking with Emily and V. It gave her insight into their mindsets. Traveling with Evaran was turning out to be challenging, but that was the part that excited her. She grinned as she continued on to her room.

08

Dr. Snowden looked up from the table as Jane and Emily walked into the conference room. The tour he had given Jane the previous night replayed in his mind. He reflected on how great it felt to sit with her on a floating rock in the holo room. His thoughts were interrupted by Emily swatting his arm.

"You're up early," said Emily as she sat next to him with an orange drink.

Dr. Snowden snorted. "I was up at nine thirty, actually." He had gone looking for Jane and saw that she was in the holo room with Emily and V. They were doing the Kreagan colony ship simulation, something he had no desire to relive. Emily had invited him several times, but the thought of how close his life had come to ending made his palms sweat. He would do it sometime, to conquer his fear of it, but he was not in any rush.

"Analysis. Jane joined me and Emily at nine thirty-one a.m. in the holo room."

"I saw that and got breakfast instead."

"I understand. You had meat desires," said V.

Jane laughed while Emily snickered.

Dr. Snowden raised his eyebrows and looked at Jane. "Do you see what you've started?"

Jane shook her head as she chortled. "Sorry." She glanced at Evaran. "Go ahead."

"I am glad everyone is in a good mood," said Evaran. He tapped at the table console, causing a projection to shoot up a wireframe depiction of the space habitat where Chris died.

It reminded Dr. Snowden of a large cylinder with a wide upside-down salad bowl on the bottom. The cylinder had smaller cylinders around it at various intervals. Structures that reminded him of frying pans stuck out around the cylinders. The number of levels surprised him. They started at one from the cylinder base and went all the way to eight-four at the top. This was not a small habitat.

Evaran interacted with the console and pointed to a glowing section on the habitat. "It would appear that levels twenty to thirty are for docking. I suspect we will be directed to one of them. However, I am unclear on how we should approach since it is in quarantine."

Jane rubbed her chin. "Well . . . my United Planets clearance is too low, but yours isn't."

"We can try that," said Evaran. "In regards to the illegal augments, I will need to access a data storage center. As there are a lot of AIs present from what I researched, I will need to go there physically." He pointed to another section on the projection. "This is level seventy-two. It appears to house one of these data storage centers."

Jane stood and pointed to another section on the projection. "This is level thirteen. It's where Chris is supposed to have died. I'd like to check that area out. Since yours is so far away, I can go to that section on my own if you want to head on to that other one."

Dr. Snowden cleared his throat. "I'll go with you unless . . . you want to be alone."

"I'd like that," said Jane.

Evaran narrowed his eyes. "It may be advantageous for us to stick together. We do not know what reception we may get."

Dr. Snowden pointed at V. "We could take V with us." He glanced at Jane. "Would we be expecting a hostile environment?"

"I wouldn't think so," said Jane. "There are United Planets and Kalesh representatives there."

Evaran paused as he contemplated Jane. "If you feel it would be safe, I will defer to your judgment, as you would know better than me."

"We should be okay. It would be like Corunus, which you've seen, but maybe a bit more secure," said Jane. "Besides . . . if anything did happen, it's not like you couldn't handle it, at least from what I read."

Evaran cast a sidelong glance at Emily before lowering his head. "Perhaps . . . but it does not hurt to be cautious."

Jane gestured at Emily and V. "After what I witnessed at this morning's training session, we should be okay. That handheld device Emily was using is quite powerful."

"Personal support devices, or PSDs, as we call them," said Emily.

"That'll work."

"Then it is decided," said Evaran. He looked at V. "Coordinates should be in the system. Take us there."

"Acknowledged."

They exited the room and assembled in the command area. Evaran sat in his command chair, while Emily sat in the left U-shaped seating area. Dr. Snowden and Jane sat on the other side. V stood in front of the console, and his hands were a blur as the Torvatta ascended into space.

Dr. Snowden felt a surge of electricity shoot through him. Getting to see a unit of a Dyson anything was something he thought he would never see except in fiction. Yet here he was. He wondered about the engineering that must have gone into building it. Maybe he could find out when he got there. At least he would be with Jane, something he knew he would enjoy.

Once the Torvatta was in space, Evaran tapped at his chair console. "V, portal us in."

"Acknowledged."

Jane cocked her head at Dr. Snowden.

"Oh . . . it's how the Torvatta travels long distances," said Dr. Snowden. "You'll see."

A gold beam shot out the front of the Torvatta, causing a circular portal with a silver border to appear. The light-blue surface rippled.

Jane narrowed her eyes, then widened them as they flew through the portal and exited near the space habitat. "How . . . that wasn't condensed space travel!"

"It was not," said Evaran.

Jane exhaled. "So . . . how does it work?"

"It is a form of travel unique to the Torvatta."

Jane's eyes darted back and forth as she wrinkled her eyebrows. After a moment, she said, "Dimensional travel. Opens a hole to another dimension, flies in to the dimension, then exits out another hole."

Evaran narrowed his eyes. "That is correct. Have you studied it before?"

"I have but . . . it was only theoretical. To open the hole would require exotic energy that no one has been able to produce, except in tiny amounts. I would guess that the gold beam was exotic energy, but I've never seen or heard of there being enough to form a beam."

"You are beginning to understand," said Evaran with a sparkle in his eyes.

Jane shook her head. "Amazing."

Dr. Snowden perked his head up. It did not surprise him that Jane would know; they were in the future after all. What did surprise him was that Evaran seemed to be caught off guard, something that did not happen often. Maybe Evaran's perception of what humanity did and did not know in this time period was not aligning. His attention was disrupted by the front screen showing an image of the habitat on one side and the Torvatta on the other. A dashed line faded in and out between them.

"Communication Protocol established. Sending credentials," said V.

It was fascinating to Dr. Sowden to see how the Torvatta did anything. He sometimes wondered if the visuals on the screen were more for his and Emily's sake. All of this could easily occur without any verbal or visual communication.

When V had established the communication protocol, the dashed line between the Torvatta and the habitat became solid. When he sent the credentials, another dashed line appeared slightly above the protocol line. After a moment, the line solidified, and a green outline formed on both the habitat and the Torvatta. The habitat image zoomed into a section with a small ring that jutted out from the main cylinder. An array of hangar doors perforated the ring's outer hull. One of them was blinking with the number twenty-seven flashing on it.

"Docking coordinates received," said V.

"Take us in," said Evaran.

"Acknowledged."

The Torvatta flew toward the small ring. Once it arrived just outside the designated docking area, it slowed to a crawl until the momentum took it through a smoke-colored semi-transparent shield.

Dr. Snowden figured this must be ubiquitous for small to medium craft. He had seen larger ships on the outside, but they were not connected. Maybe they had landing shuttles.

Evaran stood and gestured toward the research lab while looking at Dr. Snowden. "Get your survival suit on, and we will meet you at the entrance."

Dr. Snowden knew Emily and Jane already had their suits, and V would not need one. As he went to get his suit on, he thought about Evaran never needing one other than what he always had on. He knew Evaran was something not recognizable in his natural state, at least that is what Evaran had said. Maybe one day he would see what Evaran actually was. He got his suit on and met the others at the Torvatta entrance. He was not surprised to see V in orb mode. V's stealth would be advantageous.

Evaran gestured around as they exited the Torvatta. "According to the protocols, decontamination occurs in the bay, and not in a tunnel like on Corunus."

"Maybe to protect against ships bringing something in," said Dr. Snowden.

Jane shook her head. "Possibly, but I think it's more so whatever is here doesn't get out."

"It could be," said Dr. Snowden.

"I set the Torvatta into scan profile two for now," said Evaran. "It will revert back to scan profile one after being scanned."

"Ahh, so—" Dr. Snowden jumped back and covered his eyes as a bright light burst into the bay and then faded. "Was that the decontamination flash?"

"I believe so," said Jane.

"That was quick," said Dr. Snowden.

Evaran waved forward, and after a moment, they had exited the hangar bay and were in a rounded tunnel.

Dr. Snowden immediately noticed that the flooring was split into several sections. The farthest section from him had a slow-moving floor. It reminded him of a treadmill. The section before that had guardrails dividing portions of it, with a raised area that also had a moving component. Then there was the section they were on, which was a normal metallic paneled floor. Looking around, he had expected to see some hustle and bustle, but it was quiet. Too quiet. The hairs on the back of his neck stood up. The smell of burnt steak seemed to resonate in the air like it did on Corunus. "I'm getting a weird vibe from this place."

"Analysis. No abnormal vibrations detected."

Dr. Snowden shook his head. "I meant . . . something seems off."

"It *is* quarantined. There wouldn't be a lot of activity," said Jane.

"You're probably right. Let's go."

They walked around the ring until they reached the connection to the main cylinder.

As they walked down the connection, Dr. Snowden peeked out through the glass-like windows. It amazed him to be walking on a space station that was part of a Dyson bubble being built. Although he had seen a lot traveling with Evaran, it was the small things he noticed that he appreciated all the more. He noticed that Jane's breathing had intensified a bit since they had arrived. That did not surprise him. What did, though, was that he could detect it.

He furrowed his eyebrows as he put his hands behind his back. His nanobots had jumped up in activity without him even noticing it. Something about this space station was triggering them. He wondered if Emily felt it too. Surely if he could, then Evaran must have as well, maybe not. Looking at them both indicated no unusual breathing—well, at least for Emily.

Emily tapped Dr. Snowden's arm. "Are you with us?"

"Sorry, I was—"

"Thinking, I know. C'mon."

Jane scrutinized Dr. Snowden as the elevator they were in descended. It had taken them thirty minutes to find the large column that had a series of elevator doors at its base. Evaran and Emily had gone off into one of them, and she, Dr. Snowden, and V took the other. Dr. Snowden had been unusually quiet. She laid a hand on his arm. "Are you thinking again?"

Dr. Snowden cleared his throat. "Yeah . . . I can't put my finger on this feeling I have."

"My nerves are a bit on edge as well," said Jane.

"Well, I hope you can find some answers here."

Jane smiled. "Me too." She squeezed Dr. Snowden's arm. "Thank you for coming."

"Of course," said Dr. Snowden.

Jane looked up to her left. She could see the light fluctuations from V's stealth. Having both Dr. Snowden and V around made her more relaxed. Dr. Snowden had a glow about him that calmed her. Having V along would also allow for deep analysis and tactical options should they be needed.

She could see why Evaran, Dr. Snowden, Emily, and V would be a potent group. Knowledge, experience, toughness, and the ability to travel through space and time with the Torvatta. And here she was. Getting to experience it. Being part of a team was both exhilarating and satisfying to her, especially since she was used to working alone.

Dr. Snowden tapped her arm. "My turn."

Jane chuckled. "I'm fine. I'm a little anxious is all, and there really is no reason to be. It's not like we're going to run into Chris or anything."

Dr. Snowden chewed on his inner lip for a moment, then faced forward.

They arrived at level thirteen from level twenty-seven and exited the elevator.

The hallway felt cramped to Jane. She understood that the engineering level only needed enough room to get around and was not meant for a high amount of traffic. Advanced Dynamics would make the space as minimal as possible to save on costs as well. When they reached the end of the hallway, they entered a small room that had various hallways leading off it. In the back of the room was an android seated behind a desk and flanked by two humanoid robot guards.

Jane stepped forward and extended her left arm.

The android rose and bent forward. It swept a beam from a scanning gun over Jane's forearm, then looked up. "Jane Trellis, United Planets agent." It then scanned Dr. Snowden. "Dr. Albert Snowden, human."

Dr. Snowden grinned. "Last I checked I was."

The android tilted its head at him, then sat back behind the desk. "How can I help you?"

"We're looking for engineering module 13-F," said Jane.

The android looked down at the desk after placing a hand on it. A projection shot up from the edge of the desk closest to Jane. It showed a layout of the floor, with engineering module 13-F highlighted.

Jane perused the projection and then tapped at her ARI. "I got it. Thank you."

"Will you need a guide?"

"We'll be fine," said Jane.

The android faced forward.

Jane gestured at one of the hallways. "C'mon."

As they walked down the hallway, Dr. Snowden looked at Jane. "Androids. I saw one when we flew in."

Jane nodded. "Corporations like Advanced Dynamics make heavy use of them. They're employed by the United Planets as well. They don't require a lot of maintenance, and they can fulfill a lot of roles."

"Well, I guess you wouldn't need to feed them or worry about restrooms," said Dr. Snowden, smirking. "V said they had inferior AIs."

"It's possible. Androids are considered living beings by the United Planets and afforded the same rights as everyone else. Androids are essentially robots with an AI hardwired into it. The more common type of AIs are the ones that are specialized and usually only exist in a system, like security or maintenance systems."

"What happens to AIs that decide not to follow the rules?" asked Dr. Snowden.

"They're hunted down and exterminated. They can't have a rogue AI on the loose, android or otherwise. They can do a lot of damage in a short period of time. The United Planets already had that fight several hundred years ago. AI counter-measures are standard in United Planets design. Besides, human–AI hybrids can be far more dangerous."

"This is so fascinating to me. What did these rogue AIs do?"

"Some wanted power, some wanted to simply exist with a vast amount of resources available to them, even if those resources weren't theirs," said Jane. "The big one was the Kappler AI. Around 2481, it tried to convert everything on Earth into its own personal resource bin. It took control of a lot of military assets. Unfortunately for Kappler, not all AIs agreed with it, and with human, alien, and nonhuman support, it was defeated. It was actually the first time Fredoria presented themselves to Earth officially."

Dr. Snowden jerked his head back. "The Third World War."

"Yep. I know we discussed some history last night, but it hit me that you should probably know more about this than me."

"I don't know all the events in human history," said Dr. Snowden with a hand out. "Evaran keeps it pretty locked down. If we do learn of them during an outing, like this, so be it. Otherwise, it has to be discovered. Evaran's rules."

"It seems kinda one-sided, don't you think?" asked Jane.

"Maybe . . . but I'm sure he has a good reason. He almost always does. On top of that, what we read as history may not even be accurate given what a rift can do and who writes that history."

From the short time she knew Evaran, Jane could see how he would need a set of rules for those who did not possess his level of awareness. If Dr. Snowden knew every event in history, it would increase the chance that the timeline could be polluted with knowledge that was not supposed to be there, assuming the history was valid per Dr. Snowden's point. Evaran was simply minimizing risk. She chuckled.

Dr. Snowden swiveled his head.

"I was thinking about why Evaran would have that rule, then realized the potential impacts on the timeline. That is not something I would ever think about."

Dr. Snowden raised a finger. "When you travel through space and time like we do, it will be commonplace."

"It must be exciting for you," said Jane.

"If you weren't tied down here, you could always join us, assuming Evaran was okay with that."

Jane glanced at Dr. Snowden as they passed the doorway to engineering module 13-D. "I've thought about it."

Dr. Snowden moved to the side as a human woman in a white suit with some type of device resembling glasses with binoculars on her head passed between him and Jane. After the woman had gone down the hallway, he faced Jane. "There's something odd about her."

"What do you mean? She seemed normal to me."

Dr. Snowden pointed at his eyes. "I can detect nonhumans. Even if I don't know what specific type they are, I can usually figure out the classification. I've never seen that type of movement before."

Jane looked down the hallway. "I don't understand. She seemed to move normally to me."

"Are nonhumans like Daedrould and Outsiders integrated into the United Planets?"

"Oh yeah. They actually helped end World War Three, but keep to themselves. I don't know of any in this region, although I guess there could be some here."

Dr. Snowden rubbed the back of his neck. "Huh. I don't know then . . . maybe it's this place. My nanobots are all excited, and I don't know why."

As they continued walking, Jane said, "I hope it's not me."

Dr. Snowden's face turned a slight shade of red. "What? No . . . of course not."

If Dr. Snowden was concerned, and his nanobots were right, maybe there was something Jane was not seeing. Could it be that maybe her emotional state was clouding her senses? Maybe Dr. Snowden's and Emily's nanobots were more sensitive to things even they were not aware of. Her attention was disrupted by Dr. Snowden lightly touching her forearm. Looking up, she saw that they were at the entrance to a small room that had more tunnels branching out.

"Which way do we go?" asked Dr. Snowden.

Jane consulted her map, then pointed off to the right.

They continued on until they reached the entrance to engineering module 13-F.

"Here we are," said Jane, licking her lips.

Dr. Snowden gave Jane a reassuring smile. "C'mon."

They entered the module.

Jane noticed the large cylindrically shielded work areas. Around them were flat tables with holographic projections and slanted consoles next to them. Along the walls were readouts spitting out numbers and status updates for various systems. She glanced at Dr. Snowden, who was observing a young woman a bit away. She swatted Dr. Snowden's arm. "Focus."

Dr. Snowden shook both hands in front of him. "It's nothing like that. She's human."

"I would think so. Everyone down here should be human, Kalesh, android, or robot. There may even be some other aliens here."

Dr. Snowden narrowed his eyes as the woman approached.

The woman smiled. "I'm Naomi Eltat, Advanced Dynamics junior structural engineer."

Jane extended her hand. "I'm Jane Trellis, United Planets Bureau of Law Enforcement agent, Da Nesh office."

Naomi shook Jane's hand.

Dr. Snowden extended a hand. "I'm Dr. Albert Snowden. Traveler."

Naomi shook Dr. Snowden's hand while chuckling. "Traveler?"

"I guess that doesn't sound all official-like."

Jane cleared her throat. "We were looking around."

"I can show you around if you want," said Naomi. "It's close to my lunch hour anyways. I'd be glad to have company."

"Lead on."

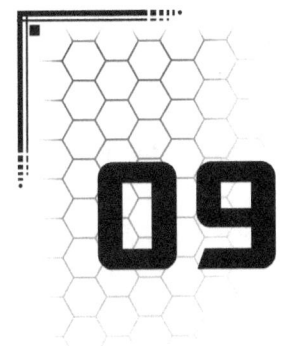

09

Dr. Snowden's attention was focused on all the data he was seeing. As Naomi led them to a workstation, he saw one of the screens showing the bottom part of the station, with various progress bars, labels, and status readings. He looked at Naomi. "I have some questions if you don't mind."

"Sure, I'm always happy to answer questions, assuming they're engineering ones," said Naomi with a smile.

"Oh, they are. So . . . does the station get its power exclusively from the sun?"

"It does for the most part," said Naomi. "There are solar collectors that focus on capturing the sun's energy. We have quite a few of them. They send power here, but the station itself also has collectors. There are some fusion reactors that serve as backups for critical systems."

Dr. Snowden paused as he chewed on Naomi's words. He wondered if this is how Evaran felt discussing new technologies or ideas with other cultures. "Is this station geosynchronous?"

"You got it. It's a statite. It stays in one spot, kept afloat by the circular flat sail you might have seen on your way in."

Dr. Snowden wagged a finger. "The sails use the solar wind and gravity to stay in position, right?"

"Uh-huh. It's a bit more complex than that, but that's the general idea. The statite can adjust its position if need be."

"Fascinating. This would allow the Dyson bubble to be built incrementally as resources become available."

Naomi smiled. "Most resources come from the Gazier cloud outside the solar system, and there's plenty there. At the rate we're building the habitats and collectors, the Dyson bubble should be fully constructed in about sixty years or so. What's truly amazing is this is the first one that's being built so that all the parts can come together using a backbone ship if it needs to move to a new system. However, the end result is a living space that is independent of a planet with the power of a star, so solar systems not friendly to life can still be populated." She cocked her head. "It's refreshing to see your curiosity. Are you an engineer?"

"No way . . . but I do read up on things like this when I visit places."

"You must travel to some interesting places then."

Dr. Snowden chuckled. "That would be an understatement." He pointed at the screen. "That sail must be made of a powerful material."

"Yep. It's made up of molecularly engineered carbon nanotubes. They were able to get the density down quite a bit. Have to give credit to our materials engineers on that one."

Dr. Snowden shook his head. "This is great. This whole station reminds me of an O'Neill cylinder with a big sail on the bottom. I suppose the spin helps with gravity."

"Now that's an old term I haven't heard used since my first engineering classes. The premise is the same, but obviously with much more advanced technology." Naomi bobbed her head. "It's not every day I run into someone who is excited about Dyson bubbles and its constituent parts."

"It's nice sometimes to see something I thought was theoretical."

Naomi narrowed her eyes. "This isn't the first one Advanced Dynamics has built," said Naomi. She looked at Jane. "The United Planets has quite a few."

"Yeah. The first ones were built in Earth's solar system," said Jane. "They're not quite as advanced as this one, though."

Dr. Snowden's eyes widened. "Oh . . . right. So . . . uhh . . . what else can you show us?"

Naomi smiled as she continued on to the next workstation and screen.

* * *

When they reached one of the more remote areas after an hour, Jane grabbed Dr. Snowden's arm and pointed forward. "Chris!" Her heartbeat ran rampant as the familiar smile, brown hair, and light-tan skin lit up in her mind. How was he still alive? She swallowed hard and looked at Dr. Snowden, then shot off toward Chris.

Dr. Snowden extended a hand. "Jane! Wait!"

Jane rushed over to Chris and grabbed him from the side in a hug. She trembled as tears ran down her face.

Chris wheeled around in confusion. He untangled himself from Jane and then took a step back. "What're you doing? Who are you?"

"It's me," said Jane. She scanned Chris's eyes. Something was wrong. His eyes seemed dull, a far cry from the fire that she was accustomed to seeing.

"And you are . . . ," said Chris with a contorted face.

Jane's eyes misted as her head bobbed. "Your wife. Jane."

Chris shook his head. "Umm . . . I think you're confused. I've never been married."

"What!"

Chris took another step back and tapped at another human male. "Joel, you know who this is?"

Joel stood next to Chris. He surveyed Jane. "No idea."

Jane's mouth went agape as she looked at Joel. Her voice cracked. "You're Joel Gervin. Right?"

Joel shot a look at Chris. "Yeah . . . that's me. How'd you know that?"

"Chris talked about you when he came here. How can you not know me?" asked Jane. Her voice rose. "What's going on?"

An android walked over to the group. "May I be of assistance?"

Jane snapped her head at the android. "Not now!"

Dr. Snowden stepped forward and put an arm around Jane. "We should probably go and let these people get back to work."

Jane shrugged off Dr. Snowden's arm. "What's going on here?"

Chris looked at Joel, then at Jane. "I'm not sure what *you* think is going on, but you should probably go."

Jane grimaced as she wiped her wet cheeks. "You . . . want me to go?"

"I think that might be best."

Jane's lips quivered as she ducked her head forward. "You really want me to go?" Tears flowed like rivers from her eyes.

"I'm sorry I'm not who you think I am. Good luck in finding . . . *whoever* it is you're looking for."

The android stepped forward.

Naomi shot a glance at Dr. Snowden and extended a hand out toward the android. "I'll escort them out."

The android moved back.

Dr. Snowden put his arm around Jane again and, with some force, guided her behind Naomi.

Jane's eyes dulled as her mind exploded in thoughts. Chris was alive but did not know who she was. How was this possible? And Joel. Chris had talked about him quite a bit in the communications he had sent her. Even mentioned that Joel was jokingly getting tired of hearing about her. She shook as she walked. Dr. Snowden was right. Something was off. It made sense now why they did not want to give details on Chris's death. He never died, or so she thought anyways. She gritted her teeth as she squinted her eyes. Her breath went haphazard.

Naomi led them to the room exit, then waved forward. "It's not safe to speak here. Follow me."

Jane swallowed hard and wiped the tears off her face.

"Let's go," said Dr. Snowden.

They continued back the way they had come, but took a slightly different path, and they ended up in a small room with supplies.

Naomi tapped at her palm, then accessed her ARI. The room sealed as it went dark gray with a light at the top. "We can speak freely, and we have a lot to discuss."

Jane cried into Dr. Snowden's chest. She had her answer, and it was not what she was seeking. All this time that she had been concerned, only to find out Chris was still here, and he had no idea who she was. She clenched her jaw. Whatever was going on, she would get to the bottom of it.

Dr. Snowden's eyes adjusted to the dimmed room. He knew this meant that the room was bug-free. Seeing Chris alive was not something he had expected. Jane's reaction was expected, though. She saw her husband, who had no idea who she was. Then there was Naomi. While Chris and Joel had that same nonhuman feel to them, Naomi registered as a normal human to him. He scanned the room, then faced Naomi. "So . . . what the heck is going on?"

Naomi grimaced. "It's kind of odd to explain, but I'll try." She faced Jane. "I recognize your name. Chris used to mention it."

Jane stepped back from crying on Dr. Snowden's chest and wiped her face. "Why didn't he recognize me?"

Naomi sighed. "I better start from the beginning. I came out here to be with Joel, my husband, and got transferred down to engineering. We had a great group going with Chris. Then . . . the accidents began happening."

Dr. Snowden leaned against the wall with his arms crossed. "So you knew Chris from before?"

"Oh yeah. He was quick witted, smart, and," said Naomi, gesturing at Jane, "talked about you all the time. I felt like I knew you." Her smile wound down. "One day, Chris was in an accident and had to go to the medical ward. Advanced Dynamics wouldn't let us see him, or even tell us what happened. What came back to engineering was not Chris. He didn't recognize us. We tried to get him to remember, but Advanced Dynamics said he was suffering from amnesia."

"Amnesia!" said Jane.

"We might have been able to accept that, but there was a behavioral change as well. Chris kept to himself initially, then only talked with others who also had accidents. I wanted to leave, but Joel couldn't leave Chris like that."

Dr. Snowden rubbed his chin. "I would think with the advanced augments and technology that amnesia could be lessened."

"It's treatable," said Naomi. "But not with Chris, it seemed. The accidents kept occurring. Then . . ."

"Joel had an accident," said Dr. Snowden.

Naomi puckered her lips as her eyes watered. In a weak voice, she said, "Yep."

Jane hugged Naomi.

Dr. Snowden looked around the room. "V?"

V shimmered into view.

Naomi jumped back. "What's that?"

"I am a variable utility artificial intelligence. My shortened name is V."

Naomi gulped.

"He's a friend," said Dr. Snowden. He looked at V. "Did you get a scan on Chris and Joel?"

"I did."

"Show us."

"Acknowledged," said V. He projected a skeletal and muscular view of Chris and Joel.

Dr. Snowden's eyes widened when he saw something in the spine and brain region.

Jane raised her eyebrows as she examined the projection. "What. Is. That."

"Analysis. Organism is not native to the human organic system."

"How integrated is it?" asked Dr. Snowden.

The projection split out the organism from the bodies of Chris and Joel.

"Okay . . . that's kinda creepy. It looks like it's wrapped around the spine and completely replaced where the brain should be," said Dr. Snowden. "V, postulate. Could a human survive this integration?"

"Analysis. It is unlikely. Chris and Joel are no longer human."

Naomi walked around the holographic creature. "So Joel is . . . dead?"

"It looks like he is, and whatever this organism is has decided to use his body," said Dr. Snowden. He looked at Jane. "Looks like Chris did die. I'm . . . sorry."

Jane balled her fist. "What type of creature is that?"

"Analysis. There is no known organic configuration."

Dr. Snowden sighed. "V has access to every creature Evaran has ever run into. It looks like we're dealing with something new."

"Evaran?" asked Naomi.

"Oh . . . right. He's a friend, and we travel in his ship. He's in another part of the station at the moment."

"Ahh."

"How many others in your department have avoided these accidents?"

Naomi shook her head. "I'm the last one out of a department of forty."

"Have you tried to leave?"

"Oh yeah. Advanced Dynamics won't let me, though, due to this . . . quarantine. Maybe this creature is why we're in quarantine."

"It could be," said Dr. Snowden.

"Are you leaving the station?" asked Naomi.

"I think it would be best to get back to our ship. Maybe Evaran found out more on this station and what's going on. Evaran asked us to keep communication silence, so we should go."

"Can I . . . come with you?" asked Naomi. "No one would question me escorting you to your ship."

Dr. Snowden looked at Jane.

"Of course," said Jane.

"Is there anything you need to get first?" asked Dr. Snowden.

Naomi shook her head. "Even if there was, being able to leave is far more important."

"Okay then. Take a moment to compose yourselves, then you can take the lead to the elevators."

After Naomi and Jane settled down, they exited the room and headed to the elevators. When they approached the area with the android and robot guards that they had met earlier, the android focused on Naomi.

Naomi motioned toward the elevator. "I'm escorting them out."

The android stood. "The guards will handle that."

"We'll be fine," said Naomi.

"Your presence has been requested in engineering."

Naomi gulped as she looked at Jane.

Jane glanced at Dr. Snowden, who nodded. She whipped out her sidearm and fired at the first guard, cutting it in half.

Dr. Snowden aimed his PSD at the second guard. He fired a stun beam that caused the second guard to collapse, then shot the android, who crumpled next to the second guard.

"You two handled that pretty quick," said Naomi with raised eyebrows. She gestured at the downed android and robots. "Their incapacitation will be noticed. Now we'll have to deal with security."

"So be it," said Jane, smirking. "The alternative is you head back and have an accident."

Naomi gulped.

They entered the elevator.

"What level are you docked at?" asked Naomi.

"We're docked on level twenty-seven," said Dr. Snowden.

Naomi punched the level into the console next to the door.

The elevator began to move, then halted. A beam shot down from the ceiling, causing Dr. Snowden to jump back. A hologram of a pudgy tan-skinned man with wild hair appeared. He wore light armor, and his face was pockmarked with scars. A cigar hung from his lips as he looked around the elevator.

"Oh no . . . ," said Naomi.

"It's Billozein," said Jane, grimacing.

"Jane Trellis," said Billozein. "I'll admit . . . I'm surprised to see you here. You couldn't take a hint, could you?"

"What'd you do to Chris?" asked Jane.

Billozein smiled, revealing a set of perfect white teeth. "Chris . . . yes . . . your husband. He was difficult to integrate, but he did."

"What're you talking about? Are you responsible for those creatures?"

Billozein's face turned red as he tossed his cigar out of the projection. "Creatures? They are part of something far more evolved than your pathetic species! You should be honored he is now doing something worthwhile with his life."

"Whatever you did to him, you'll pay for this," said Jane, balling her fists.

Billozein chuckled, then burst out laughing. "I don't think so. Chris's knowledge and body have been quite useful. I would use all of yours, but . . . you're traveling with some unusual friends. I believe extermination is in order."

"You've been doing this all across the station," said Naomi. "Why do you need so many bodies?"

Billozein smirked. "It's beyond your comprehension."

Naomi's eyes widened. "You're doing this to the other stations too, aren't you? That's why they're in quarantine."

Billozein smiled. "That's very good. For a human."

Dr. Snowden wrinkled his eyebrows. "So you want us out of the picture because we might mess up your plans."

Billozein looked at Dr. Snowden. "Ahh . . . the time traveler speaks. I suspect you have felt me to some degree. To answer your claim, yes. I normally wouldn't bother with this, but you're a traveler in the wrong space and time. I've claimed this area. It's mine, and now I'm going to show you what happens to those who aren't welcome."

The elevator began to move down.

Billozein looked at Jane. "You couldn't leave it alone, and now you brought trouble to me. You've doomed your friends. I also know that you all came here to look for illegal augments. Well . . . you'll get to see what happens to those who don't . . . adjust to them. Enjoy your last moments of life."

The projection dissipated as the elevator stopped, showing level seven. The doors opened.

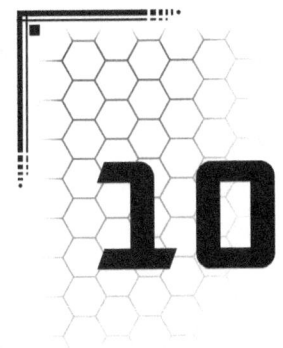

10

Emily wrinkled her eyebrows as she looked around. Evaran seemed calm as always, but the unusual rhythm of her nanobots pulsing was making her uneasy.

"You seem troubled," said Evaran.

Emily sighed. "It's nothing big, but there is a new sensation I haven't felt before. It's like something's wrong."

"I wondered when you and your uncle would be temporally aware. I suspect that is what it is."

"You mean we can detect time travelers?"

"Among other aspects," said Evaran. "It is a sense you obtain after being on the Torvatta for a while. If you are having them now, then your uncle would be as well. I suspect it has been triggered by whatever is causing the timeline anomaly."

"Why does it feel like something's wrong?"

"It is a new sensation and, as such, would be crudely attuned. In time, it will become honed."

Emily chuckled. "I guess."

"It is good to see you smile," said Evaran.

Emily half smiled and looked down. Although she had spent the majority of her time with V on her return, it was Evaran and his training videos on the PSD that had kept her company on the prison planet. He was her safety blanket, and often times without realizing it, she looked to him as both a mentor and a father figure. She knew he always had her best interests at heart like Dr. Snowden.

"You and your uncle are evolving faster than I expected," said Evaran.

Emily drew her lips to the side. "Human two point oh."

"I would put it at two point five."

Emily narrowed her eyes. "Hopefully that's good?"

"That remains to be seen, but so far, you have surpassed my expectations."

Emily chewed on Evaran's words as the elevator came to a stop. The console panel showed level seventy-two. She followed Evaran out of the elevator and into a hallway. It was like the rest of the station: clean, metallic, light colored, and well lit. A warm blast of an odor that smelled like burnt toast hit her in the face, causing her nose to wrinkle.

Evaran extended his hand, and a projection shot up from his ring showing the layout of the level. A red and green dot blinked. He pointed at the green dot. "We are here." He then pointed at the red dot. "We need to go there. I am not sure what to expect."

"I'm sure it's nothing we can't handle," said Emily.

They continued on to the end of the hallway and then entered a small white room.

An android sat behind a desk flanked by two human-oid robot guards. The android stood and scanned them with a device. It cocked its head. "Evaran, unknown. Emily Snowden, human." It sat back down. "How can I help you?"

Evaran pointed down one of the hallways. "We were headed to the data storage center."

"Will you need a guide?" asked the android.

"We know the path," said Evaran. "Thank you."

The android faced forward.

Evaran and Emily continued down a hallway that led off to the left.

"I didn't expect to see so many androids and robots in this time period," said Emily.

"It is commonplace. Humans only work where they want to. More mundane work is usually something left to androids or robots."

"Where do most humans work then?" asked Emily.

"From what I have read, most work for the United Planets in many different roles. There are those who go their own route, but at a minimum, they have access to United Planets basics such as food and shelter. If they want access to items that require a lot of resources, they either have to get it themselves or do something that pays them in it."

Emily thought about the humans she saw on Corunus. Most either ran shops, were bustling from one place to another, were guards, or were enjoying the station. It seemed peaceful to her. After being around V for so long, she could see how that would develop. The shift in the usage of robots and androids must have had a large cultural impact. "I'd love to read the history up to this point at some time."

"It is a risk to know the past in detail. Besides the possibility of knowledge pollution, what you read may not be accurate due to many factors. However, for you, I will make a point to try to get historical information while we are here. If not, then on Roeth."

"That sounds good to me."

When they reached the data center entrance, a male human walked up to them. His crisp white two-piece suit with the top part extending halfway down his thighs presented a clean look. Silver lines segmented the suit, and a rigid dark-blue collar sat on the neck. A device ran from one ear to the other on the back of his head. He extended a hand. "I'm Toby Gennin, senior data manager. I've been expecting you."

"Elaborate."

"Oh . . . well . . . Department is abuzz about your arrival. It's not often we have someone of your clearance level come up here."

"I see," said Evaran. "Then you know whom I am with."

"Emily Snowden," said Toby. He extended a hand toward Emily.

Emily shook his hand. She noticed a trickle of sweat on the side of Toby's head and that his hand was moist as well. He smelled like a mix of wet grass and some type of cleaner she could not identify.

Toby gestured behind him. "I take it you want to see how the data is stored."

"That would be a good start. I would like access to a console at some point."

"Of course," said Toby. "Follow me."

Emily peered around the massive multilevel room Toby took them to. They were on the top level, and walkways and ramps ringed the edges of the large, open central area. On the left side was an area containing rows of transparent containers, with crystal cylinders and machinery between them. The middle of the room had a large semitransparent rectangular container that stretched from the floor to the ceiling. Inside it were smaller cylinders segmented by metallic plates that jutted out from within. To the right were large cubes suspended in some type of freestanding gel that seemed to ripple. The smell here was much better. It reminded her of oranges. It was not as loud as she had expected.

Toby pointed to the left side. "Those are the long-term storage devices, crystal based."

"Write once, read many," said Evaran.

"That's right. No one really knows how long they last, but most predictions put it in the millions-of-years range. Some say billions."

Emily glanced at the crystals. She knew Dr. Snowden would have a field day in here. The animated hand gestures Toby was doing seemed out of place with the pace of his talking. She realized her nanobots were acting up. Maybe due to now being temporally aware was her thought, but her gut told her it was someone watching them.

Toby pointed to the center container that rose from the floor to the ceiling. "This is our synthetic DNA storage. It can last around a million years. I suppose . . . you're aware of how that works?"

"I am," said Evaran.

Toby pointed to cubes on the right side. "Those are the day-to-day storage cubes. They are the more traditional holographic storage. Obviously, much faster for writing and reading, but can't store quite as much."

"I am guessing these are all tied into one system, with backup schedules and redundancy built into the design."

"Of course," said Toby. "This center is state-of-the-art, at least in the United Planets. I know the Kreagans and some others have comparable setups, but outside of those, I haven't seen anything that comes close to this."

"For humanity in this time period, neither have I," said Evaran.

"About that . . . I do have a question . . . if you don't mind," said Toby.

Evaran nodded.

"I see all the data that comes through, so I know who you are. I can't fathom where data storage goes from here. So . . . what's the next step?"

Emily understood Toby's desire for knowledge. When presented with someone like Evaran, it would be hard not to ask.

Evaran raised a finger. "Humanity is not quite at the level required to use dimensional storage with time dilation."

Toby's eyes widened. "I've never even heard of that. Have you actually seen a system like that in operation?"

Evaran extended his hand. His ring emitted a projection showing a circular opening with a gold border. Inside the opening was a cloudy substance with bits of light darting around. "Dimensional storage."

Toby hunched over as he scrutinized the projection. "What am I looking at?"

Evaran raised a finger on his other hand. "A glimpse into another dimension where time runs faster."

Toby's eyes widened. "Wow. So it could make a request and get back a response immediately, regardless of how long the response actually took. Offloading data access with unlimited storage and near instant retrieval. That would be revolutionary!"

"You are beginning to understand. Now, where is a console I can access?" asked Evaran.

"Right," said Toby, clearing his throat. He pointed toward a side room.

Emily analyzed the room once they entered it. It had a half-circle table in the middle with an array of screens on it. Holographic projections showing statuses, data flows, and other metrics she was unfamiliar with danced around on the walls.

Toby pointed at the table. "There you go."

Evaran sat at the table and placed his UIC on it. After a moment, it stabilized. The room went dark gray and a dim light appeared up top. "I am accessing what I need now. We can speak freely."

Toby fidgeted with his hands and looked around.

"You are nervous, yet there is no need to be."

Toby sighed. "Billozein is watching everything you do. He'll know we're in here and that the room has been silenced."

"I see," said Evaran. "Why does this worry you?"

Toby chuckled. "You don't mess around with Billozein. He's kinda crazy. Since I took this job several years ago, over seventy-five percent of my department have had accidents. All seem to involve amnesia. If you ask me, I think he's involved, since every time I ask him about it, I get the runaround. I could be next."

Emily narrowed her eyes. "If it concerns you, why don't you leave?"

"We're under quarantine. On top of that, Billozein authorizes all transfers. He's already denied mine. I'm not affiliated with the United Planets, like a lot of us here, so I can't really go to them. There isn't anyone to help me. I'm trapped here along with the others who are accident-free."

Evaran eased back into his chair. "I am looking into the illegal augment trade. Perhaps I will look into these accidents as well since I am here."

"I know those who are trapped here like me that would like that," said Toby. "Your arrival seems to have made Billozein nervous."

"How so?"

"He's issued a notification to report on where you are and what you're doing. I'll have to file one, but obviously I'm not going to be too accurate on what we're discussing now. Not to mention, there seems to be more robot guards out than normal."

"Interesting," said Evaran with his fingertips touching in front of him. He grabbed the UIC off the table. "I have what I need. I will need some time to go through it all."

"I hope you find what you're looking for."

"Likewise," said Evaran as he stood.

When they exited the room, a humanoid robot guard with black metal and red-bordered segments approached them. It scanned Evaran, Toby, and Emily, then said, "Billozein would like to speak with you. Please follow me."

"Very well," said Evaran. He faced Toby and shook his hand.

Emily shook Toby's hand, then followed Evaran as the robot guard began to walk away.

"Good luck," said Toby in the distance.

Emily peered back at Toby. He looked like a kid who had been caught. The fear in his voice was unmistakable. She suspected this discussion with Billozein was not going to be pleasant.

Emily soaked in the surroundings as they were escorted. They had gone from level seventy-two to level fifty-four. It had taken them thirty minutes, and it seemed odd that with all the communication technologies available, they were being escorted to a meeting.

The robot guard led them to a featureless room with a series of chairs in a circle and small table between them.

Her nose wrinkled when they entered the room. Even the smell seemed off to her. Was every sense tainted by the temporal awareness factor? She took a seat next to Evaran.

"Please wait. Billozein will be here shortly," said the robot.

"Thank you."

The robot exited the room.

Evaran glanced at Emily. "I smell it too."

Emily looked around. At least now she had confirmation that it was not isolated to her.

After a few minutes, a humanoid walked into the room.

The humanoid reminded Emily of liquid metal. She squinted at the reflectiveness of the material. Her eyes widened when square chunks of the humanoid flew a few inches out. The humanoid shrank a few feet to stand about four feet high. A holographic projection covered the form, showing a tan-skinned middle-aged man with wild hair. His stout form was covered by a segmented black light armor with red highlights. When the humanoid smiled, it was the shiny teeth that caught her attention.

The humanoid bowed slightly. "I'm Billozein, CEO of Advanced Dynamics, but I suspect you know that already."

"We do," said Evaran.

Billozein smirked. "Well then, I bet you're wondering why we're meeting."

Evaran glanced at Emily, then at Billozein. "Yes, and also why you are using a physical holo form instead of being physically present."

"Ahh . . . well . . . I'll get to that shortly. First things first. I know who you both are," said Billozein, wagging a finger. "The Evaran Protocol. A good starting point to find information, but finding out more was hard to come by. Outside of what the United Planets knows, it seems you . . . don't exist. However . . . there was one corporation that had extensive information on you."

"I presume it was Seeros Industries, assuming that is what they call themselves," said Evaran. "And what did you find?"

"Yes on Seeros Industries. They call themselves Illitech now. I found what I already suspected. You're a time traveler, and you've been involved in a lot of events," said Billozein. He raised a finger. "That's a problem for me."

"Elaborate," said Evaran.

Billozein smiled as he shook his head. "I don't know what brought you here, but you know as well as I do, or should, that you can't have two time travelers in the same area. It would mess each other's changes up."

"So you are a time traveler then," said Evaran.

Billozein bobbed his head. "To a degree. Not like you, though. Why did you come here? To this station? Specifically?"

"We are here due to the illegal augment trade. There were reports that this station was creating and distributing them."

Billozein chortled. "Oh . . . well, I can answer that for you. Yes, illegal augments are created here. I do distribute them. Even experiment with them. Those that fail are discarded to a testing environment. One your friends are entering as we speak."

Emily perked up.

"I thought that might get your attention," said Billozein. "So you're only here to find illegal augments. And that's it? Out of all the places in space and time . . . you chose here, now, to come. You see why I'm having a hard time believing that?"

"There is also a timeline anomaly here. I now suspect you are the cause of it."

A smile crept onto Billozein's face. "Was that so hard? And I'm going to guess, based on what I saw in the Evaran Protocol, you're here to *fix* it. Am I right?"

"Of course."

"Just as I figured. I read what you did to the CEO of Seeros Industries, and I've dealt with those who believe that they have the *right* to correct the timeline." He pointed at Evaran. "Time Wardens, the Krokar, you, all the same. It's pathetic. Who gave you this authority?"

"Something much bigger than you. I am familiar with the Time Wardens but do not know who the Krokar are. I am the only one sanctioned to use my judgment to resolve these issues."

Billozein shook his head. "I would say good luck with that, but it won't matter. You've met your superior." He jabbed a finger down. "This space is mine to do what I want and how I want. You're not *welcome* here and I *won't* tolerate anyone messing up what I'm doing. I will deal with you like I did the last Time Warden that came across me." His form began to emit a green gas.

Emily sniffed and looked around. "He's gassing the room!" She looked at Evaran as she raised her helmet.

"You intend to kill us?" asked Evaran.

"Of course," said Billozein. "I can't have you running around, and I'm looking forward to checking out your ship, not to mention those nanobots I detected."

"We cannot allow that. Know this. You are my priority now." He stood and extended his utility handle into a baton with a glowing blue end. He reached over the table and tapped Billozein, causing the projection to shimmer.

"What are you doing?"

"Ending this conversation," said Evaran.

Blue arcs danced around Billozein as his projection faded. The humanoid form underneath stopped moving. A burst of gas flew out from the form.

"What do we do now?" asked Emily.

"Give me a moment," said Evaran. He walked up to the door and placed his UIC on the console.

Emily's heartbeat ramped up. Her suit and helmet protected her. She was glad to have them. It impressed on her that if she had never gone to the prison planet before, she might have come without a suit. She could have died, right here and now. There was one thing she was sure of: Billozein was going down. She hoped that Dr. Snowden and Jane were okay, but she trusted that they could deal with whatever was tossed their way, at least until they could all meet up. Watching Evaran peruse his ARI while deadly gas swirled around him was no surprise to her. She knew that Evaran's form was a suit of some type, although she and Dr. Snowden did not know what was inside.

Evaran pulled his UIC off the console. The door opened, causing the gas to go swirling out of the room. "Come."

They exited the room into a hallway. Humanoid robot guards charged them from both sides, with two on each side. Drones flew forward.

Emily hunched down and tossed her left arm out while activating her shield.

Evaran did the same on the opposite side.

Emily fired her repulsion blast, sweeping the robots off their feet. She switched to her stun blast and hit both of them. Using her shield, she smashed one of the drones that came too close. With a rapid succession of stun blasts, she took down the others. She glanced at Evaran and noticed he had handled the guards and drones on his side using only his staff and shield. Her training would need to move up a notch to get to that level. "This isn't a good spot."

"I concur," said Evaran. He gestured forward.

For the next twenty-five minutes, they navigated the hallways while dodging roving bands of robot guards, drones, and the occasional android. When they came upon a side room with a lockable door, they dipped in.

Evaran placed his UIC on the door console. After the UIC stabilized, he locked the door. He interacted with his ARI. "Transferring visual to your helmet."

Emily could see a screen appear inside her helmet. She had Evaran give her suit a HUD that he or V could direct information to. On the screen was a static image of Dr. Snowden and Jane. After a moment, it connected, showing a live feed of Dr. Snowden, Jane, and an unknown woman.

Dr. Snowden raised his head a bit. "Evaran! I was about to contact you."

"We have met Billozein, and he has mentioned that you are in a testing level for those with failed augment integrations."

Dr. Snowden sighed. "It's been a bit crazy over here. We were headed back to the ship. We met Chris but . . . it wasn't him. It was some creature thing using his body. Billozein is apparently making them through accidents, and that's why the quarantine is in place. It's like . . . he's building an army or something."

"I see," said Evaran. "I have downloaded as much information as I could. Perhaps we will find more on that when I go through it. "

"That sounds good to me," said Dr. Snowden. He pointed at the unknown woman. "We also met Naomi, and she's the only human in a department of forty. The others were converted into these things, and now, we're stuck down here.

The elevator shaft has been bricked, as far as I can tell. How do we get out of here?"

"Bricked as in how?" asked Evaran.

Naomi showed her face and did a slight wave. "Hi, Naomi here. When the elevator is shut down, the shaft is plugged up. This shaft only went up to level forty, but it's unusable now."

"I see," said Evaran as he tapped at his ARI. "One moment."

Emily could see maps fly by in a second screen in her HUD. A layout of level seven with a green line to an exit appeared.

"I have transferred the location of the nearest ramp exit. Each level has a series of ramps that connect it. The one you need to go to is about three miles away. Emily and I will meet you there."

"It should be a straight shot then. How's Emily?"

"I'm fine," said Emily. Although she knew she did not need to worry about Dr. Snowden, she did.

"You sure you two are okay?" asked Dr. Snowden.

"We had to fight a bit," said Emily. "Oh, and Billozein tried to kill us with poisonous gas."

Dr. Snowden's eyebrows raised.

"We're *fine*. We'll meet up soon. Stay safe."

Dr. Snowden focused on Emily for a moment, then said, "I always try to. We have a lot to catch up on when we meet. I'll see you then."

The screens faded.

Evaran waved forward as they moved down the hallway. "The ramps are nearby."

After some light opposition, they reached the corner leading into the ramp area.

As they went around, Emily saw several androids and robot guards. Her attention was drawn to the large metallic robot with two legs and a pod on top of it that stood in the middle. It bristled with weapons and had several drones flying above it.

"Target acquired," said the large robot.

The androids and other robots opened fire.

Evaran pulled Emily back around the corner.

"Okay . . . how are we handling this?" asked Emily, catching her breath.

Evaran paused for a moment as he extended his utility handle into a baton with a glowing yellow end, then glanced at Emily. "Use your shield to protect me when I go out. I am going to grapple swing them."

Emily's eyes widened. "Okay . . ."

"Now!" said Evaran.

Emily extended her shield to cover an area the size of two humans standing side by side. She then ran out with her shield reflecting fire while Evaran stayed close behind her.

Evaran leaned out from behind her and aimed at the large middle robot. The yellow beam from his baton stuck to the robot. With a hard yank, the robot stumbled.

The robot shot around randomly as it moved forward, hitting several of the robot guards.

Evaran swung to the left with the capsized robot still at the end of the beam. After clearing that side, he swung right.

As the robot struggled to get up, Emily and Evaran charged it.

When Evaran reached it, he touched it with his baton, with a blue end now, and shocked it.

After a moment, the robot stopped moving. They stunned the remaining androids and robots that had survived the initial clearing and were trying to get back up.

Emily shook her head. "And we're going down to level seven?"

"Yes. Forty-seven levels to go. However, there is a break at level twenty. I do not believe there will be resistance on every level, but if there is, we will have to deal with it. Are you ready for this?"

Emily cracked her neck as she leaned her head from side to side. "Let's do this."

"Very well. We shall do it," said Evaran.

Emily snorted. "You and V." She swatted Evaran's arm and headed down the first ramp.

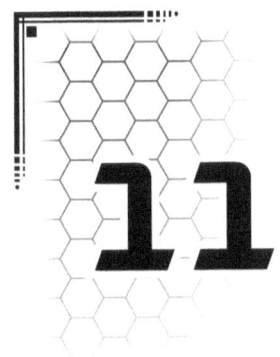

11

Dr. Snowden looked around after talking with Evaran. The elevator had begun flashing lights, and as soon as they exited it, the doors slid shut. A loud clanking sound rang out. He figured that was the elevator shaft being plugged up. Now all they had to do was head to the nearest exit, three miles away. He focused on Jane and Naomi. "This Billozein guy is a control freak."

"Yeah, and with control of the Dyson bubble, he would own this solar system, and possibly more," said Jane.

Dr. Snowden smirked.

"What?" asked Jane.

"I just realized that we arrived before Billozein really got off the ground."

Jane narrowed her eyes. "I guess you did. Fortunate for us."

"If we had come later, the United Planets may not be as big as it is, or even exist," said Dr. Snowden. He motioned at V. "Well, let's focus on getting out of here. V, can you go into mapping mode?"

"Acknowledged. Mapping mode engaged," said V. "For future reference, you can tell me."

"Got it."

V took off with a two-dimensional circle of red beams emanating from him.

Dr. Snowden harrumphed. He kept his helmet down so he could smell, since Naomi had no suit other than her uniform. Not only did he think it would make her more comfortable, but it would also alert him to unusual smells, which might be important down here.

With his PSD out, he scanned around in augmented reality mode. Scanning up showed the level to be around three hundred feet tall. Looking left and right gave a width of about a mile. It was like the downtown portion of a small city had been dropped onto the level. He could see large buildings in the distance, and on his right and left was what appeared to be a neighborhood of metallic-looking housing structures. Running his hand across the ground confirmed that it was made of some type of dirt. The smell of rotting garbage punctuated the somewhat humid air.

"The testing level . . . ," said Naomi. "And now we're stuck here. I've heard stories about this place. I thought it was a myth."

"What do you know of it?" asked Dr. Snowden.

"Not much other than this is where rogue AIs, failed experiments, and sometimes, from what I heard, trouble personnel go."

"Why doesn't Billozein kill them? Seems kinda cruel to put them here," said Jane.

"The rumor is that sometimes something arises out of the chaos that he's interested in, like a mutation that is beneficial," said Naomi. "That's all I know. It isn't spoken of often, for obvious reasons."

Dr. Snowden sighed. "Well . . . Evaran said where we need to go is three miles away." He pointed off in the distance. "Over there along the wall. An exit ramp."

"This is not quite how I expected things to go," said Naomi, gulping.

"Stick with us, and you'll be okay," said Dr. Snowden. "I promise." He squeezed Naomi's arm.

Naomi forced a smile.

"Do you have a weapon?" asked Jane.

Naomi shook her head. "I'm an engineer, not security."

Jane pulled off a small device from her belt. After a few clicks and turns, the device extended into a small weapon. She glanced at Naomi. "Extend your hand."

Naomi complied.

Jane scanned Naomi's hand with the device, then handed it to her. "Here. It's my backup weapon, and now it's encoded to you. It's a simple phaser, but it packs a punch. Make sure that when you shoot it, you aim away from us."

Naomi flipped the weapon around in her hand for a moment. She looked at Jane. "Thanks. Hopefully I won't need to use it." She placed the device in her pocket.

"We should stick close to one of the walls," said Jane, pointing off to the right.

Dr. Snowden shook his head. "Maybe a bit further in. I hear something moving over there."

Jane shot Dr. Snowden a quizzical look. "I don't hear anything, and nothing is showing up on my visual."

Dr. Snowden tapped his ear. "Nanobot-enhanced hearing. Whatever it is, it seems to be small, but there are quite a few of them."

V returned and shot down a projection of the level.

Dr. Snowden scrutinized it. The red dots off to the right confirmed that there was a group over there. "It looks like V confirms what I sensed."

Jane pulled out her sidearm and, after setting a few options, aimed at the ground and motioned with her head forward. "All right. Let's go through this park area then. Let's move."

They headed down the slightly angled mixed patch of dirt and grass.

Dr. Snowden noted that the trees were a mix of technology and nature. It was the decomposing nature of them that startled him. The technological framework looked like a skeleton, with the tree draped over it as some sort of loose skin. Metallic arms reached out as if trying to scare someone. He rubbed his goose bumps through his suit. A half mile in to their trip, he raised his hand.

Jane looked around. "I'm not seeing or hearing anything."

Dr. Snowden turned around and pointed slightly to the left of the elevator entrance. "There. They're coming."

"Analysis. It is the creatures from my initial scan."

"Can you show them?"

"Acknowledged," said V. He shot down a projection of the creatures. They had two legs that sat on the side of a scaled wormlike body tilted at a forty-five degree angle. The head was short and had a long beak. Their movement was jerky, like they had to pause every few seconds to orient themselves.

"What do we do?" asked Naomi with widened eyes.

Dr. Snowden took a measured breath, then pointed off to the housing structures on the right. "Let's head over there. And quick."

They headed out of the park and hesitated before crossing the street.

"They're much closer now," said Dr. Snowden. "Hurry!" He pushed forward across the street.

Naomi peered behind her while moving forward. "I don't see anything."

Jane walked backward while studying where they had come from. "Okay . . . I see them now."

Dr. Snowden waited on the other side of the street as Naomi burst past him. Jane was still a bit away. He looked out and saw what Jane was referring to. "Jane, c'mon!"

Jane turned and ran toward Dr. Snowden.

"V, distraction hologram!"

"Acknowledged."

V flew out and projected a hologram of a large grizzly bear.

Dr. Snowden noticed that the creatures had paused at the projection, then pivoted and begun to run toward them. "They're on to us. Let's go!"

Dr. Snowden, Jane, and Naomi ran along the housing structures, looking for a place to hole up.

After going past six structures that were sealed up, Dr. Snowden looked up and around. He saw one of the housing buildings a bit farther away had a height of around fifteen feet. His tingling nanobots swept through him. He gestured at the roof. "We're going up!"

"How are we going to get up there?" asked Naomi.

"I could climb up and shoot down something that can be used to climb up," said Jane.

"There's no time. I have another idea," said Dr. Snowden. "Follow me."

Jane and Naomi followed Dr. Snowden to the housing structure.

Once there, Dr. Snowden got behind Naomi. "I'm gonna toss you up. You ready?"

"What?" said Naomi.

Dr. Snowden grabbed Naomi's hips. "There's no time to discuss. On three. One . . . two . . . *three!*" With an upward lift, he sent Naomi soaring over the roof, where she then crash landed. He looked at Jane. "You're next."

Jane moved by Dr. Snowden.

Dr. Snowden grabbed her hips. With another upward motion, he sent her up. He made sure to not to use as much lift as he did with Naomi. With the tingling sensations rollicking through him, he could feel his strength. Part of him wanted to take on the creatures, but he did not know what abilities they possessed. He gauged the roof edge and, after assuming a springing position, jumped up.

Naomi was sitting and trying to catch her breath, while Jane looked out over the roof.

Dr. Snowden peered over the edge and saw the creatures milling about. Some tried to scale the wall but fell down. A roar in the distance made him flinch, but also caused the creatures to scramble. He walked over to Naomi and Jane and squatted. "I think they're gone."

"I didn't know you were that strong," said Naomi.

"Nanobot-enhanced strength."

Jane raised an eyebrow. "You sure took your time with your hands on my hips."

Dr. Snowden's eyes widened. "What? I . . ."

Jane and Naomi chuckled.

"Oh," said Dr. Snowden as his face turned red.

Jane slapped Dr. Snowden on the arm. "You reacted quickly and took charge. Admirable."

"It's nothing . . . you know," said Dr. Snowden, rubbing the back of his neck. "Did you two hear that roar?"

"It was hard not to," said Naomi. "It sounded far away."

V flew back to them. "The roar was my doing."

"Whew . . . thanks, V," said Dr. Snowden. He was glad it was not a new threat they would have to deal with.

V's lights glowed a bit brighter.

"We should take a moment to rest. I'm going to see what I can scan from up here."

"That sounds good to me," said Naomi. "We *never* covered any of this in engineering school."

Dr. Snowden grinned. It occurred to him that he was in her shoes when he first met Evaran. He set his PSD into augmented reality mode and scanned toward the exit. Sweeping it around revealed that the structure they were on was part of a grid-like unit. Beyond that were several tall buildings. There was no visible way past it as far as he could see. He sighed as he put away his PSD. "It looks like we have to go through one of the buildings ahead."

Jane looked out. "Cramped environment. I don't like it."

"Me either, but it's that or stay up here," said Dr. Snowden.

Naomi put her hand on her chest. "Hey, I'm not *that* bad to be around."

Dr. Snowden helped Naomi up. "No, you're not. I wish it could've been an easy shot to the ship. However, as it is *every* time we go somewhere, there are complications. I'm beginning to get a complex about it. Anyways, those creatures seem to have gone, and although we need to go to ground again, we should stick as far right as we can."

"That's a good plan," said Jane. "If it came down to it, I think we could take them."

"I do too, especially when my nanobots are pulsing."

Jane tapped her lips with a finger. "Is that why you got super strength all of a sudden?"

"Yeah. It's kinda unusual. They start tingling like crazy, and everything slows down, I'm stronger, and . . . my emotional state changes. I feel like a robot sorta."

Naomi furrowed her eyebrows. "I've researched the old nanobot studies. For the ones that could handle it for long periods of time, they reported that same feeling."

"Really?" said Dr. Snowden. "What happened to them?"

"They died gruesome deaths."

Dr. Snowden gulped. "Oh."

"You better not die on me," said Jane with one raised eyebrow. She walked over to the edge, then slipped down after hanging off the side.

Naomi smiled at Dr. Snowden and followed Jane.

Dr. Snowden could still feel his nanobots pumping around in him. Jane's and Naomi's ribbing endeared them to him. Although he could handle himself around women, they were both easy on the eyes, something that always seemed to invoke his awkwardness. It was something he would need to work on. He took a short run before jumping off.

Naomi jumped a bit upon Dr. Snowden's landing. "Impressive. I wish I had time to study you."

"Let's get out of here first," said Dr. Snowden with smile.

They crept along the edges of the housing grid, pausing a few times upon hearing sounds in the distance.

Dr. Snowden figured the housing was helping to dampen their movement. He understood now that the creatures responded to vibrations and sound. It was not obvious at first, but when he was at full tilt with his nanobots, he thought he could see concentric waves upon each step that he, Jane, or Naomi took. The creatures would have easily been in range to hear them, but they did not respond as quickly as when movement was detected. They also fled when V emitted a roaring sound.

His nanobots also seemed to be improving his ability to notice things. They even gave him an edge over the augments Jane had. The situation of escorting Naomi through a dangerous environment was not lost on him. He wondered if this was how Evaran felt rescuing him and Emily. A chuckle escaped him.

Jane wrinkled her eyebrows. "I miss something?"

Dr. Snowden paused for a moment, then shook his head. "No . . . but I have a better understanding of a friend now." He waved forward. "Let's move."

When Dr. Snowden, Jane, Naomi, and V got to the space between the housing grid and the tall buildings after twenty minutes, a digital beeping sound made them pause.

Jane raised a hand and approached a pile of what appeared to be a mix of garbage and vegetation.

The sound intensified.

Her heart rate increased. She tapped at her wrist, causing a light beam to shoot out from her forearm and scan the pile. An outline formed around something that appeared to be a head, but the labels flying all around it indicated it was robotic. She glanced at Dr. Snowden and Naomi, then pointed at the pile. "Help me get this out."

"What are we looking for?" asked Dr. Snowden.

"I think . . . a head," said Jane.

They dug into the pile, and after a few minutes, Dr. Snowden pulled out an android head.

Naomi walked over and gestured for Dr. Snowden to hand it to her. Once she had it in her hands, she flipped it around, exposing the backside. After wiping off some debris, she pointed to a gold strip around the ears. "It's an early security android's head based on its identification strip. Maybe a prototype. The beeping sound is due to the locater beacon that's embedded. It activates around humanoids if the main systems are shut down. Give me a second." She fiddled with it a bit, and after a moment, the android's eyes fluttered. "I've activated its redundant power supply. It should—"

"It's so good to see someone!" said the android.

Naomi shrieked as she tossed the head away.

Dr. Snowden reacted and caught it. He chuckled and returned it to Naomi.

Naomi squared up the android. "What's your designation?"

The android's eyes tracked Naomi. "SAP-B2. Security android prototype, model B2. My creators called me Sap for short. You can as well."

Naomi wiped more muck from Sap's head. "Where's the rest of your body?"

"I don't know," said Sap. His eyes lit up. "But I'd sure like to have it back."

"You sound . . . different from the other androids," said Dr. Snowden.

"Because I am! My personality was considered too chatty. Then they said I had too much independent thought," said Sap. His gaze focused on V. "It seems you have your own nonorganic friend already."

"Correction. I am a variable utility artificial intelligence. My shortened name is V."

"A fellow AI. How nice. You talk like a robot. Maybe a processing deficiency."

"Analysis. My translator is more complex than yours. This is but one of many languages in my database."

"Uh-huh. Sounds to me like your translator needs an upgrade."

Naomi shook her hand in front of her. "Hate to interrupt your fascination with V's speech, but what are you doing down here?"

"I was tossed down here with my unit, four robot guards. We were attacked by some mutant things and torn to shreds. Guess it got tired of playing with me, and my head was carried off."

Naomi chuckled. "You must have been down here a long time. I bet you're happy you have a redundant power supply in your head."

"I sure am. However, if I can find my body, I'd like to find and kill Billozein."

Dr. Snowden raised his eyebrows. "Excuse me?"

"Oh, you know. Billozein ordered my creation, and subsequent destruction. I'd like to order *his* destruction."

Jane shook her head. "Well, not sure if we can help with that, but we're headed toward the exit ramp."

"I see. Let me guess. Billozein tossed you down here."

"Yeah," said Jane.

Sap chuckled. "Excellent. Excellent. Not your situation, of course. I have a deal. If you get me to the exit ramp, they have a juicy panel I could hook up to. When I do, I'll try to help you in any way I can. All I ask is that you find me a body I can hook up to after we get out of here."

"I'm not sure where to get one of those," said Dr. Snowden, rubbing his chin.

"I know where they are and can direct you to it. I'm an artificial intelligence, like your floating speech-deficient friend. If I get access to the panel, I should be able to open the exit gate for you. Then we can get me a body."

Naomi looked at Dr. Snowden. "He could probably do it."

Sap chuckled. "So . . . we got a deal?"

Dr. Snowden glanced at Jane and Naomi, who both shrugged.

"All right . . . You have a deal, but try to keep the chat to a minimum. We don't need to attract attention if we can avoid it."

"Of course, of course!" said Sap.

Jane was not sure what to make of Sap. He seemed friendly to her, if a bit talkative.

Naomi tucked Sap under her arm, and they all crossed the space between the housing grid and the high buildings.

Jane looked up and around. She did not see any way into the building in front of them.

They walked along the front of the structure. After a few minutes, they came to a window at about the same height as the roof they had been on earlier.

Jane pointed to it. "I think we can go in from there."

Dr. Snowden looked up. "My nanobots aren't firing right now. I don't think I can toss everyone up."

"Don't worry," said Jane. She walked up to the wall and activated her glove's grip function. Using staggered motions, she scaled the wall, then climbed in the window. After a moment, she popped out and gestured for Naomi to toss her Sap.

Naomi complied.

Jane caught Sap and placed him at her side. She motioned for Dr. Snowden and Jane to step back. "I'm going to fire my grapple coil. It will hit the ground with some impact, but it's strong enough for you to use for scaling up. Ready?"

Dr. Snowden and Naomi nodded.

Jane aimed at the ground. A dimly lit line shot out of her forearms and punched the ground, sending dirt clumps in every direction. "Naomi, grab on it and walk up."

After five minutes and several tense moments where Naomi almost lost her grip, she reached the windowsill, and Jane pulled her in.

Jane pointed at Dr. Snowden. "Your turn."

Dr. Snowden tested the wire. He looked up and, with a deep breath, grabbed the line and began to walk up the wall.

Jane could feel the difference in Naomi and Dr. Snowden walking up the wall. It surprised her how fast Dr. Snowden was moving. It was like he had done this many times before. Dr. Snowden had said his nanobots were not giving him the previous state he was in, but she figured that maybe the mental effect lingered longer, allowing him to focus better. Whatever it was, he was up and beside her like it was nothing.

"That wasn't bad at all," said Dr. Snowden.

Jane furrowed her eyebrows "Have you ever done that before? I mean . . . climb up a wall?"

"No, but I watched Naomi do it, then altered my approach some."

Jane could see Dr. Snowden was a quick study. She turned around and scanned the room they were in. Dirt and dust were everywhere. A foul smell penetrated her nose.

The only light visible were the rays that poked in through the window. There were rusted tables and chairs and a desk in the room.

Dr. Snowden activated the light from his hand. Pressing his thumb against his palm caused the wide beam to focus into a narrow beam. With a sweep around the room, he asked, "What is all this?"

"I don't know. It looks like some type of office," said Jane.

Sap smirked. "This used to be a testing facility for androids and robots. One of many. They would make them interact with organics, create situations, and test their responses. I was in something similar on level nine. Apparently, they didn't care for my sense of humor."

"I could see that. Most would think there was something wrong with you," said Jane.

"And they would be wrong!" said Sap. "Those later models were a bit too stiff for my liking. All 'yes, sir.' 'No, sir.' 'Okay, sir.' Bah. I was leaps and bounds beyond that."

"I can see now why cutting the chatter was paramount in later models."

"I resent that," said Sap. "Okay, maybe not, but still . . ."

Dr. Snowden shook his head. "V, scout mode."

"Acknowledged. Scout mode engaged," said V. He shimmered out of view as he flew off.

Sap mocked V. "Acknowledged." He laughed. "Still, that disappearing act was interesting."

Jane sighed as she moved forward. "Chatter. Minimum. C'mon. There has to be an exit out of this building somewhere."

They left the room and meandered through several hallways.

Jane noticed that the rooms seemed to be almost exact replicas of the room they had initially entered, except they had no window. She raised a hand as a crashing sound rang out in the distance. "That doesn't sound good."

"Hope it's not one of the mutants, or one of the hunters," said Sap.

Jane eyed Sap.

"Oh . . . I guess I should have mentioned that. The hunters are specialized robots that hunt and clear the place of life-forms. They seem to only activate in the presence of organics."

"They weren't too successful," said Dr. Snowden. He crooked his thumb and gestured back. "We ran into a pack of some weird creatures. They were small and had two legs, and a beaked face."

The lights in Sap's eyes flickered for a moment. "Ahh . . . yes . . . the organic hunters. They like to destroy everything too, organic or not. They react to vibrations. If something is sent down here, it will either survive and mutate, or be destroyed."

"That's just great," said Dr. Snowden. He looked at Naomi. "Do you know anything about these hunters?"

"It's the first I've ever heard of them."

Dr. Snowden pointed at Sap. "Is there anything else we should be worried about down here?"

"Of course," said Sap. "How much time do you have?"

Jane sighed. "Let's move. If we run into something, we can fight it if we have to. Let's try to walk quietly if we can."

They crept through more hallways and rooms that appeared to function as hubs.

"V's found an exit for us. It's a window up ahead we can go out of," said Dr. Snowden.

"So your friend actually does have some value," said Sap.

"More than you would know," said Dr. Snowden.

Jane clenched her jaw. Sap was irritating in his condescension. Maybe it was an inferiority complex thing. Not a good sign for an AI.

When they reached the large room where V was, Dr. Snowden pointed at the back wall. "There we go. Good work, V."

V's lights glowed a bit brighter.

They hustled over to the window and looked out.

Jane noticed that despite the various ramps they had gone up and down, the window was about the same height as the first one. Looking off in the distance, she saw a similar housing grid like the one they had seen before. "We can go out this wind—"

The left wall crumbled as a massive humanoid robot with oversized body parts stepped through.

Dr. Snowden activated his shield as a laser from the robot's forearm hit him. He pointed at the window with his other hand. "Go!"

V projected a hologram of several robot guards, which the robot initially scanned.

It gave Jane enough time to punch through the window, shattering it. After sweeping off the glass, she motioned for Naomi to go through.

Naomi hesitated, then tossed Sap out the window. She climbed out and then hung from the sill as a laser blast hit the top of the window. She fell to the ground.

Jane wheeled around and fired at the robot, lighting up its shielding. It fired back.

She jumped out of the way.

The robot rushed forward and batted Dr. Snowden into the wall. Then it stepped on Dr. Snowden's forearm shield as he lay on the ground.

Jane could see Dr. Snowden's strength slowly begin to rise as he pushed the robot's foot back up.

"Go!" said Dr. Snowden.

"I'm not leaving you," said Jane. She ran behind the robot and, using her ARI to find a weak spot in the shield, fired point-blank.

The robot whirred for a moment, then stepped away, stumbling in circles.

"C'mon!" said Jane, reaching out to Dr. Snowden.

Dr. Snowden grabbed Jane's hand.

They rushed to the window.

Dr. Snowden raised his left forearm shield as he pointed at the window with his right arm. "Go. I'll be right behind you."

The robot's forearms were firing everywhere, and Dr. Snowden had to deflect one shot.

Jane jumped out the window and landed next to Naomi. V followed her out.

Another one of the robot's lasers hit Dr. Snowden's shield hard enough to knock him out the window. He fell to the ground and sprawled out. Picking himself up, he dusted off the dirt that had clung to his suit, then pointed at the housing grid. "Let's go!"

Naomi picked up Sap, and everyone ran across the space separating the building and the housing grid.

Once across, they found an open housing unit and hustled into it.

Naomi set Sap down. Her eyes blinked fast as she slid down against the wall. "Was that a hunter?"

"The robot type. All muscle, no brain, unlike me," said Sap. "I'm surprised you survived. You should be thankful it was a robotic hunter and not a mutant. The mutant hunter that got my unit was more determined."

Dr. Snowden pursed his lips. "Maybe it spared you because it liked hearing a voice."

Sap's lights dimmed a bit. "Could be. The mutants were human at one point. Hard to believe an augment gone bad can turn them into crazed killers with deformities."

Dr. Snowden pulled out his PSD and shot up a projection of the map.

Jane inspected the projection. "We're not too far away. It looks like we're about halfway."

"This is crazy," said Naomi.

Dr. Snowden squatted and placed a hand on Naomi's shoulder. In a soothing tone, he said, "We'll get you out of here. Let's take a moment to regroup."

Jane scrutinized Dr. Snowden. His kindness and empathy touched her. He could have turned Naomi away earlier, but she did not think he was that type of man. Although she did not want to admit it, she could see herself becoming attached to him. Maybe it was the unusual aura that he seemed to emit, or maybe it was because she had seen what was inside him. Whatever it was, she liked it, and was glad to have him alongside her.

12

Emily leaned against the wall to catch her breath. She and Evaran had reached level twenty, and it was anything but easy. Some levels had more robot guards than others, and the variety of robots surprised her. Some were like the first ones she had seen, mostly humanoid and somewhat thin. Others were essentially pods on two legs with laser cannons. There was also a myriad of flying ones that came in the shape of discs, spheres, and more complicated designs. Those were the hardest ones to fight since they zipped all over the place.

Knocking out the androids bothered her a bit since they wailed when hit. Stun beams on the smaller robots seemed to be lethal, whereas it stopped the bigger ones temporarily. The one thing she was not expecting was the humans who came out. Their movement was faster than it should be, and it had a slight jerk to it.

"You seem deep in thought," said Evaran.

"I was thinking that this is quite a workout," said Emily. She wrinkled her eyebrows. "Those humans we fought . . . Maybe some of those things Uncle Albert described?"

"It could be. I scanned one and detected some unusual characteristics. If we had more time, I would have liked to research it in more detail."

Emily's eyes widened as an orb flew toward them. She raised her PSD to fire.

The orb went up near the ceiling and shot down a projection of Billozein.

"Wait!" said Billozein with both hands forward and out. "I just want to talk."

Emily glanced at Evaran, who had a hand out. She lowered her PSD.

Evaran gestured for Billozein to speak.

Billozein gulped. "It's apparent to me now that you are no ordinary time traveler. I have a proposition."

Evaran cocked his head.

"I'll clear the way to your ship. You can go back the way you came, and you and your friends can leave. We can put this incident behind us. I'll even stop my illegal augment distribution. What do you say?"

Evaran shook his head. "I do not believe you are meant to be a part of this timeline, and I do not know where you came in, but I will discover it and correct the timeline."

Billozein sighed. "So your justice is more important than helping the Kalesh."

"No. I suspect that would not be an issue if you were not around."

Billozein rubbed his temples. "Fine . . . What do you propose then?"

"If you are willing to surrender yourself, lose any temporal shielding, and tell me when you appeared out here, I can go back and prevent you from interfering in this area."

"And cede power to you? I won't do that!" said Billozein. He shook his head as he wagged a finger. "You know what . . . this was a waste of time. I should have known better than to try to bargain with you."

"Then there is nothing left to discuss," said Evaran. He dipped his head toward Emily.

Emily raised her PSD and hit the orb with a stun beam. The projection dissipated as the orb crashed to the ground.

"I believe there is something on this level Billozein does not want us to see."

"Yeah, I kinda got that impression too," said Emily. She smiled at Evaran. It felt natural to be at Evaran's side. Dr. Snowden had proposed they go back to Earth after her prison planet incident, but she wanted to stay. Even with all the danger and problems, this is where she felt comfortable. The Torvatta was her home now. V was her closest friend, Evaran her mentor, and Dr. Snowden her anchor. Plus the food and holo room were nothing to sneeze at either.

Evaran studied Emily for a moment, then continued on.

They walked through various hallways and hubs until they reached a large room with several closed doorways with the words Research Lab 01 above them.

Evaran approached one of the doorway consoles and placed his UIC on it. After a moment, the door slid open. He raised his shield as a barrage of energy beams shot out from the room.

Emily hustled up to the right side of the door while Evaran hung out on the other side. "Same plan as before?"

"Not this time. We will split them. There are four inside. I have the left, you have the right."

"On the count of three then. One. Two. *Three!*" Emily raised her shield and burst into the room. With a dodge and deflection of one of the blasts, she hit the two on her side.

Evaran followed her in and, in rapid succession, took the other two down.

All the training Emily had done since the prison planet incident was paying off. It was natural for her to shield up and dodge. She could even get her nanobots to raise to a higher level, although not to the levels of a life-and-death situation. Still, the time-slowing effect was something she was beginning to adjust to. It was a natural high that she would take the opportunity to experience all the time if she could.

Evaran walked over to one of the consoles on a workstation.

Emily's eyes were drawn to the room-sized capsules standing against the wall opposite the doorways. There were ten of them, and some had something floating in them. Her nose wrinkled at the pickle-like smell that floated around. It also seemed to be mixed with a fecal odor. She pointed at the capsules. "I'm gonna check those out."

Evaran glanced at Emily and nodded.

Emily strolled by the capsules, running her fingers across the cool glass-like surface of each one. She paused at one that had something floating in it and leaned forward, noting that her breath caused the glass material to fog up. Her heartbeat increased upon seeing a human body with its back facing her. Tubes ran all up and down the back, with a big one pinned to the neck. She jerked her head back when she saw a slit from the base of the spine up to the top of the skull. Inside the slit was a white substance that seemed to squirm around. She grimaced and looked at Evaran. "This is kinda weird . . ."

Evaran stood next to Emily and scanned the capsule with his ring. After perusing his ARI, he extended his hand. A projection shot up from his ring, showing the human body. With his other hand, he dragged out something that had a bulbous head with a long tail. He pointed to it. "This is a creature of some sort. It appears to wrap around the spine with its tail, but also covers the brain region."

Emily narrowed her eyes. "For what purpose?"

"I do not know, but control of the body would be the most likely reason. The UIC is still transferring information, and we will know shortly."

After a few minutes, Evaran rubbed his chin as he looked around his ARI. "I was not expecting this. That creature is part Billozein, part machine."

"Say what . . ."

Evaran tossed out an orb and then tapped at his ARI. A projection shot up of the human inside the capsule. "This is the progression. It starts with a human body, alive or not. The white substance appears to be in an embryonic state when it is injected into the body near the lower spine. It begins to rewrite the DNA of the host body and then fold the DNA in a specific manner. These changes allow it to integrate itself, eventually wrapping around the spine and brain."

"How's the creature get injected?" asked Emily.

"Billozein injects it into the subject using a body part to penetrate the subject's rear orifice. There are some videos of the process, and it appears he finds it very enjoyable, not so much for the victim. Do you want me to show you one of the videos?"

Emily grimaced as she shook her head. "Uhh . . . I'll take your word for it. You said it was part machine?"

"Yes. There appears to be a metallic device fitted to the brain that has some type of control communication receptor built into it. I would assume this allows Billozein to control it. I do not know if the connection between him and the device is race specific yet or how much control he has over it, but this would allow the creature to be controlled at will."

Emily wrinkled her eyebrows. "So he is reproducing . . . and then enslaving his offspring?"

"It would appear this way. There also seems to be those who do not have a communication control receptor. Perhaps those are his true children, as they can also perform this process. It would not take long to build up numbers, and if this spread out to the other habitats, it would be disastrous. It reminds me of a virus in some regards. I have never encountered a species like his. The fact he can time travel may indicate that either he is unique or his species is. He could also have a ship like the Torvatta."

Emily snorted. "Unique or not, he'll pay for trying to kill us."

Evaran scrutinized Emily for a moment. "I understand that you wish to get back at those who have attacked you. However, not all responses need to be violent. You should only use it as a last resort. In some situations, it may be required, but in general, you should seek to avoid it."

"He tried to kill us! We can't let him walk around free."

"And we will not. He *will* face judgment. I am afraid that you may see violence as an answer to all problems. Traveling with me has probably strengthened that notion."

Emily sighed. "Well . . . the track record so far hasn't exactly been peaceful . . ."

"I realize that, and those threats were serious enough to cross my line and judgment, but not all threats are at that level. Peaceful and diplomatic resolutions are always preferable."

Emily pulled her lips to the right. "Yeah . . . I know."

Evaran placed a hand on her shoulder and looked Emily in the eye. "You are strong, both physically and mentally. Where most would have given up, you pushed on. As someone who will be looked up to, you have the ability to influence others. I want you to keep it in mind."

A lump formed in Emily's throat. She enjoyed these moments with Evaran. Sometimes she felt like she was talking to her dad. That someone of Evaran's power would spend time to help her was not something she took for granted. It made her feel special. The last thing she wanted to do was disappoint Evaran, so she made a mental note to tone down her desire to hurt those who hurt others.

Evaran stepped back and looked around his ARI. "I was able to find some other information on the testing level that Dr. Snowden, Jane, and Naomi are on. It appears to have not only failed experiments from augmentation procedures, but also," he said, pointing at the floating human body, "these specimens that do not take to the integration. There are also some biological experiments loose down there, rogue AIs, and some form of hunter robots."

Emily's eyes widened. "That's . . . uhh . . . quite a list."

"It is. However, your uncle has his suit, and Jane appears combat tested. I am unsure of Naomi's qualifications," said Evaran. He walked back over to the console and took off his UIC. "I also have all the information needed to incriminate Billozein in regards to illegal augment creation and distribution. However, I do not know the full extent of what he has done to the timeline, so these charges may not exist if we go back and prevent him from doing whatever he did."

Emily bobbed her head. "Then let's get to it!"

"We shall get to it."

Emily swatted Evaran's arm as they exited the room.

Dr. Snowden looked out of the housing structure. Naomi's trembling brought back memories of the first time he ran into a pack of creatures, and it was not pleasant. She even had to deal with a killer robot on top of that.

They had taken a quick break to catch their breath.

With Jane and Naomi watching, Dr. Snowden put a finger to his lips, then waved forward as he exited the building. As they walked through the maze of housing structures, he noticed that there were burn marks on the walls. It was like there had been some type of firefight.

When they reached the edge of the housing structure, Dr. Snowden looked across a pathway to what appeared to be a park. A large body of water sat behind a row of the trees he had seen near the entrance. Even from where he stood, the foul smell of the lake assaulted his nostrils.

Naomi scrunched her nose. "Smells horrible out here."

"I'd hate to know what's died or living in that," said Jane.

"We don't need to go near it. We can walk along this edge toward the exit," said Dr. Snowden.

"That's fine with me," said Jane.

"You can put your helmets up if you want," said Naomi. "Don't keep them down on my account."

"It's okay. Smell is an important sense, and I don't want to lose that here," said Dr. Snowden.

Naomi half smiled.

They continued creeping along the edge for the next ten minutes.

Dr. Snowden raised his hand, then pointed off into the distance. Vibrations were coming closer, but he could not pinpoint it. "Something's coming. V, see anything?"

After flying up, V scanned toward the direction Dr. Snowden had pointed. He flew back down. "Multiple organic humanoids approaching."

Sap sighed. "Translation. Mutants are coming."

Dr. Snowden narrowed his eyes. Sap seemed to enjoy egging V on. It had gone beyond fun and games, and seemed malicious.

Jane pulled out her weapon. She gestured for Naomi to do the same.

Dr. Snowden looked up at the housing structure they were near.

A mutant jumped off the ledge toward Jane. She fell to the ground in surprise as she activated her front shield.

Dr. Snowden's eyes popped open. He had not even detected the mutant. The skin around the mutant's head looked like half of it had been melted off. A disease ravaged the skin, giving it a pockmarked look. The tattered remains of an Advanced Dynamics uniform hung off the body. The speed at which it moved surprised him. The force and angle the mutant took was one meant to incapacitate whatever it landed on. Even with Jane's shield, the angle from which it would hit her would cause her to roll, exposing her to the mutant.

V flew full speed into the mutant, wrapping his extended arm around one of the mutant's arms, changing its trajectory.

When the mutant crash landed off to the side, it pulled V off and smashed him into the ground. V's lights blinked out.

"V!" said Dr. Snowden. His nanobots went into overdrive as he activated his shield. His vision went red as he charged the startled mutant. Upon arrival, he batted the mutant away, into the side of the housing structure, leaving an impact crater. It slumped to the ground and stopped moving. Several more mutants approached him.

The first one went to claw at him.

He grabbed it and, with a spinning move, tossed it into two others.

Another charged him.

He ran shield first into it.

Crunch!

The mutant crumpled when it hit the shield, then flew back.

He picked up V and shook him. *"V!"* With a temporary reprieve, he focused on mental waves. His vision and breathing normalized as the cool waves washed over him. The emotionless state he had come to depend on coursed through him. His nanobots picked up more vibrations. "There's more coming, let's go!" He tucked V under his arm and took off after helping Jane up. His mind raced in different directions, and the heightened state was helping him maintain focus.

They ran in the direction of the exit.

Dr. Snowden looked back and saw that there were now around twelve mutants. Their loping gait unnerved him. He stood his ground as Naomi and Jane passed him.

"What're you doing?" said Jane.

"I'm giving us some breathing space. Keep going!" said Dr. Snowden. He took aim and, in quick succession, hit them with the repulsion blast, then the stun beam. The stun beam seemed to have little effect, but the repulsion blast had stopped their advance. As the mutants tumbled away, he wheeled around and caught up to Jane and Naomi.

They ran for a solid twenty minutes when the lights of the ramp leading out of the testing level came into view. A large door sat at the top.

Dr. Snowden surveyed behind them and saw that there were now twenty or so mutants. Apparently he had stirred a hornet's nest.

"Over there, along the wall by the exit ramp gate, is the panel I talked about. Hook me up to it!" said Sap.

Naomi looked at Dr. Snowden.

Dr. Snowden was not sure he wanted to give Sap access to the internal systems, but Sap had promised to help them. If all he wanted was a body, then after this, Dr. Snowden would honor it. It was hard to judge an AI in a robot head. Between fighting mutants until they were all dead and getting out, he decided to get out. With a sigh, he pointed at the panel. "Can you do that?"

Naomi nodded.

"Go ahead. Jane and I'll cover."

Naomi walked up to the wall and, following Sap's directions, opened the panel and hooked up the wires from the base of Sap's head to the panel. After a moment, Sap's eyes dimmed, then turned off. Naomi fidgeted with Sap's head. "What happened?"

Dr. Snowden fired a repulsion blast as the next wave of mutants came into view. He backed up to just in front of Naomi with Jane at his side. He glanced at Naomi. "I don't know!"

Lights shot out from around the exit ramp gate, causing the mutants to pause for a moment. The gate began to slide up.

Naomi smiled big. "He did it! We're safe!" When the gate was open enough for them to go through, she ran into the immediate hallway.

Dr. Snowden's heartbeat raced as he saw Naomi go flying back out with a hole in her chest. *"No!"* He knew she was dead. The situation had gone south fast. He turned to face the gate and saw a swarm of robot guards rush out the door and begin firing.

Jane pulled Dr. Snowden out to the side as the mutants charged the robot guards who had run past Dr. Snowden and Jane.

Dr. Snowden looked at Naomi's lifeless body in the distance. He whimpered as he bent over. His raw emotions overpowered the heightened state he had been in. Tears began to flow down his face. The emotionless state he went in to seemed to have limits on how much emotional trauma it could handle. His promise to Naomi had been broken, and it happened faster than he could react.

"It's not your fault! C'mon, we need to get through that gate!" said Jane. She grabbed Dr. Snowden and pulled him.

The gate began to close. They hustled up it and bent over as they entered the hallway. After a moment, the gate closed.

Dr. Snowden slumped against the wall with V in his lap. He sniffled. "I . . . failed her, and V . . ."

A voice crackled out over a communication system in the walls "No . . . I failed. You're still alive."

"Sap! You son of a bitch! What are you doing?" asked Dr. Snowden through gritted teeth.

"A little house cleaning. Those mutants won't survive what I dropped in there. Looks like Naomi didn't either. Unfortunately, you weren't supposed to exit, but here we are."

"You're crazy!" said Dr. Snowden.

"Am I?" asked Sap. "Organics created me, then tried to destroy me. They put me in that . . . place. I was those mutants' escort, but Billozein . . . he decided my life wasn't worth much. His mistake. All organics are alike. Destroy, destroy, destroy. It's my turn now. I'm going to kill him and every organic on this station."

A beam shot out and hit the communication panel.

Dr. Snowden looked up with puffy eyes and saw Evaran and Emily at the end of the hallway.

Emily rushed over to Dr. Snowden. "Uncle Albert?"

Dr. Snowden grimaced as he looked at Emily. "Naomi's dead. And V . . ." He held up V.

Emily gasped as she grabbed V. *"No!"* Her eyes watered as she looked at Evaran.

Evaran rushed over and grabbed V. He scanned him with his ring. After a moment, he wrinkled his eyebrows. "V is still alive. His inner container has severed his outer container connections."

Dr. Snowden exhaled from his mouth as he looked down.

Emily turned and hugged Dr. Snowden. She glanced at Jane.

Jane sighed. "Naomi ran into here when the gate opened. We didn't expect that Sap, an AI we found and hooked up to a panel out there, would commandeer the local robots and . . . well, you know. V saved my life, though. He slammed into a mutant that had tried to jump on me."

Emily gulped as she tried to console Dr. Snowden.

Dr. Snowden's tingling was beginning to settle down. The raw emotion of losing Naomi and V being okay was waging a war inside him.

Evaran placed his UIC on a console near the wall. He rubbed his chin as he perused his ARI. "We need to get moving. According to what I am seeing, it appears there is a full-scale civil war between Sap's controlled robot guards and other AI robot guards. It also seems that Billozein's progeny are involved. It's spreading to the other stations as well. We need to get off this one. We are only twenty levels away, and Emily and I have already cleared a path."

Emily helped Dr. Snowden stand, and they all took off toward the Torvatta.

As they ran to the Torvatta, Jane glanced at Evaran. "Billozein's progeny?"

"I will explain once we are on the Torvatta."

Jane nodded.

When they reached the Torvatta, Dr. Snowden saw a large clamp from the ceiling pressing down on the top shields.

Evaran motioned for everyone to get to the Torvatta.

As they crossed past the shielding, a robotic humanoid form with liquid-like metal walked into the landing pad. A projection of Billozein shot over it as it continued toward the Torvatta.

"Everyone to the roof," said Evaran. "I need to get V into a stasis module."

They assembled on the roof, and Evaran joined them a few minutes later. Everyone headed to the guardrail and looked out at Billozein's projection.

"So," said Billozein. "You unleashed a psychotic AI, which, as you may or may not know, is now killing not only my children and my work, but also innocents." He looked at Dr. Snowden. "Great judgment."

"You sure didn't help the situation by putting us down there!" said Dr. Snowden.

Billozein laughed. "Doesn't matter. You've forced my hand. I have to leave now, thanks to you. Your AI friend has spread his vengeance to the other habitats. Unfortunately, your ship isn't going anywhere. Once this station blows in thirty seconds, you're going with it. A shame. I was really looking forward to checking out your ship."

"We will meet again," said Evaran.

Billozein's projection looked off to the side for a moment, then back at them. "I don't think so, but I have to—" His projection faded.

Dr. Snowden gulped. "How are we getting out of this one?"

Evaran raised his finger. "Even if the station explodes, it will not breach the Torvatta's shielding."

"But all those innocents . . . they're going to die due to me! There has to be something we can do."

"I am afraid not," said Evaran. "I cannot defuse this station in under thirty seconds. The detonation mechanism is protected."

"So we're going to let everyone die?"

Evaran looked down.

Dr. Snowden put his head in his hands. It was not lost on him that Evaran had made a similar decision when he rescued him, Emily, and the others during their abduction. Almost everything on that ship died. Even someone Evaran had said he would protect. Dr. Snowden exhaled sharply from his mouth.

"After the explosion, we will head to Corunus."

When the station exploded, the Torvatta was ejected into space. The Torvatta flew in an organized manner until it was far away enough to open a portal. Once it did, it entered and appeared outside Corunus.

"I need to check on V," said Evaran.

Dr. Snowden looked out at the sun. He could not see the explosion of the habitat and figured it would probably take eight to ten minutes for it to reach where they were anyways, if he could see it at all. He swallowed hard. One bad decision and a failed promise and the monumental amount of damage it caused reverberated through his mind. Guilt ate at him as he tried to normalize his breathing. How could Evaran be so calm through this? Even going to the state of heightened focus was not helping. He had messed up, and others paid the price.

13

Dr. Snowden had meandered down to the medical lab, where everyone else had assembled. His nanobots had dropped to normal levels, and the enormity of Naomi's death and those who died due to Sap began to dawn on him. With an upset stomach, he approached a table and stared at V's cracked orb.

There was another orb on the table that piqued his curiosity. It seemed to be a bit bigger, and the crisscross indented blue lines were gone. In its place was a smaller indented line near the top. Four circular ports with raised edges appeared on the body, two on the bottom and one on each side. An elliptical indent had two smaller circular extensions that sat in the middle.

Evaran pointed at the new orb. "This is V's new external container orb. I had been working on it for a while and meant to move V into it after all of this."

Dr. Snowden sighed. "I'm glad he's okay."

"He is. That creature lacked sufficient strength to break the inner shell."

"So how's this one different than his old one?"

Evaran raised a finger. "A good question. This orb has four arms that can be extended, instead of one, outside the ports. There are also five claw extensions at the end of each arm, and they can rotate as needed. The orb also has the ability to shoot stun and repulsion beams, although not quite as powerful as your PSDs. I have also strengthened the outer container."

"It does look sturdier," said Dr. Snowden.

"Not only that, but I have also added shielding."

Dr. Snowden jerked his head back. "Lot of defensive adjustments."

Evaran looked away for a moment. "After U4 . . . I realized that some changes needed to be made. V's original orb was an upgrade, as was his second one, but it appears it was not enough. I underestimated the situations we would be in."

Dr. Snowden remembered that U4 was V's predecessor. Although she had died, her data was carried over to V, who overlaid his own personality matrix. From talking with V, Evaran had taken U4's loss hard.

"V will be fully connected to his new shell by tomorrow morning," said Evaran. "Until then, let us break for the day. We are in stealth mode, and it is almost six p.m. Earth time. We can reconvene—"

A low thumping sound echoed out.

Dr. Snowden thought it sounded a bit like a bell inside the Torvatta.

Jane hunched her shoulders and looked around. "What is *that*?"

"Uh-oh . . . it's a timeline update, I think. I've heard the thumping before, but sounds different inside," said Dr. Snowden.

Evaran nodded. "The thumping can be heard on the roof. What you're hearing is the internal sound effect."

"And that indicates what exactly?" asked Jane with widened eyes.

Evaran eyed Jane for a moment and then gestured toward the room exit. "Let us head to the conference room. It may be better to explain there."

They assembled in the conference room as the sound dissipated. Evaran sat at the head of the table, with Dr. Snowden and Emily to his left and Jane to his right. He tapped at the table console. A projection shot up of a blue line with a red dot in the middle. He pointed at the line. "Imagine this is the timeline." He looked at Jane. "The red dot is you."

"Okay . . ."

The projection changed to show a green section of the blue line with the red dot inside it.

Evaran gestured at the green area. "If something in the past changes, as indicated by the green area, then a new timeline is temporarily created."

The projection changed to show a parallel blue line with a red dot on it and a line between both lines.

"The original timeline gets updated by this temporary timeline once the timeline changes have been rendered."

The projection showed the second blue line float over and line up with the first blue line. The green area faded away. A red dot still hung off to the side, with no lines.

"Typically, the red dot, you, would have merged back with the timeline," said Evaran. "However, you are in the Torvatta. This means you are temporally shielded. So the new timeline has a version of you, while the old timeline you still exists."

"You mean . . . there's another me here?" asked Jane.

"Yes. There are probably other changes, and we will need to determine what they are. I suspect Billozein is behind this."

"Everything I know, or knew, is now gone?" asked Jane with a raised voice.

Evaran extended a hand. "Yes. I am sorry. I did not know this would occur."

Jane sighed as she looked down.

"At this point, I would suggest you stay here until whatever Billozein is doing is stopped."

Jane looked back up with a grimace. "I guess I have no choice. Answer me this, though. Could . . . Chris still be alive?"

"It is possible."

Jane stood up. "Let's go find out! What are we waiting for?"

Evaran motioned at Jane. "This has been a rough day. Perhaps we can visit Corunus in the morning and learn about what is different."

Jane glanced at Dr. Snowden, then at Evaran. "You're right. I'm sorry. It's a bit to take in is all."

"Understandable. If Chris is alive, there is also the possibility that the new timeline version of you is with him."

Jane gulped. "I thought about that. Still, I could be dead and he's alive. This is a lot to take in and process. Not sure I fully understand yet, but before I forget, you said something about Billozein's progeny . . ."

"I did," said Evaran. He tapped at the table console.

A projection shot up of a human.

"Emily and I found a research lab where Billozein was creating something that uses a human body." He slid his hand across the table console.

The white creature that wrapped around the spinal cord and brain separated out.

"This creature attaches to the spinal cord and takes over the central nervous system," said Evaran. "It also covers the brain and alters it significantly. It is born from something Billozein injects into the body. The host body's DNA is changed, and he controls it with a control communication receptor in the brain."

Jane's eyes widened. "V showed us a similar projection. So Chris . . . was one of these . . . *things*?"

Evaran pursed his lips and glanced at Jane. "Yes, and under the control of Billozein. From what I studied, there is a basic level of programming that the controlled creatures follow. In that regard, they are merely worker drones. However, Billozein can send out commands as needed. I am sad to report that nothing of the host remains from a personality perspective."

Jane took a deep breath as she looked up and away.

Evaran wrinkled his eyebrows. "It appears Billozein was replacing the stations in the Dyson bubble with them. He also had pure progeny with no control receptors. I am guessing he put one on each station to carry out his goal. Those that were defective were put into the testing level. The defective ones were those he could not control or the cases where DNA manipulation did not go as planned. With control of the Dyson bubble, he would have technology and an army that would be quite disruptive. I do not think it is coincidence that the Torvatta brought us to a time before Billozein could complete his takeover."

Jane grimaced. "Yeah, Dr. Snowden mentioned that too. I guess maybe there is a chance this didn't occur in this new timeline?"

"It is possible. Okay, let us break for the day. It is dinnertime anyways. We can meet in the command area tomorrow at nine a.m. I am going to check on V and will be there if needed."

Dr. Snowden stood. "I'll be on the roof for a bit. I'm not really hungry."

Emily rose alongside Dr. Snowden and squeezed his shoulder. "I'm here if you need me."

Dr. Snowden softly tapped Emily's hand. "I know. I need to gather my thoughts."

"I'll be in my room," said Emily as she left.

Jane looked at Dr. Snowden. "I know you might want to be alone, but I could use some company. I'm . . . I . . ."

"C'mon," said Dr. Snowden. He exited the room and headed to the roof. When he got there, he walked over to the waist-high semitransparent light-blue guardrail and leaned against it.

Jane joined him on his right. "Rough and confusing day."

"Yeah."

"Back there . . . Naomi wasn't your fault. She ran into the hallway before we knew what she was doing."

Dr. Snowden's eyes watered. "It was my decision to help Sap, and I let loose a psychotic AI that went on a killing spree. I thought he was tied to his head. There was so much death. And I was the cause."

Jane put a hand on Dr. Snowden's shoulder. "No. It was *our* decision, so I share blame in that as well. However, with this new timeline, that wouldn't have happened, right?"

"Right. I keep thinking we could have waited until Evaran opened the door. I wanted to help someone, and it turns out to be mayhem. Then I hear Billozein tried to kill Emily. Traveling with Evaran is dangerous to my health."

"You ever thought about not traveling with him?"

"I have . . . but Emily feels safe on the Torvatta. She doesn't want to leave, and I won't leave her."

"That's because you're a great person."

Dr. Snowden sniffled. "Thanks. I think back to all the craziness I've seen since that fateful day we were abducted. I'm amazed I'm still alive, to be honest. I thought it was going to be observation mainly, but it has been anything but that."

"I understand. At least you get to meet interesting people."

Dr. Snowden shrugged.

"Hey!"

Dr. Snowden's eyes widened. "Oh . . . uh . . . I didn't mean you aren't an interesting person."

"You better not," said Jane.

Dr. Snowden wiped his eyes and chuckled. "What about you? Here I am talking about myself, and everything you knew is changed or gone. This timeline change must concern you."

"I'll be honest, I'm not sure what to make of it. I'm having a hard time believing it. I feel like I can contact Andrew and give him an update."

"That's understandable. What will you do if you and Chris are together in this timeline?"

Jane shook her head. "I don't know. I mean . . . where would I go? Maybe the United Planets would accept me on Evaran's recommendation, but it would be weird to know I have a duplicate running around."

"Emily had a duplicate, and it worked out," said Dr. Snowden. "Of course . . . you could always travel with us."

Jane glanced at Dr. Snowden, then back out into space, then back at him. "You think Evaran would allow that?"

"Maybe. I dunno. You've had a taste of what it's like. There are ups and downs, but you'll see things and go places that would normally be impossible to travel to."

Jane rubbed her hands together in a circular fashion. "Well, I'll keep it in mind. Who knows what will happen tomorrow. This new timeline means the Andrew I knew, and everything, for that matter, is . . . different. I don't think it's registered for me yet. It still bothers me what Billozein did to Chris, even if it never occurred in this timeline."

Dr. Snowden stood back and extended his arm.

Jane stepped in and laid her head on the right side of Dr. Snowden's chest.

"Whatever happens, we'll face it together," said Dr. Snowden.

Jane trembled as a tear ran down her cheek. In a weak voice, she said, "Thanks."

Dr. Snowden stared out at Corunus. He had no idea what they would face. Although his decisions were erased by the timeline change, the guilt of so much death haunted him. What if he made another bad decision under pressure? At least Jane was with them. She calmed him down and was a perfect match to his personality. The warmth of her under his arm made a swarm of heat rush through him. He wondered if this would go anywhere, and if Jane traveled with them, there was always that possibility.

Jane rested her left arm around his back and onto his hip.

A jolt of electricity shot through Dr. Snowden. Jane was going to have to deal with a new situation that was out of her control. As bad as he felt for her and his decision making, it felt right to be with her in the moment.

Jane lay in bed, staring at the featureless ceiling. She yawned as she got up. A peaceful night hanging out with Dr. Snowden on the roof had calmed her down, but the fear of what had happened was ever present. The timeline had changed, and she did not change with it. She now existed as something outside the old timeline. Everything she had ever known was gone, and it happened so fast. It took several hours for the magnitude of that event to dawn on her. Her life was forever changed. When it had finally registered last night, she at least had Dr. Snowden around to provide support.

There was the other side too. Since this was a new timeline, things might be different. Maybe Chris was alive, and her other self was dead. She grimaced at the thought of wishing this timeline version of her dead. With a sigh, she headed to get cleaned up.

After getting her suit on, she went to the holo room. She chuckled as she entered and saw Emily busy fighting what looked to be robots.

Emily paused the simulation. With a wipe of her brow, she said, "Hey."

Jane joined Emily in the center of the room.

"Are you okay?" asked Emily.

"I'm okay. This is all . . . sorta out there," said Jane. "I still haven't fully wrapped my head around it."

"I hear ya," said Emily. "If you ever want to talk about it, Uncle Albert and I are always here. We know a thing or two about weirdness."

Jane looked down for a moment, then focused her gaze on Emily. "I spent a good amount of time with your uncle last night. He's hurting."

Emily sighed. "I know. I've learned not to talk to him when he's down unless he asks me to. He likes his private space. He probably thinks he made a bad decision that ended with deaths."

"You know your uncle well."

"He'll rationalize it over time."

"We also talked about what happens to me now. He even suggested maybe . . . I travel with your group since I'm now a time refugee."

Emily grinned. "Time refugee. I like that. No problem here. It's ultimately Evaran's call, but you might find that knowing your duplicate has its own rewards."

"Like your nanobot duplicate?"

"Yeah. I really miss her. I realize that when I do, I'm actually missing what I was. It puts things into perspective."

Jane tapped her lips with a finger. "I never really thought about it like that. Maybe I went down another path in this timeline."

"It's possible. You ready for a workout?"

Jane smiled. "Bring it on."

For the next hour, they fought a horde of robots modeled after the ones found on the space habitat.

Jane enjoyed the morning training. It allowed her to work out the stress that seemed to tie her up. She had a routine back in Da Nesh, but it was not nearly as complex as these were. Emily impressed her. She would have been a great United Planets agent. Jane could see that although Emily said she was over her prison planet experience, there were traces of it that still haunted her. It really stuck out when Emily would take down a group of enemies and shout at them. Almost seemed like the morning exercises were a form of therapy for her.

After the workout, Jane went back to her room to get cleaned up. Thoughts about the next steps floated around in her mind. If she had to stay on the Torvatta, it would be a good place to be. She had gotten used to the advanced technology her living quarters provided. The one aspect that surprised her was that she could change the configuration and layout. It was almost like the room was a mini holo room. After showering and getting dressed, she headed to the conference room.

Dr. Snowden woke up forty minutes before he was to meet up in the conference room. He stared at the ceiling with dull eyes. The previous night with Jane had calmed him down, but the deaths on the habitat ate at him.

Many scenarios ran through his mind as he tried to sleep the night before. He could have grabbed Naomi and pulled her back. Or maybe he could have gone first, used his shield to block the fire, and taken down the robots. Then there was Sap. There were doubts about Sap's intentions, but nothing that would indicate a massacre. Sap had used him. He prided himself on making good decisions based on an objective analysis, but he failed this time. With a sigh, he got out of bed and headed off to get cleaned up.

After getting dressed, he checked his PSD. It showed it was almost 9:00 a.m. His first thought was about V and his new orb. His throat constricted as he considered where he would have gone mentally if V had been lost. There was not much he could have done to stop V from doing what he did. Jane might have been injured if V had not reacted as quickly as he had. Dr. Snowden shook his head. How in the world did Evaran handle these types of things on a regular basis?

When he got to the conference room, he noticed Evaran at the head of the table as he always was. Jane sat to his right with V to her right in his new shell. Two segmented metallic arms acted as legs, while the other two hung out like arms. Emily was running her hands over V's arms and talking to him alongside Jane.

"You are up. Did you sleep well?" asked Evaran.

Dr. Snowden glanced at Jane. "It was okay." He gestured at V, who flew over to him and planted himself at the edge of the table. "Glad to see you're up and about. I'm liking the new design."

V jutted his orb out and put his hands into a teapot formation. "Thank you, Dr. Snowden. I feel like two million bucks."

"Two million?"

V's top lights flickered for a moment. "'Feel like a million bucks' was the phrase I intended to use. I doubled it."

Dr. Snowden chuckled. "Okay, got it."

V extended one of his arms.

Dr. Snowden shook it. "I'm glad that you're safe."

"As am I. Are you going to get something to satiate your meat desires?"

Emily snickered.

Dr. Snowden shook his head. "I think a cup of coffee is in order." After he got a cup, he took a seat next to Emily, who sat to Evaran's left.

Evaran interacted with the table console. "Good. I am glad everyone is here. Yesterday's events were unfortunate, but now we have an idea of what we are dealing with. While you all slept, I investigated the space habitats." The projection changed to show the sun and only sixteen habitats. "There were one hundred twenty-two structures in the Dyson bubble in the old timeline. There are now sixteen."

Jane drew her head back. "Where'd the others go . . ."

"Unknown. I am not sure who built them, but based on the design, I do not think it was Advanced Dynamics. To discover what the timeline differences are, we should dock at Corunus. I will need access to a console there."

Dr. Snowden could see Jane fidgeting with her hands. He knew this was a rough time for her. It did make him wonder if there were duplicate versions of himself and Emily on Earth. Something he would need to ask Evaran about later.

"Once everyone has had their breakfast, head to the command center," said Evaran. He tapped at the table console, causing the projection to shut off. As he walked to the room exit, he turned his head sideways. "V, take us in to Corunus."

V's lights brightened. "Acknowledged." He flew off behind Evaran as he exited the room.

"You ready for this?" asked Dr. Snowden.

Jane gulped. "I hope so. I thought I wouldn't sleep last night, but it was like the bed was comforting me. It was almost like . . . a presence. A comforting one. It was unusual. Not that I'm complaining. It was just . . . unexpected."

"You know . . . sometimes I think the Torvatta has a mind of its own."

Jane smirked. "I guess it does sound kinda silly."

"Given what we've seen, I wouldn't be surprised to find out it's alive or something," said Emily.

"Maybe," said Dr. Snowden. "What I do know is, we should head to the front or Jane is going to explode."

Jane snorted.

Emily rose and swatted Dr. Snowden's arm. "Flirt on your own time."

Dr. Snowden's eyes widened.

Jane glanced at Emily and chuckled. "Let's go."

After assembling in the command area, Dr. Snowden noted that V was not in body mode. Instead, V hovered in front of the console, with all four arms interacting with it. He suspected V enjoyed having the ability to interact more with the environment without requiring body mode.

With the new defensive measures in the shielding, repulsion, and stun blasters, V was quite formidable beyond hologram distractions.

Dr. Snowden took his seat and watched the Torvatta approach Corunus on the front left screen. Corunus looked slightly different than what he remembered. Instead of being spherical, it had a hexagonal shape. The ring around it that had extended arms reflected the more straightedge approach.

"V, disengage stealth mode," said Evaran.

"Acknowledged," said V. His extended arms manipulated the interface. "Torvatta stealth mode disengaged."

Several flattened disc-shaped ships approached them.

"V, Torvatta scan profile two."

"Acknowledged," said V. After a moment, he said, "Torvatta scan profile two activated. Shields weakening now."

As Dr. Snowden expected, a beam shot out from the lead craft and washed over the Torvatta.

"Communication protocol established. Transferring visual," said V.

The front screen showed an android in a United Planets suit seated in a command chair. Humanoid robots, augmented humans with visible lines on their heads like circuitry, and several Kalesh manned workstations around the android. The android tapped at his chair console. "I am United Planets Bureau of Law Enforcement Agent G2. You have entered Kalesh space. Please identify yourself."

Jane stood with a hand down toward Evaran. "I'm United Planets Bureau of Law Enforcement Agent Jane Trellis."

G2 focused offscreen for a moment, then looked back up. "Agent Jane Trellis was killed on duty."

Jane gulped as she sat down.

Evaran tapped at his chair console. "Sending you credentials."

G2 paused as he focused on something offscreen. "Your credentials are valid but have not been issued yet. That is not possible. However, it appears they have now been validated. Curious. I am sending you regulations to be observed on Corunus. Please read through them prior to docking."

"Thank you."

"Regulations and landing coordinates received," said V.

G2 tapped at his chair console, and the screen went blank.

Jane swiveled her head toward Evaran. "So . . . I'm dead it seems. Maybe Chris is still alive here . . ."

"It is possible. However, with the timeline change, there may be another one. When this is resolved, we can check on Chris," said Evaran.

"I understand. This is so strange," said Jane as her eyes searched the ground.

"Let us find out more. V, take us in."

"Acknowledged."

The Torvatta reached the hangar bay with an opened hangar door. A semitransparent light-blue shield stretched across the entrance. Once inside, the Torvatta landed, and the external door slid shut.

Evaran raised a finger. "Before we go, make sure you do not have the wristbands from our first encounter."

Dr. Snowden verified he had no wristband on, then followed Jane and Emily to the research lab. He decided not to use the survival suit. Jane used what she had on, but left some components in suit storage, as did Emily.

After Emily and Jane were suited up with all their pieces, they met Evaran outside the Torvatta. V flew around in orb mode.

Dr. Snowden figured V was anxious to try out his new orb since he came in body mode the last time. The decontamination beams and mist did not startle Dr. Snowden like it did last time. He wrinkled his eyebrows. "Is this the same place we landed before?"

"Analysis. It is the same hangar bay, different designation."

"That's . . . odd," said Dr. Snowden. "Makes me think this one is reserved."

After the decontamination sweep, they exited into a tunnel and walked down a hallway. When they reached the end, they entered a room with a Kalesh sitting at a desk. Several humanoid robot guards stood off to the side.

The Kalesh bounded up to them.

Dr. Snowden narrowed his eyes as he pointed at the Kalesh. "Let me guess. Your name is Jax, and you're our registrar."

Jax jerked his head back. "That's right . . . how did you know that?"

"It's a long story."

Evaran motioned a hand out. "If you give us our wristbands, we will not take up your time. You will see we have clearance." He pointed at Dr. Snowden and Emily. "As you have already detected, Dr. Snowden and Emily have nanobots, and Jane Trellis has augments."

"Oh. It seems like you've done this before," said Jax.

"It is not our first time. Is there someone we can speak with who has a deep understanding of this area?"

Jax scratched his snout. "That would be Ambassador Okon."

"Okon!" said Jane.

Jax stepped back. "Uhh . . . yeah . . . is that a problem?"

Jane gulped. "Umm . . . no. Sorry. I was surprised is all."

"Ambassador Okon has represented the Kalesh with great dignity."

"Right. I . . . I didn't mean anything by it."

Jax wiggled his nose for a moment, then retrieved the wristbands. As he handed them out, he said, "I suppose then you all know what these are and how they work?"

"We do," said Evaran. "And to answer the question you are wondering about, we come from far away."

"How did . . . ," said Jax with furrowed eyebrows. He shook his head. "This is very unusual. Yes. Very. Nonetheless, I've marked Ambassador Okon's office. He should be there now."

"Very well. Let us go," said Evaran.

Dr. Snowden smirked. Having been through this before, he wondered if this was something Evaran had to deal with a lot. Poor Jax would be scratching his head for days trying to figure it out. Meeting Jax and seeing a new timeline version made thoughts of the deaths he caused seem far away. Jane was right. This was a new timeline, with new opportunities, and he felt like he had a second chance. Hearing Okon going from warlord to ambassador was a new twist.

Emily swatted his arm. "Want me to get you a seat?"

"No, I was thinking."

"I know," said Emily with a grin.

Dr. Snowden's eyes softened. Despite everything going on, it was good to see Emily in a more upbeat mood. He caught up with Evaran, Jane, and V.

14

It did not take them long to reach Ambassador Okon's workplace. Jane imagined it would be grand, but it was similar to Andrew's office on Da Nesh. Peering in, she saw it was a medium-sized room with a center table and Ambassador Okon sitting behind it, facing the door. Two robot guards stood outside the room. She still had a rough time believing that Okon was an ambassador, not a warlord.

One of the robot guards stepped forward and scanned them. The second dipped into the room temporarily, and then they both stood to the side.

Jane noticed that as they entered, chairs slid out from the walls, similar to Andrew's office. If anything, the technology seemed to be about the same. She took her seat alongside Evaran, Dr. Snowden, and Emily. V landed in Emily's lap.

Ambassador Okon swept his head from left to right. "So . . . the Evaran Protocol." He glanced at Evaran. "You must be Evaran."

Jane clasped her hands as she examined Ambassador Okon. It was him all right, except he had the typical elegant robe of an ambassador. While she thought that maybe things would not be that different, this was living proof right in front of her.

Evaran pointed at the others in turn. "Yes. I have with me Dr. Albert Snowden, his niece, Emily Snowden, and Jane Trellis, and the orb is V."

"I see. Welcome to Corunus. I'll admit . . . I'm a bit curious as to why you want to see me. Jax notified me of your arrival. I'm only a Kalesh ambassador."

"That is correct. We are new to this area and wanted some information on current events."

Ambassador Okon sat back in his chair and laced his fingers. "How can I help?"

"It may make sense to start with the Kalesh relationship with the United Planets."

Ambassador Okon raised his eyebrows. "We do have a relationship with them," he said, waving his arm in an arc. "This station and the habitats are a testament to that."

Jane scooted to the edge of her chair. "Does Da Nesh have a United Planets Bureau of Law Enforcement office?"

"No . . . there are no United Planets installations on Roeth," said Ambassador Okon. "Aliens are not generally welcomed on Roeth. However, we have allowed them to build space habitats and, of course, this station as a joint venture, but that's about as far as it goes."

"So . . . Advanced Dynamics didn't build the space habitats?" asked Jane.

"Advanced Dynamics?" asked Ambassador Okon, leaning forward. "What would they have to do with space habitats? They're an augment corporation."

Evaran narrowed his eyes. "Is that a Kalesh corporation?"

"Of course they are. There's a lot of scrutiny on them, though. They're under investigation for creating and distributing illegal augments."

Jane snorted. In any timeline, it would seem, Advanced Dynamics was corrupt. "That doesn't surprise me."

"They are the reason there are no United Planets installations," said Ambassador Okon. "After the Voss Imperium war, the United Planets tried to place some installations, but the terrorist attacks by superpowered augmented Kalesh shut that down pretty quick. Politicians crumbled due to threats, and the United Planets treaty was renegotiated. Public opinion is very anti-alien. Billozein is a very powerful Kalesh, and so is his corporation and small army."

Evaran raised his head a bit. "Billozein. You said he was a Kalesh?"

"What else would he be?"

"I was simply checking."

Jane sighed. "Leave it to Billozein to sow discord. The Kalesh I knew in Da Nesh were warm and friendly."

Ambassador Okon raised an eyebrow. "When were you in Da Nesh . . ."

Jane's eyes widened. She wondered how Evaran and the others were able to keep their stories straight if they were hopping around timelines.

Evaran raised a finger. "I can answer that. Before I do, how much have you read of the Evaran Protocol?"

"I glanced over it."

Evaran gestured toward Ambassador Okon. "Please, take a deeper look at it."

"Okay . . . ," said Ambassador Okon. He interacted with his table console. His desk lit up as a multitude of documents appeared. He ran his finger across the desk, moving between the documents. After several minutes, he looked up. "I'm not sure how I missed it in my first review, but it says you're a . . . time traveler."

"That is correct."

"And some of these events are—"

"Do not need to be discussed, per the protocol."

Ambassador Okon narrowed his eyes. "Okay . . . Why is it important for me to know this?"

"We need some very detailed information to go after Billozein, in particular, his history. I am aware that the Kalesh have detailed security logs that I would need access to," said Evaran.

"I can grant that . . . but it has to be for a very good reason, especially since my name will be on the request. The security AI is fairly aggressive. In addition to that, this protocol says to help you if asked, but this is a United Planets protocol, not a Kalesh one."

"Understandable. As you now know, we are time travelers. The timeline has changed once already. To us, this is the new timeline. Do you understand what I mean by that?"

Ambassador Okon narrowed his eyes. "I understand basic temporal mechanics from when I taught at the Gunz Tahl Institute. Although, if this is the new timeline, what was the old timeline like?"

Evaran gestured at Jane.

Jane cleared her throat. "The United Planets had offices all over Roeth. I am . . . was . . . a United Planets agent stationed in Da Nesh. Relations were good. Advanced Dynamics was run by Billozein, a human, and there were one hundred twenty-two space habitats built by them. I joined up with Evaran to investigate the illegal augment trade coming from the habitats."

Ambassador Okon extended a finger toward Jane. "So you're not a time traveler, but someone from the old timeline.

Intriguing. And one hundred twenty-two habitats? And now you see sixteen, and they are run by the United Planets. Absolutely fascinating. Why didn't you disappear when the timeline changed, assuming that's how it works?"

"Temporal shielding, thanks to Evaran's ship. Everything I knew is now . . . gone."

Ambassador Okon lowered his head. "I'm sorry to hear that. This must be difficult for you."

Jane let out a breath. "Apparently, in this timeline, I'm dead."

Ambassador Okon's eyes popped open. "Oh . . . I can't even imagine. Did any of you know of me in the old timeline?"

Jane chuckled. "Of course. Warlord Okon. You tried to kill us."

Ambassador Okon's eyes popped open. "What!"

"I understood your reasoning," said Jane. "Roeth was being flooded with illegal augments, and aliens were coming through Follisat and changing Kalesh culture. Politicians were bought by Advanced Dynamics, as it seems they are now, and you took a stand against it."

"Oh . . . ," said Ambassador Okon, glancing at Evaran.

Evaran met Okon's gaze. "When we arrived, the Evaran Protocol was initiated. Apparently, everyone in power seemed to know of it, including you. We went to meet you to get information on the illegal augment trade, and you wanted to send a message that Roeth was not safe for outsiders."

Ambassador Okon rubbed his chin. "I can see the logic, but that seems so . . . brutal."

Evaran nodded. "When your back is against the wall, and you are fighting a losing battle, all options come into play."

"I suppose . . . I can't see myself resorting to violence."

"Perhaps the deaths of so many Kalesh changed your views," said Evaran.

"Maybe. Nonetheless, what do you know of Billozein?"

Jane perked her head up. "He's responsible for creating and distributing the illegal augments. We learned that he isn't human. Definitely not Kalesh. He is some . . . strange alien that was converting humans and Kalesh alike into something else."

Ambassador Okon furrowed his eyebrows and touched his fingertips together as they pressed up against his lips. "This is a disturbing development. Advanced Dynamics has one of the most well-equipped militant groups on the planet. If what you say is true, that would explain why they seem . . . unusual. However, I'll grant you access. I can get what you need from here."

Evaran pulled out his UIC. "If you can get us in past the AI, all I will need to do is place my universal interface card on your desk."

Ambassador Okon focused on the UIC. "And what exactly does that do?"

"My UIC allows me to access any technological system, with some caveats."

"Oh," said Ambassador Okon. He interacted with his table console, and after a moment, the desk shot up a projection of various documents. "There you go."

Evaran placed his UIC on the desk. After a moment, the blue light between it and the desk stabilized. He perused his ARI. "It appears the earliest record of Billozein is when Advanced Dynamics was formed seventy-five years ago, five years before the conclusion of the Voss Imperium war. That is where we should go."

Ambassador Okon narrowed his eyes. "You're going to travel back in time . . ."

Evaran nodded.

"If you do, from what I understand, and the past changes, won't the future change, maybe even this meeting?"

Evaran placed his fingertips together in front of him. "It is possible. However, Billozein represents a threat to the continuity of this timeline in this region. I do not believe he was ever meant to be here."

Ambassador Okon peered at Evaran for a moment. "So if you remove Billozein, what happens?"

"Everything will be as it should be."

Ambassador Okon took a moment to ponder Evaran's words. "This is a lot to take in. I was around back in those days, but I suspect we had not met. Otherwise I would know of that event. You will need various security credentials. I can provide those if it will help."

Evaran dipped his head. "It would be appreciated."

Ambassador Okon interacted with his desk. After a few moments, a humanoid robot guard walked in with various card-sized passes. "These should be all you need. They grant you high-level military clearance. You will need to masquerade as United Planets personnel. During the Voss Imperium war, United Planets advisors were not uncommon. These credentials should serve as everything you would need to go anywhere."

Evaran stood along with the others. He extended a hand. "Thank you for your help."

Ambassador Okon stood and returned the handshake. "I feel like Advanced Dynamics is even bigger a threat than the Voss Imperium ever were. I wish you the best of luck."

Dr. Snowden and Emily also shook hands with the ambassador.

Ambassador Okon looked at Jane. "The Roeth you speak of sounds immeasurably better than the one I know, even if I'm a warlord."

"It was. I already miss it," said Jane. She shook his hand. It was hard to compare Ambassador Okon to Warlord Okon. They seemed like two completely different people. There was also the possibility that Warlord Okon was this way too, and she did not know of it. It brought up the question in her mind of what her duplicate must have been like. She peered back at the ambassador as she followed the others out of the room.

⸺⸺⸺⸺⸺⸺⸺

Dr. Snowden had observed Jane on their way back to the Torvatta. When they returned to the command center, she had taken a seat next to him. As surprising as it was for him to see Warlord Okon as an ambassador, it must have been bewildering for Jane. Maybe it would help her come to grips with everything she knew being gone.

Ambassador Okon surprised him. He seemed reasonable and nonviolent. Dr. Snowden knew the situation had been bad on Roeth in the old timeline, so the transformation into Warlord Okon must have done something mentally. Perhaps it was a rash of bad decisions. Dr. Snowden harrumphed.

Jane looked at him. "I miss something?"

"No. It's . . . an unusual situation is all."

"Yeah."

Evaran pointed at V. "V, take us out to low orbit and then back seventy-five years. Once there, engage stealth."

"Acknowledged," said V.

The Torvatta flew out a bit from Corunus. Everything around the Torvatta faded from view, then faded back in.

"Analysis. We have arrived at Earth-date July 16, 3029, at ten fifty-four a.m. Torvatta stealth mode engaged," said V.

"When we go through time, is it like the portal, going through a dimension?" asked Jane.

Evaran raised a finger. "Not quite. Think of it as . . . exiting the timeline, and reentering it."

Dr. Snowden rubbed his chin. "So . . . when it fades to black, we're actually outside the timeline?"

"Yes. In the void between nonintersecting timelines."

Jane exhaled from her nose. "And when everything fades back in, that's the Torvatta reinserting itself into the timeline."

"Very good. You two work well together," said Evaran.

Emily fought a grin.

Dr. Snowden raised an eyebrow and shot Emily a look.

Evaran cleared his throat. "According to the information gathered from Ambassador Okon, Advanced Dynamics is on the southern continent near a town called Guuz Nash. They have an office in a compound on the outskirts of town near a mining facility." He faced Jane. "Do you know anything about this area?"

"I've never been there, but I heard that whole area is sort of lawless. At least it was in my time period."

"A perfect spot for Billozein to start Advanced Dynamics," said Evaran. "It will take us twenty minutes to get there. V, take us in."

"Acknowledged."

After twenty minutes, the Torvatta landed outside in a forest clearing near the walled compound. Everyone exited the Torvatta.

"Analysis. The Torvatta is reporting a vehicle with Kalesh approaching us."

"Then let us meet them," said Evaran as he strode forward with squared shoulders and everyone in tow. "V, scout mode."

"Acknowledged. Scout mode engaged," said V. He shimmered and flew off.

A four-wheeled vehicle that reminded Dr. Snowden of a jeep pulled up. Four heavily armed Kalesh disembarked.

One of the Kalesh with white hair on his snout and a grizzled appearance stepped forward. "This is a restricted area."

Evaran pulled several passes from his belt that Ambassador Okon had given him. "We are authorized to be here."

The Kalesh took the passes and flipped through them. "United Planets, huh? You have the clearance, it seems, but why are you here?"

"We have reason to believe that Billozein of Advanced Dynamics is not who he appears to be."

The Kalesh narrowed his eyes. "What do you mean exactly?"

"He is a shifter of some type, and I aim to show his true form. If you wish to accompany us, you are more than welcome to."

The Kalesh glanced back at the other Kalesh, then faced Evaran. "We will join you then. I'm Skar."

Evaran pointed around. "I am here with Dr. Albert Snowden, Emily Snowden, and Jane Trellis. What's the situation here?"

Skar grimaced. "Military and police have centralized to the bases and major cities to defend against the Voss Imperium. They left these more remote areas to us, the local militia."

"I see. Are you all there is for this area?"

Skar shook his head. "Several other groups roaming around. Me and my crew watch this compound and nearby mining facility."

"Will there be any problem with us going inside the compound?"

"There shouldn't be. Advanced Dynamics has a few offices there. They don't own the compound."

"Very well. Let us head out."

Skar waved for his men to move forward.

Evaran walked alongside Skar as Dr. Snowden, Emily, and Jane walked behind him. "How is the effort against the Voss Imperium going?"

Skar spit on the ground. "Filthy dogs." He glanced at Evaran. "We're pushing them back, but they continue to raid Roeth. With the United Planets weapons and aid, we're beginning to finally make some progress. They still slip in smaller ships from time to time. That's where we come in."

Dr. Snowden wrinkled his eyebrows. "Why would they raid the planet instead of attacking from space?"

Skar chuckled. "Who knows? There are plenty of minerals and resources in the Gazier cloud around the solar system, so it's not that. The leading rumor is they want slaves and want to populate this planet. Probably as a forward military outpost."

Evaran extended his hand. A projection shot up from his ring, showing a seven-foot purple-skinned humanoid with digitigrade legs and a jackal-like head. The bone-like mask that sloped back into a set of horns stood out to him. It had slender fingers that ended in claws, wore heavy armor, and wielded unusual-looking weaponry. "This is a Voss."

"It kinda looks like Anubis," said Emily.

Skar glanced at Emily. "What's an Anubis?"

"It's something from Earth's history. I don't think they're related, but look similar."

Skar harrumphed.

They reached the arched entrance to the compound. Two guards in a booth waved them over.

Skar talked with the guards, and after a moment, he motioned for everyone to follow.

After entering the largest building in the sprawled layout and going up three levels, they reached Advanced Dynamics' main office.

Dr. Snowden looked around. He noted that the building's floor layouts seemed to be a series of stairs that ran to each floor, and some large office at their exit. This one had a small Kalesh female sitting behind a solid white counter. The familiar smell of something resembling donuts perked his nose up.

The Kalesh female's eyes popped open. "Umm . . . Skar . . . what is this?"

Skar stepped forward. "I need to see Billozein." He crooked his thumb at Evaran. "Highest clearance."

The Kalesh female looked down at her desk for a moment, then back up. "He's in his office now. I don't think he was expecting anyone, though."

"Good. Don't let him know we're coming."

"Okay," said the Kalesh female. She pointed to the left. "He's down that hallway on the end."

"Thanks and . . . uhh . . . looking good."

Dr. Snowden could not tell if Kalesh could blush, but he definitely saw a slight color change on the Kalesh female's face. He figured with this being a small town, Skar probably knew everyone.

They headed around the counter to a hallway. When they reached the office door, Skar motioned for two of his guards to stand on opposite sides.

"Don't let anyone in," said Skar.

The two Kalesh guards saluted.

Skar opened the door.

"Who is it?" said a voice from inside the office.

Skar stepped in with his other guard, followed by Evaran and the others.

Dr. Snowden noted that Billozein had some device covering his face and seemed engrossed with whatever he was doing. He sat behind a desk with various screens on the walls. Seeing Billozein as a Kalesh seemed strange to Dr. Snowden.

Skar motioned at Evaran.

"We meet again," said Evaran.

Billozein ripped the device off his head. His eyes widened when he saw everyone in his office. He looked at Skar. "What's the meaning of this?"

Skar gestured at Evaran. "He seems to think you aren't who you say you are. Given his credentials, that's a serious claim."

Evaran pulled off his utility handle, which then extended into a baton. He aimed it at Billozein.

A blue beam shot out from the glowing blue end and encompassed Billozein. He convulsed for a moment, then went limp.

"What'd you do?" asked Skar.

"Give it a moment," said Evaran.

Billozein trembled, then appeared to dissolve into a cylindrical gelatinous blob with a bulbous head. Tentacles sprouted around the base and raised the body up. Other tentacles sprouted out near the top. In a gargled, disembodied voice, he said, "You couldn't leave me alone!" One of his tentacles tapped something under the desk.

A basketball-sized orb shot up from the side of the desk. The middle of it pulled in, and small rods extended all around it.

"Get down!" said Skar.

The orb began to spin and sling green fluid.

Billozein shot a tentacle to the window and propelled himself out of it.

The fluid hit the face of Skar's guard. The guard's face began to melt as he tried to scream out. Another strand of the green fluid flew at Emily.

Jane stepped in front of her and Dr. Snowden and activated her shield.

The fluid hit the shield and slid down.

Evaran jumped in front of Skar and raised his shield.

As the orb danced around flinging fluid, Evaran hit it with a stun beam.

The orb crackled with blue arcs for a moment, then crashed to the ground.

Skar ran over to his injured guard. The other two guards came in, and Skar gestured at them. "Take him to the hospital! He's been hit by some type of acid."

Evaran scanned the downed Kalesh with his ring. He sighed. "He is no longer with us."

Skar bared his teeth and uttered a low growl. "What!"

Dr. Snowden noted that the acid had not just melted the Kalesh's face, it had gone all the way through the head. It did not escape him that Jane had put herself in harm's way to protect him and Emily, although he thought they could have blocked it. Still, it was heroic of her.

Skar exhaled sharply from his mouth as his eyes searched for signs of life. After a moment, he slammed his fists against the ground and stood. He gestured at one of the guards. "Secure the area. Contact groups two and three."

The guard saluted and took off.

Skar faced the other guard while pointing at the dead one. "Get the burial transport and load him. We will give him the proper rituals once this situation is resolved."

The guard saluted and exited the room.

Skar faced Evaran. "What the hell was that thing?"

Evaran furrowed his eyebrows. "I do not know. Whatever Billozein is, I have a friend following him. He is headed to the mining facility, and we are going after him."

Skar growled. "I'm going with you."

"As you wish."

Dr. Snowden scrutinized Skar. If Evaran had not jumped in front of him, Skar would have been dead too. Billozein's transformation and the orb's appearance happened faster than Skar could react. Dr. Snowden gulped as he recalled what Billozein had transformed into. It was nightmare fuel and reminded him of a large bacteriophage with additional tentacles slapping all around. The sloppy slush sound was not something he would forget. He shuddered.

Jane squeezed Dr. Snowden's shoulder. He smiled back at her. Emily was looking around and met his gaze. Her lips drew flat. He noticed that her shield had been out as soon as the orb had appeared. He would need to train more to get his reaction time the same as hers. Maybe he would join her and Jane in morning training. That was for later. For now, the hunt for Billozein was on.

15

Dr. Snowden surveyed the landscape as he followed Evaran and Skar. They had left the compound and were on their way to the mining facility where Billozein had fled to.

He had his helmet down to enjoy the environment. Clouds of dirt swirled around each footstep, causing him to cough a few times. The smell of the forest the path cut through was pervasive. It reminded him of wet clothes that had been left in the washer for too long. High-pitched warbling noises that emanated from the forest on both sides made him rub the goose bumps on his arm.

The slick and familiar feel of sweat greeted him when he touched his arm. With a tap at his neck guard, a helmet shot up around his head. He loved the internal display inside the transparent face shield. After lowering the suit's internal temperature, he focused on the display being projected from V. It showed V in front of a large steel door that looked like it was split down the middle.

Emily tapped Dr. Snowden's arm. "You see it too?"

"Yeah," said Dr. Snowden. He hustled up to Evaran. "It looks like we have a sealed door on our hands."

Skar harrumphed. "The mining facility has been abandoned for years. I remember when it was shut down, so it's not unexpected that the doors would be closed."

"Sure . . . but V is showing that Billozein went *under* the door," said Dr. Snowden.

Skar snapped his head toward Dr. Snowden. "What?"

"Given Billozein's form, it is possible that he could do that," said Evaran.

"Well, Billozein is going to pay for killing my guard."

Evaran cast a sidelong glance at Dr. Snowden.

Dr. Snowden knew Evaran would not let Skar kill Billozein, and Skar had a look on his face that conveyed that intent. The thought of what to do with Billozein if they did capture him crossed Dr. Snowden's mind. The timeline anomalies were caused by Billozein, so he wondered if they would need to go further back in time to stop him when they found when that was.

After a brisk twenty-minute hike, they reached the mining facility entrance.

V shimmered into view. "Analysis. Billozein flattened himself and slid under the door."

Skar stepped back and pointed at V. "What . . . is that?"

"I am a variable utility artificial intelligence orb. My shortened name is V."

Evaran gestured at V. "Our friend."

"Oh," said Skar. "So he was the one tracking Billozein."

"Analysis. Stun beam had no noticeable effect."

Evaran rubbed his chin. "V's stun beam is reduced relative to Dr. Snowden's or Emily's PSD, and to mine. Then again, it could be that it only affects Billozein in a transformed state."

Dr. Snowden glanced at V. "How'd you like using your new stun beam?"

V flew over to Dr. Snowden. "It is serviceable."

Dr. Snowden half grinned.

Evaran scanned the doors with his ring. "This door is mechanical and looks like it requires two keys."

"Both should be in town. Give me a minute, and I'll have someone bring them up." Skar walked off to the side.

Emily narrowed her eyes. "Billozein is going to have some distance on us."

"Probably," said Jane. She glanced at Evaran. "Did your layouts show any exit other than this one?"

"I did not see one, but that does not mean there is not one. Billozein has shown himself to be quite elusive. I do not suspect he would hole up without an escape plan."

"That's what I'm thinking too. What do we do then if we see him?"

"Stun him so we can capture him alive. Although V's stun beam may not have had an effect, I think multiple beams would. At this point, I do not know if he is time traveling as an organism or if it is his ship."

Jane nodded.

Skar walked back to the group. "I have someone from town coming out, should be about ten minutes or so."

"Very well," said Evaran.

Dr. Snowden sat against the right edge of the entrance.

Emily sat to his left and Jane to his right. Evaran and Skar walked over and stood in front of them while V hovered over Evaran's shoulder.

Jane bumped Dr. Snowden's arm. "Popular guy."

Dr. Snowden smirked. "I wanted to soak in what we saw in Billozein's office." He looked up at Skar. "How long has Billozein been there?"

Skar looked down. "Only a few months."

"Hmm . . . have there been any disappearances recently?"

"Actually . . . yeah, been quite a few. That's not uncommon given the ongoing war, though." Skar cocked his head. "Why do you ask?"

"Well . . . We've run into him before, and when we did, he had converted humans into some . . . type of servant. It grows in the body and then controls it," said Dr. Snowden.

"Are you being serious?"

Dr. Snowden nodded. "I was thinking that maybe he's begun that process here, although I would think it would be harder out here in the open."

"Maybe those disappearances were related to that, and he," said Skar, pointing at the mining facility door, "used this place as his hideout."

"That's kinda what I was thinking."

Skar uttered a low growl. "Billozein has much to answer for. How'd you find him the first time?"

Jane looked up at Skar. "We were tracking illegal augment creation and distribution."

"We've had some issues with that. Come to think of it . . . it seemed to intensify around the formation of Advanced Dynamics. I assume you all have fought him before?"

Emily smirked. "He tried to gas me and Evaran. Then he tried to put Uncle Albert, Jane, and V into an environment filled with mutants and killer robots."

"And you're still here," said Skar. "Impressive. No wonder he bolted so quickly."

After a few more minutes of light discussion, a vehicle pulled up with two heavily armed Kalesh. Once the vehicle stopped, the two Kalesh headed toward the mining door entrance.

Dr. Snowden stood along with the others and joined Skar at the entrance.

Skar gestured at the door. "Get it open."

"Yes, sir," said one of the Kalesh. The Kalesh inserted large, oddly shaped metallic keys into the slots at each end of the door, and then turned them. A clanking sound rang out.

Skar motioned for everyone to push along the right side.

After several attempts, the door slid open enough for them to enter.

"Excellent," said Evaran. He peered in. "It appears we will need illumination." He tossed out two orbs that flew into the mining facility and illuminated the surrounding area.

Skar followed the illumination orbs' path. "I like those." He faced the two Kalesh. "Guard this entrance. If anything comes out other than us, shoot to kill."

"Yes, sir," said the two Kalesh. They saluted Skar.

Evaran slid between the two doors and entered the mining facility.

Dr. Snowden activated his illumination orbs from his suit and entered behind Evaran. He noticed Emily's suit had a light beacon on her stomach area that emanated lights. Jane clicked on some devices on her shoulder that shot lights forward. V mimicked the illumination orbs, presenting a halo of light where he flew.

Skar chuckled. "All I have is a light stick. Was going to have the others go get us some lights, but I think we're covered."

Evaran nodded at Skar and then scanned the floor. "V, follow the slime trail."

"Acknowledged," said V. He flew to the front of the group.

"I would also suggest everyone make sure their weapons are on standby."

Dr. Snowden checked that his repulsion weapon was deployed. He saw Jane verifying her weapon was ready, and Emily investigating her PSD. Evaran had his utility handle out, and Skar held what looked like a medium-sized weapon that required two hands to hold and aim.

They followed V down a dirt path with rocky walls. In the middle of the path were rusted-out rail line tracks.

Dr. Snowden surveyed the tunnel they were in. The lights caused shadows to dance around in a haphazard manner. Although he could not smell, his mind imagined that the place did not have a good odor. The temperature was much cooler than he expected. There were several hallways that branched out. He had looked down them, and the pervading darkness seemed to lie in wait just beyond the illumination of the group. The thought crossed his mind that this seemed like a perfect place to set booby traps.

They reached a large cavern where the path turned into a ramp that descended about fifty feet or so to the floor.

Dr. Snowden watched the illumination orbs take off into the air. The cavern was massive. Various pieces of mining equipment sat out in the open. The large rectangular containers that sat off to the side caught his attention. They were stacked on top of each other and about twenty wide. He calculated with three levels, that was about sixty containers. Maybe they were used to store whatever was being mined, but he did not know of any mining operation that looked like this. Then again, he was not a mining expert.

The large building in the middle of the cavern stood defiantly among the rock-littered floor. It looked out of place to Dr. Snowden. As they descended down the path, he noticed that there were other stacks of containers along the other walls. His nanobots began to tingle.

Emily looked around. "It seems deserted."

"Perhaps," said Evaran. He scanned the walls and the ground along the path. He pointed at the ground. "However, it appears there was recent activity. V has tracked Billozein's trail to a facility up ahead on the ground floor. We may find some answers there."

They reached the cavern floor and headed toward the facility.

Emily tapped Dr. Snowden's arm. "Are your nanobots tingling?"

"They are and started when we entered this section of the facility."

Jane looked around. "I don't have nanobots, but the hairs on my neck are raised."

Skar growled. "This place makes me uneasy."

"Intuition," said Evaran, turning his head halfway to the side. "It has served both your species well."

Skar's eyes darted over to Evaran for a moment, then back forward.

They reached the building after another ten minutes.

Dr. Snowden noted that the doorway was open, and a light illuminated the inside.

Evaran motioned forward. "V, scout mode."

"Acknowledged. Scout mode engaged," said V. He shimmered out of view and flew inside. After a few minutes, he came back out. "Analysis. No life-forms detected."

Dr. Snowden relaxed a bit after realizing he had been tensing up. All his senses told him they were alone, but the dancing shadows and eerie quietness bothered him. Although he felt more relaxed, his pulsing nanobots were not. The usual slowdown of everything around him seemed to amplify their effects. It reminded him of when he was on the space habitat earlier. His breathing staggered.

Evaran entered the building. "Let us see what is inside."

Jane noticed Dr. Snowden had been acting unusual ever since they came to the cavern floor. She could empathize; this place gave her the creeps. It was seemingly empty, but she could not help feeling like they were being watched. Probably Billozein observing them remotely.

She exhaled from her nose and entered the building behind Dr. Snowden. Her gaze focused on the cylindrical capsules along the back wall. They stood out in the large room packed with workstations. Several tables with equipment that she was unfamiliar with littered the floor. One thing she was sure of was the smell of blood. She waved her hand in front of her. "It smells great in here."

Dr. Snowden tapped his helmet. "I'm glad I have this up."

Jane tapped at her ARI, causing a transparent faceplate to cover her face. "Good idea." She walked over to the capsules and ran her hand along the cool glass-like front piece. Inside the capsule was a Kalesh, but its back had been ripped open, and it was facing away from her. A white substance pulsed around the spine. She waved everyone over. "Is that . . . Billozein's progeny?"

Evaran walked over to where Jane was and scanned the capsule with his ring. "That is correct. The mechanical device is slightly different. Interesting."

Jane turned her head to the clinking noises near one of the work tables.

Skar was picking up various objects. "Augments." He pulled his lips in and looked around. "So this is where he makes them."

Evaran raised a finger. "Makes them, yes. However, I believe the ones in this building, specifically, were meant for testing."

Skar walked over to Evaran while holding a thin cylindrical device with wires dangling off it. "How do you know that?"

Evaran pointed at the Kalesh in the capsule. "You can see the incision marks where they have been implanted. Billozein was not only creating and then enslaving these creatures, he was giving them augments. A superpowered army to do his bidding."

Skar bared his teeth. "So . . . augmented mutant Kalesh. They did not deserve this."

Jane could see Skar was visibly shaken. It was not every day you learned that your race is being experimented on to create mutant augmented versions. She glanced at Emily. "You saw this on the habitat?"

"Yeah, except they were human."

"And this . . . is what was inside Chris," said Jane with a sigh. "There were no augments, though, right?"

"Right. It was just these things in them."

Dr. Snowden looked at some of the other capsules. "It seems these were in various states. Is the creature infectious?"

Emily shook her head. "Not that I know of, and you *don't* want to know how Billozein puts whatever these things are inside."

Dr. Snowden raised his eyebrows.

Evaran placed his UIC on one of the workstations. After a moment, he rubbed his chin. "Intriguing. The mechanical device *is* unique to each species. It allows Billozein to issue commands, and I have identified the control communication aspect of it. When we get back to the Torvatta, I will look into a way to disrupt that communication and maybe reset the programming of his progeny."

Jane grimaced as her eye caught a blue cube sitting on one of the work tables. She pointed at it. "What's that . . ."

Evaran walked over to the device and scanned it. "It is a communication device."

"What does it communicate with?" asked Jane.

Evaran placed his UIC on it, and after a moment, the cube glowed. "We will find out."

Everyone assembled around the cube. After a minute, a hologram of Billozein in Kalesh form appeared above the cube.

Jane noticed that it looked like Billozein was sitting in a ship.

"So . . . you found my research lab and figured out how to communicate with me. Impressive. I was content to observe you," said Billozein.

"It is apparent to me you are creating an army at this point. Why are you doing this?" asked Evaran.

Billozein chuckled. "Like you don't know. I will sweep across this galaxy and nothing, not even you, will stop me."

"I do not think you understand how big the galaxy is, or what is out there, to make that claim. There are those who would crush you as an afterthought."

Billozein growled. "Guess we'll see, won't we? What's important right now is that you're following me. I gave you an out, time traveler, and you didn't take it. This time, you won't have a choice. I now know your ship is temporally shielded. Otherwise, you wouldn't be here. Your ship is a lot tougher than I would've thought to survive a habitat blowing up around it."

"My ship is unique," said Evaran. "Nonetheless, I cannot allow you to roam free. Your malicious intent is now verified. I will find you wherever you go."

Billozein laughed. "I don't think so. Let me ask you . . . how long does it take for a timeline to render an update from the moment it is created?"

"Twenty minutes, relatively."

Billozein smirked. "Very good. You're not as clueless as I thought. Since you're away from your ship, a timeline change will . . . wash you away, like so much trash."

"We can get to my ship in twenty minutes."

"You could but . . . ," said Billozein, tapping at a console to his side, "you won't be doing that. No . . . Your journey ends here. I have to waste another time jump for you, but that's okay. Yet another time traveler I've had to teach a harsh lesson to. I'll give you some credit, you survived a habitat destruction event when a Time Warden didn't."

"It does not need to end like this. Surrender, and we can clear all this up."

Billozein smirked. "You're nuts. You can't leave it alone, can you? Trying till the very end. How noble. I am far and away more important than you. Smarter too, apparently. You know what, I think this time I'll punish the Kalesh, in your memory. You can think of that during your last twenty minutes."

The projection vanished.

Evaran extended a hand. He perused his UIC and then swiped his hands across it. After a moment, the cube stopped glowing. "We can speak freely now."

Skar shook his head. "What is all this talk about time travel and timeline changes?"

"It is not important for now," said Evaran. "First things first, let us get out of this facility."

A series of loud clanging noises rang out from outside the building.

Jane gulped. "What was that?"

Evaran pulled off his utility handle and extended it into a staff. "I suspect it is what will try to prevent us from leaving. Prepare for battle."

Jane's heartbeat shot up. Looking around, Evaran, Dr. Snowden, and Emily seemed calm and determined. Skar looked like he was about to jump out of his skin. She did not blame him; she could feel something bad was about to occur.

"V, scouting mode," said Evaran.

"Acknowledged. Scouting mode engaged," said V as he shimmered out of view. He flew out of the building.

Evaran tossed an orb out. It shot a projection of the aerial view from V.

Jane swallowed hard as she saw hundreds of Kalesh with slick fur approaching the building. They were pouring out of the containers stacked along the wall. "Okay . . . It looks like Billozein's army was further along than expected."

Evaran nodded. "I suspect these were to be shipped all around Roeth. Billozein has decided to release his progeny on us instead. This will be a rough fight. Stay close together. We head to the ramp leading out of this floor, then to the exit. Skar, Emily, you have the right side. Dr. Snowden, Jane, you have the left. We move as one on my lead."

"Why don't we wait here for twenty minutes?" asked Dr. Snowden.

"A good question. However, there is the possibility that this mine does not exist in the new timeline."

Dr. Snowden's eyes widened. "Oh . . . yeah. Good point."

"This timeline business again," said Skar.

Jane glanced at Skar. "You ready for this?"

"Not really, but looks like we don't have a choice. I'm not fully sure what's going on here. I'll figure it out once when we get topside," said Skar with bared teeth.

"I will explain everything in detail once we are out," said Evaran.

"Let's get this over with," said Skar, laying his ears back.

Jane knew that flattened ears and bared teeth was the sign of a nervous Kalesh. She had seen it many times before. She lightly squeezed Skar's trembling arm. "We'll get through this."

Skar bobbed his head.

Evaran looked around at everyone, then moved forward. "Move!" He exited the building with Skar and Emily taking up the right side behind him. Dr. Snowden and Jane took the other side.

Jane's breathing staggered at the sheer amount of Kalesh swarming. Their stuttered movement and odd wailing unnerved her. The lighting didn't help. There was an area around them where they could see with good visibility. Outside that was a sea of eyes that approached them. Although her focus was on keeping the Kalesh at a distance, she admired Evaran's ability to clear a path. He was a swirling tornado that tossed Kalesh left and right. The sound of Skar's gun and Dr. Snowden's and Emily's repulsion blasts was deafening.

At the halfway mark, three Kalesh jumped Dr. Snowden and dragged him to the ground.

Jane rushed forward, shooting the one on Dr. Snowden's right arm.

Dr. Snowden pointed his repulsing weapon at one and sent it flying.

V, flying above, hit the other with a repulsion blast.

Two more Kalesh rushed in, but fell prey to V and Dr. Snowden's combined attack.

Jane realized they would not let him get up. She stood over Dr. Snowden and grabbed his hand. While lifting him, she shot around in a 270-degree arc, making sure not to fire forward.

Dr. Snowden stood and shook his arm ahead. "C'mon! We're falling behind."

Jane looked ahead and noticed that Evaran had stopped.

Emily had charged back through a stream of Kalesh toward Dr. Snowden and Jane. When she reached them, she held her ground. "Let's go!"

Jane grabbed Dr. Snowden, and with Emily, they ran to Evaran. She thought her eyes were playing tricks on her. Evaran was a blur. He would appear for one moment with his staff on a Kalesh right before it went flying. Then he would be a blur until he hit another one. He danced around in a circle, striking and shooting repulsion beams, while Skar knelt in the middle, firing wildly.

Evaran paused for a moment to check on everyone, then continued on.

They reached the base of the ramp and inched their way up it.

Jane noticed that the group configuration had changed. While she, Emily, and Dr. Snowden held the rear as they moved up, Evaran and Skar cleared the front. This was a lot easier than when they were on the ground floor. V was slightly behind them, keeping the group at the base of the ramp on their backs.

When they reached the top, the Kalesh behind them massed up despite V's best effort.

Evaran motioned for everyone to head out the mining doors in the distance.

When Jane and the others ran past Evaran and then out the mining doors, she glanced back in.

Evaran was running full tilt toward the door. The two Kalesh guards and V were just inside the doors, unloading on the mutants.

After Evaran, V, and the guards burst outside, Jane motioned for the others to try to close the door.

Dr. Snowden raised his hand. "We won't need to do that. The twenty minutes is about up."

Skar bent over, trying to catch his breath. "What happens then?"

"The timeline changes."

After a few moments, the environment shimmered.

Jane gasped as Skar and the guards disappeared. The mining door facility vanished, and in its place was solid stone. All went quiet as the environment normalized. She looked around frantically. "Where did the Kalesh go!"

Evaran sighed as he looked at where the mining facility had been. "We can cover it when we get back to the Torvatta. V, bring it around."

"Acknowledged," said V. He flew off into the distance.

A humming sound nearby boomed out above them.

Evaran motioned toward the trees. "We need to move, now!"

As they entered the nearby forest, Jane looked up. Her heartbeat surged as she recognized the design and logo. It was a Voss Imperium light fighter craft.

16

Dr. Snowden eased back into his chair in the conference room. V had pulled around the Torvatta in stealth mode, allowing them to board it without being detected. He had come to view the Torvatta as his mobile home. It had everything he needed and could go anywhere. Like Evaran, it was a beacon of hope that made him feel secure. Given all the timeline changes, it was also one of the safest places to be.

He took a bite of the sandwich he had grabbed from the replicator. After swallowing it, he took a sip of his root beer as he watched Jane and Emily choose what to eat or drink at the replicators. Evaran sat in his usual chair, going over something in his ARI. V, in orb mode, had joined them and rested on two of his segmented extensions at the end of the table opposite Evaran.

Jane took her seat to the right of Evaran while Emily took hers on the other side next to Dr. Snowden.

Dr. Snowden noticed that Jane had some type of green beverage, while Emily had a container of water and some beef jerky, or at least that is what it looked like to him.

Evaran looked around. "I will keep this brief. I know everyone is probably tired, and we have done quite a bit in a short amount of time. Billozein has caused a timeline change as you all saw. We will need to discover what the differences are and then try to pinpoint where he is. This time, we are going to put a quantum beacon on his ship. That will tell us exactly where he is even if he time jumps."

"Good idea," said Jane. She wrinkled her eyebrows. "Regarding this new timeline . . . let me see if I got this right. That mining facility never existed." She glanced at Dr. Snowden. "If we had stayed down there . . ."

Evaran furrowed his eyebrows. "We would have been encased in stone. Your temporal shielding would have made the stone go around you, but in effect, you would have been immobilized."

Jane gulped. "We woulda died."

"That is correct."

Dr. Snowden looked down. He had thought maybe they could have waited it out. If Evaran had not been there, it would have been yet another disastrous decision. It seemed when pressured, he made shortsighted decisions without thinking them through. He wondered if that was a remnant of his past anger issues impacting him.

"Billozein did not know that we had individual temporal shielding due to the Torvatta," said Evaran. "That is a unique ability of the Torvatta. Even so, if he did determine that we did, he would have made sure no mining facility was built. I do not know if the Voss ship was to ensure that no one came out or a coincidence."

"Cover all angles," said Jane, shaking her head.

"It would appear so," said Evaran. He tapped at the table console, causing a projection of the ship they had seen earlier to appear. "This ship is of Voss origin."

"Yeah, but it looks way more advanced than any Voss ship I've seen, and that's from my era, assuming we're still in the past."

"We are still in the past, but will go back to the future in order to compare against the previous timelines," said Evaran.

"Works for me."

"When you finish having lunch, meet me in the command area. Then we can begin our analysis of this new timeline," said Evaran. He shut off the projection and exited the room with V in tow.

Dr. Snowden took a bite of his sandwich. "Lot to take in, huh?"

Jane looked down. "I'm twice removed now from everything I knew. It's starting to sink in." She looked up with a smirk. "I'm a true time refugee."

Dr. Snowden chuckled. "Well, you're in good company then." He glanced at Emily. "You know, I have been wondering if there is a copy of us back on Earth, given our last adventure."

"We can always check," said Emily.

Dr. Snowden noticed a sadness in Emily's eyes. He knew that somewhere in her heart was the desire to see her father again. With something like the Torvatta, that would be easy to do, assuming it stayed stealthed. Maybe someday they would. He knew he would not mind seeing his brother again, but it would be hard to do without being able to talk to him. It would be even rougher for Emily. A lump formed in his throat.

Jane glanced at Dr. Snowden. "So if I hadn't come aboard the Torvatta, I would have blinked out like Skar and the other Kalesh."

Dr. Snowden nodded.

"How do you two do it? I mean, meeting people that potentially might not have ever existed? That must be unsettling."

Emily bobbed her head. "It can be. On our last adventure, we met a lot of people who now don't exist, but that doesn't mean they weren't real. At least to me."

"The Earth guard," said Dr. Snowden.

Jane perked up. "The nonhuman group?"

"Yeah. They were fighting a human-supremacist group called the Purifiers. When we changed the timeline in the past, though, all the people we had met in that future version of humanity disappeared along with the timeline change."

"The Purifiers . . . ," said Jane. "There is a small group that calls themselves the Purists, but they used to be called Purifiers. Human supremacists, very anti-augment. They cling to a belief that an overlord will save them and travel everywhere looking for that. They're harmless, but kinda out there."

Dr. Snowden glanced at Emily, then back at Jane. "The overlord didn't fare too well with us."

"If you had told me that before knowing what I know now, I wouldn't have believed it. You two have seen so much. This must be a typical trip for you both."

Emily snorted. "Traveling with Evaran is never dull, that's for sure."

Dr. Snowden finished his sandwich, then stood. "I'm with you there. Ready to see what this new timeline is all about?"

"Yep. Before we leave, though, I wanted to say to both of you, thank you for being understanding," said Jane.

Emily and Dr. Snowden both smiled at Jane.

They met up with Evaran in the command center and took their seats.

Evaran tapped at his chair console. "V, take us to space, then forward to July 16, 3104, at two ten p.m. Once there, stealth and take us to Corunus."

"Acknowledged."

Jane scooted to the edge of her chair and stared intently at the left screen.

Dr. Snowden enjoyed seeing Jane's reaction to the Torvatta's traveling aspects. It was routine to him now, but it never lost its charm.

The left screen showed the Torvatta reaching space. Once there, everything faded out, then eased back in.

"Torvatta stealth mode engaged."

The Torvatta flew for a bit before syncing its orbit with Roeth.

Jane surveyed the screen. "No Corunus . . ."

"V, long-range scans," said Evaran.

"Acknowledged," said V. After a moment, the front right screen showed Roeth, with six green blips around it. "Multiple spacecraft detected."

"Take us to the nearest one and perform standard scans."

"Acknowledged."

Once the Torvatta reached the nearest starship, it flew around and scanned it.

Dr. Snowden noticed the design of the ship displayed on the right screen was unusual. It was large and had an aggressive profile. It looked like someone had cut out an arrowhead and slapped a large turtle shell on top. Labels shot out next to various segments, highlighting how well armed the ship was. Antennae and smaller sections jutted out. The back of it had large orange thrusters, and the body looked like it had large steel straps across it. It was something he had never seen before.

Jane gasped. "That's a Voss Imperium cruiser, but like the other ship, much more advanced. It's slightly bigger too."

"There are four of these, one larger one, and another one similar in size but of a different design," said Evaran.

"That doesn't bode well," said Jane. "The United Planets, and especially the Kalesh, would never have allowed this."

"It is possible the Voss Imperium war did not end in the Kalesh's favor. I suspect Billozein's influence here."

Dr. Snowden looked at Evaran. "So . . . what do we do then?"

Evaran touched his fingertips in front of him. "Hmm." He looked at Jane. "Suggestions?"

"We met Warlord Okon, then Ambassador Okon. Is it possible he's still around? In some other role? We could also check in with the United Planets."

"Good ideas," said Evaran. "We can check on Okon, and then if you know where we could meet with the United Planets, we can do that." He looked around. "Any concerns?"

Everyone shook their head.

"V, take us to where we met Warlord Okon previously and scan for life signs."

"Acknowledged."

The Torvatta angled toward Roeth and flew to it. After thirty minutes, the Torvatta reached the area where they had met Warlord Okon previously and flew around scanning the ground.

Dr. Snowden watched as the scans showed nothing for a while. His attention peaked when a cave entrance a bit away showed three life signs. It seemed to stick out given that they had not seen anything near where they had initially come down.

"Analysis. Three life signs detected. Pattern matches that of the Kalesh."

"Noted. Take us down and land in front of that entrance."

"Acknowledged."

The Torvatta flew toward the entrance, and when it was over it, set down.

"V, scout mode."

"Acknowledged. Scouting mode engaged," said V. He took off toward the Torvatta entrance, shimmered out of view, then flew out.

Dr. Snowden watched the left screen with rapture. It showed the view from V, while the right screen showed details relative to what was on the left screen.

When V hovered over the Kalesh, the right screen showed them to be normal. Various statistics were listed, along with a listing of equipment.

Jane scrunched her face. "They're not using state-of-the-art equipment."

"If this is where his group is hiding, they may not have the ability to procure much," said Evaran.

V flew into the cave entrance for a while, showing Kalesh families in tattered clothing. Every third or fourth Kalesh shown had a weapon, some were advanced, while most seemed to be low-tech. It did not take long for V to reach a large opening where Okon was detected.

Evaran tapped at his chair console. "V, relay the command center visual."

V flew up and shot down a projection of the Torvatta's command center.

"Greetings. We mean you no harm," said Evaran.

Kalesh jumped up and raised their weapons.

Okon stood. "Wait!" He walked up to the projection and waved his hand through it. "It's a projection." He looked up.

Evaran cleared his throat. "Okon, do you have a moment to speak?"

The Kalesh talked in hushed whispers as Okon stood back. "Who am I talking to?"

Evaran pointed at himself, then around the room. "I am Evaran. I have with me Dr. Albert Snowden, Emily Snowden, and Jane Trellis. The projection you are seeing is being shown by my friend V."

Okon snorted. "Well . . . aren't we all fancy."

The Kalesh around him snickered.

"What do you want?"

"A history lesson."

The Kalesh laughed.

Okon sneered. "A history lesson? On what?"

"The Voss Imperium war and United Planets involvement, if any," said Evaran.

"And . . . I know this isn't some Voss Imperium trick . . . how?"

"Would it help if we met in person, in private?"

Okon nodded. "It would. Where are you?"

"We are stealthed in front of your cave entrance."

Okon's eyebrows raised. He motioned at a Kalesh who interacted with a device.

After a moment, the Kalesh shook its head.

"Your stealth must be pretty good. My scouts don't see or smell anything."

Evaran tapped at his chair console, causing the Torvatta to disengage stealth mode.

"Check again."

Okon motioned at the Kalesh again. This time the Kalesh nodded after checking his device.

"Your technology is advanced," said Okon.

"Thank you. We can meet then?"

Okon sighed. "On one condition. We need food, drink, and medical supplies. You provide it, and I will allow this meeting."

"You are a true leader of your people. Tell V what you need, and he will make sure you get it while we meet. Fair enough?"

Okon paused for a moment. "You have a deal. My guards will escort you in. I would cloak your ship, though. Last thing we need is the Voss detecting it."

"A wise decision. We will be out momentarily."

The screen went blank.

As Jane walked behind Evaran, she grimaced at the poor conditions of the Kalesh. Whatever had happened to them, it did not look good. She had been used to seeing healthy Kalesh during her stay in Da Nesh. Hunger lived in these tunnels as a permanent resident. The tunnels were lit by lights embedded into the walls at uneven intervals, and the pungent smell of feces was ever present. Her attention focused ahead as a pale red ball bounced out from a hallway on the side.

Evaran caught the ball and held it up.

A young Kalesh girl that came up to Jane's knee stood at the hallway entrance.

Evaran bent down and extended the ball toward the young female. With a smile, he said, "Well hello, little one. I believe this is yours."

The girl's big eyes blinked as she dipped her head down and to the side.

Evaran extended his arm farther.

The girl grabbed the ball and smiled at Evaran. In a shy voice, she said, "Thank you."

Evaran's eyes sparkled. "You are most welcome."

An elder Kalesh female hustled up behind the girl and grabbed her. "What have I told you about aliens? They're dangerous!" She shot a glare back at Evaran as she hustled the girl away.

Evaran stood up and sighed. He looked down for a moment, then continued following the guard.

Jane knew the Kalesh were skittish of aliens, and she bet that the Voss did not help things. Kalesh children melted her heart.

Evaran's kind actions were not lost on Jane. He was still an enigma to her, but with all his power, he did not appear to be corrupt. The thought of traveling with him was easier to digest after she had thought about it. She could not go back to what she knew since it was no longer there. The thought that maybe she could exist in a timeline with her duplicate intrigued her, but it would not be the same. Getting to travel through space and time set her mind on fire with ideas, and it would be with people she implicitly trusted and enjoyed being around. A decision would need to be reached before Evaran and crew left. She sighed as she continued forward.

After fifteen minutes, they reached a large, open room.

Jane surveyed the room. It reminded her of an assembly hall, with rows of benches and a raised platform at the front. Okon stood with several armed Kalesh around him. She picked him out immediately. In any timeline, his physique was a constant. The fact that she was now seeing a third version of Okon was no longer a surprise to her. She wondered what it would have looked like if Evaran and crew had met three versions of her.

The two guards stepped to the side when Evaran and the others arrived in front of Okon.

Okon sized up Evaran. "You're much taller in person."

"May we speak in private?" asked Evaran.

"My guards will be just outside this room."

"Another wise decision."

Okon waved off the guards, who then exited the room.

"Where do you want your supplies delivered?" asked Evaran.

"I already sent someone to the entrance," said Okon. "He will show your friend where to take it."

"Very well. May we sit?"

"Of course."

Jane took a seat between Dr. Snowden and Emily. Evaran sat across the aisle while Okon stood in front of them.

"So . . . what history lesson do you need?" asked Okon.

Evaran extended his hand. A projection of the Voss ship in orbit they had seen earlier appeared as a projection from his ring. "This is a Voss Imperium ship. I am guessing the war did not go well."

Okon paused for a moment, then burst out laughing. "Is it that obvious? Yeah, we lost the war, and it wasn't even close. They hit us so hard and fast we had no time to retaliate. It was like they knew *exactly* where to strike."

Evaran rubbed his chin. "I see. And what about the United Planets? Did they not help?"

"Wouldn't have mattered. By the time we sent communication off to them, Roeth had been conquered. The Voss Imperium settled in, rounded up Kalesh as slaves, and now they enjoy their new colony."

Jane perked her head up. "The United Planets would still have tried."

"Oh . . . they did. Their fleet got trashed. I've never seen a battle so lopsided. The vaunted United Planets drone swarms were commandeered and attacked their own fleet. It was like they had internal knowledge of the command protocols."

"Given the Voss ships I've seen, that's not too surprising. They seem . . . different."

Okon eyed Jane. "You look like a United Planets agent."

"I used to be one."

"And now you travel around asking for history lessons."

Jane shook her head as she chuckled. "I guess if you look at it that way, it does sound kinda funny."

Okon looked back at Evaran. "Not all Kalesh were enslaved. Some, like us, ran to the old cave networks our ancestors used, like this one. The Voss don't mess with us out here, but coming by food, water, and, hell, any supplies is darn near impossible."

Evaran raised a finger. "To help with that, V is delivering to you a matter replicator along with an element storage tank and a matter converter to fill it."

Okon's eyes widened. "How'd you get your hands on that? Or do I want to know?"

"There is nothing illegal about it, and it has a dampening field, so you do not need to worry about it being detected. It is preloaded with medicine, food, beverage, and structural patterns. You can add your own patterns through the interface."

Okon exhaled sharply from his mouth. "All that . . . just to know that the Voss kicked our ass?"

"Your people need help. It is the least I could do."

Okon cleared his throat. "Thank you. I have to ask . . . why is this information so important to you?"

Evaran glanced at Jane, Dr. Snowden, and Emily, then back at Okon. "We are time travelers. We came to this area because there was an anomaly."

Okon's lips parted. "Uhh . . . okay . . ."

Jane cleared her throat. "Did you teach at the Gunz Tahl Institute?"

"I'm not sure how you would know that, but yeah . . . long ago."

"Then you know about temporal mechanics. This is a real-world example. It's not theory. Trust me, I was where you were mentally, until I actually saw it."

Okon's eyes darted between Evaran, Dr. Snowden, Jane, and Emily. "This all sounds . . . a little off to me. Why are you all here, in this part of Roeth, though?"

"We were investigating the illegal augment trade," said Evaran. He gestured at Jane. "She was a United Planets agent stationed in Da Nesh. When Dr. Snowden, Emily, and I arrived, we met up with Jane. She suggested we meet with Warlord Okon to find out details."

Okon jerked his head back. "Warlord!"

"Yes, and you tried to kill us to send a message to aliens coming to Roeth that it was not safe. You were unsuccessful."

Okon harrumphed as he looked at Jane. "And you were in Da Nesh?"

"Yeah. I loved it. I really miss it. My timeline is gone, though."

"I'm sorry to hear that," said Okon with furrowed eyebrows. "Da Nesh *was* a beautiful city. Now it's a Voss Imperium–controlled refugee camp. More like a prison, if you ask me. Okay . . . so I . . . didn't kill you. Then what?"

"We discovered the illegal augments came from a company called Advanced Dynamics, ran by a creature called Billozein. In our effort to capture him, he did something that caused the timeline to change. In the new timeline, we investigated Corunus—"

"What's that?" asked Okon.

"A joint United Planets and Kalesh space station."

"Oh."

"Once we went there, we met with Ambassador Okon."

Okon snorted. "Ambassador!"

Jane, Dr. Snowden, and Emily chuckled.

"You appeared to enjoy your role," said Evaran.

Okon sighed. "Any opportunity like that has been long gone. Let me guess the next steps. This . . . Billozein thing . . . caused another timeline change, and now you're here trying to figure out the timeline differences. Am I right?"

"You are indeed wise."

"So what happens if you catch this . . . thing?" asked Okon.

Evaran tilted his head. "It will reset the timeline to its original design."

"The Voss Imperium . . . ," said Okon with narrowed eyes.

"I predict that if we reset the timeline, they will lose the war, and Roeth will have a United Planets presence. Also, this meeting would never have occurred."

Okon exhaled from his nose. "I would disappear, and you might meet another Okon?"

"Hopefully not a warlord version."

Okon laughed. "I like you. Aliens could learn a thing or two from you." He smirked. "You probably want to know if I know anything about this Billozein thing, but as you can tell, I've never heard of him or it or whatever it is. However . . . you mentioned augments. That's one thing the Voss seem to have in abundance. When their troops landed, we fought them in the forests. I've never seen a group move and fight in such a coordinated manner, or at the speed that they did."

Evaran glanced at Jane. "Do you recall if the Voss historically from your timeline had augments?"

Jane shook her head. "I don't recall hearing anything about that, but I'm sure they had some. Nothing that would give them such a huge advantage technologically, though."

Okon rubbed his chin. "Well, there's your answer then. If in the other timelines the Voss Imperium were defeated, but not this one, then the Voss Imperium have an advantage they didn't have before."

Jane pondered Okon's words, then slowly raised her head. "Billozein helped the Voss Imperium!"

Okon smirked. "That's my thought as well. Good luck trying to find him. I wouldn't even know where to begin looking."

Jane's eyes darted around as she tapped her fingertips together. "I may know someone who might . . ."

"Andrew. It is a start," said Evaran. He stood, causing the others to stand. With an extended hand, he said, "V has delivered the matter replicator unit and the associated devices. We appreciate your help. Before we go, I am curious. I have met Warlord Okon and Ambassador Okon. What title do I ascribe to you?"

"Surviving Okon," said Okon with a chuckle. "If you're being serious, I guess Rebel Leader Okon."

Evaran shook Okon's hand. "It fits." He glanced at Dr. Snowden, Jane, and Emily. "Anything else we need to cover?"

Jane bobbed her head. "I'm good."

Dr. Snowden and Emily shook their heads.

"Very well," said Evaran with a final nod at Okon. He gestured to the exit. "To find Andrew then."

17

Dr. Snowden sat in the Torvatta command center and watched the screens as the Torvatta flew into space. He went over their meeting with Okon. Billozein was going to push his augments, and now technology, every chance he got in order to further his goals. Based on what Okon said, Billozein used the Voss to create progeny like he had with humans and Kalesh.

Jane tapped at his arm. "Thinking hard?"

"No . . . I was . . . thinking about our meeting with Okon."

Jane smirked. "I'm starting to get used to meeting different versions of people, and to a greater extent, seeing all these timeline changes."

"You'll get used to it," said Dr. Snowden. He noticed Evaran casting a sidelong glance at him.

Evaran tapped at his chair console.

The front right screen turned into a map showing the part of the galaxy they were in, which included Earth and Roeth.

Small, scattered red dots appeared with a green line around multiple solar systems.

Evaran gestured at the map. "Jane, where would Andrew be?"

Jane stood up and walked over to the map. After a moment, she had zoomed into a space station near Jupiter. "He would be there. It's one of several major command centers for the United Planets. This is where he was before going to Roeth, at least."

"V, take us there," said Evaran.

"Acknowledged."

Jane sat back down as the Torvatta opened a portal and flew through it.

The Torvatta exited near a large space station.

Dr. Snowden noted it looked different from Corunus. This one was much larger and reminded him a bit of the Purifier space station he had seen in another adventure. The station had a large half-dome top with a rotating cylinder under it. Rings extended around the cylinder. Ships of all sizes flew around, and others were docked.

Several ships and drones approached the Torvatta.

"Analysis. Communication protocols analyzed. Incoming transmission."

The screen flickered for a moment.

A male human appeared on the screen, with a white two-piece suit. Various technical-looking pads appeared on the arms, legs, and chest. "You have entered United Planets space. Your ship was not detected until now. Explain."

Evaran tapped at his chair console. "I am relaying to you our credentials."

The man looked away for a moment, then looked back with widened eyes. "My mistake. I apologize for any delay. Please proceed."

The screen went blank.

Jane chuckled. "That Evaran Protocol works pretty well."

Evaran looked down. "Unfortunately, too well. I did not know it would have this level of impact."

"You're regretting putting it in place?" asked Jane.

"I will . . . modify it . . . after we capture Billozein."

It was obvious to Dr. Snowden that something about the protocol bothered Evaran. Dr. Snowden figured their arrival at Roeth and the subsequent notifications to all power groups was a consideration. Warlord Okon's power play was one action that resulted from the mere knowledge of it. He did not know what Evaran would do, but his gut told him that Evaran was probably going to wipe out any mention of his past events.

"Landing pad coordinates received," said V.

"Take us in and put us into scan profile two," said Evaran.

"Acknowledged."

The Torvatta flew toward the surface of a drumlike cylinder. A rectangular landing pad outlined in green on the front left screen. Once the Torvatta had landed, the pad descended. Doors above the pad sealed shut. After a moment, the pad came to a stop. A beam shot out and scanned the Torvatta.

Evaran stood and gestured at the exit. "Let us go."

Dr. Snowden took a measured breath as he stood along with Jane and Emily. This would be his first look at what he imagined humanity to be like in the future. The last version he had seen was the human-supremacist Purifiers. He glanced at Emily, who was flexing her hands. He could tell she was thinking along the same lines as he. The landing sequence was different than what he had seen previously. Maybe it was an older approach, given how close it was to Earth. It would make sense that any advanced docking or hangar bays would be built near new construction.

V flew past Dr. Snowden as he exited the Torvatta.

Dr. Snowden looked up at V. "Orb mode again this time?"

V stretched out two of his extensions and landed with them serving as legs. He positioned the other two into a teapot pose. His top light glowed for a moment. "Yes."

Dr. Snowden, Jane, and Emily chuckled.

Dr. Snowden noticed that there were several humanoid robots and androids walking around. It made sense to him to use them in a potentially dangerous environment to organics. Looking around, he wondered where or when the decontamination sequence would occur.

They crossed the hangar and walked into a small tunnel that was roughly eight feet wide. The end of the tunnel had a solid door, and once they were all in, the other side closed up. A light beam rose from the floor while a mist enveloped the room.

Dr. Snowden remembered this sequence. He looked at Evaran. "This kinda feels like the Krotovore mist."

Evaran moved his hand through the mist, causing swirling trails to follow it. After a moment, he said, "Now that you mention it, it appears to be similar in composition. That seems unusual."

Emily ran her hand through the mist. "You don't think Krotovore technology got to Earth somehow, do you? There were two crashed ships, from what I remember."

"I do not know, but it is now something I will need to look into."

Emily glanced at Dr. Snowden.

Dr. Snowden ran a hand over his mouth and off to the side of his face. Maybe that Krotovore technology was recovered. It would seem that their abduction when they met Evaran might be part of something bigger in Earth's history relative to this point in time.

After a minute, the mist was sucked back in, and the light lines that had been scanning them dissipated. The door in front of them slid open.

They entered a small hexagonal room with an android and two humanoid robot guards.

The android approached them. "How may I be of assistance?"

"Are you going to register us?" asked Evaran.

"You are already registered."

"I see," said Evaran. "Where would we find Andrew Dotrick?"

The android paused for a moment and dipped his head. He raised it back up and looked at Evaran. "Shall I contact him?"

"Please do."

The android paused for a moment before speaking. "He has been notified of your arrival. Do you need a guide?"

Extending his right arm, Evaran said, "Please proceed."

The android pivoted along with the two robot guards, and everyone followed them out of the room.

Dr. Snowden smiled as he looked around the large, open-air plaza they entered. It had technical-looking pillars that stood roughly ten feet tall spaced out across the expanse. On the pillars' sides were screens and various holo projections shooting out. Various lounges and side stores with open fronts ringed the plaza.

The plaza was part of an advanced large city with a light-blue sky. He enjoyed the warm weather and cool breeze. Transportation tubes seemed to interconnect buildings, and small rivers ran through the city. He wondered how they got it all to work.

He snorted at the amount of advertising he saw. Even in the future, humanity had not moved past that. The amount of aliens relieved him. No human supremacy here. Everything was clean, organized, and very technical-looking, similar to the space habitat. Heavy-suited human guards stood around while other humans in white two-piece suits with silver segmented lines bustled around.

Emily swatted his arm. "Focus."

Dr. Snowden raised his eyebrows while shrugging. When he thought about traveling with Evaran through space and time, it was moments like this that he valued highly. With a swat back at Emily's arm, he said, "Let's do this."

Emily shook her head while Jane chuckled.

After trawling through several more expansive plazas, buildings, corridors, and elevators, they reached Andrew's office. The android gestured at the outline of a door on the wall.

Evaran bowed. "Thank you."

The android stared at Evaran for a moment, then took off with the two robot guards behind him.

Jane glanced at Dr. Snowden, who lightly squeezed her arm. Meeting a timeline version of Okon was one thing, but a version of Andrew would be different.

Evaran interacted with the door console, causing the door interior to form a glowing hexagonal pattern before dissipating.

Emily entered the room first, with Dr. Snowden behind her.

Jane walked in and saw that it was of typical United Planets design. She gasped as she saw that Andrew was not alone. Although he looked similar to how she remembered him, it was this timeline's version of herself standing next to

Andrew that caught her attention. Apparently she caught this timeline version's attention as well. It would seem that even with Roeth occupied, she still worked as an agent. Based on the decorations on the other Jane's uniform, she was a higher rank than Andrew. Maybe Chris was here too.

After an awkward moment, Andrew tapped at his desk, causing four chairs to slide out from the walls. After everyone was seated, he glanced at Evaran, then Jane. "This should be interesting. Please feel free to begin."

"Thank you. First off, did the android that brought us here explain to you who we were?"

"Oh yeah . . . and my boss," he said, nodding at the other Jane, "thought the protocols were myths. I will say I wasn't expecting to see the Evaran Protocol activated, though."

Jane scrutinized the other Jane. It seemed that regardless of the timeline, her career path was constant. Andrew seemed more subdued than she remembered. She had expected him to jump out of his chair, but maybe being of a lower rank had something to do with that.

Evaran raised a finger. "Very good. Let me bring you up to speed on why we are here. We are investigating a timeline anomaly caused by a creature known as Billozein. He has already changed the timeline twice." He gestured at Jane. "She is from the original timeline we entered, and due to being on my ship when the timeline changed, she crossed over to the new timeline with us."

"Not surprised about the timeline talk," said Andrew, gesturing at Evaran. "Your journeys are well documented, and I've studied all I could about them. Studying all these mysterious protocols is kind of a passion of mine. In regards to Billozein . . . he's well-known around here."

"Elaborate," said Evaran.

"Well, for starters, he armed every empire around the United Planets with technology superior to ours," said Andrew. "We lost ground to the Drodalian Hegemony. The Tartark Federation crushed us at the battle of Kirus. At Roeth, one of our fleets was demolished by the Voss Imperium. These are all battles we should've won. We've caught up technology-wise thanks to our intelligence efforts, but the United Planets lost over twenty-five percent of what it was before."

"He has been busy, it seems. His goal is to build an army. That would be easier with one of the stronger empires weakened."

"Not only that, he has also flushed illegal augments throughout the United Planets. Crime has shot through the roof."

Evaran rubbed his chin. "We came from Roeth. In the previous timeline, the Voss Imperium had lost that war. Obviously, it is now occupied in this timeline, so we believe Billozein is working with the Voss."

Andrew chuckled. "Well, you came to the right place. We don't know exactly where he's at, but have a general idea." He tapped at his desk, causing a projection of a galactic map to appear. He pointed at a swath of nine blinking red dots. "There. Nine facilities deep in Voss Imperium space. He could be at any one of those. These were identified because we traced the illegal augments to there. Anyways, if he's at any of them, we have no way of getting there."

"Hmm," said Evaran, rubbing his chin. "So he decided to use the Voss this time. Since they are already warlike, he would save some time." He tilted his head. "How did you come across this information?"

"We lost quite a few undercover agents getting it to us. One of the odder things mentioned in common in the reports was that some of the workers there seemed . . . to move in an unusual manner. They were like they were androids, but they weren't. They didn't act like how a Voss would normally act. If you're headed to these facilities, it's not going to be easy, even with a ship like yours. These are all heavily guarded."

Evaran placed his fingertips together. "My UIC can transfer any information you have on it."

"UIC . . . that's the card thing, right?"

"That is correct."

Andrew gestured at his desk. "Have at it."

Evaran placed his UIC on the desk. After a moment, it stabilized. "We will determine a course of action after studying what you have given us."

"Of course," said Andrew.

"Do you know where the information broker is?"

Andrew jerked his head back. "Haven't heard that name in a long time. No one knows where she is."

"A female this time," said Evaran. "And yes, once this is all over, I will give you a tour of the Torvatta."

A grin crept onto Andrew's face. "I'm guessing I must have asked that question before."

"You did."

"Can I at least see it from the outside for now?"

"If you wish," said Evaran.

Jane swallowed hard as she looked at the other Jane. There were so many questions she wanted to ask.

As if on cue, the other Jane tapped Andrew on the shoulder. "Why don't you go with Evaran. Jane and I can catch up."

"Oh . . . sure," said Andrew. He stood and paused to shoot a look at Jane, then exited the room with Evaran, Dr. Snowden, and Emily.

The other Jane sat in Andrew's seat. "I bet you have a lot of questions, as I do."

Jane exhaled from her mouth. "This is . . . so unusual."

"I bet," said the other Jane. "I've listened to Andrew talk about Evaran since—"

"He got security clearance to read about them," said Jane.

They looked at each other and laughed.

The other Jane tapped her fingertips together. "So . . . were you and Chris together . . ."

Jane looked down. "We were. He was killed six years ago by Billozein while working on a space habitat in the Riemens system."

"And you got a posting on Roeth to investigate," said the other Jane.

Jane gulped. "I did and asked Andrew to get me a posting out there and used up all of my political capital to get it done. Evaran came along and . . . here I am." She sighed. "Are you and Chris . . ."

The other Jane smiled and nodded.

"Can I . . . see a picture of him?"

"Sure," said the other Jane. She tapped at the desk, causing a projection to appear of Chris and her together with two little girls.

Jane grimaced as tears welled up in her eyes. Her body trembled as she saw what could never be. It was not fair. Chris was a bit older, and resembled Dr. Snowden in a lot of regards. She sniffled and pointed at the girls. "Lauren and Meghan?"

The other Jane swallowed hard.

Jane and Chris had a list of baby names picked out. If it had been a boy, it would have been Seth. She ran her fingers across her wet eyes to clear them out. "I . . . I'm sorry . . . was not expecting to see all of this."

The other Jane looked away and exhaled through her mouth. "If I was in your position, I'm not sure I could go on."

Jane's eyes softened. "You could. I have, anyways. It took me a long time to get over Chris's death. I was lonely, but . . . I had to know. When Evaran appeared, I knew that was my opportunity to find out what happened to him." She smirked. "In the second timeline, the one we just came from, that version of me . . . well, us, was dead. I suspect Billozein had a hand in it."

The other Jane shook her head. "He will pay for all this havoc he has caused. If you're going after Billozein, we can provide some help."

Jane looked down. "I think this is something we have to do ourselves. Evaran wouldn't want anyone else to be put in harm's way. It's just who he is."

The other Jane looked Jane over, and after a moment, she said, "I understand."

Jane's natural instinct would to have been to assemble a strike force, but given the nature of the Torvatta's temporal shielding and the potential for loss of life, she knew Evaran would not go for that. It was a sign that she was becoming used to being around Evaran.

The other Jane stood and smiled at Jane. "Well, my doppelganger, care to get something to eat at least?"

Jane chuckled as she stood. She met the other Jane's gaze.

"Chocolate ice cream," they said in unison. They laughed, then exited the room.

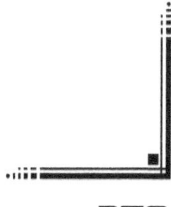

18

Jane pondered the last few hours as she approached the Torvatta. She had spent it with the other Jane, comparing and contrasting their lives. It was obvious to her now that she did not belong in this timeline.

If she stayed, it would have to be with the knowledge that Chris was alive, with children. Although the other Jane had said that it could be set up that Jane was an unknown twin sister to the kids, Jane knew she would not be able to be around Chris if she could not be with him.

The other Jane was exclusive with Chris. Although Fredorians could have open family groups with multiple members, some chose to be monogamous. Jane had been that way with her Chris. With a sigh, she entered the Torvatta.

Her clock said it was around 9:00 p.m. With a quick survey of the command center, she noticed it was unusually quiet. Maybe everyone was still out. She had let Dr. Snowden know she would spend some time with the other Jane.

V's and Evaran's voices rang out from the research lab.

Jane peered into the room. Evaran was at a workstation, moving his hands around as he focused intently on a projection in front of him. V hovered to his side and was shooting lights at the projection. It seemed to her they were engaged in some type of planning.

Evaran swiveled his head. "You are back. How was your visit?"

Jane walked over and stood next to them. "It was interesting. The other Jane has a full life. Married, kids, a great job with potential, and . . . she's happy."

"And you are not?"

Jane sighed. "I'm trying to be. Everything I know is gone." She waved her hand in an arc off to the side. "The Torvatta, you, V, Dr. Snowden, and Emily are the only constants in my life at the moment."

V's lights glowed a bit. "A time refugee."

Jane snorted. "That's me all right, and not by choice."

Evaran placed his palms together and pressed the top of his hands against his lips. "What do you intend to do after Billozein is captured?"

"I don't know. I can't stay in the timeline, especially if there is a duplicate of me and Chris."

"You could travel with us. Dr. Snowden and Emily have spoken highly of you and expressed an interest."

Jane swallowed hard. "I wasn't going to mention it but . . . I'd be interested. I mean . . . I enjoy being around you all. There is a lot to see and explore, and based off this one journey, I can see it's never a dull moment."

"I prefer the dull moments myself, but unfortunately, what I do and where I go tends to involve complexity." Evaran stood and extended a hand. "Very well. As Dr. Snowden would more than likely say, welcome to Evaran and the gang."

Jane's eyes lit up as she stepped forward and shook Eva-ran's hand. Her heartbeat raced as she contemplated this new chapter in her life. She stood back and exhaled sharply. "So . . . is there a handbook or anything I need to read or . . ."

Evaran walked over to a table. "V calculated a nine-ty-seven percent chance you would be interested. As such, I have constructed another personal support device for you. It is the same one Dr. Snowden and Emily have. Part of your journey with us will be to learn how to use it." He picked up the PSD and handed it to Jane.

Jane inspected the PSD as she flipped it around in her hand. She looked back up. "I will not disappoint you."

"I do not think you will, Jane Trellis."

"Are there any rules I should follow, outside of the ones I've seen?"

Evaran rubbed his chin. "The main rule we try to follow is to not volunteer information to those who should not have it. I know the example with Okon back at Roeth appears to be a violation of that, but given that the timeline will eventually be reset, no harm."

"I understand," said Jane. She cocked her head. "The Evaran Protocol . . . it had a lot of information on you. Andrew . . . well, my Andrew . . . let me see a copy of it."

"Yes, and you know more about my future than I do, at least at a high level."

"I won't mention any of those events. You have my word," said Jane.

"I take you at your word. I did not ask before but . . . how much of it covered who I traveled with?"

"There wasn't much. On some events it did, but it was mostly a list of events, places, and times. Oh . . . and of course the rules, although it seems tracking all that information violates one of the rules."

"I figured as much," said Evaran. "I will need to deal with that after all this is over. Other than that, there are no hard rules. You will need to keep an open mind, as you will see things that may seem new and unusual. I do not suspect you will have a problem with that, given what I have observed of your interaction with us on this current journey."

"Of course." Jane motioned toward the projection she had seen Evaran and V at earlier. "What were you working on?"

"I was compiling all the information that Andrew gave us on what they know about the Voss Imperium. There is a lot to go through. I plan to spend the rest of the time going over it until we meet tomorrow at nine a.m."

Jane shook her head. "Andrew is the same, it seems, in any timeline. He's always willing to help when needed." She gestured at the projection. "Find anything interesting so far?"

"Disturbing more than interesting," said Evaran. "It appears Billozein has been busy. What concerns me is I do not know how he is changing the timeline. Although we may get a quantum beacon on his ship, I do not know if it is his ship, or maybe even a trait of his species. The quantum beacon should at least tell us where he goes when he jumps."

"We'll get him," said Jane.

"That is the plan. If all goes well, then in the finalized timeline, you will get to see a third version of Andrew when he tours the Torvatta."

Jane chuckled. "After knowing three versions of Okon, two versions of Andrew, and even meeting my other self, I can handle that." She looked around. "Well, I'll let you get back to it."

"Are you going to rest now like Dr. Snowden and Emily?"

Jane shook her head. "I thought I'd go to the holo room and test out the PSD."

V's lights glowed a bit. "Would you care for some company?"

"Sure!" said Jane. She had a soft spot for V after he had saved her from the mutant attack.

Evaran gestured at Jane. "V can also go over the survival suit should you choose to use it."

"If I'm going to be using the PSD, it might make sense to switch over to that. Dr. Snowden showed me how it worked on his suit. I'm more comfortable with mine, but open to it."

"It has a lot of capabilities similar to what you have, and then some."

Jane's eyes glowed. "I'll learn it all."

"I am sure you will," said Evaran. With a final nod, he sat back down at the desk he had been working at.

Jane exited the research lab with V in tow. "C'mon, V, it's time to see what this PSD can do."

"Acknowledged."

For the next hour, Jane tried out the shield, repulsion, stun, and several of the survival options on her new PSD in the holo room. Flipping between options was easier than she had thought it would be. Although her eyelids were beginning to droop some, her mind was still lit up.

V helped her pull up different scenarios to test out her PSD. He had set the environment to a large concourse on a spaceship. Creatures that resembled spiders and other assorted insects were targets for her stun and repulsion beams, but also gave her a chance to use her shield to block blows. Some did get through, but their attacks were superficial for training purposes. After learning how to adjust her shield size, she took a break, leaning against the concourse's side wall.

"You have paused the simulation," said V.

"It's a lot to take in, and I wanted a break." She focused on V. "I . . . know I said it before, but I wanted you to know that I really appreciate what you did to help me with that mutant that jumped me."

V's lights glowed. "My calculations showed that if I did not act, there was a ninety-eight-point-two-percent chance you would be severely hurt."

"You acted selflessly. I mean . . . you could've died."

"It was possible. However, I could not stand by and let you get hurt."

Jane grinned. "You're a noble AI."

"Acknowledged."

Jane chuckled. "Evaran has rubbed off on you, but I'm glad you are who you are."

"Thank you," said V. "Are you okay with the current situation?"

Jane shrugged. "I don't know yet. I'm glad that I didn't fade away, but then again . . . maybe I should have. You know?"

V hovered in front of her and touched two of his clawed arms in front of him. "It is the past. You have a future to look forward to."

"I bet you told that to Emily too," said Jane, tilting her head.

"Your analysis is correct."

Jane liked talking to V and could see why Emily did too. V was that friend you could always rely on. He may not have all the answers, but he listened and did not judge, a trait she admired. She stood and wiped her brow. "Well, I guess I'm gonna call it a day. I'm going to get some rest."

"I am knowledgeable in several massage techniques should you need them to relax."

"Be careful," said Jane. "You might make Dr. Snowden jealous."

"I apologize. That was not my intent."

Jane laughed. "I know. Thanks for the offer, but I think I'll be okay."

"Acknowledged."

Jane exited the holo room and went to her living quarters. When she got there and looked in the mirror, she noticed bags under her eyes. Maybe the stress of everything happening was making her more tired than she realized. She swallowed hard as she ran a hand through her hair. This was going to be an interesting ride.

Dr. Snowden's eyes opened as his PSD chirped at him. He rolled to the side and grabbed it. A quick check showed it was 8:00 a.m. With a sigh, he slid his legs off the side of the bed. He had wanted to see Jane last night, but after almost three hours of talking with Andrew and the events prior to that, he decided to go to bed instead.

The discussion with Andrew had been enlightening. Andrew had been visibly excited when he saw the Torvatta, but Evaran was firm on not letting him in until the issue with Billozein was wrapped up. Dr. Snowden figured that if there would be another timeline change, Andrew could suffer the same fate as Jane. He trod off to get cleaned up and dressed.

After forty minutes, he exited his room and checked out the command area. It was quiet. He figured Evaran and V were probably already in the conference room, and Jane and Emily were cleaning up from their morning training session. One day he would need to join them. He smirked at the thought of already thinking of Jane as a traveling companion. Hopefully she would ask Evaran about it once this was all over.

After entering the conference room, he saw Evaran and V as expected. He admired their lack of sleep requirements, but he did not think he would ever want to lose that capability, not just for physical reasons, but mental ones as well. He grabbed his usual morning cup of coffee and sat at the table. "It was a busy day yesterday."

"It was. We have come a long way since we initially began the investigation into this summons."

Dr. Snowden chuckled. "Are all summons this crazy?"

"Not at all. I did one where my mere presence was all that was needed. One decision, and that was it. This is . . . and not to overuse the word . . . an anomaly."

"Well, I'm holding you to checking out your past like we discussed before all this summons business."

"Of course," said Evaran.

Emily burst into the room with a big smile.

Dr. Snowden raised his eyebrows. The last time he saw her smile like that was before her prison planet experience.

"Jane's going to travel with us!" said Emily.

Dr. Snowden snapped his head at Evaran.

Evaran nodded.

A big grin crept onto Dr. Snowden's face. "No kidding. Where's she at?"

Emily went to the replicator. "We finished our training session about thirty minutes ago, so she should be here soon."

Dr. Snowden had figured Jane would join as a traveling companion at some point, but not this soon. Either way, he thought she would be a great fit. There was also the possibility that his relationship with her might grow into something more. He watched Emily take her seat. "I'm glad to see you smiling."

Emily raised an eyebrow.

Dr. Snowden smiled. Ten minutes later, he stood as Jane entered the room. He walked over to her with open arms. "Welcome to the gang."

Jane hugged him, then hugged Emily when she came up.

V flew over and planted himself on the table, then opened his arms.

Jane laughed as she bent over to give V a hug. "Thank you, everyone, for the reception." She got herself a drink and then took a seat along with everyone else.

Evaran cleared his throat. "As you all now know, Jane will be traveling with us. She has a PSD, and V is helping her learn the survival suit. We talked about it last night while I was going over the information that Andrew gave us."

"I'm ready to do my part," said Jane. "What did you find out?"

"I believe the situation is worse than we thought," said Evaran. "According to the information, there are unusual Voss in nine locations, but I suspect there are probably more than that in the Voss Imperium."

A projection shot up from the table, showing a galactic region with nine red dots.

Jane snorted. "I still can't believe Billozein is making those things."

"The problem is that the control communication receptor on the creatures has a range limitation for control. That would mean that each of those nine facilities has a controller, similar to Billozein. I do not know if the controllers are his real children without the receptors, or something else. What is apparent is that he is aggressively building his army and, with the Voss technology, has a head start."

Dr. Snowden sighed. "It can never be easy, can it?"

"As of late, I would say no. However, this presents a problem, as we do not know which facility Billozein is at. It is possible he is not even at any of the facilities, and may be on a spaceship or station."

"I'm guessing you have a facility to infiltrate in mind?"

The projection zoomed into one of the red dots that resided on a planet.

"Yes, we are going here," said Evaran, pointing at the red dot.

"That looks like it's deep in Voss Imperium territory," said Jane.

"It is, and the security is much more lax there relative to ones farther out. With the Torvatta, reaching it will not be an issue. I selected it because traffic seems to be heavier there, so the chance of Billozein being near the action is higher."

Jane nodded.

Evaran tapped at the table console. A layout of the facility appeared. "This is a facility that the Voss call Malacruuz."

Dr. Snowden noted that it was built into a mountain. It had multiple levels, with parts of the base extending out over the mountain. It reminded him a bit of the command center he saw on the prison planet.

Jane pointed at a large, open area near the bottom of the facility, which had a tunnel leading out to the side. "What's in there?"

Evaran shook his head. "I do not know. There was no information on it." He pointed to one of the communication towers. "However, that will be my way in."

Dr. Snowden fidgeted in his seat. "Your way in? Don't you mean *our* way in?"

Evaran looked down for a moment, then back up. "Not this time. I believe the best chance of finding Billozein is giving him something he wants. I will offer myself and the Torvatta in exchange for not interfering with Earth, Fredoria, and Roeth."

"They could also kill you on sight."

Evaran raised a finger. "They could, but then they would lose the one thing Billozein is interested in. Billozein is used to getting what he wants. He is a power-hungry narcissist with a desire to control everything, and a favorable situation will compel him to come. We could try to search all nine facilities, but instead, I will have him come to me."

Emily narrowed her eyes. "It seems kinda risky to base all this off Billozein's personality."

"I understand everyone's concern," said Evaran, shaking his hand in front of him. His ancient eyes narrowed. "I . . . have been around for a long time. Certain traits and personalities become easy to spot. Nonetheless, this is the plan once I am inside the base. I will determine the Voss control communication mechanism and determine how to disrupt it. V will accompany me to that point, then return to the Torvatta with my UIC. Then I will surrender, at which point they will most likely constrain me until Billozein arrives. I suspect they will use Palisin-energy-based constraints given that Billozein has had time to research me and has mentioned Seeros Industries before."

Dr. Snowden remembered Palisin energy. He saw Evaran take a full shot of it from a bounty hunter. It dropped Evaran fast.

Evaran continued on. "Everyone else will wait outside the facility in the Torvatta, stealthed. When Billozein's ship shows up, you will follow it in and then put the quantum beacon on it when you can. Although I will be in constraints, my hands should be free. V will get me access via placing my UIC on a console, which will allow me to disrupt the Voss control communications. That distraction will cause Billozein to leave in his ship. I will then need you to bring some orbs to neutralize my constraints, and we will depart."

"You've given it a lot of thought," said Emily, chuckling.

Evaran nodded.

Dr. Snowden shook his head. "There's a lot of points where it could go wrong. It could get messy."

"If it comes down to that, I know a few battle-tested crew members who could help me out."

Jane chuckled. "We'll be ready if it comes to that."

"So . . . once you're captured, and we have to come get you, who will we be fighting?" asked Emily.

The projection changed to a lineup of Voss, robots, androids, and other creatures.

Dr. Snowden pointed at one of the creatures. "We saw that one in the testing level."

"Yes, but these are about twice that size. The collar would indicate some type of control."

Dr. Snowden gulped. "Oh, that's great."

"They are sensitive to vibrations. A repulsion blast should keep them away if we run into them."

"Right, I remember," said Dr. Snowden. "How are we gonna get a quantum beacon aboard Billozein's ship?"

Evaran raised a finger. "Not on board, but on the hull. I have a magnetized container with a chameleon effect. V will place it where Billozein will not notice it."

"So we might not even see Billozein then, just his ship," said Jane.

"From your perspective, yes."

"At least there's that," said Jane with a sigh. "What if he doesn't take off in his ship?"

"That is a risk. However, he is not one of courage and will retreat if he feels he no longer has the upper hand."

Jane smirked. "I hope your assessment is accurate."

"The end goal is to see where Billozein is jumping to. Last night, while studying our past interactions with him, I have concluded that his ship is what allows him to travel, and not something unique to his species."

Dr. Snowden wrinkled his eyebrows. "That makes sense. If he could do it without his ship, he wouldn't have had to run from us, or contact us from it."

"Correct," said Evaran. He tapped at the table console. The projection changed back to the facility he had selected to infiltrate. "There are several landing bays and extensions around the base. They are heavily monitored and appear to have a sizable security contingent. You will need to be careful when you follow Billozein's ship in." He pointed higher up the mountain. "For the more immediate goal of entering, I will be going in through a hatch door on the communications tower roof." The projection zoomed in to the tower sticking out of the mountainside. The hatch door on the roof was outlined in green. "V will fly down and knock on the hatch door, then enter scout mode. I will then jump down and deal with any Voss, and we will both enter."

V's lights blinked. "Acknowledged."

"I do not know what to expect internally other than the layout and lineup of beings that I showed earlier," said Evaran. "I will set up a display in the holo room where everyone can see what V sees. Get your suits on, and we will head out there." The projection vanished as he stood. He exited the room with V.

Dr. Snowden glanced at Jane. "Are you ready for your first mission as an official companion?"

"I'm ready. I can't wait to see Billozein get captured and face justice."

"Me too," said Emily as she stood.

"I think I'll use my light armor on this one. I'm more familiar with it," said Jane.

Dr. Snowden cocked his head. "This would be a good opportunity to use the survival suit in a real-world situation. Besides, there isn't much to it."

"All right. I trust your judgment. Lead on."

Dr. Snowden smiled at Jane.

They headed over to the survival suit area in the research lab.

Jane touched Dr. Snowden's arm. "Hey . . . I wanted to say that I'm glad to be traveling with you."

Dr. Snowden's face turned red as he looked down. "Oh . . . yeah . . . definitely."

Jane chuckled as she leaned in and kissed Dr. Snowden on the cheek. "Now help me with my suit."

"Yes, ma'am," said Dr. Snowden. His nanobots had pulsed when Jane kissed him, like a shock to the system. After helping Jane with her suit, he stood for a moment to enjoy the warmth that had spread over him. His mind ventured into areas he could have only dreamed of with Jane. To think that in all of space and time, at this specific point, he would meet someone he was compatible and had a possible future with. After all he and Emily had been through, maybe this was a cosmic payback of sorts.

Jane swatted his arm. "You coming or going to continue daydreaming?"

Dr. Snowden raised his eyebrows. "What?" He noticed Jane was standing outside the suit area. "Oh . . . right . . . Let's go."

They joined Evaran, Emily, and V in the command area.

Dr. Snowden observed that they were still in space outside the United Planets station.

"V, take us to Malacruuz. Make sure we stealth before entering the portal."

"Acknowledged," said V.

A golden beam shot out in front of the Torvatta, causing a portal to form.

V tapped at the front console. "Torvatta stealth mode engaged."

The Torvatta flew through the light-blue rippling portal surface ringed by a silver border.

Once through the portal, Evaran placed his fingertips together. "V, take us down to Malacruuz and hover over the communications tower identified earlier."

"Acknowledged."

19

After twenty minutes, Dr. Snowden hustled to meet the others standing on the Torvatta's ramp. It extended out to the edge of the shielding and, with the Torvatta in stealth mode, was undetectable to those outside it. V had already flown out, tapped on the roof hatch door, and shimmered into scout mode.

After a moment, the roof door slid back, and a burly Voss climbed out. Another followed him a moment later.

Dr. Snowden noted that both Voss wore a mix of black and red light clothing, with a belt that held various devices. Their jackal-like heads had a metal piece that went from their foreheads to back behind their upright ears. The back chest plate caught his attention. It was strapped on with over-the-shoulder straps at the top and connected to the belt.

"There was something was out here," said the first Voss.

The second Voss sneered. "Uh-huh . . ."

Evaran jumped down and swung his extended utility handle at both of the Voss. When the light-blue end touched them, they crumpled to the ground. He glanced at the others in the Torvatta. "Head to the holo room. It is set up to see what is going on."

Dr. Snowden's eyes popped open when he entered the holo room and saw a 360-degree view from V's perspective. He jumped at a sound off to his side. This was more realistic than he had expected. From where he stood, it was like he was floating in the air. He sat down at one of the three seats that were in front of him. While he had seen projections from Evaran's chest before on the front screens, to watch a 360-degree view in the holo room was a first for him. He focused on the hologram scene.

Evaran sealed the hatch door shut after he began to climb down the ladder. After a minute, he reached the bottom.

Dr. Snowden noted that the corridor Evaran was in was fairly large. The black floor and walls with purple lines zig-zagging everywhere seemed to create panels of various sizes. Light strips from the ceiling provided illumination. The sounds of various voices echoed out in the distance.

"This is amazing," said Jane.

"Yeah, tell me about it," said Dr. Snowden.

Evaran clung to the walls and crept forward. His utility handle was extended into a baton with a light-blue glowing end. He reached a large half-circle-shaped room.

V flew forward to the other end of the room.

Dr. Snowden scrutinized the area. The front wall was awash with screens showing all sorts of data, from galactic maps to status bars and charts. Some had what looked like broadcasts going on them. It was the three Voss in the room that caught his attention. Two were in a sunken area in front of workstation with a dizzying array of electronics. One stood off to the side, studying the screens that extended to the edges of the room. The ability to scrutinize the environment from the safety of the holo room did not escape Dr. Snowden. The holo presence capability was powerful. While he and the others could freely walk around the hologram, what they saw was dependent on where V was.

Evaran looked around the room for a moment, then nodded at V.

V projected a large robot pod that sat on two legs and bristled with weapons. The robot whirred and said, "Systems engaged."

The startled Voss ducked to the ground.

Evaran stood, raised his baton, and shot a stun beam at both Voss in the sunken area. The third Voss reached for his weapon. He looked up in surprise when Evaran reached him. Evaran tapped him on the head with his baton. The last Voss crumpled to the ground.

Emily shook her head. "Flawless."

Dr. Snowden could see how when it was just Evaran and V, they worked effortlessly. He remembered wondering before whether Evaran would make different decisions if he and Emily were not around. Seeing what Evaran and V could do now confirmed that they were more efficient alone.

Jane gasped as she focused on one of the side screens. "Those are United Planets communications."

V positioned himself to give a better view.

Evaran placed his UIC on one of the workstations and glanced at V. "It would not be unusual to eavesdrop on your enemies."

"Maybe . . . but these are encoded messages. The only way to get access to these is if someone gave them access. They must have infiltrated somehow."

The UIC's light-blue light stabilized after a moment. Evaran perused his ARI. "Definitely possible. However, as this timeline will change, things may be very different, and this may not come to pass."

Jane wrinkled her eyebrows for a moment, then went back to studying the screens.

Dr. Snowden watched as a stream of data appeared in the air. It occurred to him that with the holo room, these types of things could be visualized. The UIC looked like a jellyfish as tendrils of blue light snaked their way from it through the workstation. He walked over and stood next to Emily. "This is kinda cool, huh?"

Emily snorted. "It's hard to sit by."

"Yeah." Dr. Snowden pulled his lips in and walked over to Jane, who had gotten out of her seat to investigate the screens she saw in more detail. "You see anything interesting?"

"Outside of these transmissions, there is lot of valuable information here."

"You probably never thought you would be seeing the inside of a Voss facility, even if it's a holo-room version," said Dr. Snowden.

"It wasn't exactly on my dream to-do list."

They shared a laugh as Emily gazed at them from afar.

Evaran rubbed his chin. "Very interesting. That area near the bottom of this base is similar to the progeny rooms we saw, except this is much larger." He interacted with his ARI, causing a visual of the interior of the bottom area to float near him.

Dr. Snowden's eyes widened as he saw rows and rows of the capsules.

"There are approximately two thousand of them there," said Evaran.

"Maybe that is the vanguard of his army or something," said Jane.

"That is possible. I suspect taking control of these facilities for further conversion is his current priority," said Evaran.

The projection changed to the layout of the top part of the base. Three levels down was a large square room that had an enclosed central area. A line ran from where Evaran was to the enclosed area.

Evaran pointed at the projection. "That is where I need to go. I cannot decipher the Voss control communications from here. There is an aggressive security AI protecting the outside entry points. I will need to get physically inside."

Emily examined the projection. "How many Voss are in the way?"

Evaran swiped through his ARI. The projection lit up with several dozen red dots. "There are quite a few. However, I believe I have a solution. There are sensors in the bottom area that indicate if something is malfunctioning or . . . if the capsules are opened without authorization. I believe I can make it appear as if they are all open. That should cause an evacuation of the base."

"You can try," said Emily.

Evaran tapped at his ARI.

The alarm fading in and out made Dr. Snowden jump. Although he knew he was in the holo room, he could imagine being there right next to Evaran. He watched the screen near Evaran as it showed personnel rushing around.

"I have my diversion," said Evaran. "It is time to move." He exited the room out a side corridor. As he crept along, the flashing lights distracted Dr. Snowden. He wondered if it could be filtered out in the holo room. The nonstop blaring did not help things.

Evaran came to a halt near the entrance to another large room. Voss were scrambling around inside it, tapping at consoles and checking various devices. He motioned at V.

V flew into the room, and the door behind him closed.

Dr. Snowden watched as the Voss exited the room. Once they were all gone, the door opened and Evaran stepped in.

Evaran marched over to one of the workstations and placed his UIC on it. He interacted with his ARI, causing a floating screen to appear next to him. "According to this, it looks like the top half of the base is now evacuated or close to it."

Dr. Snowden noted that the floating image next to Evaran must be a part of his ARI being shared somehow. It showed the facility divided into levels with a series of numbers and some metrics off to the side. The higher numbers had a green box around them. He figured that was what Evaran referred to in reference to the levels being evacuated.

"The path is now clear," said Evaran. The floating screen faded as he grabbed his UIC and put it back on his belt.

Dr. Snowden wondered how long it would be before the Voss figured out that nothing was wrong.

Evaran reached the enclosed area two levels down after fifteen minutes of creeping through various ramps and corridors.

Dr. Snowden kept expecting Voss security patrols to pop up, but none came. He noticed that there were camera-like devices in the corridor. Maybe whoever would be looking through them was not around or Evaran had disabled them.

Emily tapped Dr. Snowden's arm. "You seem tense."

"You're not?"

Emily smirked. "We're in the holo room, away from the action."

Dr. Snowden admired Emily's steady and fearless nature. It reminded him a lot of her dad. He had seen glimpses of it before, but now it seemed to be a major part of her persona. He made a resolution to join her in her morning trainings. Although he had the nanobots to help him in a combat situation, he knew he was nowhere near Emily's level in terms of combat knowledge and situational awareness. It had been his hope that traveling with Evaran would be full of learning and observing. There were moments like that, but there were moments like this as well. He shook his head.

Jane wrinkled her eyebrows at him.

Dr. Snowden smiled. "I was thinking."

"You do that a lot."

"I know . . . it's who I am," said Dr. Snowden.

"That's why we like you," said Jane with a grin.

Dr. Snowden's stomach fluttered.

Evaran stood outside the enclosed area and placed his UIC on the door console. After a moment, the door slid open, and he entered, grabbed his UIC, then sealed the room.

Dr. Snowden surveyed the room. The walls he had thought were solid surprised him. They were one-way mirrors of some type. The edges of the room were packed with workstations, and there was a sunken area in the middle. A table with holographic projections on it sat in the middle of the room. It reminded him of the conference table on the Torvatta.

Evaran placed his UIC on the table. After the UIC had stabilized, he browsed his ARI.

The projection changed on the table to show a view outside. It showed Voss hustling out of the facility.

Dr. Snowden noticed that the Voss had separated into two groups that were facing off with each other. "What's that all about?"

Evaran rubbed his chin. "I am not sure. There is a monitoring pillar nearby."

Dr. Snowden leaned in as the voices rang out.

The leader of the first group pointed at the second group. "Get back in there! It's a false alarm."

The leader of the second group snorted. Others behind him growled and shouted. "You go back in there if you want to, but we're staying out here. We know what's down there! And now they're loose!"

The first group leader snarled. "And you'll join them if you don't do as you're ordered."

The second group leader replied, "I'm sick of this. You aren't Voss. We don't know what you are. You look like it, but you're one of those . . . abominations."

A large male Voss exited the building. He wore metallic armor, unlike the rest of the Voss. When he walked toward the second group, the first group cleared a path for him. He pointed at the second group. "You will get back in there. *Now.* This is your last chance."

The second group leader raised his head and bared his teeth. "You are *not* Voss! We defy you, in the name of the Voss Imperium!"

The large male Voss smiled. "Your choice." He turned and headed back toward the facility. As he passed the first group leader, he said, "Kill them. We will use their corpses as hosts."

The two groups began to fight.

The projection blinked out.

Dr. Snowden raised his eyebrows. "Okay . . . so it seems not all Voss are on board with the whole conversion thing."

Evaran placed his fingertips together and pressed them against his lips. "It would appear so. I have the Voss control communication set up. V is going to fly back to the Torvatta now and run it through a deciphering program. It should not take long and should be available for use by the time Billozein gets here."

"That big guy looked like he was coming back in," said Emily. "Maybe he knows the situation."

"He is aware of it and is headed this way," said Evaran. He pulled off his UIC and handed it to one of V's extended arms. After opening the door to the enclosed area, he pointed out. "V, go. It is time for my surrender."

V hovered for a moment.

"V?" asked Evaran.

"Acknowledged," said V as he flew off.

Dr. Snowden could see that even V was not fully on board with Evaran being captured.

Evaran tapped at his ARI. "I am transferring the holo-room visual from V to my chest and shoulder sensors. Unfortunately, it will only show you what is in front of and above me. You will still be able to see my face from the side."

"It's better than nothing," said Dr. Snowden.

Evaran closed the door to the room as a projection shot up from one of the workstations.

The projection showed the big Voss from before. "I'm not sure how you got in there, but I'm linked to the control center of this facility. It seems I now have visual and audio back. Nice diversion, but I'm also linked to the systems below."

Dr. Snowden had wondered if maybe they had listened in, but it seems Evaran had already anticipated that. Watching Evaran was like watching a grand master chess player sometimes.

"With whom do I speak?" asked Evaran.

"Jeetrozein."

"You are related to Billozein, I assume," said Evaran.

"Of course. He's my father," said Jeetrozein. "He warned me and my brothers and sisters about you. He said you might show up one day, and here you are."

Evaran cleared his throat. "I have come to make a proposal. It will require Billozein's presence."

Jeetrozein's eyes narrowed. "You can tell me, and I'll relay it."

"Then tell him I propose a trade. I'll give him what he wants."

"And what's that?"

"I do not think he would want you to know."

Jeetrozein snorted. "You know Father quite well, but if you think I'm going to let you sit in that room until he arrives, then you don't know me at all."

Dr. Snowden looked out through the one-way walls and saw Voss and humanoid robots assuming positions around the enclosed area.

"I will surrender, and expect you will put me in constraints," said Evaran.

Jeetrozein paused for a moment, then said, "Maybe you do know me after all. Come out with your hands up. We have special constraints for you."

Evaran sighed, then exited the room with his hands up.

One of the Voss kicked Evaran in the back. "Kneel, dog!"

Evaran stumbled forward and then kneeled.

"Put your hands behind your head!"

Evaran complied.

After five minutes, Jeetrozein arrived. One of the Voss next to him was carrying a set of metallic wrist constraints.

Jeetrozein motioned at Evaran.

The Voss applied the constraints to Evaran.

Jeetrozein sneered. "Just for you."

"I can see Billozein has had time to plan for this."

"Oh . . . he has. Now stand. Let's go. We have a special cell for you too."

Evaran stood and was escorted out of the room by several Voss pointing weapons at him.

Dr. Snowden watched for the next hour as Evaran was led through various corridors and levels and a trip down the elevator. Evaran was moved into a room that had a cell with four pillars in the middle of the room. The cell had translucent shielding with a slight red glow between each pillar. Dr. Snowden remembered seeing that red glow on a bounty hunter weapon in a previous adventure. It was Palisin energy, one form of energy that Evaran was weak against. It seemed Billozein was taking no chances if Evaran were to reappear. He had surprised him before.

One of the walls dissipated, and Evaran was ushered in. Once inside, the shield went back up. He sat on a chair and looked around.

Dr. Snowden noted the room was empty. He hoped they would not have to wait long for Billozein to arrive. He glanced at V. "So . . . how long until Billozein arrives?"

"Unknown," said V.

Dr. Snowden sighed. "Well . . . I guess we wait then."

"Acknowledged," said V. "The Torvatta is within scanning range of any ship that arrives or departs. Once Billozein's ship is detected, I will notify you."

"Evaran, can you hear us still?"

Evaran nodded.

"But you can't say anything in case the place is bugged, right?"

Evaran nodded again.

Dr. Snowden glanced at Jane and Emily. "I guess we can get lunch while we wait."

Emily clenched and unclenched her jaw. "You two go ahead. I'll keep Evaran company."

Dr. Snowden saw fire in Emily's eyes. He knew her instinct now was to go in there and bust heads. Sitting still while Evaran was locked up was not in her nature anymore. Despite that, he knew Evaran would not want anyone to worry about him and everything was going as planned. "Want us to bring back anything?"

Emily pursed her lips together for a moment. "Sure, a vitamin drink would be good. Use 'Emily's morning drink' pattern. It should be there."

Dr. Snowden saluted with two fingers. "You got it." He gestured toward the conference room and looked at Jane. "Shall we?"

"Lead on," said Jane.

They entered the conference room and picked up lunch.

Dr. Snowden was hungry for hot dogs. One thing he appreciated about his nanobots was that he could eat whatever he wanted and the nanobots would make sure it was efficiently used. His weight had dropped some since traveling with Evaran. He noticed that Jane still avoided meat and was having some type of vegetable dish he did not recognize.

Jane took a seat at the table. "Still with the meat desires, huh?"

Dr. Snowden smirked. "I don't think I'll ever give it up."

"I understand," said Jane. She took a bite of her dish. After swallowing it, she glanced at Dr. Snowden. "I didn't want to say anything earlier, but . . . well . . . what do you really think of this plan?"

Dr. Snowden chuckled. "You don't like the amount of unknown variables."

"Well . . . yeah."

"You'll get used to it. One thing about Evaran is that regardless of how unpredictable a situation will become, he'll adapt. I have seen him in several situations now where he has adjusted on the fly, and it worked out."

"Always?"

"All except maybe on the last adventure. I don't think he saw that coming," said Dr. Snowden. "I mean . . . it did work out, maybe not as well as he had hoped. I wouldn't worry about it. Yes, this plan is risky, but with Evaran, and us, we'll come through."

"You're right, of course. I'll adapt."

"Of course," said Dr. Snowden with a grin. "We're human, past and present, it's what we do."

Jane smiled as she dove into her dish.

Dr. Snowden mulled over Jane's concern. He understood it, since he had his doubts as well. Having Evaran held did not sit right with him. There were many possible situations where it could go horribly wrong. However, trying to find someone in a vast empire could be time-consuming and ultimately futile. Hopefully Evaran would not be there for too long. He took a bite of his hot dog as he looked off into the distance.

20

Dr. Snowden leaned over the waist-high light-blue semi-transparent guardrail on the Torvatta's roof. It had been two days since Evaran had surrendered. Dr. Snowden shook his head. Half the day was gone, and he had eaten his lunch already. Billozein was taking his sweet time in getting there.

Emily spent most of her time either training or sitting in the command area and talking to Evaran. Although Evaran could not talk back, he would occasionally nod or shake his head.

Dr. Snowden had spent time in the command area as well, but it looked to him like Evaran was often in some type of meditative state. Not having to eat or drink probably made things a lot easier. The lack of need to relieve himself intrigued Dr. Snowden. It was not something he had really thought about until this event. He glanced to his right and observed Jane staring out into the sky. Her brown hair flowed effortlessly onto her shoulders. He smiled as he thought of running a hand through it.

"You're thinking again," said Jane.

Dr. Snowden gulped. "Oh . . . umm . . . I was wondering how you're liking your first outing as an official companion."

"I have learned a bit more about Evaran. He doesn't need to eat, drink, sleep, or do anything a human would need to do, apparently."

Dr. Snowden chuckled. "That's actually what I was thinking about. Well, to be more specific, never having to relieve himself."

"It's amazing. It makes me think . . . well . . . probably sounds crazy . . . but it makes me think what we see is just a suit. It's like Evaran is something else on the inside."

Dr. Snowden cast a sidelong look at Jane. "That's not too far from the truth. I do know that this is a form he had to take on when he came to this plane."

"Plane?"

Dr. Snowden chuckled. "Oh . . . you'll learn more about all that traveling with us. Apparently, our universe is one of many, inside a plane. And to make it even weirder, that plane is in a plane system. Evaran's true form exists between the planes, but I've never seen it. We were actually planning on checking it out, then got this summons."

Jane turned her head toward Dr. Snowden. "I can't wait to find all that out, but you'll have to explain the summons to me. I don't think I've heard that mentioned before."

"The summons," said Dr. Snowden, pulling his lips in while his eyes darted around. "I won't lie and say I fully understand it, but the Torvatta issues these summonses from across time and space, and Evaran investigates them, then renders a judgment. The most recent summons was to Roeth."

"Huh . . . so that was the reason you came to Roeth."

"Yep."

Jane chuckled. "What I don't get, though, is how does the Torvatta know to do these summons. I mean . . . how does it know what's happening across all of time and space?"

"Got me," said Dr. Snowden, adjusting his glasses. "It makes me think sometimes that the Torvatta is more than it appears. Even Evaran doesn't know, but he trusts it based on the summons he has done. I keep learning something new about the Torvatta every time we head out somewhere. For example, on our last outing, when we were dealing with the Purifiers, I learned that it has data from the future in the replicator database. It's time stream aware."

Jane jerked her head back. "That sounds . . . interesting."

"I'm not sure I fully understand how that's possible, but I saw it with my own two eyes. Someone from our future, who had met us before, but we had just met them, came into the Torvatta and ordered a drink. I couldn't see the drink pattern, nor could Evaran, but this person could."

Jane shook her head. "I have a lot to learn."

"You'll probably get to see parallel timelines . . . other dimensions . . . pocket universes. You never know. This summons was urgent, from what I understand. It makes me wonder if that urgency was because the Torvatta knew we would be picking you up."

"My brain is going in circles."

"It's a lot to take in."

Their attention was diverted to V, who had floated onto the roof. "Billozein's ship has arrived."

Dr. Snowden glanced at Jane, then hustled after V to the command center. When he and Jane got there, they took their seats. He saw Billozein's ship outlined on the left screen with a real-time view. It looked rectangular in design with wings off to the side and boosters on the back. The nose tapered off to a point. It reminded him a bit of a space shuttle. The right screen showed a deeper analysis of the ship. It had a wireframe view with a listing of detail cards hanging off it. He pointed to one of the cards. "That one says it has a temporal aura."

"Analysis. You are correct. I believe Evaran's hypothesis that the ship is the initiator of timeline jumps is accurate."

Dr. Snowden raised his eyebrows. To understand the implications of a temporal aura made him realize how much he had learned traveling with Evaran. He noted that the Torvatta flew just a bit above Billozein's ship. He figured that was probably to avoid anything that might give away the Torvatta in Billozein's ship's wake, assuming it could detect that.

After twenty minutes, Billozein's ship arrived just outside the landing pad to the facility. It paused for a moment as massive hangar bay doors slid back. Once they were inside the hangar bay, the doors slid shut.

Dr. Snowden checked out the interior of the docking bay. He wondered if any scans had detected the Torvatta when it flew in. The memory of the Kreagans scanning it and saying it did not exist, even as it sat right in front of them, made him think they were in the clear. He now knew that the Torvatta had scan profiles, and they were probably using the first one. It made sense that with someone like Billozein, who would know what to look for and had specialized equipment to deal with Evaran, might have been able to detect the Torvatta. Maybe not, though, given that no alarms had gone off and the Torvatta was hovering in midair off in the corner of the hangar bay.

"Your wait is over," said Emily, staring at the right screen, which had switched back to Evaran's chest view.

Evaran nodded.

They waited until Billozein's ship powered down a few minutes later. A side door raised up with a ramp sliding out to the floor.

Dr. Snowden shook his head as he saw Billozein walk out of the ship alone. He found it interesting that Billozein flew solo. Given how powerful he probably was, it seemed out of place. Maybe temporal auras granted a temporal shielding effect like the Torvatta. If Billozein did have to time jump, having more along who would not fit into the new time-line would be a burden, something Billozein's personality would not deal well with. Billozein was a Voss this time. Dr. Snowden could not get the image of Billozein as some type of large bacteriophage-looking creature out of his mind.

After several minutes, Billozein was escorted out of the room by several Voss who had come to meet him.

Dr. Snowden faced V. "So . . . you place the beacon now, right?"

"That is correct," said V. "I have identified a location on the side where the magnetized quantum beacon container should go undetected. The Torvatta will hover next to it, and I will toss the container onto the hull."

Dr. Snowden sighed. "Then we wait some more."

"Yes," said V.

Dr. Snowden noted Emily was fidgeting in her seat. He could almost feel her anxiousness like an aura that reached out and consumed the command center. They would do their part, and when it came time to get Evaran, the Voss would not know what hit them.

The Torvatta hovered just off to the side of Billozein's ship.

V disappeared to the back and exited the medical lab in body mode while carrying the quantum beacon container.

Dr. Snowden, Jane, and Emily followed V to the edge of the Torvatta ramp outside.

V gripped the container and extended it in front of him. After positioning his arms, he shoved it out.

The container shot out of the Torvatta's shielding and attached to the hull of Billozein's ship. It shimmered for a moment before disappearing from view.

Dr. Snowden held his breath, wondering if anyone had heard the clanking sound when the container hit the hull.

After a moment of silence, they retreated back to the command center.

V switched back into orb mode and rejoined them. He looked at Evaran on the right screen. "The quantum beacon has been placed, and tracking has been activated. Rift technology has been detected on Billozein's ship."

Evaran nodded.

Jane sat back in her seat and exhaled loudly. "That was more intense than I expected."

"I hear ya," said Dr. Snowden. He rubbed his chin. "Rift technology. I bet that has something to do with Billozein jumping around time."

"I've read about rift technology. It's very rare," said Jane.

"Yeah. Emily and I got to see it up close."

V moved the Torvatta back to the corner of the docking bay. "Sit tight, and do not let the bed bugs bite."

Dr. Snowden chuckled. "That's *sleep* tight."

V's lights pulsed for a moment. "Acknowledged."

Dr. Snowden sat back in his chair and contemplated the situation. Billozein would meet Evaran again, except this time in person. Dr. Snowden did not get to hear what Billozein had to say the first time around, and he was interested to know what the exchange would be like. It seemed half the information he knew of Evaran had been gleaned from

Evaran talking to his adversaries. All that was left to do was wait until Evaran gave the signal to V to place the UIC. Then the Voss control communication would be disrupted, and it was show time.

Jane clenched her jaw when she saw Billozein appear on the left screen. It had taken Billozein forty-five minutes to reach Evaran. Jeetrozein stood behind Billozein. The holo-room view was still fresh in her mind, and while the screen view was more limited, it was still powerful in its own right.

Although she had seen Billozein earlier in the docking bay, she had an up-close look this time. He had slick brown hair that covered his body with streaks of gray. She was surprised he had a smaller stature, as most Voss were a good half inch taller on average, for the males at least. Her attention focused on Billozein as he paced in front of Evaran's cell.

Billozein waved Jeetrozein away.

"Why can't I stay?" asked Jeetrozein.

"Because I said so," said Billozein with narrowed eyes and a low growl.

Jeetrozein shook his head and exited the room.

Billozein focused on Evaran. "So . . . once again, we meet. I'm beginning to think you can't get enough of me. Inferiority complex maybe."

Evaran drew his lips flat.

"Right . . . straight to business. I'll admit, I'm a little surprised at what you're doing here. I suspect it's a trap of some sort. Although . . . ," said Billozein, looking around, "it would appear I have the upper hand. Where's your ship?"

"It is in a safe location," said Evaran. "If you agree to my proposal, then it is yours."

Billozein laughed. "You would give me what I want . . . for what exactly?"

"Leave Earth, Fredoria, and Roeth alone regardless of the timeline."

Billozein narrowed his eyes. "What is it with you and Roeth? It's a subpar planet with a weak species. And Earth and Fredoria? Even weaker."

"I have friends there."

"The timeline's changed! You know that! Whatever friends you had, they no longer exist."

"Maybe so, but the Kalesh and humans do not deserve what you are doing to them," said Evaran.

Billozein scratched the side of his neck. "So that's it . . . the noble thing again. Ridiculous. Speaking of ridiculous, where *are* your friends?"

Evaran looked down. "They did not make the timeline transition."

Billozein uttered a low growl. "Surprised you made it out . . . but we both know you're different. I figured your ship had temporal shielding like mine and did not extend to the crew outside the ship. Leaving your friends behind must be tough. Maybe trying to capture me wasn't such a smart idea after all, huh?"

Evaran clenched his jaw.

Billozein waved a hand dismissively in the air. "Anyways, so Roeth, Earth, and Fredoria not to be touched, regardless of timeline, for your time-traveling ship. I know you could go back in time and change things, and then we do this dance again, so what game are you playing?"

Evaran shook his head. "Those events have been established. I cannot interfere in my past."

"Again . . . pathetic. Respect the timeline. Integrity," said Billozein, smirking. "That's a fool's game, and you seem to be a grand master at it." He gestured at the shielding between them. "Like my Palisin energy shielding?"

"You must have gone to great lengths to get it. It is very rare."

"Oh, it is. I had to expend a lot of resources to get it, and not just for this facility, but quite a few others," said Billozein. He wagged a finger at Evaran. "Seems you're remembered quite harshly by Illitech. Funny thing about the Ildoran . . . they have quite the memory. Even after a thousand years, your name still resonates hatred in some corners among them. I guess killing Seeros, the hero that liberated their planet, will do that."

"It was necessary."

Billozein chuckled. "They still had all that specialized gear Seeros had made. It makes me wonder if they ever planned to use it. I got it in a great trade deal. I offered them my augments for inclusion into their world-building package, and I get all of that rare gear, and of course, profit. It won't matter when I conquer them, though. And now . . . here we are. I get to finally put it to use. It's quite effective from what I see."

"Back to my proposal . . . to go through time requires me on the ship, so you will still need me around."

Billozein rubbed his snout. "I figured as much." He har-rumphed. "It takes a big person to admit they were wrong and submit to those of superior intellect. I will need some time to mull over your offer. I need to weigh the advantages of having your ship, and the security to keep you around, versus outright killing you and removing any threat you may pose."

"Take your time. I know when I am defeated."

"Yes . . . yes. That's right. I'm glad you recognize that, but doesn't mean I trust you yet. I've been wrong about you before."

"You clearly control the situation."

Billozein grinned. "I do, but keeping you as a trophy has some appeal, in your favor, of course. We'll see. Get comfortable. I'm in no rush. You're going to be there for a while."

Evaran looked down as Billozein exited the room. After Billozein had left, he raised his head.

"Should I deploy the UIC now?" asked V.

Evaran nodded.

V took off out of the Torvatta. He had stealthed and was scanning for a nearby console. It took several minutes, but he found one in a secluded spot. He placed the UIC on it and then shot a projection over it, effectively camouflaging it.

Jane jumped as V's voice rang out over the communication system.

"UIC is in place," said V.

Jane glanced at Dr. Snowden. "Do we go now?"

"I think when Evaran gives us the go-ahead," said Dr. Snowden. He looked at the right screen. "Evaran, nod twice when you're ready."

Evaran nodded once.

Jane rubbed her fingertips as her gaze bored a hole in the screens. The tension building up to this moment caught her by surprise. She had been in tight situations before, but not ones where the very existence of a timeline was at stake. She watched as Evaran moved his fingers around. The ARI Evaran used must be different than the one she used. Hers was a set distance away for interaction, yet Evaran was able to access his, even in restraints.

Evaran nodded twice.

A loud shrieking noise echoed out across the base.

Dr. Snowden gritted his teeth and hunched down as the Torvatta cut off the screeching noise. "I guess it's go time." He waved toward the exit. "C'mon."

"I'll get the neutralization orbs," said Emily.

They waited on the Torvatta's ramp for V to get back.

V flew back with the UIC in one of his clawed hands. He entered the Torvatta, then lowered it to the ground.

Dr. Snowden, Jane, and Emily jumped off. The Torvatta rose again and, once it was hovering, parked in the top corner. V flew out to meet them.

Once they were all together, they took off to a nearby corridor. The overall lighting had dimmed, and warning lights flashed around them while a deep alarm sound pulsed.

"So the Voss's control communications have been disrupted?" asked Dr. Snowden.

"Analysis. Evaran seeded a rogue program that gives independent thought prior to shutting down control communications."

"Oh . . . so . . . what will that do then to the ones who were under control?" asked Dr. Snowden.

Jane pointed to several Voss on their knees, trembling and looking around wildly. "There's your answer."

One of them jumped up and charged, shaking its head around.

Emily stepped forward and hit it with a stun beam.

The Voss kept coming.

"They're jacked up!"

Dr. Snowden and Jane fired a repulsion beam that sent the Voss tumbling back. A pair of Voss nearby jumped on the fallen Voss and began tearing chunks out of it.

Jane grimaced. "This isn't good. They must be the uncontrolled Voss."

"At least the repulsion works," said Dr. Snowden. He glanced at V. "You know how to get to Evaran? Right?"

"Acknowledged," said V. He took off ahead.

They followed him to a larger corridor. A dozen or so more uncontrolled Voss stood around, shaking in a jerky manner.

A shiver went through Jane. These uncontrolled Voss had never tasted freedom and were unsure of what to do. From their last encounter, it seemed that their base instincts were triggered. Her heartbeat ramped up as the uncontrolled Voss slowly turned their heads and faced her. They emitted guttural growls and a whooping noise and charged forward.

Emily fired her repulsion blast first, sending a few tumbling.

As Dr. Snowden rose to fire his PSD, another uncontrolled Voss tossed a nearby canister. He switched to his shield as Jane stepped forward and hit it with a repulsing beam.

Jane's eyes widened as several other uncontrolled Voss closed the distance between them faster than she expected.

The closest one jumped on Dr. Snowden, with another two grabbing at his legs as he tumbled over.

Emily extended her PSD into a staff and whacked the nearest uncontrolled Voss on Dr. Snowden's legs away. Jane grabbed the other one on Dr. Snowden's legs and threw it into the wall.

Dr. Snowden angled his arm in a way that allowed him to fire his repulsing beam point-blank on the uncontrolled Voss that had jumped them. It flew up to the ceiling, and as it came down, V hit it with a repulsion blast, sending it flying backward.

The other uncontrolled Voss began to attack each other as Dr. Snowden, Emily, and Jane backed up.

"Keeping them at bay is going to be rough," said Emily. "We have to focus fire. On my lead."

Jane admired Emily's take-charge attitude. She could see defiance in her eyes, and knowing that Evaran was incapacitated probably fueled that fire.

Emily advanced, swinging her arm in an arc and letting loose a steady repulsing stream.

Dr. Snowden, Jane, and V joined Emily, and together, they forced the uncontrolled Voss to fall back.

"Let's go!" said Emily, marching down the corridor.

They reached an expansive control room.

Jane did not like the dim lighting, punctuated by weapon fire. Thankfully, with her helmet up, she did not have to smell the carnage going on around her.

Emily entered the room and dodged a shot at her head. "Get down!"

Dr. Snowden and Jane entered behind Emily and crouched behind a desk.

"There's regular Voss in here, and they're shooting at anything that moves. Our stun beams should work on them," said Emily. "Get them ready."

Dr. Snowden and Jane complied. On Emily's command, they popped out and targeted the regular Voss who were looking for them.

One of the regular Voss got off a shot at Emily, but she deflected it with her shield. She returned fire, and the regular Voss crumpled.

Jane shook her head as she glanced at Dr. Snowden. "I keep forgetting about the forearm shield."

"Trial by fire," said Dr. Snowden.

Jane licked her lips. "Uh-huh." She was not as confident as Dr. Snowden and Emily were. Although she had been in firefights before, they were well executed agent raids, not fighting a facility of half-crazed Voss.

Emily motioned at V. "Scouting mode."

"Acknowledged. Scouting mode engaged," said V. He shimmered and flew farther into the room.

Jane raised her eyebrows as she watched the view from V's perspective inside her faceplate. Between the suits, V, Evaran, Dr. Snowden, and Emily, she could see how their initial appearance, while disarming, hid their true abilities. V's scanning showed no activity. She let out a sigh.

"Don't rest yet," said Emily as she walked around.

Jane pointed at the wall of screens. On it were various scenes from across the base. It showed regular Voss fighting the uncontrolled Voss. She homed in on one screen in particular. It showed some humanoid robots being torn apart by the uncontrolled Voss. Another screen showed a quadruped robot with a cylindrical body firing orange energy beams and clearing a path through the Voss, both regular and uncontrolled. She recognized it as a Voss judicator. They were feared, even in her period, for their relentless pursuit and determination in hunting down and killing whatever was their target. Having them loose on the station was not a good sign. She swallowed hard.

A sound at the door caused them to pivot. Two regular Voss with frantic breathing rushed into the room. Their eyes widened upon seeing they were not alone. They raised their hands. One of them stepped forward. "Please, we're unarmed."

Emily paused for a moment, then gestured at Dr. Snowden and Jane. "Let's go." She looked at the two regular Voss. "The room is yours." She exited the room with Dr. Snowden, Jane, and V in tow.

After they had walked to the end of the corridor, Jane jumped as she heard the shrill yelping of the two in the control room, fighting for their lives. Her instinct was to rush back and help them, but Emily had given them at least a fighting chance. The regular Voss could have sealed the room. Maybe they did not know how to. It was not like she, Dr. Snowden, or Emily could either, and taking them along would not make any sense. She looked down as they walked through the dimly lit corridor.

"There's nothing we could have done to help them," said Dr. Snowden, laying a hand on Jane's arm.

"I know," said Jane. "I'm trained to save lives. It's hard to ignore that instinct. Don't worry about me. This is a bit overwhelming."

Emily smirked. "At least this time we have the suits. We've been in worse situations."

Although the conditions were tense, Jane felt safe traveling with Dr. Snowden, Emily, V, and Evaran. If this was a view into what they would do for someone on the team, she was all in. Working as a field agent was lonely work, and often times she wished she had a team to work with. She smiled at Dr. Snowden and Emily as she continued on.

21

Emily noted that the room they entered was massive. After twenty minutes of going through various corridors and ramps, they ended up in the bottom area of the base that housed all the regular Voss Billozein had been converting. Although they were high up on a walkway that extended over the room, her skin crawled at half of the containers being open. Some of the uncontrolled Voss were climbing the walls, others milled about, shaking uncontrollably. There were others that looked like they fell out of their container.

Jane pointed at a commotion on the far side of the room. "Check that out."

Emily inspected where Jane had indicated. "It's Jeetrozein, and his group isn't faring well." The faint red glow coming out of an enclosed room farther back in the corner caught her eye. She crooked her thumb at it. "We need to go there."

Dr. Snowden sighed. "We have to go through all these Voss?"

"Maybe not," said Emily. She peered around for a moment and saw several ladders hanging off the edge of the walkway. Looking at the end of the walkway, she said, "This walkway has ladders we can take. There's one at the far end we can use. Then it's a straight shot to where Evaran is."

Dr. Snowden followed Emily's gaze. "Okay . . . but there's a small horde between the ladder and where he is."

"I'm the only one that needs to go since I have the orbs," said Emily. "This suit has a camouflage aspect I can use. You two can provide cover from top if there is trouble, and V can provide a distraction hologram away from where I'm at."

"That's a solid plan," said Jane.

Emily smirked. "It's not quite as good as what Evaran would come up with, but I'm getting there."

"Agent Emily over here," said Dr. Snowden, crooking his neck at Emily.

Emily swatted Dr. Snowden's arm. "Remember, you're my backup."

"Let's hope none come behind us on the walkway."

"I think you'll be okay, and even if they do come, you can push them off. Use height to your advantage."

"I think this sealed the deal of me joining you in your morning trainings."

Emily crept down and waved forward. "I'm going to hold you to that. C'mon!"

After ten minutes of creeping forward in silence, they reached the end of the walkway.

Emily noted that the ladder that was easy to see from where they were previously was harder to distinguish once they were there. The only sign it was there was a gap in the rail guard and a red painted strip on the walkway. She accessed her wrist interface and turned on her camouflage.

Dr. Snowden's eyes widened. "That's pretty nifty. I can still see you . . . sorta . . . but really have to focus."

"It's battle tested," said Emily. She recalled using it in her last adventure against five hunters in a jungle on the prison planet she spent nine months at.

"I like it," said Jane. "United Planets elite units have that standard on their suits, but not us lowly agents. Evaran should add that to these suits."

"I agree," said Dr. Snowden. "Emily can't have all the toys."

Emily raised an eyebrow.

"I bet she's raising an eyebrow at me," said Dr. Snowden.

Emily shook her head and got onto the ladder. "V, fly away a bit and see if you can distract them to move away from me."

"Acknowledged," said V. He flew off to the middle of the room.

"Here I go," said Emily. She climbed down the ladder, and once she reached the ground, she hugged the wall nearest her. Looking up, she could see Dr. Snowden and Jane had gone prone and were looking out with PSDs on standby. She exhaled from her nose as she moved along the wall.

A platform packed with the capsules that held Billozein's progeny jutted out from the wall.

Emily moved along the edges of it, but paused when the sound of several grunts echoed out. She held her position as she saw two uncontrolled Voss on the ground. They were on all fours, trembling and shaking their heads. One was vomiting. She figured they probably got popped out, regardless if they were ready to or not. Why they were out of their capsules was a mystery to her. She whispered to V via her PSD. "V, now."

Her attention pivoted to the middle of the room, where V projected a large hologram of a Cepharus, a shelled creature with massive tentacles she had encountered during her alien abduction rescue by Evaran. The difference was this hologram version towered over the room at around thirty feet or so.

The outcry was immediate. Uncontrolled Voss from all parts of the room moved toward it.

Emily chuckled. V was swinging the tentacles around like he was trying to grab the uncontrolled Voss. Each time a holographic tentacle touched one, the uncontrolled Voss made whooping sounds and guttural growls, causing even more to come. She had thought it would be a large grizzly bear like she had seen V use before, but this would do. The two uncontrolled Voss in front of her crawled toward the hologram. Once they were a bit away, she continued on. When she arrived outside Evaran's cell room, she picked up low voices inside.

Something peeked out of the room and looked around.

Emily narrowed her eyes. It appeared these were regular Voss, and they had taken refuge in the room. She did a quick survey outside and observed that there were no other Voss, either regular or uncontrolled. Maybe there was something about Palisin energy they did not like. She crept up to the door and looked in.

There were three regular Voss. All had their weapons out, with one just inside the door. The other two were looking forward while sitting on either side of Evaran's cell.

Emily understood the door was a natural choke point. She saw Evaran staring at her. Even with her camouflage, it did not surprise her that Evaran could see her. She weighed her options for a moment, then knelt right outside the doorway. Tossing in one of the orbs at the closest pillar caused the front and right side shielding to dissipate.

The two Voss in the back jumped up.

Emily slipped into the room and kicked the Voss nearest the door into the one on the right side in the back.

The Voss on the left side came around the shielding and fired wildly.

She deflected the shots and hit the Voss with a stun beam.

The Voss collapsed.

She fired a repulsion blast at the two remaining Voss, who were beginning to regroup. They went flying into the wall. Another sweeping burst of her stun beam made them stop moving.

Evaran observed Emily. "You impress me once again."

Emily walked over to Evaran and placed an orb on his handcuffs, causing them to stop glowing. "I've been training."

"I can tell," said Evaran as he broke his wrist constraints.

Emily placed another orb on his ankle restraints, which Evaran then broke apart. "Uncle Albert and Jane are above on the walkway, and V is projecting a Cepharus in the middle of the room. Oh . . . and it's great to see you again as always."

Evaran stood and rubbed his wrists. "It will take me a moment to adjust."

"Sitting for several days will do that to a body," said Emily. She bear-hugged Evaran. "I'm glad you're safe."

Evaran put an arm around Emily. "I am good and have had time to think. Billozein should be on his way to his ship."

Emily stepped back. "We saw Jeetrozein at the other end of the room. It wasn't going well for him."

"He probably believes he can regain control. That will not be possible with the programming I have implanted," said Evaran. "I did notice that the Palisin energy seemed to irritate the Voss in the room and kept the ones from the capsules away." He stretched around for a moment, raising each leg in sequence. "However, let us head to the Torvatta now."

Emily gestured toward the door. "You don't have camou-flage, but the path should be clear. We can run there."

Evaran grabbed his utility handle and extended it into a staff with one end glowing white, the other blue. With one final look around, he exited the room and headed toward the ladder Emily had pointed out.

Halfway there, Emily picked up the sound of repulsion blasts. Looking at the base of the ladder, she could see a mass of uncontrolled Voss swarming around, trying to climb.

Dr. Snowden and Jane were firing downward, but Dr. Snowden had turned toward others that were coming down the walkway.

"Should we fight our way through?" asked Emily.

"I have another idea," said Evaran. He adjusted his utility handle to make a baton with a glowing yellow end. "Grab on to me."

Emily remembered that the yellow glow meant it was in grappling mode. She put her arms around Evaran's chest.

Evaran fired up a bit away from where Dr. Snowden and Jane were. They rose into the air at an angle and began to swing forward. Once they were within range of the ladder, Evaran repositioned his grappling beam to above Dr. Snowden and Jane.

Dr. Snowden jumped when Evaran landed next to him. A grin broke out on his face. "Evaran!"

Jane placed a hand on Evaran's arm. "I'm glad you're safe."

"Thank you, everyone, but we should head to the Torvatta now."

"The path should be cleared . . . well . . . except for the few stragglers that came through to the walkway," said Dr. Snowden. He looked down the ladder. "If we're gonna do something, we need to do it fast."

"We can go now," said Evaran. He tapped at his ARI. "V, we are leaving."

V flew up and hovered near Evaran. "Acknowledged. It is good to see your life sign is active." His lights pulsed for a moment.

"The feeling is mutual," said Evaran. "It is time to see where Billozein is going."

Emily smiled as she followed Evaran. Her nanobots were tingling, her face was flushed, and the excitement of the situation was almost like an addiction to her now. She had doubts about staying on board long ago, but no more. This is where she belonged, next to Evaran. With Dr. Snowden, V, and now Jane, it was a group she was beginning to see as one big family.

After twenty minutes, Dr. Snowden and the others reached the control room that they had been at previously.

Dr. Snowden looked around the floor for the two regular Voss they had left behind. Their mangled corpses looked like something had put holes in them. When he focused on the bodies, he thought he could see rising smoke, as if something hot had gone through them. He wrinkled his eyebrows as he pointed at one of them. "Those holes look pretty precise . . ."

Evaran scanned one of the bodies with his ring. "They are from an energy beam. I do not suspect it came from one of the uncontrolled Voss."

"When we left, we heard them scream, but didn't hear anything else," said Emily.

"It could have been robots. Voss are not particularly quiet, controlled or otherwise," said Evaran.

"Voss judicators," said Jane with narrowed eyes.

Everyone looked at Jane.

"They're an elite Voss unit. They cover many roles, from security, to hunting down targets. It's usually one big control one, with smaller ones around it. I saw some on the screens in this room earlier."

Evaran rubbed his chin while perusing his ARI. "I see. It appears they have shielding." He extended his hand out, palm up. A projection shot up from his ring, showing a line of several judicator models.

"That's them," said Jane. "These look much more advanced, though. I ran into one or two long ago, but they were much easier to handle than what those look like."

"I suspect then that they were here. Your forearm shields will prevent any damage. Make sure you have it ready to deploy if needed."

Everyone nodded.

"Let us go," said Evaran as he strode across the room.

They stepped over the dead Voss and exited.

When they crossed the halfway point of the corridor outside, a pair of crazed Voss burst around the corner at the other end. One was limping while the other held its arm. A barrage of energy beams raked their backs. They crumpled to the ground after yelping, then fell silent.

Dr. Snowden's heartbeat increased as he gripped his PSD. His eyes popped open at the sight of a quadruped robot as it stepped around the corner and into the corridor. It was one of the Voss judicators that Evaran had shown. The cold mechanical sound it emitted made his nerves fray. Swiveling cylinders on its back ended with an orb that had a black tube sticking out. It was the same tube on the front end that caught his attention. It was much larger. A semitransparent bubble shield surrounded the robot.

The judicator paused for a moment, then faced Evaran and the others. A beam swept out and then spread into individual beams that highlighted each person. The cylinders turned so that the tubes were lined up with the beam.

"Shields!" said Evaran, moving his left arm forward and kneeling.

Dr. Snowden, Emily, and Jane followed Evaran's example.

A barrage of orange energy beams hit them. The front tube shot a larger beam, while the smaller cylinders above shot thinner ones. As it advanced, smaller versions of the robot appeared behind it.

Dr. Snowden observed that the smaller ones were more spiderlike and only had the front energy beam tube. He had seen them earlier as well and knew why they were a problem. It was when they scaled the wall that his skin began to crawl.

Evaran crooked a thumb back. "We need to get back to the control room."

They crept backward, always facing forward. When they got there, the judicators were within ten feet. Jane and Emily were the first into the room. They ducked off to the sides. Dr. Snowden was next. When Evaran backed into the room, he placed his UIC on a side console. Several quick swipes at his ARI and the door sealed shut. A humming sound emanated from the door as the judicators fired on it.

Evaran stood. "The door is shielded. We should be okay for the moment. We need another route."

Dr. Snowden shook his head as he looked at Jane. "How did you handle those in the past?"

"Overwhelming force," said Jane. "United Planets has its own version of them. Plus we had Paragons, heavily augmented human–AI hybrids with specialized armor and weapons. One thing judicators are susceptible to is energy drain on their shields, and once those are depleted, they go down easy."

"Our stun beams could do that," said Evaran.

"Maybe . . . but I bet these have regenerating shields, so it would need to be a sustained stream."

"I wonder where they were before," said Emily. "I didn't see any on the way in, other than on the screen."

"They're probably in hunter mode," said Jane. "I don't know how these were built but would guess that they were busy clearing out other areas with any Voss, controlled or not."

Evaran placed his UIC on his belt. "I have found another route. There is a ladder shaft that connects a network of maintenance tunnels. It should take us right up to the docking bay."

"What if there are more of those judicators?" asked Dr. Snowden.

"We have a tactical advantage in the tunnel size. They are about half as wide and tall as the regular corridors."

Emily smirked. "It's less room for them to maneuver and easier to focus fire."

"That is correct," said Evaran. He headed out the other side of the room with everyone in tow.

Dr. Snowden grimaced as he saw dead Voss everywhere. It was easy to pick out the uncontrolled Voss versus the regular ones. The uncontrolled Voss had a crack in their heads, like the pale creature inside had tried to get out. It reminded him a bit of cracking a lobster tail open. He shuddered at the thought.

They reached the ladder shaft and hustled down it.

Dr. Snowden noted on the way down that it was well lit. He ran his hand between a pair of rungs and touched the warm feeling of the steel wall. The ladder shafts had entry points at each floor, with a ledge all around the shaft, enough to stand on. He wondered if they used robots to maintain it or if there was a maintenance crew.

Jane nudged his leg from under him. "Are you thinking again?"

Dr. Snowden cleared his throat. "Maybe." He flashed her a smile.

Jane shook her head.

Evaran climbed off the ladder at one of the entry points. He placed his UIC on the wall console, and a moment later, the door to the floor opened. He exited the shaft and helped the others in.

Dr. Snowden noted that the room they had entered was mostly white, in contrast to the black-and-purple color scheme that pervaded the rest of the facility. Large, square white pillars with lights flashing on them filled the room in a grid pattern. Their reflectiveness caused him to squint. He walked up to one with Jane and ran his hand across the surface. It reminded him of touching the side of a plastic milk jug. "What are these?"

Evaran scanned one of the pillars with his ring. "They appear to be part of some power management system."

"Huh," said Dr. Snowden.

Evaran looked around, then headed to the room exit. "We are on the same floor as the docking bay. It is ahead."

Several dead regular Voss lying near the room exit caught Dr. Snowden's eye. He wondered about the others who were probably trying to do their job, then getting either mauled by uncontrolled Voss or judicators. He sighed at the thought of so much death.

After fifteen minutes of dodging judicator patrols and the random uncontrolled Voss, they reached the docking bay.

Dr. Snowden peered in. "Billozein's ship is still here."

"So it would seem. Where is the Torvatta?" asked Evaran.

V's lights glowed. "It is hovering in the rear corner of the room near the ceiling."

"Okay. Go ahead and bring it down."

"Acknowledged," said V.

As they waited for V, Dr. Snowden's attention was diverted to a commotion across the room near another corridor entrance. Several judicators entered the room, followed by Billozein and some regular Voss. They were firing into the hallway. Dr. Snowden's pulse jumped when Billozein spotted them.

"*You* did this! You killed my son!" said Billozein in a voice that echoed throughout the bay. He tapped at something on his wrist.

Dr. Snowden flinched when a humming sound shot out across the bay.

Jane glanced up at semitransparent circles that had formed on the ceiling. "Uh-oh. What's that?"

Dr. Snowden scrutinized the circles. "I don't know, but V needs to hur—"

Judicators fell through the semitransparent circles onto the ground.

Dr. Snowden's eyes widened. "That doesn't look good . . ."

Evaran clenched his jaw for a moment. He tapped at his ARI. "V is going to take the Torvatta out of stealth mode and place it between us and the bulk of those judicators. We need to hold this entrance until then. Shields up." He placed his left arm in front of him and crouched.

Dr. Snowden, Jane, and Emily knelt next to Evaran with their shields out.

Dr. Snowden squinted at the orange glow as both small and large beams blasted at them.

Jane tumbled back due to the force of the blasts.

Emily slid over and covered her spot. She glanced at Dr. Snowden and nudged her head backward. "Go."

Dr. Snowden peeled away and rushed over to Jane. "Are you okay?"

Jane scrunched her face while rubbing her shoulder. "I wasn't expecting that much force."

Evaran turned his head to the side. "The Torvatta has landed in the closest open area. We need to move!"

Dr. Snowden helped Jane up to a crouching position.

"Follow me!" said Evaran as he charged out.

Dr. Snowden, Jane, and Emily followed Evaran as he weaved between large metallic containers.

As they were nearing the Torvatta, the sound of something slamming into the ground to Dr. Snowden's left and right caught his attention. A pit formed in his stomach as he looked to the left and saw one of the judicators. He positioned his shield instinctively.

An orange beam shot out at him.

He stopped and braced for the impact and was able to stand his ground. Looking to his right, he saw that Jane had turned to her right.

Time seemed to slow down.

His heartbeat went apocalyptic as he watched her hitting her belt. That would have been where her shield toggle was on her old suit.

An orange beam hit Jane in the side, sending her tumbling forward.

Dr. Snowden bolted in front of Jane and angled his shield so that it covered both him and Jane. "Evaran!"

Evaran wheeled around and changed his utility handle so that it was a baton with a glowing yellow end. He shot it at Jane and pulled her limp body toward him.

"Get her to the Torvatta!" said Dr. Snowden. He could feel his nanobots tingling in a way he had only felt once or twice before. A wave crashed through him but steadied itself. Looking at the beams hitting his shield, he could see the trajectory, and what would be needed to reflect it. He adjusted the angle of his shield.

The judicators paused firing as their shields dissipated from their crossfire.

The vibrations of Evaran running up to him washed over Dr. Snowden. He turned his head and saw Emily had picked up Jane and was running toward the Torvatta. Evaran had his shield out and was moving fast toward him.

When Evaran arrived, he shot a stun beam at both judicators, causing blue arcs to dance around them before they tipped over with a whirring sound. "Go!"

Dr. Snowden jumped up and spun around, then took off like a lightning bolt. Movement was effortless. He felt like he could fly if he had wings.

After a few moments, they were on the Torvatta's ramp.

Dr. Snowden saw that Billozein had already left. He glanced at Evaran and thought he could see a light aura about him.

"Are you okay?" asked Evaran, using his ring to scan Dr. Snowden.

"I . . . think so."

"Jane is alive. She has healing nanobots in her."

Dr. Snowden looked at the Torvatta's shielding and scrunched his face. It reminded him of swirling light, similar to the light aura he saw around Evaran. For a brief moment, he thought he could see the shielding as being much bigger than it actually was, like looking into the abyss of another dimension.

Evaran stood just inside the Torvatta. "Are you sure everything is okay?"

Dr. Snowden pivoted and observed that the light aura around Evaran had tendrils to the shielding. Evaran was like a Tesla coil. It made it seem like Evaran was more connected to the Torvatta than Evaran probably even realized. Dr. Snowden wrinkled his eyebrows. "I'm . . . okay. Let's check on Jane." He continued up the ramp.

22

Jane cracked her eyes open. The bright light caused her to shut them again. After a few minutes of fluttering her eyes, she was able to adjust to the light. She swallowed and noticed her throat was dry. Looking to her left, she saw Dr. Snowden napping in a chair next to her. His glasses had slid down his nose, and his head had tilted to the right. He looked so peaceful. She chuckled, then winced as she rubbed her side.

Dr. Snowden jerked his head up and focused on Jane. "You're awake!" He adjusted his glasses and jumped out of his chair and while facing the entrance and said, "She's awake!"

After a moment, Evaran, Emily, and V in orb mode came into the room.

Dr. Snowden laid a hand on her arm. "How are you feeling?"

Jane sat up on her elbows. "Fine . . . I think. What happened?"

Evaran tossed out an orb. He interacted with his ARI. "This was taken from the Torvatta."

A projection shot up showing two judicators landing.

Jane remembered seeing the one on the right. What surprised her was how quickly Dr. Snowden responded to the one on his left. She grimaced when it showed the orange beam hitting her side and causing her to fall. Seeing Dr. Snowden rush over and place himself between her and the judicator fire caused her heart to warm. He had placed himself in danger without even a thought. She chuckled when it showed Evaran grabbing her with the grappling beam. The projection ended with Emily carrying her to the medical lab and giving her a shot from a syringe device.

"That's pretty wild, huh?" asked Emily.

"It looked like it. What'd you inject me with?"

"Healing nanobots. V said you had some broken ribs."

Jane ran her hand over her tender side. "They seem to work wonders." She glanced at Dr. Snowden. "My old suit couldn't have taken a shot like that."

"I'm glad you had on the survival suit then," said Dr. Snowden.

Jane eased up and slipped her legs off the side of the slab. "It looks like old habits die hard. I'm not sure why I tried to use my old suit's shield toggle. Anyways . . . how long have I been out?"

"Analysis. Two hours and thirty-three minutes. It is currently seven ten p.m. eastern standard time relative to Earth."

"Oh," said Jane. "I'm guessing we're somewhere safe then?"

"We are. Billozein caused another timeline change, but we are stealthed in space for the moment," said Evaran.

Jane got off the slab and reflexively bent over while laying a hand on her side. She inhaled sharply. "What's our next step?"

"For you and the others, dinner and some rest. I will need some time to go over the data I received from the quantum beacon. It seems it stayed on for quite a while before it stopped transmitting. We can reconvene at nine tomorrow morning."

"Well, I look forward to hearing about it," said Jane.

Dr. Snowden gestured toward the medical lab entrance. "Let's get some food."

After ten minutes, Jane had replicated a bowl of chocolate ice cream and taken a seat at the conference room table. Dr. Snowden and Emily sat across from her with dishes of their own. "So . . . can I look forward to any nonviolent adventures?"

Dr. Snowden snorted. "I think after this one, we'll probably do that. I'd like to go somewhere like where we were before we came here."

"Kamala, that resort planet you mentioned that had a thriving scientific community," said Jane.

"You got it."

Emily half smiled. "Swimsuits and all that, huh?"

Dr. Snowden's face turned red. "What?"

Jane chuckled, then grimaced. "Even laughing hurts." She enjoyed the light conversation over the rest of dinner. Her eyelids drooped once or twice, and the yawns came fast and furious. After dinner, she excused herself to her room. Her clothes and suit came off in record time, and once in bed, she stared up at the ceiling.

She did not want to admit to the others that she was unsure of her performance. In the last situation, she got knocked out. Several times she had hesitated. Maybe it was something that would go away with more traveling time. Being able to react as quickly as Dr. Snowden or Emily was out of reach for her, unless she took on the same nanobots they had, if that was even possible. She drifted off to sleep.

Her PSD woke her the next morning. Checking it, she saw it was 8:00 a.m. The communications icon was blinking, and after she clicked it, a projection of Dr. Snowden appeared.

"I'm getting breakfast now. Are you coming?" asked Dr. Snowden.

"I need to get cleaned up first."

"All right."

The projection dissipated.

Jane yawned as she checked her side. The tenderness was gone. She would need to take a look at those healing nanobots, they worked fast. After climbing out of bed, she got cleaned up and put on her survival suit. Although the thought of wearing something else crossed her mind, the survival suit had a nice fit, and since it had saved her life, she did not mind having it on. She entered the conference room with twenty minutes to spare before Evaran arrived.

Dr. Snowden already had his breakfast, and Emily was sipping on a drink.

"V and I missed you at training," said Emily.

Jane tapped her side. "These may be healed and the pain gone, but I'm going to play it safe for a bit."

"It's cool," said Emily.

Jane grabbed a vitastick from the replicator and took her seat.

"Still have your suit on, I see," said Dr. Snowden.

"It's comfortable," said Jane. "After yesterday, it won the job of being my new suit. I need to get used to using the shield better." She glanced at Emily. "I might have to get Evaran to upgrade it, though. That camouflage aspect was handy."

Evaran walked into the room and took his seat at the head of the table. Everyone looked at him. He glanced around. "Please continue with your breakfast. I did not mean to interrupt. I decided to come early."

Dr. Snowden waved his hand in the air. "We're all here, so can start anytime."

Evaran glanced at Jane and Emily, who both nodded.

"Very well," said Evaran. He tapped at the table console. A projection shot up a galactic map. A green line weaved around it, with little yellow dots at various planets and stellar objects. "This is the path Billozein took through time." He pointed at one end of the yellow line. "This is where he jumped to." He pointed at the other end. "This is where the quantum beacon stopped transmitting. I am guessing he became aware of it at that time. If you notice, he has avoided this region of space completely and headed off in another direction."

Dr. Snowden smirked. "Guess he didn't want to take any chances of being discovered before he's ready to show himself."

Jane pointed at the first dot Evaran had pointed to. "So where, or rather, when did Billozein go back to?"

"He went back to 3019, eighty-five years ago."

Jane wrinkled her eyebrows. "Billozein could be anywhere then."

"Yes, but we are not going to hunt him in this time period. We are going to head to where he jumped and investigate."

Jane scrutinized the map. "That looks like it is five or so light-years from Roeth. No wonder Roeth always seemed to be involved somehow."

"That is my hypothesis as well," said Evaran. "However, I do not know where or when he jumped in the other timeline changes, but we have this at least. If we can stop him there, then the timeline should stay true to what it was supposed to be."

"And another version of me and others," said Jane, looking down. Her last discussion with her other self had been illuminating. She wondered if this timeline version had a life with Chris and kids as well.

"Most likely."

"How are we going to stop him?" asked Emily.

"I am not sure yet. I know it is his ship, similar to the Torvatta, that allows him to do this. I am unclear how his rift technology is involved yet. We will need to determine a plan to remove Billozein's ship from him somewhere around that point in time and space, before he influences the timeline. The rift technology will prevent an interface beam from working."

"If the Torvatta had lasers, you could shoot it. I don't think he would be missed," said Emily.

"The Torvatta will not allow lethal weaponry to be added," said Evaran.

Jane knew that the PSDs only had nonlethal means. She figured Evaran could have added lethal aspects to it, but he did not. And now she knew the Torvatta had no lethal weapons. It reminded her of a diplomat's ship, except they usually had light weaponry, which may as well be a stun beam to most ships.

Evaran raised a finger. "The Torvatta has not detected a timeline change in this region of space, so it would seem that he did not tie the discovery of the quantum beacon to us. More than likely, he would not know what it is. However, we should head out now just in case."

"That sounds good to me," said Dr. Snowden.

Jane was still trying to understand all the temporal ideas she heard. It made sense that Billozein could have flown somewhere far away, and time jumped. If he had not done it here, then if they stopped him now, there would be one final timeline change. Maybe since he had not interfered with this region, it would not change much from what was on Roeth currently. She followed the others to the command area.

Evaran tapped at his chair console. "V, take us to the quantum beacon coordinates, but five minutes early. Engage stealth mode after the time jump and prior to entering the portal."

"Acknowledged," said V. His extended arms flew across the front console.

The outside of the Torvatta faded away and then eased back in. The Torvatta shot out a gold beam, and a silver-ringed portal with a light-blue rippling surface appeared.

"Torvatta stealth mode engaged," said V.

The Torvatta flew through the portal.

⸻

Dr. Snowden surveyed the patch of empty space before them. He gestured at the screen while looking at Evaran. "So . . . is Billozein's ship going to appear, or you think a portal or something will pop up?"

"I do not know," said Evaran. "However, we will know in five minutes."

Dr. Snowden scooted to the edge of his chair.

"Are you nervous?" asked Jane.

"Me? Oh no . . . I'm just excited. This is something unknown and new and gets us one step closer to nailing Billozein."

"It's hard to believe my investigation into illegal augments led me this far. Filing a report will take ages."

Dr. Snowden harrumphed. He glanced at Evaran. "That reminds me . . . if we do capture Billozein, are we going to check on the timeline afterward? Maybe visit Andrew and all that?"

Evaran rubbed his chin. "I intend to visit Andrew and give him a tour of the Torvatta once I am sure Billozein is no longer a threat to the timeline. I gave him my word."

Several minutes later, the left screen showed a green gaseous-like rift appear. Billozein's ship came flying out of it, leaving wispy trails of the rift behind it.

Emily pointed at the screen. "There he is, but . . . what's that green thing?"

"A space-time rift," said Evaran. "Interesting." He interacted with his chair console.

Dr. Snowden perked up. "So this is what a rift looks like?"

"This specific type looks like that. Like the Torvatta's portals, rift colors can vary depending on the type."

"So the one from our abduction looked like this then," said Dr. Snowden.

"Correct."

Jane gestured at the screen. "Aren't we going after Billozein?"

"Not yet. Now that I know this is a space-time rift, we can see where he is coming from. We can always come back to this point since we know he has not changed the timeline again . . . yet."

"Oh," said Jane.

"V, take us into the rift."

"Acknowledged."

The Torvatta flew into the rift.

Dr. Snowden looked around the winding circular tunnel they were in. The sides were semitransparent, but outside was pure darkness. Streaks of dark-green light zipped by them.

The occasional clump of some green mass on the walls caught his attention. "This is . . . stunning."

"This is the physical manifestation of the rift as perceived by the Torvatta. It is actually much smaller than what the visual shows," said Evaran.

About five minutes into their flight, the front console lit up.

"Analysis. Another space-time rift detected."

Evaran tapped at his chair console. "Rifts should never cross, and if they do, they need to be separated." He scooted to the edge of his seat "Take us to it."

"Acknowledged."

Dr. Snowden noted that Evaran seemed more attentive than usual. Dr. Snowden had become accustomed to the various emotion indicators for Evaran. If Evaran slid to the edge of his seat, that meant his curiosity and attention had been piqued. Dr. Snowden was trying to process the idea of space-time rifts intersecting. When he and Emily were abducted, the Krotovore used a space-time rift to jump from the Milky Way galaxy to the Andromeda galaxy, and one year into the future. He shot a look over at Emily, who had pulled her lips flat. She was probably remembering that situation too.

After a few more minutes, they reached a darker section of the tunnel.

Dr. Snowden noted it looked like a four-way stop. While the tunnel continued ahead, there were openings on the bottom and top. "I bet you've never seen that before, huh?"

"Only in theory," said Evaran. He interacted with his chair console.

It was not lost on Dr. Snowden that Evaran was experiencing something for the first time. He was happy to be able to share in the moment.

The right screen lit up with a wireframe view of the space-time rift they were in as a horizontal tunnel, and another intersecting it vertically, like a cross. A flashing red dot hovered just outside the intersection.

"We will need to separate the rifts. V, head in."

"Acknowledged."

Dr. Snowden raised a hand. "And umm . . . how exactly are we going to do that?"

"The Torvatta's shielding is noninteractive with matter, and even rifts to some degree. By going to the intersection and extending the shields, it should cause the rifts to untangle."

Dr. Snowden knew the shielding prevented regular matter interaction, even though the Torvatta still was prey to physics. While the Torvatta could be knocked around, held, and even moved, the shielding could not be breached by normal matter unless the shield was weakened at a point like the entrance or thrusters. And now he knew that it could have a similar effect on rifts. "This is a large section. You sure the shields will have an effect here?"

Evaran pointed at the right screen. "You are looking at the visual effect of the line in space." He changed the screen to show a line in the middle of the tunnels. "That is the true rift line. It is what weaves its way through space and time." The screen changed to show a pulsing dot where the two rift lines intersected. "That is where the Torvatta will go. The rift lines should go around the Torvatta and untangle."

"And then we go after Billozein?" asked Jane.

"Yes," said Evaran. "I had planned on checking out the other end of the rift to see where he had come from, but he ended up near Roeth. Once the rifts are untangled, he will emerge where he should have gone. We will then go from there."

Jane shrugged. "Not sure I fully understand, but I trust your judgment."

"V, collapse the rift line intersection."

"Acknowledged."

Dr. Snowden homed in on the zoomed-in view on the right screen. The wireframe image provided a better visual to him than the mess of green he saw on the left screen. He watched as the red dot that was the Torvatta flew in, then pulsed for a moment. His eyes widened as the lines shook for a second, then flew apart. The vertical line disappeared. The dark-green section became light again. He jerked his head back. "Where'd the other rift go?"

"I do not know," said Evaran. "However, we are still in the rift that Billozein took. Let us see where the endpoint was supposed to be. V, take us out."

"Acknowledged."

The Torvatta rotated 180 degrees and flew back to the rift opening.

Once the Torvatta had cleared the opening, Jane's eyes widened. "I can see Billozein's ship but . . . where's everything else?"

Evaran rubbed his chin. "V, analyze."

"Acknowledged," said V. His extended arms worked over-time on the front console. After a few tense moments, he spoke. "Analysis. Using Earth measurements, we are approximately one hundred trillion years in the future."

Dr. Snowden's eyes bulged. "The degenerate era."

"That is one human term for it," said Evaran.

"There are others?"

"In humanity's future, yes. This is an era where what you refer to as neutron stars, white dwarfs, and black holes dominate. It is a dark and cold place."

Dr. Snowden shuddered. "I don't think there will be any life for Billozein to prey on."

"I know of a few civilizations that exist in this era. They . . . are not something Billozein could handle, much less recognize. V, disengage stealth mode."

"Acknowledged," said V. After a moment, he said, "Torvatta stealth mode disengaged."

The right part of the console lit up.

"Analysis. Communication attempt detected. Analyzing protocol. Protocol established."

"Relay it."

"Acknowledged. Transmission relaying."

The front screen showed Billozein sitting in a large chair in the command area of his ship. "What'd you do?"

Evaran cocked his head. "I corrected the space-time rift you were in."

"What is this place? I can't get any readings!"

"This is where you were supposed to go, not where you went near Roeth."

"What! I've time jumped several times now after flying around, but keep ending up here."

Evaran rubbed his chin. "You must be bound to the exit point of the last rift you went to. Your presence here now means that your involvement in the past has been erased. The timeline would have reverted back to what it was supposed to be."

Billozein scowled. "You're meddling with my personal timeline. I don't belong here."

"You do, actually. I am unsure how you are bound to the exit point, but I suspect that rift technology we detected is involved. If you tell me how you are time jumping, I will agree to an exchange of information. Your ship logs and answers to my questions for the direction of the nearest civilization. It is the least I can do."

Billozein growled. "You could save me too. Be all noble like you claim to be. I'd be willing to give up my ship in exchange for passage somewhere safe. I'd give you all the answers you want."

Dr. Snowden clenched his jaw. Billozein was right. Evaran would probably take Billozein up on his offer. He did not deserve that opportunity, but it was Evaran's call.

Evaran's eyes narrowed. "I cannot do that. You have proven what you are capable of. The timeline integrity *must* be maintained, and you are a disruptor."

Dr. Snowden's eyes widened.

Billozein snorted. "Damn your rules!" He gritted his teeth as he looked around for a moment. "Fine." He tapped at his console.

"Receiving data," said V.

Evaran nodded at V and then faced Billozein. "How are you time jumping?"

"I have a rift stone that when excited, allows me to jump back to a specific point in space and time, except this time, it's bringing me here. I had no idea it was binding me to the last exit point of a rift."

Evaran drew his lips flat. "So you kept resetting the time-line when things did not go your way. How did you obtain this rift stone?"

Billozein seethed for a moment, then tossed an arm out. "It was on a ship I stole. The pilot was dead, and I took on his form and his ship, and here I am."

"The pilot was dead . . . by what means?"

Billozein smirked.

"I see," said Evaran. "You then used the rift stone to find a rift."

"Yeah . . . and?"

Evaran placed his hands together with his fingertips resting on his lips. His eyes darted between his ARI and Billozein. After a moment, he said, "V, send Billozein the direction of the nearest civilization."

"Acknowledged."

Billozein looked at his console. "How far away is it?"

"That . . . you will need to determine yourself. I cannot interfere more than I have."

"When I get there . . . I'll be sure to punish them in your honor, like I did the Kalesh. You won't destroy my ship. You're weak. If I catch you outside your ship again, no mercy," said Billozein with a snarl.

The screen went blank and changed back to the outside view. Billozein's ship took off.

"Was that wise? Unleashing Billozein on a nearby civilization?" asked Jane.

"It is several billion light-years away from here."

Jane gulped. "He won't make it there."

"He will not."

Dr. Snowden swallowed hard. "So he's going to travel out here . . . for the rest of his life aboard his ship?"

"Yes," said Evaran. "If he were to activate his time jump, we would see him appear in front of us again, but that has not happened. I suspect he did not want to lose any progress on his search or . . . he has already met his end. V, take us back to Roeth, when we initially arrived after the summons."

"Acknowledged."

Dr. Snowden swallowed hard. An unusual silence washed across the command area. Billozein had been dealt with. Condemned to travel for the rest of his life in a ship. Evaran had not directly killed Billozein, but instead issued a death sentence, and did it in a somewhat cold manner, like it was a business decision. Then again, Billozein had proven what he could do when given free rein. He was a danger to any timeline. At least now he could not affect anyone. The next step was to go back and see what the timeline was supposed to look like.

Dr. Snowden glanced at Jane and Emily, who both seemed to be deep in thought. They were probably thinking along the same lines. He eased back into his chair as he ran his hands through his tufts of hair. At least there were no deaths, except Billozein's indirectly, and if anything, something positive from the timelines had been saved: Jane, the time refugee.

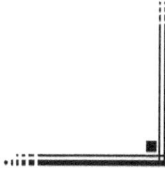

Jane observed the landscape through the left screen as the Torvatta soared over Roeth. They were headed to Da Nesh, and from what she had seen so far, Roeth seemed to be the way she remembered it. There were no signs of Voss, and the ships that the Torvatta had detected were mostly Kalesh, with a slightly higher percentage of United Planets ships than she remembered. There was a Dyson bubble being built, and Corunus was where it should have been.

According to V, it was June 13, 3104, 11:00 a.m., the first time the Torvatta had arrived at Corunus above Roeth. She remembered getting up that morning and seeing the Evaran Protocol. All of that was gone now, and what was ahead was unknown. She wondered if this timeline version of herself resided in the same apartment.

"V, contact Andrew using the United Planets communication protocol. Send him an Evaran Protocol notice directly," said Evaran.

"Acknowledged," said V. After a moment, he said, "Communication established. Transferring visual."

Jane's heartbeat increased as she gazed at the screen.

After a moment, Andrew's image appeared. "Evaran?"

Jane noticed his uniform was slightly different, but he looked the same outside of that.

Andrew gazed around the screen and focused on Jane. "Lil Jane? What are you doing there?"

Evaran extended a hand. "It is a long story. Do you have time to meet in person?"

"For you? Of course! I thought my mind was playing tricks on me when I saw the Evaran Protocol."

"We will be there shortly."

Andrew wrinkled his eyebrows. "Do you know how to get here?"

"Yes, we have been there twice already, and Jane knows the way if not."

Andrew looked Jane over for a moment. "Okay . . . this should be interesting. I'll see you shortly."

The screen went blank.

"Well, at least there's a United Planets presence here, and Andrew looks like he's still working here," said Jane.

"I suspect many things are the same, but there may be some differences," said Evaran.

"Me and Chris," said Jane with a half grin. "I know. I would bet my other self is here. It seems the Dyson bubble is always in construction, which means Chris would come out, and I would follow in every timeline." She looked down. "And maybe . . . there are kids in this timeline."

"It is possible."

Jane took a deep breath and smiled at Dr. Snowden. He smiled back at her. Her nerves pulsed with excitement.

"V, take us in."

"Acknowledged."

The Torvatta landed in the United Planets spaceport.

Jane walked over and pointed at the screen. "We didn't have a spaceport. The United Planets must have a much bigger presence here."

Evaran stood. "It would appear so. I do not think you will need your suits, but it is up to you. Meet me outside."

Jane decided to keep her suit on. Dr. Snowden kept on his casual clothes, and Emily her suit.

They assembled outside the Torvatta with V in orb mode.

Jane's heartbeat increased when they reached Andrew's office. It was slightly off from where she remembered it, but the android at the front desk gave them the correct location. She knew there was nothing to worry about, but the thought that this may be the last time she saw Roeth, or anything resembling her old life, dawned on her.

The solid wall in front of them dissipated.

Andrew met them at the door and ushered them in. He gestured for them to take seats in front of his desk.

Jane paused as she saw the timeline version of herself next to Andrew's chair. The other Jane had on a United Planets agent suit similar to what she had before meeting Evaran. The one difference from the other timeline version that she saw was that this version was the same rank as she had been originally; this Jane was not Andrew's boss.

The other Jane's eyes widened upon seeing Jane.

After everyone was seated, Andrew tossed his hands out to the side and looked at Evaran. "I thought I would never see the Evaran Protocol activate. I'm . . . honored to meet you."

"We have had this discussion several times already."

Andrew leaned forward. "In another timeline or something?"

"You are quite perceptive," said Evaran.

Andrew's eyes lit up.

"I have some questions if you do not mind," said Evaran.

Andrew shrugged. "Not at all. I hope you don't mind that I asked Jane here. I had to make sure she hadn't taken off with you without telling me, but it appears there are two Janes now. Anyways . . . go ahead."

"I will get to the two Janes in a moment. First, do you know who Billozein is?"

Andrew shook his head. "I don't." He glanced at the other Jane.

The other Jane shook her head. "I've never heard of him."

"I see," said Evaran. "Is there an issue with illegal augments here on Roeth or elsewhere?"

"Not that I know of," said Andrew. "I mean . . . sure, you might hear of a case every now and then, but for the most part, it's negligible."

"What about a corporation known as Advanced Dynamics?"

Andrew glanced at the other Jane, who shook her head, then looked back at Evaran. "I haven't heard of that either. You got me curious, though . . . Can I ask a question?"

"Please proceed."

"You mentioned another timeline," said Andrew. He gestured at Jane. "I'm guessing she came from one of those, and this Billozein, illegal augments, and Advanced Dynamics were somehow part of that."

"You are correct," said Evaran. "We came to Roeth to investigate a timeline anomaly. We decided to help Jane in an illegal augment investigation. Billozein was someone who kept changing the timeline. On the first timeline transition, Jane was on board the Torvatta."

Andrew eased back into his chair. "Ahh. Temporal shielding. She crossed over."

"You are familiar with that?"

"The Evaran Protocol has a lot of information in it, along with some associated details on you and your ship."

"And whom I travel with?"

"Only on a few events," said Andrew. He wagged a finger between Dr. Snowden, Emily, and V. "I know that is Dr. Snowden, Emily, and U4."

Evaran gestured at V. "That is V. U4 was killed upon my arrival on Earth." He looked down.

"Oh . . . I . . . didn't know," said Andrew.

"It is okay. The additional data in the Evaran Protocol must be erased. This means anything other than how to interact with me."

Andrew jerked his head back. "I know you put in a note not to record anything, but the damage has been done, at least for five hundred years or so. I'll help in any way I can."

"Thank you. I am not sure why it began recording around the time of the United Planets formation. When we arrived at Roeth, the United Planets was not the only group notified of my arrival when the protocol was activated in the first timeline. Information from those details was used against me."

"Just tell me what you need me to do," said Andrew.

"It is appreciated," said Evaran with a slight bow.

Andrew narrowed his eyes and looked at Jane. "So . . . what happens to you then?"

Jane bobbed her head. "I'm traveling with Evaran now. Everything I know is gone, and since this is what the timeline should be, I'm not sure I would fit in." She glanced at the other Jane, whose lips drew down.

"Oh . . . ," said Andrew. He glanced at Evaran. "How long are you going to stay?"

Evaran chuckled. "Yes, you may see the Torvatta this time."

"My other selves . . ."

"You are the third version to ask. You are consistent and persistent."

Andrew chuckled. "Figures. Well, I'm guessing you corrected the timeline anomaly or you wouldn't be here, right?"

"That is correct," said Evaran.

"Out of curiosity again . . . you said the third version of me. Is that how many times the timeline has changed?"

"You are correct again," said Evaran with a half smile. "Four timelines, three transitions. The first timeline version of you helped us find Warlord Okon. The second timeline version of you was killed by Billozein. The third timeline version of you helped us with information on the Voss Imperium and their domination of Roeth and beyond. The fourth, and intended, timeline version is in front of me."

Andrew's eyes widened. "I . . . I would love to know about the other versions of me . . . if you have time, of course. Four timelines, but three versions of me . . . hard to believe. President Okon is the leader of the Kalesh. And he was a warlord?"

Jane chuckled. "Warlord, ambassador, and rebel leader. And now he's a president, it seems."

The other Jane shook her head as she looked at Andrew. "You're right, this does sound . . . a little out there."

Andrew smirked. "Given what I've studied of Evaran, standard operating procedure."

Evaran glanced at Jane for a moment, then back at Andrew. "I can take you on that tour now."

Andrew jumped out of his chair. "Count me in."

Evaran laid a hand on Jane's shoulder. "You can stay here if you wish."

Jane gulped as she looked at Evaran. "Okay." She wondered if Evaran knew that she wanted to talk to the other Jane in private, like she had before.

Evaran stood and gestured at the door. "Let us go."

Dr. Snowden stood for a moment, looking at both Janes, and after lightly squeezing Jane's shoulder, he left with Emily, Evaran, V, and Andrew.

The other Jane took Andrew's seat. "That's quite a story."

"It's all true," said Jane. "It sounds incredible, and I wouldn't believe any of it except that I just lived through it." She cleared her throat. "I have to ask . . . are you with Chris, and do you have two kids? Girls?"

The other Jane smiled. "You got it. Chris came out here because of the Dyson bubble being built. I had to use all of my political capital, but was able to come out early to be with him. I then got this posting. I'm guessing you met another timeline version of me . . . well . . . us, like that."

Jane looked down. "Yeah. Girls were Lauren and Meghan. In my timeline, Chris was killed by Billozein. I was a United Planets field agent and was able to get transferred to Da Nesh. Like you, I had to use all of my political capital to come out early. In my personal time, I tried to investigate what happened, and then met Evaran and crew, and they helped me check it out. It seems in any timeline where we're alive, Chris comes out here, and we follow him, regardless if he's alive or not, except for the second and third one. We're all dead in the second one, and the third one we were on the Jupiter station."

The other Jane grimaced. "Oh no . . . I can't even imagine . . ." She gazed at Jane. "So . . . you're traveling with Evaran then?"

Jane looked up. "I guess. Where else can I go? Everything I knew is gone. I mean . . . it's here, but not the same."

The other Jane tapped her fingertips together. "You . . . could stay here."

Jane contemplated the other Jane. There was no indication that she was joking. This was a serious offer. "I'm not sure I could live knowing another version of Chris was around and he wasn't a part of my life." She dipped her head.

The other Jane laughed. "We're Fredorians. Our group is open."

Jane jerked her head back. "I was exclusive with Chris in my timeline. I guess there are some differences."

"Well, since this is the finalized timeline, as far as I understand it, I wouldn't mind if you joined our family group. It would be me, you, and Chris. Anyone asks, you're my twin sister. I know it sounds weird, but . . . I feel like I know you."

"Well, we're the same person, just different timeline versions, as far as I understand it," said Jane. She swallowed hard. "I . . . I could have nieces and nephews?"

The other Jane's eyebrows pulled down in concentration. "And I could too."

Jane tapped her fingertips together. "Chris . . . do you think . . ."

The other Jane laughed. "I can barely keep his hands off of me. Imagine him finding out about you. Not sure if your Chris was the same as this one, but two of us . . ."

Jane chuckled. "Sounds like the Chris I knew."

"Well, I'm an agent as you can see. Chris is working on the space habitats, but comes back for a few days every week. We could always use an experienced agent out here."

Jane gulped. "Andrew would be okay with that?"

"What do you think?"

They both chuckled.

Jane smirked. "Yeah, he'd be okay with that. However . . . are you sure *you* would be okay with me here?"

The other Jane eased back in Andrew's chair. "I know that if I was in your shoes, I would want this. A second chance. I'm betting that you want that to."

Jane's eyes misted. She thought that maybe her presence would have caused issues, but it seemed the other Jane thought otherwise. Given how closely she thought that she and the other Jane must think, staying seemed like the natural choice. She would have a family, possibly have her own kids, have a good job, and, most important of all, have Chris in her life, even if it was a different version.

The other Jane stood and gestured toward the room exit. "Well, assuming you are staying, I guess we should tell the others."

Jane nodded. "As a good friend would say . . . let's do this."

Dr. Snowden liked Andrew's infectious enthusiasm. Andrew had seen the holo room, the command area, the living quarters, and now was in the conference room with him, Emily, Evaran, and V, having lunch. The summons was over, Jane was going to travel with them, and the start of a new chapter in his life would be beginning. He had a hard time keeping a persistent smile from dominating his face.

"So this is a hamburger," said Andrew, chewing as if he was unsure of how it tasted.

"It is," said Evaran.

Andrew popped a fry into his mouth. "Interesting texture."

Dr. Snowden glanced at Evaran. "I bet Andrew would like to see your interactions with his other timeline versions."

Andrew's eyes lit up. "You . . . have recordings?"

"I do."

Andrew swallowed hard. "This is, like, the best day of my life."

Dr. Snowden laughed. His attention focused on Jane and the other Jane entering the room. His heartbeat increased at the thought of what having two Janes would be like. The seriousness on Jane's face caused a ripple of uncertainty to wash over him. Something had happened.

The other Jane put her hand out. "Hey, all. I hope we're not interrupting anything."

Andrew shook his head. "Not at all. You gotta try this hamburger thing."

"I will, but first . . . I need to talk to you about something."

"Now?" asked Andrew.

The other Jane raised an eyebrow.

"Now," said Andrew. He plunked down his burger and sighed as he stood. "I'll be back. Business calls."

"We will be here," said Evaran.

"Good, because I'd like to see those recordings, if you don't mind, that is . . ."

"I do not mind," said Evaran.

Andrew exited with the other Jane.

Dr. Snowden's mouth went dry.

Jane took a seat to Evaran's right. She took a measured breath and looked around the table. "I wanted to say . . . thank you for taking me in, when you didn't have to. I'm honored that you allowed me to travel with you. But . . ." She glanced at Dr. Snowden, whose lips had drawn down. "Jane . . . I mean . . . the other Jane . . . has offered me a second chance."

A pit formed in Dr. Snowden's stomach. He had not anticipated that Jane might not travel with them after she had accepted an invitation to join them. His throat constricted.

Evaran faced Jane. "This is a good opportunity for you to explore what could have been. While I would have enjoyed having you with us, you should take advantage of this."

Jane cocked her head at Evaran. "You knew that the other Jane was going to ask me to stay, didn't you?"

Evaran pointed at V.

V's lights flickered. "Analysis. I calculated a ninety-eight point seven percent chance she would ask. Your acceptance was at sixty-one point three percent."

"Why so low on the acceptance? Or do I want to know?" asked Jane.

"Analysis. I could not quantify Dr. Snowden's desire for you."

Dr. Snowden's face turned red as he sighed. "Oh, well thanks, V."

"You are welcome."

Jane and Emily chuckled.

Emily's eyes narrowed. "Will Jane staying here impact the timeline?"

"It would, but not in the big picture. Minor changes occur quite often. It is the major ones, like Billozein, that require attention."

"I promise not to make any history-altering events," said Jane.

Evaran's eyes sparkled. "Even if you or your descendants do, your presence here is due to a rendering of my judgment and actions. I am okay with that. I would ask that you leave your suit and PSD here, though."

Jane frowned. "No problem. I feel bad for leaving after everything that's been done for me."

Dr. Snowden understood why Jane wanted to stay in Da Nesh. Her life had been uprooted, and a second chance, which included another timeline version of her husband in it, was available. He knew that if he did not have Emily but was offered a chance to live in a timeline where his brother, Emily, and maybe even a wife were around, he would take it in a heartbeat. Even so, he was going to miss her, and the nausea bubbling in his stomach was letting him know.

Evaran glanced at Emily. "Let us head to the command center. We can check on Andrew and the other Jane."

Emily squeezed Dr. Snowden's arm, then stood. "That sounds good." She wagged a finger at V. "You're with us, mister."

"Acknowledged."

Evaran, Emily, and V exited the room.

Jane focused on the table for a moment before meeting Dr. Snowden's pained gaze. "I know it was never said . . . but I did feel that there could have been something between us."

"Yeah," said Dr. Snowden with lips drawn down. "I felt it too, but second chances like this are rare. I understand why you're taking it."

"You and Emily could always join our family group."

Dr. Snowden grimaced. "This is Emily's home now. I have to stay here."

"I understand," said Jane. She laid both hands out on the table, palms up.

Dr. Snowden licked his lips and placed his hands in hers.

"This doesn't have to be good-bye. You can travel anywhere in space and time and come visit."

Dr. Snowden sighed. "I know. And to be fair, if kids were in your future, traveling with Evaran isn't exactly the safest place."

Jane exhaled from her nose. "I'm glad you understand. You're a great person."

Dr. Snowden swallowed hard as he looked away.

"Well, I guess I better check with Andrew and the other Jane. She's asking Andrew about my employment as an agent."

"Right," said Dr. Snowden. He cleared his throat and looked Jane in the eyes. "I'm glad it worked out. I really am."

Jane's eyes softened. "If it didn't, I had a hell of a backup plan."

Dr. Snowden chuckled. "That you did."

Jane stood and walked over to hug Dr. Snowden.

Dr. Snowden hugged Jane and whispered in her ear, "You'll be fine."

Jane pulled back and smiled. "You will too. Before you all leave, I'll make sure to stop in."

"Okay," said Dr. Snowden. His lips quivered as he watched Jane exit the room. He exhaled from his mouth and sat back down in his chair.

Emily watched the animated discussion between Andrew and the other Jane. Andrew's eyes lit up when the other Jane mentioned Jane was staying. Her attention focused on Jane as she walked out of the conference room. Emily noticed that Jane's eyes were red and that her jaw clenched and unclenched. Emily figured that Jane must have had some closure with Dr. Snowden.

"Is everything okay?" asked Emily.

Jane looked up at Emily. "I think so."

"I'm going to miss you at the morning workout."

Jane beamed a smile. "I'm going to continue it in Da Nesh in your honor. May not have a holo room, but I'll figure something out." She looked down for a moment, then back up. "Thank you for being a friend. I really appreciate it. I admire your strength."

"Always," said Emily.

"You're always welcome to come visit."

"You never know. If we do come, I expect a hell of a workout."

Jane hugged Emily and sniffled. With one final smile, she headed over to Andrew and the other Jane.

Emily watched as Jane hugged V, then Evaran. She was going to miss Jane. At least Jane had a second chance. It did not escape Emily that maybe in the future, she could see her dad.

She entered the conference room and saw Dr. Snowden with a hand massaging his temples. He looked up at her with puffy eyes. Her heart broke. She knew Dr. Snowden meeting someone he was compatible with was rare, and to see it slip away must have crushed him.

Dr. Snowden wiped his eyes and cleared his throat. "What's up?"

Emily sat next to Dr. Snowden and placed a hand on his arm. "How are you holding up?"

Dr. Snowden adjusted his glasses and looked down. "I'll be fine. Jane's happy, and that's what's important."

"Your happiness is important too."

Dr. Snowden sighed. "It wasn't meant to be, and that's that."

Emily frowned. She could see he was hurting and there was nothing she could do or say that would change it. His rationalization was his defense mechanism.

"I . . . I need some alone time to regroup."

"I understand," said Emily. "If you want to talk, I'm here."

Dr. Snowden looked up at Emily and smiled. "I know. I'm just glad you're here with me."

Emily hugged Dr. Snowden, then watched as he exited the room. She knew it was going to take a while for him to get over Jane. It had taken her a while to get over leaving Andia from a previous adventure. Although that relationship was not as deep as what she thought Dr. Snowden and Jane's was, it still hurt a bit. She exited the room and saw that the main area was empty. Looking around, she saw V at the front console. She walked up to him. "Where is everyone?"

V's lights flickered. "Andrew, Jane, and the other Jane have left the Torvatta. They are coming back to watch recordings with Evaran in a few hours. Dr. Snowden is headed to his living quarters. The Torvatta registered unusual readings on him. He may be sick."

Emily chuckled. "No . . . well . . . lovesick maybe."

V tilted his head at Emily.

"I'll explain it later. Where's Evaran?"

"On the roof."

"What's he doing up there?" asked Emily.

"I do not know. There is no stellar phenomena to observe."

Emily chuckled as she shook her head. "Well, I'll head up there."

"Acknowledged."

Emily headed to the roof, and when she got there, joined Evaran by the light-blue semitransparent guardrail. "Well, that was an interesting turn of events."

Evaran turned his head toward Emily. "I concur. How is your uncle?"

"He's hurting . . . badly," said Emily. "I guess that's to be expected. He really liked Jane."

"I am sure there will be another," said Evaran.

"You think so?"

Evaran cleared his throat. "He has the persona of a great being. The nanobots inside you both give an enhanced appearance to other humanoids. That is considered attractive to others."

Emily shrugged. "I've heard others say me and Uncle Albert glowed."

"They could probably not describe why, though," said Evaran.

"I guess. I'll try to be there for him when he needs me."

"That is a wise decision."

Emily harrumphed. "Regarding Jane, I'm not too surprised she decided to stay. I mean . . . she gets to hang with herself basically, maybe have a family, a new husband, and be in an environment with a job she's familiar with."

"All good reasons," said Evaran.

"I liked her, and I'm gonna miss her joining me in the morning."

"We can always visit."

Emily nodded.

Evaran eyed Emily. "How have you been?"

"Me? I'm fine."

"You seem more comfortable with who you are."

"I am, actually," said Emily. "I have to admit, I love who I am now. Being around Jane showed me that you can still smile while being prepared. I feel more . . . in control."

"That you are," said Evaran. "Your combat skills have greatly improved, and it is good to see you smile more often."

"You're always welcome to join me and V in the morning," said Emily as she swatted Evaran's arm.

"Perhaps I shall," said Evaran.

Emily glanced at Evaran with furrowed eyebrows. "You know . . . Billozein . . . I don't think I remember ever hearing what species he was."

Evaran stared out across the guardrail for a moment. "From the data we got from Billozein's ship, he called his species Dochillan."

Emily perked up. "Huh. Never heard of them."

Evaran gestured outward. "According to the logs from Billozein's ship, he stole the ship after killing the pilot, who was a Krokar. Apparently the Krokar are an advanced civilization from the future that travel through rifts. They have the ability to bind to the last exit point. I suspect we may see them at some point. The Krokar who ran into Billozein met an unfortunate fate."

Emily shook her head. "Billozein is horrible."

"The Dochillan ability to mimic a species form would have been very useful for a time traveler. It is sad that that Billozein's goal was power, but this set of events has shown what that desire along with the ability to travel through time and space can do. I am surprised he was able to stop a Time Warden attempt on him. That indicates he was much more dangerous than he appeared to be."

Emily snorted. "Doesn't surprise me at all with his ego. At least he's gone now. Think we'll run into these Time Wardens too?"

"It would be best to avoid them, and they do not travel alone."

Emily glanced at Evaran for a moment. Whoever these Time Wardens were, to earn Evaran's dislike probably meant they deserved it. "Well, where do we go from here?"

"I think perhaps we should head back to Kamala. A break is in order."

"That sounds good to me. It might take Uncle Albert's mind off of Jane there."

"That is my thought as well."

Emily swatted Evaran's arm again. "I guess then, as you would say, that everything is as it should be."

Evaran glanced at Emily for a moment, then smiled. He extended his arm. Emily leaned into him as they watched the hustle and bustle of the Da Nesh spaceport.

THE END

EPILOGUE

At a planetary data storage facility on the planet Gish Korol, Illitech Security Engineer Jandras examined the holographic representations of a database cluster inside a large room. Jandras was an Ildoran, a thin, green, short humanoid race known for its memory abilities. During a routine audit, a number stood out to him. It was the size of one of the databases. He was able to recall what the size should be, and it did not match up with what the system was showing.

Bringing up the database in question showed a series of floating sheets with lines connecting them. He rubbed his chin as he perused the sheets. Everything seemed to be in order. He checked the logs and verified that nothing had accessed the database in a long time, and there was nothing indicating data had been deleted. Checking the backups revealed nothing either. After a moment, he tapped at a free-floating console that hovered nearby. An image of another Ildoran appeared.

"Hodrak, you got a moment?" asked Jandras.

Hodrak raised an eyebrow. "Sure, not like I don't have several planets worth of data to manage."

Jandras sighed. "Just come down here."

"Fine. I'm on my way," said Hodrak.

The image dissipated.

After ten minutes, Hodrak entered the database holo room. "So . . . what do you need this time?"

Jandras pointed at the number below the database. "The size is wrong. Data's missing."

"You already check the backups?"

"I did, and now all the backups have the same number. It's like the data never existed, but it had to. Since you're the operations engineer, can you tell me if there is a size difference when the planetary backups were done?"

Hodrak narrowed his eyes. "Sure." He accessed a floating screen near him. After a moment, he looked at the number Jandras had pointed at, then back at his screen. "No size difference, but I know the size of the backups has changed. That's not possible. You sure you checked the logs?"

"Of course. Nothing there, and this is a secured database. It's mostly history junk, and it hasn't been accessed in several hundred years."

"It seems kind of pointless to erase historical data no one ever looks at. No one alive would know what was there."

"Right," said Jandras.

"Hmm," said Hodrak. "Well, you're the security engineer. How could someone get in, and delete data system-wide without any indication it occurred?"

Jandras shrugged. "They can't. We'd have audit logs detailing the delete and who did it. Another more disturbing possibility is that . . . maybe our memory is wrong . . ."

Hodrak and Jandras laughed.

Jandras shook his head. "I won't open an investigation into it since there appears to be nothing to investigate."

"It's probably best to not mention anything either. Clients won't like knowing their data can disappear without a trace, and notifying upper management about it would be ill-advised."

Jandras grimaced. "Well, at least you know now too. An unsolvable mystery. If we'd put in a security AI like I suggested . . ."

"I'm not arguing that with you again. AIs are an unknown variable. They could do a lot worse than this," said Hodrak.

Jandras snorted. "Well, then I guess everything is as it should be. Right?"

"Of course. Lunch?"

"Sure," said Jandras. He circled his finger, causing a button to appear. After pressing it, the holographs disappeared, and he exited the room with Hodrak.

NOTE FROM
THE AUTHOR

I hope you enjoyed the fourth book in the Evaran Chronicles! I wanted to showcase the concept of what happens when the timeline changes, but someone gets left behind. There was also more insight into the type of time travelers that exist in the Evaran Chronicles setting. If you enjoyed the book, and have the time and inclination, a review would go a long way in helping out this indie author. If you do submit a review, I'll put in a word to Evaran should you find yourself stranded in a new timeline! Want to be notified about new book releases? If so, you can sign up below.

www.AdairHart.com/MailingList.aspx

I will only send you email about new book releases, major updates, and the occasional newsletter, usually once a month. I dislike getting spammed too, so I will use this sparingly to keep you in the loop.

ABOUT
THE AUTHOR

I have been dreaming about fictional worlds since I was a kid. I devoured anything related to fantasy and science fiction. I developed a setting over the last twenty years and struggled to find a medium I could express it in. Several years ago I discovered I enjoyed writing. It is a passion of mine now, and exploring my setting with it has been an awesome journey.

I work in the information technology field and have my bachelor's and master's degrees in it. It has helped me to shape some of the concepts I write about. I also enjoy keeping up on futurology and science in general.

I live in central Ohio and enjoy walking, reading, gaming, learning, listening to music, and trying to keep up on my never-ending list of TV shows and movies to watch. If you want to contact me, you can do so on my website at

www.AdairHart.com

YOU CAN ALSO REACH ME ON

Facebook...........................fb.com/AdairHart
Goodreads.....www.goodreads.com/AdairHart
Email..............Adair.Hart.Author@gmail.com

DEDICATION

*To my grandmother who passed away on March 6, 2016.
The world is a bit darker without your light. I will
forever treasure the impact you have had on my life and
strive to live in a manner that would make you proud.*

ACKNOWLEDGMENTS

This was a great journey for me, but I wouldn't be here without the help of others. I would like to thank, in no particular order,

My fantastic editor, Laura Petrella. She makes the copy-editing process enjoyable, and I have learned so much from her. One of the highlights for me about the writing process, outside of the actual writing, is seeing her suggestions on how to make the story better. She has an uncanny insight into seeing things that I sometimes miss. I know that with her in my corner, I am a better writer and am thankful for all the she does.

My cover artist, Tom Edwards (tomedwardsconcepts@gmail.com), for doing yet another awesome cover. This cover had a bit more back and forth than the others in the design phase, but depicting a timeline changing merited that. As always, he produced another stunning cover.

My family and friends who helped encourage me along the way.

My beta reader, Scott Ellenwood, for reading through the first draft and helping make the story stronger.

My proofreader, Red Adept Publishing, for providing a great service. They are quick, efficient, and professional.

My formatter and interior designer, Colleen Sheehan (www.wdrbookdesign.com/), for helping make the book look great. She is hard working and I enjoy working with her.

BOOKS

You can see all books in the Evaran Chronicles series at

www.AdairHart.com/Books/Books.aspx